LIBER MALORUM

Children Of The Apple

Woven by
Sean Scullion

LIBER MALORUM
Children Of The Apple
Woven by Sean Scullion

1st Edition

Published and distributed in the U.K. by
PagAnarchy Press
20 Queens Park Road
Brighton BN2 0GL

ISBN-13: 978-0-9557984-0-5

Cover image by Madeleine Mourron. Cover design by Martha Muffin.

All participating contributors can be contacted via the publisher.

It begins.

ents

This book is dedicated to:

My Ancestors
Seen and Unseen
Known and Unknown

and to my Teachers
for Feeding my RAW
Imagination

"Yeah Malus, don't worry about the kitchen. I'll do it in the morning," Michael sighed. "I think instead of blaming the Illuminati, I'll blame someone easier – the Lizard men." They both laughed again and Malus went over to give Michael a hug.

In his shaken-up state, Michael tried to imagine Lizard Men in his living room. He chuckled, *Impossible. This whole Illuminati thing; this whole conspiracy thing; the whole magic and initiation and Witchcraft and everything - it's all bullshit. We can't just create myths and religions as we go along... can we? We can't just re-write history as we see fit. This Illuminati crap is a myth, but it is also a myth that we can align ourselves with 'the energy of the universe'. What the fuck is that anyway? What the fuck am I doing here?*

Con

PART II

INTERMISSION

PART III

List Of Illustrations

Acknowledgements

Transcription of William Blake's *A Poison Tree* copyright © 2007 the William Blake Archive. Used with permission.

New Falcon Publishing, for permission to publish excerpts from Robert Anton Wilson's *Ishtar Rising* and *Cosmic Trigger.*

The Multidisciplinary Association for Psychedelic Studies (MAPS) for permission to republish *Homage To the Awe Full See-er* written by Dr Timothy Leary. MAPS is on the web at http://www.maps.org/

Excerpt of William J Murray's excellent book, *Anarchic Harmony: The Spirituality of Social Disobedience* © Loompanics. Used With permssion.

Excerpts of Robert Shea's and Robert Anton Wilson's *The Illuminatus! Trilogy.* Permission granted by Writers House LLC on behalf of the Estates of Robert Shea and Robert Anton Wilson.

Hakim Bey has made all of his work copyright-free including his essay *Sorcery: THE UNIVERSE WANTS TO PLAY* which appears within.

Excerpt from *Ritual Magic: What It Is & How To Do It* by Donald Tyson © 1992. Llewellyn Worldwide, Ltd. 2143 Wooddale Drive, Woodbury, MN 55125-2989. Used by permission of the publisher. All rights reserved.

Excerpts from the *Principia Discordia* are in the public domain. READ IT !

All contibuting authors retain full copyright of their stories. You can contact them via the publisher at www.paganarchy.net

Every effort has been made to trace copyright holders for all copyrighted material in this book. The weaver regrets if there has been any oversight and suggests the publisher be contacted at www.paganarchy.net in any such event.

FOREWORD

This space reserved for Bob.

TRANSLATIONS

LIBER	
Children Of	(Noun, PL)
Book Of	(Noun)
Unimpeded	(Adj.)

MALORUM	
Evil	(Adj.)
Apples	(Noun, PL)
Apple Tree	(Noun, Singular)

PROLOGUE

"Scratch under the surface of this 'well to do' society and you will find a filthy, scandalous underworld; a circus that rehearses in the protection of the nights' shadows; where sounds are muffled and activity slips away unnoticed...

"Keep it secret... Keep it safe... Let it become strong, twisted and entwined and let the roots become so deep that they break apart all other matter."

- Anneli Stollar, from *Her Travel Diary*

~

"And there never was an apple, in Adam's opinion, that wasn't worth the trouble you got into for eating it."

- Neil Gaiman and Terry Pratchett, from *Good Omens*

FRUIT OF THE DEVIL

Cigarettes, juice and chocolate - just what I need for a heart-broken, hung-over afternoon. In the late April sunshine Bernadette set out on the short walk from her Clapham apartment to the corner shop. *Oh fuck, what now?* Blocking her entrance to the shop was a well-dressed but angry-looking man with a particularly shiny head. He held aloft a placard depicting a large green apple with a red slash through it. Beneath the apple was a cross signifying that he was a Christian of some kind. *But what kind of Christian would put a slash through an apple?*

There were weirdos and creeps everywhere and a modern woman had to avoid communicating with people all the time simply to maintain sanity. Bernadette decided that she would not communicate with this strange man. Alas, as she approached to walk past him and into the shop he stepped out in front of her. *What the hell could this freak want? I do not need this!*

Bernadette felt a nervous rush when she realised he was about to answer her unspoken question. "Kind miss," he said in a very polite Oxbridge accent. Bernadette ignored his advances as best she could as she tried to step around him. "Kind miss," he repeated. "For the sake of your soul, please stay well clear of apples." Bernadette said nothing and did all she could to avoid eye-contact as she accepted the piece of paper thrust into her hand.

Instead of going into the shop, she continued walking in the same direction. *Damn! I didn't get chocolate!* Once she had turned the corner and was out of the man's line of sight, Bernadette read the flyer:

Apples are the sin of the World and the Fruit of the Devil.
Shun apples as you would shun the Devil himself.

We all know that original sin was created by Eve eating
the apple given to her by Satan, the evil devil ruler of Hell.
Forbidden from that day forth,
it is a sin to eat apples!

To eat an apple is to transgress against the Almighty
and to wish upon yourself
eternal misery and damnation!!!

It is time for you to request, nay DEMAND,
your local fruit and vegetable store to
IMMEDIATELY STOP
supplying apples.
Tell your grocer they are performing
the work of the DEVIL.

Contact your local church groups to
campaign against this malevolent fruit
and together we can beat the
FRUIT OF THE DEVIL
once and for all.

For Heaven on Earth, the only option is to destroy the apple.

AMEN

For more information contact Father Ryan Duffy by phone, dial 0800 NO APPLES

What a fucking weirdo! Bernadette crumpled the pamphlet. There were no rubbish bins nearby so she put the crunched paper into her bag to be disposed of properly later...

Matt: “Contradiction is the key to enlightenment.”

Anna: “No, it's not.”

01.

THE ORCHARD OF BECOMING

<Frater Kaotec>

I don't know where I am or how long I've been here. It feels like I've been here for eternity, wherever 'here' is. This is where I belong, for now. It's a nice place to be. I'm very happy, floating free in the breeze. Not that I'm alone, I'm very well connected. And my connections go deep down, right into the Earth, from where I draw my power. A power I share with my neighbours, who are happy and free like me. It feels good and the light, so clear and fresh, is the breath of life. Yes, this is a wonderful place to be.

Sometimes I dream about a past, a past that was not so happy. There was a time when I was attacked by those who would dislodge me from this happy union. Hostile forces, disconnected, disunited, dis-eased. I could feel their presence, cosmic excrement, exerting will for will's sake, weak dominators. And there was something deeper too, a desire for unity frustrated which twisted into sickly resentment. Atomisers. Such monsters sought faux unity in possession and dominion. But they are gone now. They failed, I suppose.

So here I stay in the breeze, in the light, feeling happy with my neighbours. Yet despite this utopic being, I also feel a vague dissatisfaction, as if something is missing. What, I don't know. I lack nothing. Everything is here, wherever here is. Is there more? More what? Just *more* perhaps? Could I become part of something bigger? Could I *become* something bigger? These are strange feelings, as if I need something more. But there is no way I could bring such things into being as I just float free in the breeze.

Something is here. The birds fly up and away. My daydreams have been disturbed. The monsters!? Come to pull apart the world? But no, this time it is different. The world is about to be shattered, but it feels good, feels right. This is no monster, no disconnected brute, but an integrated force of nature. A force that is about to sever my connection with life, destroy my world, shatter my very unity. Yet for some strange reason I am happy. This is my destiny. I am needed. Although about to be cut off from my old world, I know I am about to be united with something greater.

Come devourer of worlds, pull me from mother's womb! Rip me asunder and make me whole again! We are united within a single destiny. We are one within the process of life, death, rebirth. We are one and the same living divinity. Take me in bliss! It is now that I realise my time in this place is over. It no longer appeals to me. What was once a paradise is now a prison. True utopia lay before me. In this moment of ecstasy I remember who I really am:

A serpent from the dark depths of the Earth, having crawled up into this tree
I had forgotten myself in its happy branches....

Eve was hungry when she plucked the fruit from the tree. Her babe was due any time now and they both needed nourishment. She hoped her babe would be as sweet as this apple. And how sweet an apple it was, and so rosy. It must have been very happy, she thought, for so would she be if she lived in such a beautiful orchard. She felt a little sadness as she wrenched it from the tree and bit into its flesh. But it was almost as if it was there for her, almost as if it was calling her. And besides, it tasted so good, so very good. She devoured it greedily.

02.
STOP THIS CRAZY THING

An unknown number of years later, Bernadette Franklin was sitting in her van parked 100 metres from the Dalston flat she would shortly be breaking into: Michael's. Feeling extremely anxious, she had to continually remind herself that she was doing the right thing: *It will be for his own good.*

Michael and his new weirdo mates would soon be leaving the house to go clubbing and he would no doubt conveniently leave the lights on. He'd always left the lights on in some idiotic attempt at feigning to be home when he went out. It was supposed to scare away the burglars, Bernadette nervously snickered to herself.

About half an hour to go. He's bound to go out soon. Bernadette mentally ran through the checklist of items she wanted to steal. First of all, she'd take his beloved laptop. Once she had that, she would grab any small computer accessories, like digital or video cameras. Bernadette had heard that Michael had been making dodgy movies and she was planning to steal a tape or two. *Fuck it, I'll steal all of them if I can.*

As well as uncovering the truth about him, there was a big part of her that wanted to *Fuck Him Up.*

She would also steal any important papers, passports and other things that would make his life hard. If it turned out that Michael had really sold himself to the Occult as he had said, Bernadette would find out once and for all. She'd heard through the grapevine that he had become involved with some very dangerous people and was now performing all kinds of strange and dangerous rituals. She had even met some of his new spooky mates once. She shivered a little and hoped the rumours were false. The Michael she had known wouldn't be so stupid.

"I'm getting initiated," had been his last words to her after they had split up. Dumbstruck, she had hung up on him. That had been six months ago and she had spent much time in the months since worrying about him and pondering what it could all mean. *Worrying, Ha! I haven't slept!*

Initiated? What's with that? Initiated into what? Michael had alluded to there being a 'global revival' of people studying the 'Occult' and 'Magick' and 'Witchcraft' and that he was going to be a part of it. Bernadette had thought she could talk him out of getting involved, as if it was just a phase he was going through. But when he'd said that he was getting initiated into some cult or conspiracy or whatever, Bernadette felt she had no choice but to cut him off. She had stopped answering his calls and emails, hoping to lure him back to the world of the sane. *But by cutting him off, I've let him get buried deeper in this strange, evil world.*

He's getting initiated? Since that ominous phone conversation six months ago, Bernadette had worried continuously. She had tried to forget it, but somehow couldn't. She'd tried everything to push Michael from her mind but he visited her sleep, haunted her dreams, his face kept appearing and vanishing in crowds. She had to know what had happened. *Has he already been initiated? He must have been - our phone conversation was six months ago... But initiated into what? The whole thing is ridiculous! Does he think he's going to rewrite history? I've got to stop this crazy thing. There is no goddamn global magical conspiracy! Pah! The only conspiracy out there is the one in his twisted imagination...*

03.
OATH OF THE CONSCIOUS METANOID
<Nathaniel Harris>

1 (3-2)

My name is Twinkle Golden-Delicious Unthank 235, being the 'new name' that was given to me upon initiation into the Order of the Imaginary Conspiracy. My 'old name' has been completely erased from memory by the Orbital Mind Control Laser. I am thirty two years old, at the last count, and male, the last time I checked. And I am an inmate of Arkham Asylum, having been diagnosed as an existential schizophrenic and solipsist. An apple a day keeps sanity at bay. If life is but a dream then my mind is obscene. Looking in the mirror at a broken reflection, I ask the nurse for another injection. Burple.

Do you ever suffer from the creeping suspicion that none of this, right now, that you are experiencing here in the present, is in any way real? This suspicion is what is known as solipsis. It means that you may be 'mentally ill'. It seems to me that I, Twinkle, am a complete fiction. I exist only in the head of you, the reader. Since I am not described, every single detail about me requires your own interpretation and imagination. Burple. Squwack. Heee heee heee! The little voice you hear inside your head is a voice of your own devising. The way it sounds, its inflections, the way in which it speaks, are all dependent on your own subjective judgements. I, Twinkle, am the voice inside your head right now. You are experiencing me, but I am not real. I am therefore completely dependent upon you for my existence, and owe you much gratitude.

Arkham Asylum is a fictional place, by the way. So do not bother trying to write to me. All attempts at rescue and escape are futile. I cannot live in your world. Your world has too few dimensions. Besides, I like it here. The nurses have short short uniforms. They give me lots of free drugs and keep me stoned all day. And my cell overlooks the apple orchard. It is very pretty at this time of year, with the blossom and all. I'll get to eat the first apple of the year. Which is quack quack supposed to be lucky. Did you know that? Make a wish.

It is *you* that has my voice in your head telling you all this. A voice that, I might point out, is most certainly not the 'voice of reason'. Just thought you should know. In all likelihood, then, you are completely insane. But it is me that sits in this fictional loony bin. Do not worry, I am not about to burple blame you for this sorry fact. Although it is you that is imagining me here, now, it was not you who dictated these circumstances or authored my misfortune. They are afraid of what can be revealed in a work of fiction, you see, and have locked me safely away.

Is a dream about a fairy a real dream? What, then, about a story concerning an Imaginary Conspiracy? Is this a real story about unreal things, a truth about fiction? Or is this an unreal story about subjective truths? Is life but a dream? If so, is it a dream about a real life, or a fictional one? What is 'truth'? Some people say nothing is true. Some people say everything is true. Do not look at me as if I am going to give you any answers. Hee! I did not author the world. If I did, I would still advise you to take anything I say with a pinch of salt. After all, I am in an asylum for people who are voices in heads. Which is probably all 'God' is, anyway. Although I can also tell you GOD is ANGRY and She's BLACK. She is also a lesbian drug addict single mother in a wheelchair. Burble. What of it?

In the end, it hardly matters. What matters is *possibility*. It is my potential to be dangerous in the future that makes me dangerous in the now. I am an idea gone mad.

2

I warn you with all sincerity. What I am about to impart may endanger you. It may place upon your shoulders a responsibility of immense weight. It may be greater than any weight that you have had to bear at any time in the past. It may be more than you *can* bear. I warn you, then, and beg you to turn back. Read no further, if you imagine even for a second that such a responsibility might destroy you, as it has me. It places me in a dilemma, then, for also I beg you to read on, for a secret may not be preserved except in its passing.

It is with great trepidation that I reveal to you now the little that I know, for I am sworn to utter silence on all these matters on the pain of death. Nay, even unto a particularly painful death, and then to worse pain that will continue even after the event of death itself. This oath is taken very seriously indeed by the agents of the Imaginary Conspiracy. Before you read any further, I will remind you that right now the quack agents quack of the Imaginary Conspiracy are watching you. They can read your mind from anywhere in the world - because anywhere in the world is all in your mind, which is exactly where they are, too. You must make a decision.

Do you have the courage to dream, create, and destroy?

If your answer is no, please read no further.

If yes, and it is your desire to embrace reality through Imagination, please follow these instructions.

Gather together twenty-three coins of any denomination and one apple of any kind. Go to a place where nobody will hear you. This must *not* be a public house, or night-club. When you have done so, you may read on. Until then, read no further. I remind you that the Imaginary Conspiracy are watching you at all times. If you read further without following these instructions, we may choose to work against you. If you make allies and friends of us, we will work with you and for you in everything that you do.

Join us.

3

Place the twenty three coins and the one apple before you, as a payment to the Order of the Imaginary Conspiracy. Then repeat the following oath clearly and loudly, so that I and my imaginary friends can hear you.

"I of my own free Will and accord do hereby most solemnly vow and swear before Discordia and all these witnesses that I will always hide, conceal and never reveal any Art or part of this Secret of our Imaginary Conspiracy, which is to be revealed to me at this time, or any other time hereafter except to an untrue and fictional initiate after finding them to be so after due trial and strict examination. Furthermore I vow and swear that I will not give it or see it given to a fool nor to a lost-it, nor to a drunkard nor to any one tripping nor to anyone who would abuse or bad use its knowledge. Furthermore I vow and swear that I will not give it nor see it given to anyone employed except to an artist, author, musician or poet. Furthermore, I vow and swear that I will not give it or see it given to anyone under 5 or above 529 years of age nor without the sum of 23 coins of any denomination and one apple of any kind, or anything of the same value being placed on the table as I do at this time before three imaginary sworn initiates after trial and examination finding them to be so. Furthermore, I vow and swear that I will not give it nor see it given to anyone after the sun sets on Friday night nor before she rises on Monday morning nor in a public house or night-club. Furthermore I vow and swear that I will always be at the call of the Imaginary Conspiracy within the bounds of three miles unless I can find a damn good excuse, such as; myself in bad health, having to sign on, my mobile telephone has no credit or I am simply too stoned. Furthermore, I vow and swear that I will not give it to my Father or Mother, Sister or Brother, nor to anyone who did not fight in the Punk Wars. Furthermore, I vow that I will not write it nor endite it, paint nor print it, carve nor engrave it, on rock nor gravel, sand nor snow, silver nor gold, brass nor copper, iron nor steel, woollen nor silk, nor anything moveable or unmovable under the great canopy of heaven; or so much as wave a single letter of it in the air whereby the secrets of our Imaginary Conspiracy might be revealed. And if I fail in any of these obligations that I go under at this time or any time hereafter, I ask to my heart's wish and desire that my throat may be cut from ear to ear with a flick knife, my body torn to pieces between two motorbikes and blown by the four winds of heaven to the uttermost parts of the earth; my heart torn from my left breast and its blood wrung out and buried in the sands of the sea-shore in the shadow of Sizewell-B where the tide ebbs and flows thrice every 23 hours that my rememberance may be no more heard among untrue and fictional initiates of the Imaginary Conspiracy. So help me Discordia to keep this solemn obligation. Nothing is true and everything is permitted. **So mote it be**."

You may now consider yourself an Imaginary Initiate. You must choose for yourself a new name - being:

The name of the imaginary friend you had as a child, the kind of apple you chose, plus the name of the street that you live on. Add to this any number between one and three hundred and sixty to represent your 'degree' within the circle of the Imaginary Order. You may imagine any hand shakes, passwords and mysteries appropriate to your imaginary grade. Try them out on any imaginary people that you meet.

4 (2X2)

The secret agents of the Imaginary Conspiracy are everywhere. We are your shopkeepers, civil servants, students, lecturers, policemen and prostitutes, priests and pop-stars, in telephone exchanges and post offices, internet chat rooms, strip bars, casinos, galleries, museums, on street corners begging for alms and selling 'The Big Issue'. We are working behind the counter in the health food shop, serving you beer in the pub, lighting your fag in a night club. We collect your rubbish, clean your public toilets, deliver your milk, fix your teeth, help you to decide what clothes to wear this season. We deliver your children, and we measure you up for your coffin. We wait, like Manchurian Candidates, ready to strike at any moment, ready to do something Imaginative with our lives, ready to say or do something inspirational and of great burple quack significance to the whole world. We are so secret that even *we* do not know who we are... It hardly matters. What is important is that you remain aware. Anything that anyone, anywhere, does or says, may be a message to you, personally, of the most profound spiritual importance. The more unlikely the agent, the more important it is that you remain aware of what they might have to impart to you. Quack quack.

Our call is to psychic re-evolution, happening not before your very eyes or beneath your nose, but between your eyes and behind your nose. Kick open the doors of perception, smash away the windows of the soul, reach out from your solipsis to the Greater Fiction, take and change whatever you desire without fear of reprisal. You have sworn allegiance to the Imaginary Conspiracy, and we shall be with you always. We are Twinkle, the Anti-Christ, and the Man Who Was Not There. We are servants of the Goddess Burble-Discordia-Eris-Quack. Only as a work of fiction may such a call be burble quack permitted.

We cannot be stopped, and once we have a hold of you we will never, ever, ever let go. We think you should know. We do not want to encourage you to be paranoid. Paranoia is a heightened awareness based upon fictional ideas distorting your perception of the real world. Rather, we seek to awaken the faculties of *metanoia.* Metanoia is also a heightened state of awareness, but it is based upon real ideas distorting your perception of the fictional world.

The Imaginary Conspiracy disguises itself as a cunning fiction so that you will instinctively seek the truths that lie behind it. They call themselves 'Discordians', 'Luciferians', 'Illuminates', and by many other names. Their secret glyph is the Apple of Avalon, sometimes whole, sometimes with a bite removed, sometimes with the encoded name of their goddess, 'Kali-Sti', engraved upon it, or their dark and destructive god, 'Mack-N-Tosh'. Always they have employed the five rayed star, seen on old churches, in Freemasonic jewels, and in the circles and summonings of the witches, magicians and sorcerers. All these people are 'in on it'. Quack. The five pointed star, or pentagram, is a sign representing the seeds within the apple, revealed when it has been cut neatly in half.

Yet all these things are *red-herrings,* so that even their initiates remain ignorant of the mysteries that have been imparted to them. In this way they programme the subconscious minds of their agents, whose conscious minds are enchanted by the fictions they have swallowed. It is through these subconscious assumptions that the agents of the Imaginary Conspiracy control the world. Burble.

5 (2+3)

You might call them 'psychic pylons' through whom such fictional initiations pass, transmitting to our imaginations like radios receiving voices of the dead. Indeed, some might say that this is what happens to dead people anyway - they become works of fiction and cease to be 'real'. Ghosts, like U.F.O.s, are banished from reason and condemned to the infernal realms of 'Imagination'.

I gained my sponsorship in the Conspiracy through a contact in a Satanic cult I joined during my years in Hackney, living amongst the artists, performers, circus clowns and freaks that had made it their stronghold back in those days. There were hedonistic indulgent parties, plenty of sex, drugs, and dramatic 'Black Masses', but of little obvious value regarding the magic or mystery they had advertised. Well, it turned out that there were a few agents of the Imaginary Conspiracy amongst this strange East End cult who were scouting for people Imaginative enough to move on to more profound initiations of a different kind. My contact was a surreal little fellow whom others called 'Doctor Na'Ton Shaitan', or simply 'The Good Doctor'. He revealed to me the true secret behind the pentagram employed in Satanic ritual, and introduced me instead to that more profound spiritual service, the worship of Our Burble Quack Lady of Burble Completely Quack Meaningless Occurrences.

He told me that his own sponsor was a fellow from Northern Ireland known only as 'The Anti-Christ', the Magi of that paradoxical cultus, The Vicious Circle. The Anti-Christ himself claims that he gained his sponsorship in the Order of the Imaginary Conspiracy from 'The Man Who Was Not There'. As in, when I was walking down the stair I met a man who was not there (he was not there again today, I wish that man would go away).

He, in turn, had been initiated by a cute little blonde called 'Daisy', whose middle name was that of our Lady, and whose parents met whilst working on the set of 'Illuminati - The Opera'. Should you ever meet her, you are well advised to give her all your money, without ever telling her why, and play very close attention to everything that she has to say. She is the untrue and fictional High Priestess of the Imaginary Conspiracy. She has the ability to reveal to you the Penultimate Quack Burble. Yet you must never make mention of the Imaginary Conspiracy, or reveal to her your knowledge of it. If you do so, you will be expelled from the Order without mention.

6 (2X3)

I braved Chapel Perilous, and dared to bite of that Apple denied our ancestors in the Garden. I swore to know, will, dare, and keep silent on all the absurdities of ritual they might employ. I learnt to value my Imagination above any mere material thing, and with it I embraced all my perceptions. I gained union between my own consciousness and that of the Universe, only to discover that 'the Universe is Mental'. And then I learnt to forget all the unanswerable questions I had asked, and all the secrets I had learnt in trying to answer them, just like the rest of humanity does. Thus, I found myself initiated into a secret society whose secrets were so secret that the secrets were secrets even from the secret society itself. I really had no idea what it was that I was getting into. Nor did anyone else.

To be honest, I'm still pretty unsure as to whether this is all some trick of the mind. If it is, there still begs the question as to who played the trick - them, me, or you? Is there even a distinction to be made between us all?

It is like the whole 'twenty three' thing that the Temple of Psychic Youth were so hot about in the nineteen eighties. Robert Anton Wilson picked up on it, too, and so did William Burroughs. You might remember them from your studies of American literature. Does the number twenty-three really occur with more regularity than any other two digit number? Is it really 'the number of coincidence' or do we just see more and more of them because we are looking for them? And why is it so often equated with acts of evil, with disaster? There are twenty three temples in the Grand Lodge of English Freemasonry. Why? Coincidence again? Is it a coincidence that occurs more regularly because more people are looking for it? Has some kind of psychic-field been created? Is it a fiction made real?

I had hoped, in vain, that my thirty second year of age might see a reversal of all this confusion. I do not know if I am undertaking a rebellion against the Imaginary Conspiracy or doing their business for them, or both.

Note: The author of this work was arrested soon after his release, performing some socially unacceptable act (reader's choice). I do not know who signed his release forms, but I do not much fancy their chances of promotion.

04.

REMEMBER SMURFETTE

*You can't just go around fucking who you like and pretending to believe in ghosts and magic simply for fun, Michael. You've made my life hell. Your new friends are all weird, breaking rules and taboos simply for the fun of it or so it seems. I'm sure there's bad karma in there somewhere. Oh fuck it, I have no idea what I'm doing but I *am* going to go through with this and uncover the truth.*

Fucking bastard.

Bernadette took a deep breath and became acutely aware of the butterflies dancing chaos inside her belly. She did her best to push the thoughts from her mind. With time to kill, she attempted to ease her nerves by turning the van radio on. The auto-tuner stopped and she heard a very crackling version of a woman singing:

> *I just got word from a guy who heard from the guy next door to me;*
> *The girl he met just loves to pet and it fits you to-a-tee*
> *So, don't sit under the apple tree with anyone else but me*
> *Til I come marching home.*

It sounded good. Bernadette liked the rhythm and decided she definitely wouldn't be sitting under any apple tree with anyone until Michael finally marched home. He would probably be quite embarrassed but she would forgive him at once.

She knew where he kept the spare key so getting into his flat would be no problem. Fighting off the nervousness, however, might be a challenge. She climbed into the back of the van, lit a cigarette and slowly exhaled smoke while keeping her eye on his flat through the van's side window.

~

Eventually, Michael came out with someone else following close behind. From her hiding place, Bernadette tried to see who it was but in the darkness couldn't see the person's face. The two silhouetted figures wore backpacks and were carrying large bags. She watched as Michael and his companion walked a short distance before climbing into a clean, white van, not unlike her own. She wondered briefly if it was Malus or Helene or one of those other Witchcraft fuck-ups. She also wondered if Michael had slept with any of them. The thought of him fucking someone slowly morphed into a vivid memory of their own powerful and passionate love-making. She remembered his smile, his cock and his body, and smiled briefly as she recalled the Smurfette tattoo on his ankle that she used to tickle.

The time we shared together was fantastic. Why did you change so drastically, so suddenly? Why, Michael? Why? I'm going to uncover the secrets of your demise and help you escape.

I hate you Michael, I hate you and I'm gonna fuck you up she intoned mentally over and over as the other white van drove off with him in it. All the while, she was trying to drown out the little voice in the back of her mind that was pleading *I love you Michael.*

05.
PASSION
<DJ Lawrence>

Love and hate are mirror reflections of the same singular emotion - attachment. Love is nothing more than the positive side of attachment with hate being the negative side of it. These thoughts ran through my mind as I furiously stabbed the central focus of my ritual - an apple with a picture of my ex-girlfriend Aiko pinned to it...

Using the apple as a psychic link to Aiko, I unleashed the full force of my attachment to her upon it. I stabbed it furiously, cursed it and swore at the 'dumb cunt' of an apple, whilst masturbating over the naked form of Aiko in the picture. She was a hot bitch and lovemaking with her had introduced me to new dimensions of carnality that I had never dreamed possible. It also brought me pain and suffering unlike anything I had ever experienced before.

My thoughts on the nature of attachment blurred subtly away as the intensity of the ritual increased. Feeling only hatred and lust, I was frothing and spitting while stroking my engorged, swollen member. My eyes focused so intently on the apple sitting on my altar that the red of the apple's skin melted and bled over the photograph, turning Aiko's supple form into shades of red.

I loved her. I hated her. But most importantly I wanted her gone, out of my life, ending this torment. My chanting grew louder and shriller, my mantra was now reaching a feverish pitch.

"Mufok xancs giwd tylep!"

"Mufok xancs giwd tylep!"

"MUFOK XANCS GIWD TYLEP!"

My rage and self-stimulation had both reached their peak. I grabbed the apple from the altar, and thrust myself into the hole I had stabbed into it. I pulled out and came over Aiko's face in the photo - much like I had done with her so many times in the past.

Still quivering from the aftermath of my orgasm, I burst into laughter as I watched my semen slide slowly down the photo, causing the ink from the digital photo to smear. I laughed even more heartily, acknowledging the fitting end to the ritual - the photo blurred away into nothing more than a hazy memory, banishing the woman who had brought so much pleasure and pain into my life.

I carefully sealed the sticky mess of an apple into a jar and placed it on my windowsill. The prime purpose of the ritual was to forge a psychic link between the apple and Aiko. At the same time, I had exorcised my passion and hatred for her, which was now trapped inside the apple. This was all magically cemented with my intention for her to receive an ample amount of pain as retribution for the misery she had caused me.

Over time as the apple rotted away, so would her life.

~

It all started about six months ago. I was sitting in a large corporate coffee shop teaching English to a Japanese scientist. My regular job is editing - fixing the crazy Japlish for the marketing firm I work for six days a week. The latest piece I've had to translate included several gems such as, "Impossible Is Nothing", "Vomit Is Never Mind" and "Pleasure unfolding bringing happiness insanity."

The job pays well enough, but teaching students privately on a one-on-one basis in coffee shops is fairly lucrative, so I do that on the side. I have precious little free time, but it is hard to say no to receiving a large wad of yen for little more than just having a conversation in English with a Japanese man. Call me a whore if you will - since really I am just being paid to do something that any native speaker of English could do.

My student was telling me about his latest project at work: a complicated organic reactor that cleans the pollution out of lakes and ponds. With the mix of complicated scientific jargon and broken English, his explanation would have been difficult to follow even at the best of times, but I was particularly distracted this time by an attractive woman sitting at the table next to me. The first thing I noticed about her was that she was remarkably tall for a Japanese girl and a cigarette was dangling out of her pouty lips. She crossed and uncrossed her legs repeatedly - occasionally offering me a brief glimpse of her panties underneath her short skirt. Sexuality oozed amply out of her pores and I found myself struggling to listen to my student's explanation of his latest invention. All of my thoughts had been stolen by the nymph sitting next to me.

As my student was finishing off his explanation of the organic reactor, the girl was struggling with her lighter to start her second cigarette. Silently I placed my lighter on her table and made eye contact with her. I lost myself temporarily in her brilliant green eyes (obviously contact lenses, as Japanese do not naturally have green pigment in their eyes). I remembered after a moment that direct eye contact makes Japanese people feel uncomfortable - it is seen as confrontational. Making eye contact with a Samurai in the old days often meant the death of the villager unfortunate (or stupid) enough to have done it. Even today, the Yakuza keep up the same tradition and making eye contact with one of them for too long can end up with you waking up with a knife in your back.

Sheepishly I broke eye contact and turned back to my now clearly pissed-off student. Fair enough for him to be pissed-off, really. He was paying me a small fortune to listen to him speak English and I was not doing my job. I did my best from then on not to look at the lovely thing sitting next to me and listened more intently to him. But even without looking at her, it was still a struggle. I could still smell her and the temptation to turn my head and look at her was consuming my thoughts. Hell, at that point I was so overcome by lust that it was all I could do to stop myself from placing my hand on her leg and sliding it up her skirt.

The remainder of the hour with the student ticked away slowly and painfully. Every minute seemed to drag on for eons as I waited for the class to finish. Finally, my student wrapped up his explanation and we scheduled the time for his next lesson. My student pulled an envelope full of cash out of his briefcase and handed it to me, holding it carefully in both hands. He held the envelope so that the lettering on it would face towards me. That is one of the things I love about Japan, such meticulous attention to detail.

I took the envelope (with both hands, according to the custom) and slid it into my own briefcase. Not knowing whether to bow or shake hands, my student did both and ran off towards the station to catch a train to get to his next of a seemingly endless chain of business meetings.

Quickly, I whipped out my cell phone and sent an email cancelling my next lesson. I was supposed to meet my next student in the next town over but I did not want to leave the coffee shop just yet. The beautiful green-eyed goddess was still there and I just had to talk to her. As I finished sending the email, I looked up and saw the girl putting her things away into her purse, getting ready to leave. I did not have much time to act! My brain was scurrying to find something to say but I panicked and sat there dumbfounded. I kept wracking my brain for something, anything to say, but it just would not come. She interrupted my train of thought - "Thanks for the lighter," she said, with a slight bow as she stood up to leave.

"Would you like to use it again?" I asked, wincing at my own words. I could not believe the way she was affecting me. I was a bold and confident man and had never found myself acting so shy and awkward around a woman before.

She took the lighter and lit another cigarette. Well, at least I had succeeded in getting her to stay in the coffee shop longer. She started talking to me, asking the same slew of questions that every Japanese asks a foreigner the first time they meet:

> "Where are you from?"
> "How long have you been in Japan?"

"Where do you work?"
"How do you like Japan?"
"Why did you come to Japan?"
"Can you eat Natto?"

Natto is a horrid Japanese invention - most likely invented by scientists attempting to create the ultimate biological weapon. Anthrax has nothing on Natto. It looks like snot and smells like feet. I have never been able to get it in my mouth and successfully swallow it. Great Cthulhu himself could not choke that shit down... So I told her the obvious - that it smells like feet and therefore should not be classified as a food product.

Relieved that she had broken the ice for me, I felt much more at ease. Her questions made me feel comfortable and soon enough my normal personality took over from the shy spaz that I had suddenly become, and I started directing the conversation myself. I asked her about her outlook on life, philosophy, various issues and so on. She turned out to be quite an independent thinker and a very interesting person. Cliché perhaps, but in Japan – one of the most homogeneous countries on Earth – those are rare and precious qualities. Down to the tiniest detail, everything in Japan stresses the group over the individual. Most Japanese people think of others first before thinking of their own wants, needs and desires. They think about things not in terms of themselves as individuals but as members of a group. Aiko was definitely not cut from the same cloth as other Japanese people I had met and talked with.

Time sped by. Glancing down at my cell phone, I noticed that two hours had already passed. Best to wrap things up now, I thought, getting her phone number and email address. Leave now after a good firm impression has been made and work on her more later. Humans have short attention spans and even when something is enjoyable, they do not want to do it for too long. After getting her number I stood up to leave and she likewise grabbed her purse and jacket. After saying goodbye outside the corporate conglomerate coffee shop, we found ourselves walking in the same direction.

"I'm going this way," I said.

"Me too," she giggled. Oh well, I sighed, may as well throw my regular routine for courting chicks out of the window, as it seemed both unnecessary and inappropriate with Aiko.

"I was just going to go get some dinner, want to come?"

"I'd love to!" she grabbed my hand and started running down the street with me. This girl really was something different.

We found ourselves at an Aussie steakhouse, slightly less corporate than the coffee shop. It seemed as good a place as any, and steak is a carnal indulgence that I truly relish. We were placed in a cosy, dimly-lit booth at the back of the restaurant. This pleased me, since a natural reaction of human beings when they are attracted to another person is for the pupils to dilate. Since the pupils also dilate in a dark room, simply being with a person in a dark room is a simple and effective method for increasing their level of attraction to you. It's amazing the things you learn when you start studying magic!

I ordered a nice thick fillet mignon - rare as possible, without being raw. Cutting into it left a sizeable pool of blood on my plate - beautiful. We continued to chat as we dined, and drank ample amounts of red wine and I thoroughly enjoyed myself. Simple physical pleasures are what I live for: a bloody steak, red wine and a copious number of cigarettes equals ecstatic bliss for me.

After our meal, as we were walking away from the restaurant, I put my arms on her shoulders and stopped her. I leaned forward to give her a little peck. Public physical contact is frowned upon in Japan, so I had no intentions of doing any more than that. Sure, being a magician means breaking social taboos and other acts of rebellion, but it also means being practical too. Breaking social taboos is an excellent exercise in self-liberation - but forcing another person into a position where they have to is a very efficient way of scaring them away. Therefore, getting what you want out of life necessitates a modicum of rule obeying.

But Aiko shocked me - as I was leaning over to give her a small peck, she grabbed me hard, pulled me towards her forcibly and kissed me roughly and passionately. As she was kissing me, she slid her hand down my pants and started stroking my cock. There were many people walking around nearby so I was equally shocked and impressed. This chick was definitely a rule-breaker. The suddenness of all this, everything mixed together, made me feel euphoric. Her blatant disregard for Japanese etiquette, her desire for me and her aggressiveness was all simply wonderful. My knees trembled.

Her free hand flicked my zipper playfully. She looked into my eyes and said, "Come on! Let's go!"

She grabbed my hand again and started running. She dragged me behind the restaurant where there was a small park. It was quite atmospheric, rows of apple trees, clusters of meticulously trimmed bushes and a tiny Shinto shrine in one corner. The benches were interesting slabs of stone that made me think of Stonehenge.

She pushed me down onto one of the slabs, and climbed on top of me. She sat herself between my legs, and wrapped her own legs around the outside of my thighs, coiling inwards over my shins, with her feet hanging back over the outside of my legs. She was coiled around me like a snake.

I laughed - I, the womaniser, was now being taken. Everything about her was serpentine; she lifted her arms above her head and swayed back and forth, grinding her crotch against mine, yet at the same time dancing like a cobra under the spell of a snake charmer. Perhaps it would be more appropriate to say that she was the snake charmer - because I was completely enchanted by her. All other thoughts left my mind. Everything was focused on Aiko.

She unzipped my pants and playfully toyed with my cock, bobbing it up and down like a spring. She looked up at me and asked if I had a condom. Of course, Murphy's Law dictated that I did not. So, a long conversion ensued about how many people we had each slept with and when the last time we had each had a blood test. We had both had blood tests recently and with the passion of the moment decided to abandon caution and fuck anyway. She pulled her jeans down to her ankles and sat down roughly on my cock. Her tightness startled me - she was snug enough that penetration actually hurt a little bit at first. Not enough to deter me, however. There was nothing gentle about it - savage and carnal.

When I told her that I was ready to cum, she quickly hopped off me and clamped her mouth on my penis. I came hard and violently into her mouth. Afterwards, she stood up, held three fingers in the air, and counted down to zero with her fingers. At zero, she swallowed then smiled at me. Damn! Her playfulness was attractive. She sat down next to me and we chatted more. She told me that she made a habit of swallowing every time she had sex - that she considered cumming in a condom to be a waste.

"Think of all the physical and spiritual energy put into making your orgasm. All the Ki within it, all the calories burnt to produce it, all the nutrients used to make it. There's a lot of power in cum. I want to ingest that power and make it a part of myself," she stated.

I was impressed. For a woman who was not a magician she had a deep understanding of magical things. She was a natural magician of her own flavour. The only difference between her and someone who actively called themselves a magician (like myself) was that she didn't formalize or ritualise what she did. She worked with energies in her own manner.

We walked back to the train station and said our goodbyes. As I turned to leave she said, "if it ends up that we both have AIDS, we can get married. We'd only have each other then after all." It was a very sobering thing to say and sent a chill down my spine. It hit home how careless I was having sex with her unprotected. Still, I did not regret it. It was, after all, one of the best experiences I had had.

Her charms definitely affected me and I was completely enamoured by her. Working two jobs (out of greed more than necessity), my free time was limited to Saturday nights and Sundays and that free time became exclusively hers. We spent the next half-year together as much as we possibly could. Occasionally, she would come over to visit me late on weeknights and we would fuck until six in the morning, leaving me with thirty minutes to catch a few winks before work. I swear she was hell bent on killing me, but it was great, and I was happier than I had ever been before. Everything about the relationship was intense.

Although she was not a magician herself, I had some of the best conversations of my life about Magic with her. We even practiced a little bit together and I taught her some basic sigil magic and elementary divination skills. I did everything I could to spoil her, buying her lavish gifts and cooking the best gourmet food for her. I felt alive and impassioned. Mundane and profane things took on new life for me. I felt energetic and lively at work and taught some of the best lessons of my career. In short, life was good.

Moreover, Aiko was very happy too. Her eyes would light up when I walked into the room. She would smile brilliantly around me in a way that I never saw her smile when she was with her friends. She went out of her way to make me happy. What impressed me the most was that she put a tremendous amount of effort into trying to understand me. She even borrowed and read my copy of *Liber Null & Psychonaut* by Peter Carroll to try to understand better what this 'Chaos Magic' stuff that I was so into was all about. That may not sound like much, but remember that Aiko was a Japanese girl who barely spoke English. Magic texts in general use language in complex and subtle ways. The effort she put into reading that book to understand me was one of the greatest compliments I have ever received. She did everything in her power to please me and please me she did. I was perpetually euphoric.

Then one day everything suddenly changed.

I did not understand it at all at the time. Aiko became completely cold towards me. When I tried to hug her, she would push me away. Our lovemaking stopped completely and her tone of voice to me was cold, contemptuous and snide. I was completely dumbfounded. No event of particular import preceded this; there was no reason at all that I could identify as the cause. Up until that point, our relationship had been very beautiful and I did not understand why the shift had come. All kinds of thoughts went through my head. Perhaps she was afraid of the level of commitment our relationship was reaching. Perhaps she had found another guy. Perhaps I had done something wrong that I did not realise. Perhaps, perhaps, perhaps...

Ultimately, I did not know, and that was the worst aspect of it. It drove me crazy, not knowing. Regardless of how many times I asked her, I got no answer. Most of the time I did not even have an opportunity to ask her since she rarely returned my phone calls and met me very infrequently. It was torture. The same girl who made me higher and more ecstatic than I had ever been before had now brought me dark and miserable despair. I felt helpless. Here I was, a supposed bad-ass Magician who was accustomed for many years to getting my own way, now completely powerless. I knew exactly what I wanted and was unable to have it.

Of course, I considered casting love spells on her but I did not desire it. I did not want to force her to love me as she had before. I knew that I would quickly find that unsatisfying. If only she had told me what was wrong, I could have fixed it. I performed every form of divination that I knew to try to find an answer but it was fruitless. My sorrow clouded my judgement and made any kind of accurate divination impossible.

Finally, after several months of torturous agony, the inevitable day came. Aiko called me after a long period without contact and said she would come to visit on the following Sunday. She sounded cheerful on the telephone but it had an empty, hollow ring to it. My intuition knew what was to come. She was coming over to break up with me. This saddened me but I knew it was a long time coming.

My philosophy has always been that if you are going to break up, do it in style. So I started preparing. I bought a dozen red roses and had them arranged in the style of Ikebana. They cost a dear fortune but looked gorgeous. I also bought a lot of Italian food from my favourite import shop and cooked an exquisite dinner for her.

Most relationships end on a sour note and for most people it is the end, when everything is at its worst that paints their memories strongest. That is why I always went out of my way to ensure that the final day of a relationship was something special. It was an act of preservation so the relationship could be remembered as the beautiful thing it once was, not what it had deteriorated into.

Aiko arrived on Sunday in the late afternoon with a scowl on her face. I was upset that the whole situation had reached this level, but it was beyond repair now, even if she did finally tell me what was upsetting her so much. I presented the flowers to her and was met with hostility.

"I don't need them," she said in Japanese, "the truth is I came here today to break up with you."

"I know."

"You know? What do you mean? How could you know?"

"How could I not know? It was obvious and has been a long time coming. I bought these flowers knowing that you would be leaving me today. Our relationship was beautiful in the beginning - the best I have experienced. Out of respect of how nice things were, please accept the flowers, and let us end this on a positive note. I want to remember the time we spent together with a smile."

Her stone face softened. For the first time in months, I saw her smile. Not just a weak half-hearted smile but the brilliantly warm smile that had made me melt before. It was the smile that had enslaved me. She talked to me like old times; we discussed many things, politics, magic, times we had spent together, cabbages and kings. I prepared the Italian food I had bought for her. My appetite was low, but I enjoyed the cuisine nonetheless. She asked to look at some nude photos I had taken of her again and a video we had made of our lovemaking.

While watching the video, she turned to look at me. I looked deep into her eyes, not flitting my glance away sheepishly as I had when we first met. I lost myself in her pools of black radiance. We kissed - softly and tenderly, not in the passionate and lust-engorged style that we usually did. I felt content at finally being able to hold her again and express my love physically. We made love - gentle and slow, and even though we were breaking up, it felt completely appropriate to make love one last time. Afterwards she asked me to take a photo of her lying naked on my bed, something for me to look at later and remember how nice things had been. It was a nice touch and I appreciated it.

We said our good-byes and I showed Aiko to the door. I closed the door behind her and closed the door on the relationship. I was confused. I did not know whether I should have felt relieved, sad, upset or content. In a way I should have felt good about the situation - I had been miserable for months. Because I could not find a reason for the relationship having turned bad and because it had been so wonderful before, I was unable and unwilling to end it. I should have been glad that at least she put an end to the misery I was experiencing. Although that was a good thing in its own way, it still did not feel good. I felt broken and empty. In the back of my mind, I could not stop thinking about what could have been.

And time passed. I tried emailing Aiko several times, but each time my email bounced. Likewise, I tried calling her a few times, but not only would she not answer - as before - now she even had my telephone number blocked. I felt insulted that she would not allow me into her life in any form. I was completely cut off from her.

Meanwhile, my thoughts about what could have been would not go away. I was becoming obsessed. Aiko consumed the entirety of my waking thoughts. I felt drained and burnt out - I could not continue like this, it would cause my death. I loved Aiko and I hated her too. My passionate love for her became a passionate hatred. I could only see one solution for my troubles - one way to remove her from my mind and reclaim my life. Curse her.

I wanted Aiko to feel the same level of torment that she had callously put me through. I wanted her to feel pain - emotionally, physically and spiritually… Simply, I wanted her to suffer. So I decided to perform my apple curse ritual on her. I started gathering the materials necessary - a shiny red apple, some of Aiko's hair that I had collected while brushing her hair one day, a copy of the photo of Aiko lying naked on my bed from our last night together, a jar to contain the final 'stabbed and loved' apple and some red construction paper for writing a sigil on.

Knowing Aiko's menstrual cycle, I chose to perform the ritual on a day when I knew she would be having her period. I also chose to perform the ritual at 3am, since at around that time she would likely be in the middle of REM sleep and thus more susceptible to the effects of a curse.

I closed the heavy steel shutters on all the windows of my apartment. They are mainly intended for security reasons but for a magician like me, they are also great for achieving complete and total darkness in my temple space.

I lit the candles in my treasured silver candelabra and lit some pungent incense that a friend, Helene, had given me as a birthday present. The atmosphere in my apartment was just perfect. I smiled - being happy with the atmosphere of my temple, but my heart felt heavy at the work I was about to undertake. With a heavy sigh I changed into my ritual robe and put some upbeat, energetic but angry Techno music on.

I began with a simple banishing ritual. I tend to dislike prefabricated rituals and feel the best method to perform a successful banishing is simply to do one completely ad lib. Just let the feeling of the moment come over you. And this I did. Starting from the North of my temple, I ran along in a circle in large strides, letting the music energize me. When I returned to the North, I drew a Chaostar in the air and summoned Azathoth using the words, gestures and images that came to me at that moment. Next, I moved to the Northeast and drew another Chaostar, this time calling forth Thanatos in an ad-lib style. I continued like this for each of the eight rays of the Chaostar - calling Plutus for the blue ray of Wealth Magic, Aphrodite for the green ray of Love Magic, Marilyn Manson for the yellow ray of Ego Magic, the Japanese striptease goddess Ama-no-Uzume for the purple ray of Sex Magic, Loki for the orange ray of Thinking / Wits Magic, and Tyler Durden for the red ray of War Magic.

After completing the circle, I sat in quiet meditation for several minutes in the centre of the circle. I stood up clear-minded, focused, and ready to perform the ritual with no regrets. I invoked two god forms together simultaneously - Ares the War God and Aphrodite the Love goddess. As

I invoked Ares, I leapt across the room in bold strides, feeling more and more martial and warrior-like. I let loose many war cries and allowed the rage naturally present in myself to flow outwards.

The invocation of Aphrodite was more visual in nature. I visualized myself as a gorgeous, voluptuous woman, with full hips and bosom and I stroked my naked body. I alternated back and forth between the god forms, decreasing the duration each time, until eventually I was oscillating between the two at no less than one second each. Then I let them merge: A new god of Love and War - Aresrodite the god/dess of passion and attachment!!

With the god form fully invoked, I turned my attention to the apple. All my rage, anger and resentment towards Aiko was directed towards the apple with the photo on it; as was all my love, lust, and infatuation for her. All my passion, all my attachment allowed full reign. And the rest of the ritual you already know.

Afterwards I felt exhausted but relieved. A great weight was finally gone. I felt like I could finally move on and forget about her. I have always felt that cursing rituals are more cathartic than anything else, and indeed that is how I felt then. All the negative emotions eating away at my insides were spent up, burnt out in the spiritual fire of the ritual.

Time passed. I did not feel happy, but I did not feel any pain either. Just numb. I did enjoy, however, the free time that was then at my disposal. Being with Aiko was great before, but it did consume the entirety of my free time. I now had time again to write, read, and study Magic. I ordered a copy of the Robert Anton Wilson book Sean had recommended. Feeling a need to make up for lost time, I worked harder than I ever had before, and I was quite productive during that time.

Then one night, while returning home from work, I walked into a crowded subway car to see the back of a girl who looked a lot like Aiko. She was on the other side of the subway car and it was crowded so I was not certain if it was her or not. I could not take my eyes off her and stared at her for several stops. The subway arrived at a popular urban district, where many of the commuters who work in Tokyo lived, and the majority of passengers got off. The girl strode over to an empty seat and sat down. Seizing the opportunity, I quickly pushed my way through to the same seat and sat next to her. I turned my head to look at her face and she did the same. We sat in silence together for several stops, just staring at each other. It was Aiko.

"Remember me?" I asked – returning to the ineptitude of speech that I had had when I first met her.

"Yeah, James wasn't it?" she replied with a sarcastic grin.

"So where are you going? You live in the other direction."

She looked at me in silence again for a while, then, "to your place," she sighed.

"Why?"

"I don't know. I really do not. It just happened suddenly tonight. When I walked into the station, I just felt this... overwhelming urge to go visit you. Nothing sparked it. It just came up on its own – out of nowhere. I ran to the platform to get the train headed your way, and here I am."

I did not reply. We sat in silence for the remainder of the train ride looking at each other. I was feeling extremely emotional – and quite confused.

The train stopped at my station. We got off and silently walked together to my apartment. I unlocked the front door and we stepped inside. Once again, we looked each other in the eyes silently. Then without saying anything at all we both leapt forward at the same time and grabbed each other in a passionate embrace. All the old emotions poured back into me as if they had never left. I loved her intensely and I could feel the same emotions emanating from her. The air was thick with it. Neither of us wanted to waste any time at all. We did not even bother to remove our shoes, instead I pulled off her panties from underneath her skirt, and we fucked right there in the doorway to my apartment. The last several months were nothing more than a faint memory of a dream dreamt years ago, distant and abstract.

Afterwards, it really felt like nothing at all had changed. We lay down on my bed and caught up with each other. She had slept with a few other people while we were apart. No surprise, considering her intensely high sex drive. I was neither angry nor jealous. I expected as much and could not blame her - her intense carnality was one of the things that attracted me to her.

I was back to the same euphoric state as before. We saw as much of each other as possible and I didn't lament the lack of free time at all. I was happy. Our relationship was stronger than before and she moved in with me.

Then, after several months, my company required me to get a medical done - standard practice for foreigners living in Japan. A week later I received the results - I was HIV positive.

Love and hate really are merely opposite aspects of the same emotion. My passionate love for Aiko turned to hate when she left me. I sent that passionate hate to her full force and the ritual was effective - I was the cause of her destruction. One of her one-night stands during the interim of our separation had given her HIV. Unfortunately, I was so blinded by my passionate hatred that I could not see how easily that passion could turn back into love. True to our agreement when we first met, we got married. Nothing left to do but to die together with the woman I love - and start working all I can on Reincarnation Magic. I hope that I will carry this difficult lesson over to the next life…

Chaos Star

06. Excerpt From ANARCHIC HARMONY <William J. Murray>

Knowledge: Society's DNA

Just as a cell perpetuates itself with information-laden DNA, society perpetuates itself with information-laden "knowledge." We are all programmed with information that is designed to keep the *organism of society* alive and functioning, so we may each fulfill our part. Just like cancer cells reprogramming healthy cells, though, this social programming completely covers up our true, reality-based programming and makes us over into ineffective, destructive beings from our very *birth.*

The only way to shed this malignant programming is by conceptually understanding that it is not inherently *true* or *superior* or even *accurate.* As individuals, we are in awe of the sophistication of our "knowledge" as a society, and obediently go about fulfilling our social programming, never allowing an obvious *reality* to give us pause; *every society, no matter how backward or advanced, considers its "knowledge" superior.*

In a hundred years, our "knowledge" will be laughed at just as we dismiss the beliefs of eighteenth or nineteenth century societies. In two hundred years, our most profound "truths" will be considered folklore and faery tales. We don't want to accept this, because it points out that this kind of "knowledge" is not true *knowledge* at all, just subjective *mythic* information. Its only purpose is to program each of us away from our *designed purpose* and into *society's* fold, perpetuating and strengthening itself.

The sophistication of society's mythic programming is surpassed only by its sheer volume. Trying to dismantle it, piece by piece, is like trying to eradicate a *ten-story building* brick by brick. It would be tremendously difficult at best, if not impossible. The only alternative is *destroying it completely in one swift act,* accepting that our entire personal belief system is based on inaccurate, destructive myths and must be replaced.

Must it be an act of faith? No! Because we have the ability, more or less, to suspend our beliefs, walk outside the tower, and look it over objectively to see if it is founded on *reality* or if it completely ignores the obvious construction of the universe. From within we can see nothing.

Suspension of our beliefs is very difficult, because it is hard to recognise just how deep and intractable those beliefs are. However, suspending them as best we can, we can look over the *principles of reality* as objectively as possible and easily see, because of their inescapable, blatant nature, that the building *must come down.*

07.
ACID DROPS

With a mighty crash, Michael's kitchen wicker stand came down, shattering plates, saucers, cups and glasses across the kitchen floor. Bernadette held her breath as the noise echoed through the flat and she watched one plate, unbroken, dance around the floor as if it were a coin she had spun.

The key had been exactly where Bernadette remembered it so she'd had no bother at all getting in. She'd entered through the back door, which led into the messy laundry room. She'd ignored the mess and walked right into the home of her ex-lover.

Commitment.

Now that Bernadette had trashed his kitchen, there could be no turning back. Collapsing the tower of crockery, she realised, was very symbolic of what she wanted to happen to the world at large, especially to Michael. *It is done and now I must go all the way.*

Crunching a shard of glass under her boot, she stepped towards the familiar fridge, hoping to steal any acid drops Michael might have stashed there. Bernadette was both relieved and upset that the old photo of her and Michael had been taken off the fridge door. The photo, of a much happier time, had been taken at a squat party in Lausanne, Switzerland where they had both gone to visit some friends a few years ago. *I wonder where that photo is now.* In its stead, there was a postcard of a bronze warrior statue.

The fridge magnets spelt out 'MILK LOVE BREAST IS DINNER. COSMIC TRIGGER. MINE IS GORGEOUS BIGGER.' She had had a lot of fun with Michael spelling out funny sentences on the fridge. For a moment, Bernadette considered writing a message, but *no, there's work to be done.*

Commitment.

Bernadette was fulfilling the prophecy she herself had made once: "Michael, you can't change the world. Your attempts will bounce back and destroy you. You trust too much. Society has its demons. You can't ignore them or they will destroy you."

"DESTROY YOU!" she shouted in her loudest whisper as she pulled several jars out of the fridge onto the already messy floor, allowing mustard to mix with shards of crockery and dabs of jam.

Alas, there were no drugs in the fridge.

Bernadette took the statue postcard off the fridge and read the back:

Dear Michael,

I'm having a great time in Iceland. The eclipse was absolutely amazing and the lesbian scene here is flourishing! We had a major Thor invocation here with the local witches. The god of thunder came and it was very fucking powerful. I hope the magic is strong in whatever you are doing and whoever you find to be with next.

Lots of Love,
Helene xxx

What a fucking bitch that fucking bitch Helene is! Michael was mine... He was all mine you fucking bitch – fucking witch. What is this thing you've gotten him into? Please don't hurt him...

Suppressing her rage and tears, Bernadette read the writing on the front of the postcard: "10th century bronze statue of Thor, the Norse god of Thunder". Bernadette tore the postcard in two and put both pieces into her backpack as she cynically laughed her way into the living room. *Ludicrous! What the fuck is he doing? And what is Helene talking about? An invocation of the god of thunder? God of my arse, more like! Science can easily prove there are no gods!*

08.

THE LAY OF BURLEY

<Douglas Ezzy>

Asgard is the home of the Gods. Late one morning a human named Burley arrived outside. He pounded on the mighty gates and demanded a meeting with the Gods. The Gods were surprised by the arrogance and hubris of this human, but intrigued by his courage. They thought a meeting might lead to something worthwhile, and decided to give Burley an audience. The gates were opened, and a feast was declared for that evening at Valholl, one of Odin's halls, where Burley would be given an opportunity to speak.

Burley spent the day exploring Asgard. The Gods allowed him to wander their walled city. He visited the halls of various Gods, including the Hall of Bilskirnir with 540 rooms, the home of Thor. Burley had a rather unpleasant encounter with the goats from Thor's chariot. He insisted on his right to ride in the chariot, even though Thor was not there and had not granted him any such permission. The goats refused to move, while Burley tried alternately commanding them authoritatively and then speaking quiet seductive words. Both strategies were equally useless. He dismounted in disgust.

Burley had a more pleasant encounter with Bragi, the God of poetry. Bragi invited Burley to join him for a midday feast, and they spent the afternoon drinking mead and reciting poetry, each amazed and thrilled to find another skilled in the art and craft of the spoken word.

At the evening feast, Burley was invited to speak. Burley said: "I bring word from a city in Midgard called Pubmootgard where the Atheisnir live. You must all come to live there as the time of Asgard has passed. A dwarf called Scientrix who lives in Pubmootgard has built a cunning machine that will consume the bridge Bifrost, and Asgard will be cut off from the world. Even now it begins to gnaw away at the roots of Bifrost."

Thor rose to his feet, already furious at Burley's treatment of his goats, and said: "This idea is crazy. If I were not in this feasting hall you would feel the weight of my hammer on your head." Thor was angry and blood flushed his cheeks.

Burley replied: "I'll gladly meet you in a duel, but be warned, Scientrix has made me a hammer mightier than yours, and it will be your head that is crushed, not mine."

The anger in Thor rumbled like a volcano preparing to erupt, and some of the Gods thought he would strike Burley there and then. The Goddess Sif moved to her husband's side and whispered in his ear. As she spoke the blood drained from his cheeks. He glared at Burley's insult, and took his seat.

Odin rose to his feet and said: "Greetings Burley, now that you have come into my hall and begun so badly, let us see if your wisdom meets up to your hubris."

Burley replied: "Who is this who addresses me with such condescension? If I prove to be the wiser, you must come and live in my city of Pubmootgard with the Atheisnir."

Odin had spoken a rune, and disguised himself from Burley. Odin said: "Gagnrad I am called, and I have travelled far and wide. I know your city Pubmootgard well, and, although it is pleasant to visit, I am not so sure I want to live there. If you lose, you must remain here in our city and use your skills as I request. Let us test your wisdom."

Burley said: "Gladly I will duel with you. Whether you wish it or not, you shall come and live in Pubmootgard."

Odin said: "Tell me this Burley, as I foresee you have great wisdom about all things. What is the earth called that lies beneath the feet of men, in all the worlds?"

Burley said: "The Aesir call it ground, and the Vanir call it ways. The giants say evergreen, the elves the growing one, and the Powers call it loam.[1] Of course, all these names are empty words. The only true name is that used by men: earth."

Odin said: "I will ignore for a moment the hubris of men. Tell me Burley, since you are so wise, how was the earth formed, and the sky above?"

Burley said: "The Gods say that the earth was formed from the primeval giant Ymir's flesh, and the sky from his skull. But we the Atheisnir know this to be a lie. The giant Big Bang formed all the worlds and their skies. Thus has Scientrix written, and all he writes is true."

Odin said: "I will ignore for a moment the arrogance of men. Tell me Burley, since you are so wise, who are the Gods?"

Burley said: "Well Gagnrad, the Gods were once but mortal men and women, doomed to die. They are now just myths and legends, and if they lived at all they were no wiser than me, and certainly less wise than Scientrix."

Odin stood silently for a moment. He could see that Thor's anger was returning and Thor was eager to teach Burley and Scientrix a little humility with his hammer. However, Odin also held great affection for Burley and the people of Pubmootgard. Burley was a great artist and Odin had admired his work displayed in many halls. Burley was also skilled in poetry and song, and could move both men and women's hearts through his recounting of the ancient lore.

Odin motioned to Thor, and whispered in his ear so that none save Thor could hear. Thor's face changed from rage to a grin and he laughed and returned to his seat. Burley wondered what had been said, but dared not ask. Odin had told Thor what he had seen that morning whilst looking out over the world from his high seat Hlidhskjalf. Odin had seen the machine that was cunning, large and dangerous, roaming the fields where Bifrost meets Midgard, the land of men. Odin had also seen that

1 These sentences are almost a word for word quote from Carolyne Larrington's translation of "The Poetic Edda", Oxford University Press, 1996, p. 110.

the machine was unable to find Bifrost, and so could not destroy it. Instead, at first it had roamed the fields, lost and confused, attacking any thing of beauty or importance, such as houses, halls, trees, rivers, or anything that resembled a bridge. However, it had developed a technical fault, and was now consuming itself.

Odin turned to Burley and resumed his questions. "Tell me Burley, since you are so wise, have not the machines created by Scientrix been the cause of great sorrow and pain in the world?"

Burley was furious and replied: "You know as well as I do, Gagnrad, that Odin himself charged the Goddess Freya with the spreading of war and discord. I do not think the wisdom of Scientrix or the brilliance of his creations can be diminished on this count."

Odin smiled and nodded in acknowledgement. Burley had spoken well. He continued: "Tell me Burley, since you are so wise, where do men go when they die?"

Burley said: "Nowhere. Their bodies return to the earth, their memories linger on in poetry and song, but they cease to be."

Odin laughed long and loudly. Such was the vigour of his laugh that the Einherjar joined in. The Einherjar are the heroic dead, warriors chosen by Odin from among those who die in battle. They wait, feasting in his hall until Ragnarok, when they will fight alongside Odin at the end of things. Odin drained his horn and smiled broadly as the warriors, equally amused, raised their horns and drained them also.

Odin said: "I will ignore for a moment the myopia of men. Tell me Burley, since you are so wise, what is beauty and where can it be found?"

Burley said: "Beauty is found in the smallest leaf of Yggdrasil, the coldest ice crystal, the dancing flames of a hearth, and the face of Freya. Beauty is an appreciation of the complexity of the world. Some say that it takes us beyond ourselves and into a relationship of love, but how can you love a tree, an ice crystal, a flame, or a Goddess?"

Odin said: "I will ignore for a moment the insensitivity of men. Tell me Burley, since you are so wise, what is love?"

Burley said: "Love is an emotion. It is wonderfully pleasurable, but is not a sound basis for understanding the world. Only rational thought can guide us and lead us without error."

Odin said: "I will ignore for a moment your disenchanted world. Tell me Burley, since you are so wise, why did you marry your wife?"

Burley said: "Out of love."

At this the whole hall broke out into roars of laughter. Odin sat down and the assembled horde began to feast and drink and talk loudly among themselves. Burley sat down confused, somewhat angry, but still determined. He banged the table loudly with his hammer. He still had things to say. But no one took any notice. It was clear he had lost the wager.

Later that night as the Gods and warriors filed out of the hall Burley was offered a bed, which he gladly accepted. He slept, if somewhat fitfully.

Early the next morning Burley rose to find a valkyrie at his side. She took his hand and led him to a green glade with an apple tree at its centre. The tree was tended by the Goddess Idun, who picks the apples and gives them to the Gods to eat. Idun's apples grant the Gods immortality. At one time Loki, the doer of good and the doer of evil, had lured Idun away from her apple tree and allowed her to be imprisoned by the giant Thjazi. Since only Idun could pick the apples, the Gods grew old and nearly died until Odin forced Loki to go and rescue Idun so she could again distribute her apples to the Gods. The valkyrie then said to Burley: "Paint what you see, this is what Gagnrad has appointed to fulfil the wager." In one corner of the glade was a large canvas and a wide selection of paints of such colour, richness, and subtlety that Burley immediately fell in love with his task.

Burley spent the day in that glade, and the days following. The valkyrie brought food and drink, and led Burley to and from his bed. Burley began painting the glade and Idun tending the tree. He could easily have fallen in love with Idun, seduced by her grace and unfeigned innocence. But he found that the greatest challenge was not to paint Idun, but the apples. Despite the vast array of tones and hues before him, the painted apples never seemed quite right.

His mind moved between the beauty before him and his debate with Gagnrad. "Why did the Gods not understand? Surely it was obvious to all that he, Burley, was right? Gagnrad had only won through clever word play. Gagnrad's argument had no substance." So his thoughts raged.

Then, on the seventh day, he remembered his wife, and their small child. His thoughts were filled with sadness and fear that he would never see them again. As he stood before his painting, his tears mixed with the paint and the apples finally found their colour. The painting was complete. He signed his name, and lay on the grass exhausted.

Later that day the valkyrie returned to collect Burley. She woke him from his slumber and led him by his hand to Valholl. He carried the painting under his arm. The Gods and the Einherjar were assembled and Burley was left standing. Odin rose to his feet and said: "Hail Burley, let us see what you have made."

Burley held his painting up and all in the hall were quiet, such was its subtlety and beauty. Odin motioned with his hand and the valkyrie lifted the painting onto the wall where it remains to this day. Burley was overwhelmed, and awed at the reception. He wept for a second time.

Odin turned to him and said: "Burley, we have spoken harsh words to each other, but your painting has spoken beyond those words and revealed your heart. You may now return to your city, and there will be peace between us. However, before you return, there is one last task to be performed."

Odin motioned to the God Bragi, whom Burley had met earlier. Bragi rose to his feet and smiled at Burley. Burley felt warmth in his heart.

Bragi began to recite a story that Burley knew well, of the great battle of Ragnarok. Burley and Bragi had recited it together on his first day in Asgard. Again their voices entwined and echoed as the words evoked deeds of courage and honour, and moments of loss and sadness. After their words finished, all were silent.

Odin was the first to speak: "Go now Burley. Return to your city. You have painted and sung with great beauty, and for that I toast you." Odin raised his horn in Burley's honour and then drained it. All the others did likewise. Burley realised that his adversary had been Odin all along, and bowed his head in honour.

Burley returned to the city of Pubmootgard with less than he had hoped, but more than he had expected. After embracing his wife and child, he went straight to his studio and began a new painting.

09.

TIMBER

Crash! A small painting of an apple orchard and a pile of books tumbled noisily off the bookshelf and onto the floor.

The first thing Bernadette had seen upon entry into Michael's living room was a stack of books on the most bizarre subjects. Her first instinct was to destroy them all. But then she thought more about her strategy and remembered her goal was to discover, not to destroy. She wanted to find out *exactly* what he was getting into. The best way to do that was to take everything relevant with her.

Bernadette walked across the familiar living room to Michael's desk to see what she could find. She had last been in here six months ago, back when they were still a couple. There were stacks of papers, as usual, plus his kitsch Smurf lamp. Pushed to one side was his laptop with a new, pink 'Capitalism Is Boring' sticker on it. There were also scattered piles of papers and letters. Most obvious was a book with a 'Treadwell's Bookshop' bookmark sticking out of it. She picked the book up and opened it to the marked page to see what Michael had been reading. She saw that he had highlighted a section with a fluorescent yellow marker pen.

There is no way to get that fluorescent marker off. I would never destroy one of my books like that. The Michael I loved wouldn't have either! With a frown, Bernadette read the highlighted text:

Goethe's Faust provides a classic example of the same breast quest conveyed in a different symbolism:

FAUST:
A lovely dream once came to me;
I then beheld an apple tree,
And there two fairest apples shone;
They lured me so I climbed thereon.

YOUNG WITCH:
Apples have been desired by you
Since first in Paradise they grew;
And I am moved with joy to know
That such within my garden grow.

Freud commented tersely on this exchange: "There is not the slightest doubt what is meant by the apple-tree and the apples." In fact, *a nice apple dumpling shop* is Cockney slang for a pair of firmly rounded breasts.

Some readers will be thinking of the Garden of Eden at this point, and they are probably right. It has long puzzled and provoked scholars that both Eve in that story, and the Goddess Eris in Greek mythology, are associated with apples and that the apples in both cases made a great deal of trouble. In the Hebrew story, Eve insists on eating a certain apple (actually, Genesis only says fruit, but the tradition has always identified it with the apple), and Yehweh, the local volcano-god, is thrown into a fury and curses her and all mankind, for reasons that are far from perfectly clear.

In the Greek story, Zeus slights Eris by not inviting her to a banquet on Olympus and she gets her revenge by manufacturing a golden apple inscribed KALLISTI ("To the prettiest one") and rolling it into the banquet hall. Immediately all the goddesses begin squabbling, each claiming to be the prettiest one and entitled to the apple; this quarrel worsens until men as well as gods are drawn into it and eventually the Trojan War results. Eris became known as the goddess of chaos and the golden apple is called the apple of discord.

Bernadette closed the book and placed it back on the desk exactly as she had found it. With an afterthought, she picked it up and read the front cover. The book was titled 'Ishtar Rising' and had been written by a certain Robert Anton Wilson. *Am I really going to do this? Should I live and let live? Or should I exact my revenge on the man who broke my heart?* Then: *It will be for his own good. This is the only way I can help him,* and with that she put the book into her backpack to be read later. Without a second thought, she put his laptop in there too.

She pulled the top desk drawer open, revealing Michael's British passport, a number of journals and a small wooden box. Opening to the back of the passport, she saw his photo stamped and laminated onto the last page. She looked at it for a few moments with mixed apprehension, guilt and a sense of duty. Memories of her love for him flooded back in causing her to close her eyes for a few moments and breathe deeply.

Such beautiful times we had, Michael. Why did you give all that up and choose madness? After regaining her composure, Bernadette opened her eyes and put the passport back in the drawer. She took the journals out, put them in her backpack and closed the drawer. *Madness...*

She then ruffled through the papers that were spread across his desk to see if there was anything else that would help her in her quest. She pushed a pile of bills and other boring-looking letters onto the floor and shoved a few hand-written letters into her backpack. Deciding what to do with each item was a task in itself, so Bernadette took her time.

In a sense Bernadette knew that by trashing his house, she was doing Michael a favour. She feared society and all of its maniacs with good reason. By scaring him now, perhaps she'd make him wise up enough to avoid some future tragedy. Any which way you looked at it, it was healthy to fear society. The world was full of corrupt politicians, evil murderers, rapists, psychopaths and weirdos. *A healthy dose of fear can really help you survive the enormity of weird shit out there, Michael.*

10.
Excerpt From THE ILLUMINATUS TRILOGY
<Robert Shea & Robert Anton Wilson>

I had been reading Pat Walsh's memos, at home, and listening to a new record from the Museum of Natural History. I was adding a few new samples to my collection of Washington-Weishaupt pictures on the wall, when the saucer appeared hovering outside my window. Needless to say, it didn't particularly surprise me; I had saved a little of the AUM, after Chicago, contrary to the instructions from ELF, and had dosed myself. After meeting the Dealy Lama, not to mention Malaclypse the Elder, and seeing that nut Celine actually talk to gorillas, I assumed my mind was a point of receptivity where the AUM would trigger something truly original. The UFO, in fact, was a bit of a letdown; so many people had seen them already, and I was ready for something nobody had ever seen or imagined.

It was even more of a disappointment when they psyched me, or slurped me aboard, and I found, instead of Martians or Insect Trust delegates from the Crab Galaxy, just Hagbard, Stella Maris and a few other people from the Leif Erikson.

"Hail Eris," said Hagbard.

"All hail Discordia," I replied, giving the three-after-two pattern, and completing the pentad. "Is this something important, or did you just want to show me your latest invention?"

The inside of the saucer was, to be trite, eerie. Everything was non-Euclidean and semitransparent; I kept feeling that I might fall through the floor and hurtle to the ground to smash myself on the sidewalk. Then we started moving and it got worse.

"Don't let the architecture disturb you," Hagbard said. "My own adaptation of some of Bucky Fuller's synergetic geometry. It's smaller, and more solid, than it looks. You won't fall out, believe me."

"Is this contraption behind all the flying saucer reports since 1947?" I asked curiously.

"Not quite," Hagbard laughed. "That's basically a hoax. The plan was created in the United States government, one of the few ideas they've had without direct Illuminati inspiration since about the middle of Roosevelt's first term. A reserve measure, in case something happens to Russia and China."

"Hi, baby," I said softly to Stella, remembering San Francisco. "Would you tell me, minus the Celine rhetoric and paradox, what the hell he's talking about?"

"The State is based on threat," Stella said simply. "If people aren't afraid of something, they'll realize they don't need that big government hand picking their pockets all the time. So, in case Russia and China collapse from internal dissension, or get into a private war and blow each other to hell, or suffer some unexpected natural calamity like a series of earthquakes, the saucer myth has been planted. If there are no earthly enemies to frighten the American people with, the saucer myth will immediately change. There will be 'evidence' that they come from Mars and are planning to invade and enslave us. Dig?"

11. ADVANCED CONSPIRACY THEORY

It used to be Aliens.
Now of course, it's 'terrorists.'
That - and the fear of being called 'unpatriotic.'

12.
Excerpt from THE ILLUMINATUS TRILOGY
Robert Shea & Robert Anton Wilson

Hagbard said, "America is the target now. They've got most of Europe and Asia. Once they get America, they can come out into the open. The world will then be much as Orwell predicted in *Nineteen Eighty-four.* They bumped him off after it was published, you know. The book hit a little too close to home. He was obviously on to them – the references to Inner and Outer parties with different teachings, O'Brien's speech about power being an end in itself – and they got him. Orwell, you see, ran across them in Spain, where they were functioning quite openly at one point during the Civil War. But artists also arrive at truth through their imaginations, if they let themselves wander freely. They're more likely to arrive at the truth than more scientific-minded people."

"You've just tied two hundred years of world history up in a theory that would make me feel I should have myself committed if I accepted it," said George. "But I'm drawn to it, I admit. Partly intuitively – I feel you are a person who is essentially sane and not paranoid. Partly because the orthodox version of history that I was taught in school never made sense to me, and I know how people can twist history to suit their beliefs, and therefore I assume that the history I've learned is twisted. Partly because of the very wildness of the idea. If I learned one thing in the last few years, it's that the crazier an idea is the more likely it is to be true. Still and all, given all those reasons for believing you, I would like some further sign."

Hagbard nodded. "All right. A sign. So be it. First, a question for you. Assuming your boss, Joe Malik, was on to something – assuming that the place he sent you did have something to do with assassinations and might lead to the Illuminati: what would be likely to happen to Joe Malik?"

"I know what you're suggesting. I don't like to think about it."

"Don't think." Hagbard suddenly pulled a telephone from under the railing of the ship. "We can tap into the Bell System through the Atlantic cable from here. Dial the New York area code and dial any person in New York, any person who could give you up-to-date information on Joe Malik and on *Confrontation* magazine. Don't tell me who you're dialing. Otherwise, you might suspect I had someone on the ship impersonate the person you want to speak to."

Holding the phone so Hagbard couldn't see, George dialled a number. After a wait of about thirty seconds, after numerous clicks and other strange sounds, George could hear a phone ringing. After a moment, a voice said, "Hello."

"This is George Dorn," said George. "Who is this?"

"Well, who the hell did you think it was? You dialed my number."

"Oh, Christ," said George. "Look, I'm in a place where I don't trust the phones. I have to be sure I'm really talking to you. So I want you to identify yourself without my telling you who you're supposed to be. Do you understand?"

"Of course I understand. You don't have to use that grade school language. This is Peter Jackson, George, as I presume you intended that it should be. Where the hell are you? Are you still in Mad Dog?"

"I'm at the bottom of the Atlantic Ocean."

"Knowing your bad habits, I'm not surprised. Have you heard about what happened to us? Is that why you're calling?"

"No. What happened?" George gripped the telephone tighter.

"The office was blown up by a bomb early this morning. And Joe has disappeared."

"Was Joe killed?"

"Not as far as we know. There weren't any bodies in the wreckage. How about you - are you okay?"

"I'm getting into an unbelievable story, Peter. It's so unbelievable that I'm not going to try to tell you about it. Not till I get back. If you're still running a magazine there then."

"As of now there's still a magazine, and I'm running it from my apartment," said Peter. "I only hope they don't decide to blow me up."

"Who?"

"Whoever. You're still on assignment. And if this has anything to do with what you've been doing down in Mad Dog, Texas, you're in trouble. Reporters are not supposed to go around getting their boss's magazines bombed."

"You sound pretty cheerful, considering Joe might be dead."

"Joe is indestructible. By the way, George, who's paying for this call?"

"A wealthy friend, I think. He's got a corner on flax or something like that. More on him later. I'm going to sign off now, Pete. Thanks for talking."

"Sure. Take care, baby."

George handed the phone to Hagbard. "Do you know what's happened to Joe? Do you know who bombed *Confrontation?* You knew about this before I called. Your people are pretty handy with explosives."

Hagbard shook his head. "All I know is, the pot is coming to a boil. Your editor, Joe Malik, was onto the Illuminati. That's why he sent you to Mad Dog. As soon as you show your face down there, you get busted and Malik's office is bombed. What do you think?"

"I think that what you've been telling me is the truth, or a version of it. I don't know whether to trust you completely. But I've got my sign. If the Bavarian Illuminati don't exist, *something* does. So, then, where do we go from here?"

Hagbard smiled. "Spoken like a true *homo neophilus,* George. Welcome to the tribe. We want to recruit you, because you are so gullible. That is, gullible in the right way. You're sceptical about conventional wisdom, but attracted to unorthodox ideas. An unfailing mark of *homo neophilus.* The human race is not divided into the irrational and the rational, as some idealists think. All humans are irrational, but there are two different kinds of irrationally — those who love old ideas and hate and fear new ones, and those who despise old ideas and joyfully embrace new ones. *Homo neophobus* and *homo neophilus. Neophobus* is the original human stock, the stock that hardly changed at all for the first four million years of human history. Neophilus is the creative mutation that has been popping up at regular intervals during the past million years, giving the race little forward pushes, the kind you give a wheel to make it spin faster and faster. Neophilus makes a lot of mistakes, but he or she moves. They live life the way it should be lived, ninety-nine percent mistakes and one percent viable mutations. Everyone in my organization is *neophilus,* George. That's why we're so far ahead of the rest of the human race. Concentrated neophilus influences, without any neophobe dilution. We make a million mistakes, but we move so fast that none of them catch up with us. Before you get any deeper, George, I'd like you to become one of us."

"Which means what?"

"Become a Legionnaire in the Legion of Dynamic Discord."

George laughed. "Now that sounds like a gas. But it's hard to believe that an organization with an absurd name like that could build anything as serious as this submarine, or work for such a serious end as foiling the Ancient Illuminated Seers of Bavaria."

Hagbard shook his head. "What's serious about a yellow submarine? It's right out of a rock song. And everybody knows people who worry about the Bavarian Illuminati are crackpots. Will you join the Legion— in whatever spirit you choose?"

"Certainly," said George promptly.

Hagbard clapped him on the back. "Ah, you're our type, all right. Good. Back through the door you came, then turn right and through the golden door."

"Is there someone lifting a lamp beside it?"

"There are no honest men on this voyage. Get along with you now." Hagbard's full lips curled in a leer. "You're in for a treat."

("Every perversion," Smiling Jim screamed. "Men having sex with men. Women having sex with women. Obscene desecrations of religious articles for deviant purposes. Even men and women having sex with animals. Why, friends, the only thing they haven't gotten around to yet is people copulating with fruits and vegetables, and I guess that'll be next. Some degenerate getting his kicks with an apple!" The audience laughed at the wit.)

"You've got to run very fast to catch up with the sun. That's the way it is, when you're lost out here," the old woman said, stressing the last five words in a kind of childish singsong... The woods were incredibly thick and dark, but Barney Muldoon stumbled after her... "It's getting darker and darker," she said darkly, "but it's always dark, *when you're lost out here*"... "Why do we have to catch the Sun?" Barney asked, perplexed. "In search of more light," she cackled gleefully. "You always need more light, *when you're lost out here*"....

Behind the golden door stood the lovely black receptionist. She had changed into a short red leather skirt that left all of her long legs in view. Her hands rested lightly on her white plastic belt.

"Hi, Stella," said George. "Is that your name? Is it really Stella Maris?"

"Sure."

"No honest men on this voyage is right. Hagbard was talking to me telepathically. He told me your name."

"I told you my name when you boarded the sub. You must have forgotten. You've been through a lot... And sad to say you'll be going through a lot more. I must ask you to remove your clothing. Just shed it on the floor, please."

George unhesitatingly did as he was told. Total or partial nudity was required in lots of initiation rituals; but a twinge of anxiety ran through him. He was trusting these people simply because they hadn't done anything to him *yet.* But there was really no telling what kind of freaks they might be, what kind of ritual torture or murder they might involve him in. Such fears were part of initiation rituals, too.

Stella was grinning at him, eyebrows raised, as he dropped his shorts. He understood the meaning of the grin, and he felt the blood rush hot as a blush to his penis, which grew thicker and heavier in an instant. Being aware that he was standing nude with the start of an erection in front of this beautiful and desirable woman, who was enjoying the spectacle, made him swell and harden still more.

"That's a good-looking tool you've got there. Nice and thick and pink and purple." Stella sauntered over to him, reached out and touched her fingers to the underside of his cock, just where it met his scrotum. He felt his balls draw up. Then her middle finger ran down the central cord, flicking the underside of the head. George's penis rose to full staff in salute to her manual dexterity. "The sexually responsive male," said Stella. "Good, good, good. Now you're ready for the next chamber. Right through that green door, if you please."

Naked, erect, regretfully leaving Stella behind, George walked through the door. These people were too healthy and good-humoured to be untrustworthy, he thought. He liked them and you ought to trust your feelings.

But as the green door slammed shut behind him, his anxiety came back even stronger than before. In the centre of the room was a pyramid of seventeen steps, alternating red and white marble. The room was large, with five walls that tapered together in a gothic arch thirty feet above the pentagonal floor. Unlike the pyramid in the Mad Dog jail, this one had no huge eye goggling down at him. Instead there was an enormous golden apple, a sphere of gold the height of a man with a foot-long stem and a single leaf the size of an elephant's ear. Cut into the side of the apple was the word KALLISTI in Greek letters. The walls of the room were draped with enormous gold curtains that looked like they'd been stolen from a Cinerama theater, and the floor was covered with lush gold carpet into which George's bare feet sank deeply.

This is different, George told himself to quiet his fear. These people are different. There's a connection with the others, but they're different.

The lights went out. The golden apple was glowing in the dark like a harvest moon. KALLISTI was etched in sharp black lines.

A voice that sounded like Hagbard boomed at him from all sides of the room: "There is no goddess but Goddess, and she is your goddess."

This is actually an Elks Club ceremony, George thought. But there were strange, un-BPOE fumes drifting into his nostrils. An unmistakable odour. High-priced incense these people use. An expensive religion, or lodge, or whatever it is. But you can afford the best when you're a flax tycoon. Flax, huh?

Hard to see how a man could make such big money in the flax biz. Did you corner the market, or what? Now, mutual funds, that was more down to earth than flax. I do believe I'm feeling the effects.

They shouldn't drug a man without his consent.

He found he was holding his penis, which had shrunk considerably. He gave it a reassuring pull. Said the voice, "There is no movement but the Discordian movement, and it is the Discordian movement."

That would appear to be self-evident. George rolled his eyes and watched the giant, golden-glowing apple wheel and spin above him.

"This is a most sacred and a most serious hour for Discordians. It is the hour when the great, palpitating heart of Discordia throbs and swells, when She What Began It All prepares to ingest into her heaving, chaotic bosom another Legionnaire of the Legion of Dynamic Discord. O minerval are ye willing to make a commitment to Discordia?"

Embarrassed at being addressed directly, George let go of his wang. "Yes," he said, in a voice that sounded muffled to him.

"Are ye a human being, and not a cabbage or something?"

George giggled. "Yes."

"That's too bad," the voice boomed. "Do ye wish to better yerself?"

"Yes."

"How stupid. Are ye willing to become philosophically illuminated?"

Why that word, George wondered briefly. Why *illuminated?* But he said, "I suppose so."

"Very funny. Will ye dedicate yerself to the holy Discordian movement?"

George shrugged, "As long as it suits me."

There was a draft against his belly. Stella Maris, naked and gleaming, stepped out from behind the pyramid. The soft glow from the golden apple illuminated the rich browns and blacks of her body. George felt the blood charging back into his penis. This part was going to be *OK*. Stella walked toward him with a slow, stately stride, gold bracelets sparkling and tinkling on her wrists. George felt hunger, thirst, and a pressure as if a balloon were slowly being inflated in his bowels. His cock rose, heartbeat by heartbeat. The muscles in his buttocks and thighs tightened, relaxed, and tightened again.

Stella approached with gliding steps and danced around him in a circle, one hand reaching out to brush his bare waist. He stepped forward and held out his hands to her. She danced away on tiptoes, spinning, arms over her head, heavy conical breasts with black nipples tilted upward. For once George understood why some men like big boobs.

His eyes moved to the globes of her buttocks, the long muscular shadows in her thighs and calves. He stumbled toward her. She stopped suddenly, legs slightly apart forming an inverse with her patch of very abundant hair at the Royal Arch, her hips swaying in a gentle circular motion. His tool pulled him to her as if it were iron and she were magnetized; he looked down and saw that a little pearl of fluid, gleaming gold in the light from the apple, had appeared in the eye. Polyphemus wanted very much to get into the cave.

George walked up to her until the head of the serpent was buried in the bushy, prickly garden at the bottom of her belly. He put his hands out and pressed them against the two cones, feeling her ribcage rise and fall with heavy breathing. Her eyes were half closed and her lips slightly open. Her nostrils flared wide.

She licked her lips and he felt her fingers lightly circling his cock, lightly brushing it with a friction strong enough to gently electrify it. She stepped back a bit and pushed her finger into the moisture on his tip. George put his hand into the tangle of her pubic hair, feeling the lips hot and swollen, feeling her juices slathering his fingers. His middle finger slid into her cunt, and he pushed it in past the tight opening all the way up to his knuckle. She gasped, and her whole body writhed around his finger in a spiral motion. "Wow, God!" George whispered.

"Goddess!" Stella answered fiercely.

George nodded. "Goddess," he said hoarsely, meaning Stella as much as the legendary Discordia. She smiled and drew away from him. "Try to imagine that this is not me, Stella Maris, the youngest daughter of Discordia. She is merely the vessel of Goddess. Her priestess. Think of Goddess. Think of her entering me and acting through me. I *am* her now!" All the while she was stroking Polyphemus gently but insistently. It was already ferocious as a stallion, but it seemed to be getting more inflamed, if that were possible.

"I'm going to go off in your hand in a second," George moaned. He gripped her slender wrist to stop her. "I've *got to fuck you,* whoever you are, woman or goddess. *Please.*"

She stepped back from him, her tan palms turned toward him, her arms held away from her sides in a receiving, accepting gesture. But she said, "Climb the steps now. Climb up to the apple." Her feet twinkling on the thick carpet, she ran backward away from him and disappeared behind the pyramid.

He climbed the seventeen steps, old one-eye still swollen and aching. The top of the pyramid was broad and flat, and he stood facing the apple. He put a hand out and touched it, expecting cold metal, surprised when the softly glowing texture felt warm as a human body to his touch. About half a foot below the level of his waist he saw a dark, elliptical opening in the side of the apple, and a sinister suspicion formed in his mind.

"You got it, George" said the booming voice that presided over his initiation. "Now you're supposed to plant your seeds in the apple. Go to it, George. Give yourself to Goddess."

Shit man, George thought. What a silly idea! They get a guy turned on like this and then they expect him to fuck a goddamn golden idol. He had a good mind to turn his back on the apple, sit down on the top step of the pyramid and jack-off to show them what he thought of them.

"George, would we let you down? It's nice there in the apple. Come on, stick it in. Hurry up."

I am so gullible, thought George. But a hole is a hole. It's all friction. He stepped up to the apple and gingerly placed the tip of his cock in the elliptical opening, half expecting to be sucked in by some mechanical force, half fearing it would be chopped off by a miniature guillotine. But there was nothing. His cock didn't even touch the edges of the hole. He took another small step, and put it halfway in. Still nothing. Then something warm and wet and hairy squirmed up against the tip of his cock. And, whatever it was, he felt it give as he reflexively pushed forward. He pushed some more and it pushed back, and he slid into it. A cunt by all the high hidden Gods, a cunt!— and by the feel it was almost surely Stella's.

George exhaled a deep sigh, planted his hands on the smooth surface of the apple to support himself and began thrusting. The pumping from inside the apple was as fierce. The metal was warm against his thighs and belly. Suddenly the pelvis inside slammed up against the hole, and a hollow scream resounded from the inside of the apple. The echo effect made it seem to hang in the air, containing all the agony, spasm, itch, twitch, moon madness, horror, and ecstasy of life from the ocean's birth to now.

George's prick was stretched like the skin of a balloon about to burst. His lips drew back from his teeth. The delicious electricity of orgasm was building in his groin, in the deepest roots of his penis, in his quick. He was cumming. He cried out as he fired his seed into the unseen cunt, into the apple, into Goddess, into eternity.

There was a crash above. George's eyes opened. A nude male body at the end of a rope came hurtling at him from the vaulted ceiling. It jerked to a stop with a horrible crack, its feet quivering above the stem of the apple. Even as the leaps of ejaculation still racked George's body, the penis over his head lifted and spurted thick white gobbets of come, like tiny doves, arcing out over George's uplifted, horrified head to fall somewhere on the side of the pyramid. George stared at the face, canted to one side, the neck broken, a hangman's knot behind the ear. It was his own face.

George went ape. He pulled his penis out of the apple and nearly fell backward down the stairs. He ran down the seventeen steps and looked back. The dead figure was still hanging, through a trap in the ceiling, directly above the apple. The penis had subsided. The body slowly rotated. Enormous laughter boomed out in the room, sounding very much like Hagbard Celine.

"Our sympathies," said the voice. "You are now a legionnaire in the Legion of Dynamic Discord." The hanging figure vanished soundlessly. There was no trapdoor in the ceiling. A colossal orchestra somewhere began to play *Pomp and Circumstance.* Stella Maris came round from the back of the pyramid again, this time clothed from head to foot in a simple white robe. Her eyes shone. She was carrying a silver tray with a steaming hot towel on it. She put the tray on the floor, knelt, and wrapped George's relaxing dick in the towel. It felt delicious.

"You were beautiful," she whispered.

"Yeah, but – wow!" George looked up at the pyramid. The golden apple gleamed cheerfully. "Get up off the floor," he said. "You're embarrassing me."

She stood up smiling at him, the broad grin of a woman whose lover has thoroughly satisfied her.

"I'm glad you liked it," said George, his wildly disparate emotions gradually coalescing as anger.

"What was the idea of that last little gag? To turn me off permanently on sex?"

Stella laughed. "George, admit it. Nothing could turn you off sex, right? So don't be such a bad sport."

"Bad *sport?* That sick trick is your idea of sport? What a goddam rotten dirty motherfucking thing to do to a man!"

"Motherfucking? No, that's for when we ordain deacons."

George shook his head angrily. She absolutely refused to be shamed. He was speechless.

"If you have any complaints, sweet man, take them to Episkopos Hagbard Celine of the *Lief Erikson* Cabal," said Stella. She turned and started walking back toward the pyramid. "He's waiting for you back the way you came. And there's a change of clothes in the next room."

"Wait a minute!" George called after her. "What the blazes does *Kallisti* mean?"

She was gone.

In the anteroom of the initiation chamber he found a green tunic and tight black trousers draped over a costumer. He didn't want to put them on. It was probably some sort of uniform of this idiotic cult, and he wanted no part of it. But there weren't any other clothes. There was also a beautiful pair of black boots. Everything fit perfectly and comfortably. There was a full-length mirror on the wall and he looked at himself and grudgingly admitted that the outfit was a gas. A tiny golden apple glinted on the left side of his chest. The only thing was that his hair needed washing. It was getting stringy. Through two more doors and he was facing Hagbard.

"You didn't like our little ceremony?" said Hagbard with exaggerated sympathy. "That's too bad. I was so proud of it, especially the parts I lifted from William Burroughs and the Marquis de Sade."

"It's *sick,*" said George. "And putting the woman inside the apple so I couldn't have any kind of personal sex with her, so I had to *use* her as a receptacle, as, as an *object.* You made it pornographic. And sadistic pornography, at that."

"Dig, George," said Hagbard. "Thou art that. If there were no death, there would be no sex. If there were no sex, there would be no death.

And without sex, there would be no evolution toward intelligence, no human race. Therefore death is necessary. Death is the price of orgasm. Only one being on all this planet is sexless, intelligent and immortal. While you were pumping your seeds into the symbol of life, I showed you orgasm and death in one image and brought it home to you. And you'll never forget it. It was a trip, George. Wasn't it a trip?"

George nodded reluctantly. "It was a trip."

"And you know— in your bones— a little more about life than you did before, right, George?"

"Yes."

"Well, then, thank you for joining the Legion of Dynamic Discord."

"You're welcome."

13.
NINJA TUNES

Michael,
Thank you for joining the Order of Dynamic Discord (ODD)! Yay!
Lots of love and laughter,
Malus & Helene.

Bernadette couldn't believe what she was reading. It was printed on the back of what looked like an oversized Joker from a deck of playing cards. *'Dynamic Discord'? I have never heard of anything so evil! He used to care so much about the world! Why would he suddenly be promoting Discord and Chaos?*

Bernadette heard a car noisily pull up outside.

Fuck! What if that's him!?

With a sudden burst of nerves, Bernadette grabbed another handful of Michael's photos, a few more journals and a dozen or so of the weirder-titled books and shoved them into her backpack. She pulled some pictures off the wall and bagged them too. In her dash, she scampered quickly out through the kitchen, over the shattered crockery, through the laundry room and out the back door. Like lightning, she bolted across the garden, up the road and dived into her van before starting it and speeding off into the night.

Phew – I've made it. Ha! I've made it! That bastard! I'll be able to find out what he's been getting into and at the same time I've got revenge for him dumping me! Ha Ha!

After speeding through the streets of Dalston, London Fields and Hackney, and laughing all the while, Bernadette started to wonder where she could go. She needed a safe place to park so she could rest and read through the stolen journals. The most obvious choice was her aunt's property, a campsite to the north of Epping Forest. This would be ideal because Bernadette knew full well it was off-season and the place was bound to be empty. *With Aunt Jacqui away, I should be able to camp for a few days with no-one bothering me.*

As Bernadette drove further away from London's metropolis, she remembered one of her endless play-arguments with Michael - *'Is it better to be a Pirate or a Ninja?'... Well I'm definitely a Ninja now! Ha ha ha!* She turned the radio on and was delighted by the sound of some extremely jazzy Japanese Drum'n'Bass. *Ha! I'm a Ninja! So bring on the Ninja Tunes!*

As she passed Epping Forest, Bernadette was surprised when she saw a group of people heading into the woods apparently equipped for a picnic. *Very odd for this time of night!* Bernadette looked at her van's digital clock and confirmed that it was 12:30am. *What on Earth could those people be doing in the woods at this time of night?*

14. THE WILD DANCE

<Indigo Niebla>

The sound of cars on the distant highway blends into the wind sliding cold through the ragged eucalypts. The glow of the city on the horizon a neon reminder of that which is left behind. The drums have started.

Hollow, echoing through the forest, they beat a summons. Here, in this place, in this time. The darkest night, turning point of the year, the moment of darkness when the world hangs suspended between life and death. We are called.

Life has led us to many strange places. Few could have foreseen our fates in childhood imaginings, the sheer gravity of our daily burdens incomprehensible to the bright minds of the young. We were to be heroes and jesters, to see the world through crystal clear lenses, to laugh, to sing, to dance with the fae. We would burn like stars, illuminated and illuminating, or shine like wraiths in the darkness. We couldn't have known...

The drums call out to long-dormant desires. Desires crushed by the forces that compel our compliance, subsumed into vacant submission. Desires that threaten the fragile balance of work and consumption. Desires that make us human, animal. The thrill of life that runs through our veins, intoxicating, toxic to the powers of suppression and repression. The drums call out. They pound out their message through the forest, entering us through our dirty, dusty feet. The sound draws us on threads of silver towards the source. From the gaps in the darkness, we emerge in silence, gathering.

In the cold light of the full moon, you can see the remnants of the children who once shone with the glow of sunrise. The rich shimmer of silks, a ruffle of feathers, the flashing of jewels. In the darkness, the colours muted and muffled, hidden under warm, serviceable wool. Even obscured by the cold light, the glimpse of richness hints at itself, so different from the grey mornings waiting for the train. We are so far away from ourselves, yet so close to where we started. Knowing, we wait.

The drums send out tendrils of sound into the night. They are joined by a new note, a sound born from human throats yet unlike any language we could name. The sounds blend into a single thing, an entity composed purely of vibrations in the air, created and let loose, to become what it may. It circles us as we wait, expectant. The perimeter throngs with strange harmonics, the sound caressing invasively as it herds us close together.

They come for us, from us. Cut off from us, they have become shadows, dark things crowding the edges, encircling. We see only shapes in the darkness, movement under cloth, flashes of white skin, or is it bone? The darkness feeds our fears, our fears feed the darkness. In the sable night lurks all we disown, all we project from our pale whiteness onto the black. We step forward to meet our shadows. The sound descends into sibilants, closer now, intimate, like a word whispered by a lover. Dark wings move in on us. Surrounded, we are led into the darkness.

We are led deeper into the forest. Ferns brush our limbs, and briars ensnare us as we walk along the narrow path. The soft humus underfoot, the moist earth's sweet smell of decay fills our noses and our lungs. We breathe in the spores from the forest floor with every breath, and breathe out life for the green things with every exhalation. We can feel the forest drawing us in, our substance moving outward to mingle with the humus underfoot, every step confusing the distinction.

We return to our source, the source of life, the forest. We spiral inwards, backwards, to a time when we were not so far removed from the life of this planet, when we knew that we too were a part of this. Before we spread like a plague of locusts, greedy, devouring. Each step brings us closer to what we were before. Each step takes us further from where we are now. The forest remembers us, accepts us, absorbs us, as we spiral into the green centre.

The drum throbs like a heartbeat. A single tone aligned with our footsteps. The Earth moves our throats to voice its song. Rising through our bodies like fluid, it emerges from each mouth round and resonant - *Ommmm... Ommmm....* We breathe out the chant, drawn from our feet and our bellies, ripe with the scent of the forest. We are the voice of the Earth.

Ommmm...

We pass flowing water, fluid, constant, chaotic. The sound of it lifts our song of heartbeat and Earth. The note blends in as those who feel it first let themselves be washed away. *Aaaahhh... Aaaaahhh...* The water flows, carrying us onward.

Aaaahhh...

We breathe, measured to our steps, in and out. From the diaphragm, the air, controlled and sweet, like pipes or flutes. High, thin air, mountain-top born, streams from our lips. The breath of life, the song of life, shaped by our mouths and our desires. *Eieeee... Eieeee...*

Eieeee...

Our path, our past, leads to the fire. Accompanied by shadows, we reach the circle, a lone torch lights the mound of white wood, or is it bone? Fire held aloft, we hold our breath, waiting. The shadow figures close in behind us, marking the boundaries. Flames plunged into the mound, which catches, writhing with fire, glowing with life. We exhale, our breath making the circuit complete, *Shahhhh... Shahhh...*

Shahhh...

Ommmm.... Aaaahhh... Eieeee.... Shahhh...
Ommmm.... Aaaahhh... Eieeee.... Shahhh...
Omaisha... Omaisha... Omaisha...

The drums pick up the new tempo of the flame, upward and outward. Our bodies move to the chant, each finding their way, sliding between the notes. Cloaks discarded, we shine in the firelight. Silk and skin, fur and metal, jewels and eyes flashing in the shadows. A carnival of colour flowing through light to darkness and back again as we spiral in toward the bonfire and back out again. Light on skin, smoke and flowing hair, bedecked and entwined. We have become what we are, creatures of the flesh, born of imagination.

Tonight, of all nights, we are here to honour the flesh. Our flesh, the flesh of the Earth. The flesh that is bound, tied with bindings of family and work, society and fear. Flesh that is driven like a machine, misused, abused and ignored. Flesh which is denigrated, denied, disowned. Set in false opposition to the spirit, our bodies have been made alien, alienated. Tonight we discard the dualism that severs body and soul, mind and matter, male and female, darkness and light.

We are here in the flesh. The word is made flesh. Our salvation resides in our bodies, our selves. This is our heresy: the sacred is here, in our bodies, our desires, in the earth below our feet and the air in our lungs and the tears in our eyes. We are whole. There is nothing to transcend. Tonight we sever the ties that bind us to 5000 years of history, weaving and swaying in the firelight, imminent.

We are given a gift, a sacrament. The flesh of the apple, cut with sharp knives to reveal the cipher of imminent divinity, the five-pointed star. Earth, Air, Fire and Water made one in Essence. Eat this, and you will not die but your eyes will be opened and you shall be as gods. We fall, joyously, choosing embodiment as the concrete emanation of the divine. Our flesh is the flesh of the Earth, the flesh of the apple, the flesh of the gods.

A high ululation breaks the moment. The sound hangs in the air like smoke in the sudden silence. There is a clatter and clashing in the darkness beyond our small circle of light. The shadows gather, and an answering cry sends ice through us all. The keening is primal, discomforting. It strikes us in ways unknown from our civilised lives, yet we understand the familiarity of it all.

Panic rushes into the circle, a burst of fury and energy, screeching and screaming. Tatters fly, swirling flame and ribbons of sparks pounce on the unsuspecting, whirling chaos through our ranks. We are dragged into the whirlwind of madness, dancing. The figure is ambiguous, androgynous. We have discarded the dualisms that inscribe the body with chains of gender. No signs to be read, no symbols to store away for future reference. We accept the indeterminacy, the uncertainty, rejoicing. S/he dances like a wild thing, nothing but sheer energy released to the purpose of this night. S/he reels us in, our shadows and all, laughing, chaotic, erotic, whirling to the pounding, racing drumbeat. We go willingly, divesting ourselves of our burdens for the sake of the wild dance.

We ride the current of the dance, stomping and wailing. We fly. We slither. We run like children in a wild game of tag, yet no-one knows who is 'it' or what the rules are. We crow and we howl, our voices carrying us where our feet cannot take us, back to some ancestral revel or forward to some archaic future. We sing in glorious discord, twisting and turning, weaving through and around each other's songs. And all around is the wild one, goading us, tempting us, challenging us to dance with the fae.

We become who we are. Creatures of flesh and imagination. In the wild dance, no signs are left to divide, to distinguish. We are all Other, other than what we were, other than what we might be. We dance, but we are the dance. We create with our bodies, our movement, our song, the power to be something more than we are, but less than we pretend. We are, in this brief space and time, free from the delusions of transcendence, alive. We know we are born of the Earth. We feel the water of life on our sweat-slick bodies. With every breath we inhale the wisdom of the forest, of life, death and decay, and continual renewal. We burn with the fire of life and desire, the one thing that joins all living beings in the dance of life. We know.

Firelight flickers on bodies glistening with sweat. Some still sway with the echoes of the wild rhythm. Some lie exhausted. Some lie entwined, limb over limb, the fires still burning brightly. The cup passes from lip to lip, rich and red, fruit of the vine, fruit of the Earth. We drink deeply of this night, inhaling the heady fragrance of smoke and incense and sweat. The soft sounds of laughter merge with the wind and the crackling of the embers, drifting through the trees like a mist before dawn.

Sunrise draws near, and we know that we must return to a world we did not create, lives we did not choose. We know that this is just one night, but in this night we have evoked a vision that will reach out, changing those it touches. While we sit here, we know that the power we have let loose on the world will persist, an echo of this night slipping through the cracks of our concrete world, whispering its invitation to join the wild dance.

15. CHOCOLATE BOX

Bernadette felt a shiver race down her spine. She had been driving through the night for nearly an hour before finally making it to her Aunt's property, a lush campsite near Epping Forest dubbed by her Aunt 'The Grove'. Bernadette had come here frequently as a child with her mother and had always had great fun. There were always other kids to play with during the summer, and during the winter the surrounding woods became an enchanted forest where Bernadette played endlessly with her cousins. Bernadette had had a falling out with her Aunt Jacqui and Jacqui's partner Profth, so hadn't been here in at least five years.

Bernadette had heard through her family that Jacqui had started living in the city for most of the year and only ran the campsite during the summer months. As this was now the end of April, Bernadette assumed no-one would be about. After driving around the campsite and car park, she was relieved to confirm that there was, indeed, nobody there.

Bernadette parked the van under a large, dark tree, climbed out and inhaled the night air. *Wonderful. The perfect spot to find out what is really going on in Michael's life.* She took another quick look around the campsite; *I wonder where my cousins are now? Where is Jamie?* Strong memories came flooding back to her of an incident, maybe five years ago, when she had tried to resolve an argument amongst members of her family; Jamie and Aunt Jacqui fighting; raised voices; stubborn gestures; slammed doors... *What was that fight over?* She couldn't remember. *I must get in touch with Jamie and tell him I love him. It's crazy that one bad instant stands out stronger than a lifetime of beautiful memories...*

Bernadette climbed back into the van before her childhood memories had a chance to return and taunt her further. *Focus. This is important.* She carefully took the books, journals and laptop out of the backpack and put them into a pile in the back of the van.

I'll look through the letters, diaries and journals first. I'll check the laptop last because I don't know how long its battery will last out here. Bernadette felt a surge of excitement: *I got away with it! A grand criminal am I! Better than a Ninja!* And then, more seriously: *I really hope I can find a way to help Michael out of this mess he has gotten himself into.*

After switching the van's camp light on, Bernadette cleared a space on her mattress where she could sit comfortably and looked over her collection of newly acquired books, journals and notepads.

23 books - not a bad stash. Bernadette relaxed for a moment and spent some time looking over some of the stranger book titles, including "The Witches' Bible", "Chaos Monkey" and "The Ethical Slut". *What the hell is an Ethical Slut?* She put the books to one side and took hold of one of Michael's hand-written journals.

Am I really going to do this? Do I really care that much? Reaching into her backpack, she grabbed her chocolate box and tobacco. As Bernadette munched on a chocolate, she felt the pain of love lost and recalled the memories of her time with Michael; memories of life being beautiful. She took a deep breath, opened the journal and told it, "okay, magic book, let's see what kind of journey you're going to take me on."

16.
JUST A LITTLE DROP
<Profth>

Sometimes one ends up in the strangest places.

The illumination is somewhat lacking here but my impression is of a snow cave – a circular chamber with ceiling, floor and walls: a featureless, dank white. I must be careful not to get too rigid in my beliefs. Number one - don't feel cold. Number two - I look white too, except where my heel has been scratched and is oozing green blood. That's weird! Looking inwards, dark suffused blue and misty lights, brighter at interchanges. Well, at least something is normal.

~

Once I went to hear a Guru, recently arrived from India. His English was limited so his western followers had taken to correcting him as he spoke:

Guru - When the rain it is falling it is creating bubbles.

Followers - Puddles.

Guru - No that is not correct at all. When the rain it is falling it is creating bubbles.

Followers - Puddles.

Guru – No a puddle is a very small thing is it not. When the rain it is falling it is creating bubbles.

Followers – Puddles.

Nobody thought to ask what the rain was falling on.

The Westerners did not know about the Indians' universal ocean.

The Indian could not envisage the Westerners' muddy allotments.

~

Anticipate problems here with the toilet facilities. Have at least discovered that shit is still brown. Two turds, like eyes, reproach me malevolently from across the cave.

~

I recall my Bumbootee Bu'twa friend in Coomba la Coomba. Bu'twa (pronounced *Bu tock twat*), before the age of political correctness, were called pygmies. Coomba is in the north west of Boonear.

Upon entering my friend's grass hut, he pulled some leaves from the wall and filled a pipe. In those days, many grass huts were made of cannabis rather than elephant grass. Some neighbours dropped in with lunch, meat and tapioca, marinated in palm oil and marijuana, followed by more pipes from the wall. It was a highly stoned group that set out later to hunt. We quickly found a monkey and the Keystone Cops arrived: Bu' twa chase monkey - monkey chase Bu' twa, Bu' twa regroup and chase monkey. My friend at this point fell head first into a large elephant turd. His stoned neighbours were soon rolling around on the ground in hysterics and the monkey, ignored, wandered off in search of dinner.

A couple of years after my stay, a group of Europeans decided things were distinctly not cool and froody for the monkeys of Coomba La Coomba; my friend was deported to a tin shack on top of an active volcano. My friend was very small. His step was small for a man but few of mankind can have fallen so low.

~

I shed a tear drop for my fallen friend and gain a drop of inspiration in return. I don't expect to get high on my prison walls, but tunnelling is feasible and the stuff actually tastes quite good.

"I'm getting out of this place if I have to eat my way out, Stan!"

"That's another fine mess you've got us in to, Ollie! Watch you don't explode!"

~

'The road goes ever on and on'. Am proceeding well, have quite a long tunnel with a steep upward slope, in case I happen to be underground. How thick ARE these walls, anyway?

~

I'm worrying about that green blood thing. The chaos magician's handbook is quite specific about not including people what are 'cabbages or something'. Now I've definitely become a something and have a distinct tendency to become a cabbage. I believe that any chaos not inclusive of cabbages can't be the real McCoy. Considering all the weird things Christians or Muslims believe, I'm really not that loopy. I could even end up as Holy Chao fodder.

I think I spoke too soon, my sickly alabaster skin appears to have transformed into a floppy oversize raincoat that drags on the ground and trips me as I walk. Went to the park and adopted my best flasher pose, quite expecting a green and putrid revelation. The fact that I am still sickly alabaster don't prove nuttin. How many leaves can you remove from a cabbage and still have a cabbage? Chucked the thing away and went back to work.

~

Changes at last: The wall became harder, then I broke through into another chamber, this time almost filled by a large, shiny, black, flat, pear-shaped object. At first I thought of a door, for pear-shaped people. On second thought, it is not only straights who use rectangular doors. On third thought, until I got here there wasn't anywhere to go to. On fourth thought, this thing ain't budging.

That's better: To one side of the obelisk, a small opening in the wall has led me through to a larger, empty chamber. This is definitely a sacred space. Five chambers radiate out from this one like petals on a flower. Four contain menhirs and the last looks like it should have one too. It's like the builders went on strike, piled their rubbish in the last room and walked out. Wrong! There's no way out of this place other than my tunnel. Am going to sit and meditate for a bit and when I get back I'll have a go at patching together a working theory for magic and the sacred.

~

O.K. Now, the fact that this is just me getting my head in order doesn't mean one can ignore the formalities. So we'll have a class of trainee wizards over there and I'll put on my gown and mortar board.

"Good morning class."

"Good morning sir."

Aw get real! What I need is structure not pomposity.

To be an effective Wiz one needs a clear working knowledge of both the sacred and the magical and the distinction between them. These are our yin and yang; without proper balance, the chi cannot flow.

The sacred power is the receptive experiencing position. It entails making contact with specific energy flows or vibrational frequencies, generally through meditation.

It contains a measure of yang, in that one can effect change by increasing or decreasing a particular energy field.

In terms of this theoretical structure, magic is performed by finding places where two or more differing vibrational structures meet, but remain out of sync. The change instigated at such a place will ripple out in all directions and must always be observed for a while to make sure one hasn't created problems somewhere else.

To give some common examples:

> Fairies play on days caught between solar and lunar calendars.
>
> Directions, elements and deities in a magic circle do not and should not fit neatly into place.
>
> Golden section numbers 1, 2, 3, 5, 8 grow harmonies. Magic numbers 3, 4, 5, 9, 1, 3 create tension, thus power.
>
> Imagine a one-wheeled chariot with the wheel properly balanced. You will stay on the road and move smoothly and quickly. Now have the same chariot with a wheel that has its hub off-centre. You will stay on the road but you will have a rough slow trip. Now incorporate a lever so you can start with the balanced wheel and build up speed. Then, when you are going at full speed you throw this lever and the wheel is changed for the eccentric one. Chances are you'll fly straight over the hedge.

~

Back to the tunnelling. I'm going to continue upwards using the outside wall of the chamber group as a ley. That was often where the Hindus got messed up. While they were all expecting to pop and be ditched in the ocean at any moment, not many got the hang of standing on the earth and walking through the world. Most of them were trying to continue upwards into some rarefied upper zone, the proverbial Indian rope trick.

~

As the little lady said when ......(Indian rope trick)........."This is a REAL DOOZEY!"

I had just gotten used to exploring my underground world, when I found it was really a vehicle in crash mode. Without warning, my stomach lurched as my home fell like a lift without moorings. This was followed by a bone-jarring collision that would probably have proved fatal if the walls were not so soft, and a couple of rolls where gravity did a full 900 degree shift. I am sitting dazed, on what used to be the ceiling, surveying my tunnel which is now proceeding downhill. Have decided to persevere in the same direction on the grounds that the shortest distance between two points is a straight line even if you don't know the point.

~

Language is a funny thing; like computers, it requires continual updating. A few years ago, when I spoke of the Matrix, people visualized a kind of crystalline spider's web, which one could enter in order to find connections to re-route or re-weave. All it takes is a couple of movies and the Matrix now conjures images of Emma Peel on speed and multi-cloned humanoid Daleks.

~

The fairground ride has just resumed.

While I fully expected that last crash to have left the vehicle a write-off, the lift has climbed back up the skyscraper. The climb was followed by a shorter drop and another roll. I am now standing on the left hand wall of the tunnel and burrowing on the level.

~

No more large movements, but a continual swaying and vibration have set in, which make me feel quite queasy. Feeling sleepy too. Have joined the owner-builder's club. Created a neat little grass hut built of Indian rope and bird's nest soup on one side. The Taj Mahal walls on the other sides I have carved into a lattice of stalagmites and magical signs.

'... and now perchance to dream.'

~

I have awoken into something more like a nightmare. My prison has fallen into the universal ocean, but it is acting more like a cork than a bubble, rocking n rolling more than Bill Haley ever did.

It feels like my body has been in too hot an oven... My front is hard brown and distinctly crusty. My back is soft and sticky, with tattered lumps projecting outward. The only improvement is in the illumination. The end where I finished digging is now emitting a gentle light in what could be referred to as "moon beam green," but is usually associated with glow-worms or corpse lights.

That's the way to go, holding firmly to a stalagmite, hooking a foot into an ankh to anchor me; a good punch to the light gives me a hole to another world.

~

It took a bit of effort to enlarge my escape hatch, but now I'm sitting on the outside of my prison feeling quite pleased with myself. It isn't the universal ocean that I'm bobbing on, or rather it is, but this particular section has a circular rim, which is immediately recognisable as a cauldron. I'm coming close to the rim now. I'm going to jump.

~

Phew! That was close. No sooner than I had a foothold on the rim, a giant witch tried to take my prison in his teeth.

Yee ha! The prison got away and the witch got a wet head. I nearly got submerged by the wash. I'm going to sit quietly for a moment (the lumps on my back are growing at an alarming rate) and get my thoughts on witches in order.

~

Just about every witch I know has this thing. It is rectangular like a normal door but has holes and lumps like my pear-shaped one. They go to their friends and say, "look at my thing, isn't this beautiful?" They look at their friends' things and ask, "why doesn't your thing have a line there like mine?" or "why is your thing red in the middle when mine is so obviously green?"

If we had words, we could give these things names - jigsaw puzzle pieces. If we had hands, we might give these things a purpose - you put them together and get a beautiful picture.

~

Talking of beautiful pictures, up there in the branches of that old apple tree, nestled in among the mistletoe a pretty lady is sitting. She appears to have forgotten her clothes, but has the most gorgeous rainbow-coloured wings. She is looking at me and wriggling in a most delightful manner.

GWION BYACH, MOVE YOUR FAT HAND OUT OF MY WAY

I'M FLYING OUT

~

Just a few years since this was written and it needs updating. Despite the efforts of the logging companies there are still a few remnants of forest (though at some distance from Coomba La Coomba).

Despite two government armies and three Christian militias all touting AK47s, there are still a few of the followers of Meli'e that have survived the genocide and continue to freak out their neighbours with their elephant dung magic.

Despite the finely choreographed pratfalls of the Bumbootee Bu'twa, nobody was fooled into seeing them as other than magical clowns.

Bu'twa tips for successful hunting :

1. *Find a suitable thicket. Remove Roebuck and leave a book full of apples in its place as bait.*
2. *Obtain a narrow-necked jar. Remove the goose. Replace it with a single apple or several nuts.*

Gently gently catchy ...

17. SECURITY AND PROTEST IN BOURNEMOUTH <Fox News>

The major story at this year's Labour Party Conference is the unprecedented security around the centre of political activities at the International Centre in Bournemouth.

In one police station located underneath the Labour Party Conference site, police officers with guns, flak jackets, sniffer dogs, gas masks, flare guns, stun grenades and plastic handcuffs seemed to outnumber Bournemouth residents coming and going from the train station.

Tens of thousands of police guarded Bournemouth's roadways, bridges, tunnels and its port, while vehicle restrictions in a 3-mile-area around the Centre ground traffic to a halt in a city already congested. Constant air and satellite surveillance was also being maintained over the city. A number of police harbour boats monitored activity along the shore-line. Security personnel were stationed at every hotel housing delegates, politicians, aides and Fox News reporters.

Hundreds of thousands of protesters and demonstrators have also taken to the streets airing complaints on a number of different issues.

"The majority of this country wants the warmongering government out of office immediately," a war-critic told a crowd that had gathered about a mile south of the International Centre site.

Police gave an official crowd estimate of the day's protest at 1,250. One Labour Party official put the size at 120,000, although it took nearly five hours for the procession to pass the Bournemouth International Centre.

Organizers claimed roughly 500,000 protesters had turned out.

The conference will host 2,300 delegates and 500 politicians and about 18,000 Labour Party volunteers will be working the event. About 50,000 visitors will descend on Bournemouth during the week while accredited media number about 11,000 including staff from Fox News. The Conference has cost about £100 million to organise. Security alone has cost the city of Bournemouth about £76 million.

Upon arrival attendees were given a list of items prohibited from the conference. The list of banned items included guns, explosives, fireworks, knives, banners, placards, leaflets, flyers and other security-related materials. Also outlawed from the conference were some less obvious items such as umbrellas, tent-pegs and recording devices. Apples were also prohibited from the conference centre because of the imminent danger that in the hands of a terrorist, they could be used as projectiles.

From http://www.foxnews.com/

18.

>>* DONK *<<

"What the fuck was that!?!?" the Grand Master of Le Templi Malorum cried. Something hard had just smacked him on the side of the face from out of nowhere, snapping him awake from his dreamy, sexy fantasy.

"What did you say, Isaac?" came the call from inside the house.

"Nothing... I'm just thinking out loud," Isaac answered his maid. He picked up and examined the object that had just whacked him and looked around for its possible source.

"An apple?" he asked the strange red-green fruit that would surely be the cause of some intense bruising. "From whence do you come?"

Isaac looked up, looked down and looked up again. He looked at the apple closely, and asked it gently, "what makes you fall with such force my little friend?"

And then, as if divinely inspired, Isaac Newton had a realisation. All the years in the laboratory, all the years in meditation, the rituals, the prayers, alchemical experiment after experiment - all of it finally seemed to make sense. It's as if all the threads of the different stories in his life had come together at once, sending Isaac into a spin, "well, Fuck Me!"

Isaac looked at his hand, in which the red and green fruit sat ever so patiently. He tossed it six inches above his palm and, as if in slow motion, it fell back into his hand. Isaac looked to the sky, stood up and called, "Great Goddess, Shaper of the universal forces, if you can hear me, I thank you with all of my heart." He held the apple close to his breast and continued. "That something so simple as an apple can contain so much wisdom is beyond me. I mark this day sacred. Great Goddess, your power and your wisdom are infinite. Blessed Be."

He looked at the fruit in his hand again. "So that's it," he told it tenderly. "My dear apple, you are surely the keeper of many, many occult secrets. The enormity, nay, the *gravity* of your inner power suddenly makes sense!" He took a noisy bite out of it and spoke through the delicious crunch, "I must tell my Templi brethren about this at once!"

From his leather case, he retrieved a notepad and started to scribble some diagrams.

19.
WHAT WE'RE LIVING FOR

Bernadette was horrified by the many strange quotes, titles and texts from the various books and letters she had taken possession of. There was a lot of obscure writing about angels, demons, spell casting, secret names, codes and rituals.

She looked at more book titles, which was a trip in itself:
Radical Ecstacy
Right where you are sitting now
and *Freedom is a Two-Edged Sword*
were some of the weirder titles.

But even more bizarre were the diagrams!

There were pictures of pentagrams, a strange-looking crossword puzzle with "The Tablet of Union" written below it, and a picture of a hopscotch pitch with "The Tree of Life" as its moniker. *How fucked up!*

There were numerous drawings of candles and sketches of naked people lying on top of each other; a photo of an apple, cut in half with the pips clearly laid out in the shape of a five-pointed star.

Bernadette scanned through the pages of one of Michael's journals. She stopped at a page containing a picture that sent a jolt of fear through her: it was the Devil. *I knew it!*

SOLVE
COAGULA
ELIPHAS
LEVI DEL

Michael is up to his neck in evil! What can I do to help him?

Michael had scribbled a note under the picture, which Bernadette nervously read:

Whilst the image of Baphomet is scary to some, indeed, the Christians would liken this image to their own devil, the picture of the God/dess is actually a very powerful alchemical symbol.

Notice the male and female arm, plus the male and female sexual organs. Baphomet can be used in rituals to bring about powerful alchemical transformations and is, in fact, very holy. See also the light moon and the dark moon. Notice the various elements in there (Wings for air, Goat for earth etc). Also notice the upward pointing pentagram on Baphomet's forehead. This is clearly a symbol of light.

Across the arms are written "Solve Coagula" which means "dissolve and congeal" or, in other words, to divide into parts and then integrate those parts back together. Pure alchemy.

If I believe what I'm told, this alchemical synthesis is what we're living for. Baphomet represents purity through the integration of different parts of the whole. I must meditate on this.

Oh my god! Devil worship disguised as alchemy! But the text makes the whole thing sound beautiful, not diabolical. No wonder it has so much appeal to Michael. No wonder he is being pulled into their web.

She turned the page to see what came next – another glued-in picture:

SOLVE
COAGULA

In someone else's handwriting, there was a note beneath this second picture:

Michael,

This is the picture you asked for. The Shadow Of BAPHOMET, God/dess of the Sabbat, stood over me as I drew it. Hir message came through very clearly: "I sit no longer, as I did in Levi's day. Now I bring the power of SOLVE COAGULA into the world, and walk among you."

Michael, you must understand. SOLVE COAGULA is an alchemical formula which means 'dissolve and reform'. It is an occult truth - things must be broken down into their components before they can be made pure. This is the death and resurrection of the Christians, if they only knew it.

Note the blazing torch upon the goat-god's brow, another symbol of transformation. Note the meeting of upright and inverted pentagrams. BAPHOMET is all things combined: male and female, light and darkness, flesh and spirit.

What must be dissolved in your life, before it can be remade? What changes do you need to make?

Minka

Holy shit! This stuff is so crazy! I haven't heard of a 'Minka' before, she must be one of Michael's new Witchcraft friends. What does she mean by 'made pure?' What does she mean by 'transformation?' When was Levi's Day? What changes does Michael need to make??? None!

Angrily opening up Michael's diary to another random page, Bernadette found a photocopy of an A4 sheet of paper glued in. After inhaling deeply and looking out into the darkness of the campsite, her eyes glanced over the page. *What am I getting into?*

She read the photocopy, which looked like a religious pamphlet.

20. THE SACRED CHAO Excerpt from Principia Discordia <Malaclypse The Younger>

THE SACRED CHAO (pronounced 'the sacred cow') is the key to illumination. Devised by the Apostle Hung Mung in ancient China, it was modified and popularized by the Taoists and is sometimes called the YIN-YANG. The Sacred Chao is not the yin-yang of the Taoists. It is the HODGE-PODGE of the Erisians. And, instead of a Podge spot on the Hodge side, it has a PENTAGON which symbolizes the ANERISTIC PRINCIPLE, and instead of a Hodge spot on the Podge side, it depicts the GOLDEN APPLE OF DISCORDIA to symbolize the ERISTIC PRINCIPLE.

The Sacred Chao symbolizes absolutely everything anyone need ever know about absolutely anything, and more! It even symbolizes everything not worth knowing, depicted by the empty space surrounding the Hodge-Podge.

HERE FOLLOWS SOME PSYCHO-METAPHYSICS.

If you are not hot for philosophy, best just skip it.

The Aneristic Principle is that of APPARENT ORDER; the Eristic Principle is that of APPARENT DISORDER. Both order and disorder are man-made *concepts* and are artificial divisions of PURE CHAOS, which is a level deeper than is the level of distinction-making.

With our concept-making apparatus called *mind* we look at reality through the ideas-about-reality which our cultures give us. The ideas-about-reality are mistakenly labelled 'reality' and unenlightened people are forever perplexed by the fact that other people, especially other cultures, see 'reality' differently. It is only the ideas-about-reality which differ. Real (capital-T True) reality is a level deeper than is the level of concept.

We look at the world through windows on which have been drawn grids (*concepts*). Different philosophies use different grids. A culture is a group of people with rather similar grids. Through a window we view chaos, and relate it to the points on our grid, and thereby understand it. The ORDER is in the GRID. That is the Aneristic Principle.

Western philosophy is traditionally concerned with contrasting one grid with another grid, and amending grids in hopes of finding a perfect one that will account for all reality and will, hence (say unenlightened Westerners), be True. This is illusory; it is what we Erisians call the ANERISTIC ILLUSION. Some grids can be more useful than others, some more beautiful than others, some more pleasant than others, etc., but none can be more True than any other.

DISORDER is simply unrelated information viewed through some particular grid. But, like 'relation,' no-relation is a concept. Male, like female, is an idea about sex. To say that maleness is 'absence of femaleness,' or vice versa, is a matter of definition and metaphysically arbitrary. The artificial concept of no-relation is the ERISTIC PRINCIPLE.

The belief that 'order is true' and disorder is false or somehow wrong, is the ANERISTIC ILLUSION. To say the same of disorder, is the ERISTIC ILLUSION.

The point is that (little-t) truth is a matter of definition relative to the grid one is using at the moment, and that (capital-T) Truth, metaphysical reality, is irrelevant to grids entirely. Pick a grid, and through it some chaos appears ordered and some appears disordered. Pick another grid, and the same chaos will appear differently ordered and disordered.

The PODGE of the Sacred Chao is symbolized as THE GOLDEN APPLE OF DISCORDIA, which represents the Eristic Principle of Disorder. The writing on it, KALLISTI, is Greek for 'to the prettiest one' and refers to an old myth about the Goddess. But the Greeks had only a limited understanding of Disorder, and thought it to be a negative principle.

The PENTAGON represents the Aneristic Principle of Order and symbolizes the HODGE. The Pentagon has several references; for one, it can be taken to represent geometry, one of the earliest studies of formal order to reach elaborate development; for another, it specifically accords with THE LAW OF FIVES.

It is also the shape of the United States Military Headquarters, the Pentagon Building, a most pregnant manifestation of straitjacket order resting on a firm foundation of chaos and constantly erupting into dazzling disorder; and this building is one of our more cherished Erisian Shrines. Also it so happens that in times of medieval magic, the pentagon was the generic symbol for werewolves, but this reference is not particularly intended and it should be noted that the Erisian Movement does not discriminate against werewolves - our membership roster is open to persons of all races, national origins, and hobbies.

21. BERNADETTE'S MAGICKAL DIARY PAGE ONE

That's just fucking stupid. It makes no sense at all. 'Open to werewolves?' What the fuck?!

Bernadette closed the stolen journal and again looked out into the darkness through the van's back window. *Here I was, worried Michael was getting into some dangerous cult or sect, but really he's just getting a bit weird. Maybe too weird. I'm not sure if the danger of the occult stuff is worse, but one thing is certain, Michael is certainly messing with his head.*

Bernadette re-opened her ex-lover's diary, found the page she had last been on, and read the pamphlet again. *It makes no sense. I'd better try to get a good understanding of this, just so I know how I can best help Michael escape from it. 'Open To Werewolves' - What the hell is he doing wasting his life with these losers, weirdos and freaks? I'd better make some notes of my own. Don't tell me he now believes in werewolves!*

Bernadette ruffled through the mess that was the back of her van and eventually found an old Red and Black journal she had 'borrowed' from an office she once worked in. *I'll copy all the passages from Michael's diary that I think are relevant into my own journal and, one way or another, I'll get to the bottom of this.*

She reached over the back seat into the front, opened the glove box and found a pen. Relaxing again into the back of the van, Bernadette flipped through the journal, and tore out all the pages that had already been used. She opened it up to the first clean page and wrote:

Page 1

In this journal, I will attempt to uncover the full truth and facts behind what Michael has got himself into.

In Michael's so-called "magical" diaries, there are many mentions of occult conspiracies, drugs, aliens, ghosts, gods and goddesses, old pagan religions, serpents, alchemy, devil-worship, government cover-ups, secret societies, oriental sex techniques and many other twisted topics. And this is simply after I have briefly flipped through a few pages! Goodness knows what I'll find once I delve in a bit deeper.

Some of the items I should research include:-

1 – Michael writes that Judaism is not really a monotheistic religion as most people suppose. He writes that the Old Testament of the bible is fairly explicit in stating that the God of the Jews acknowledges that there are other gods – but he forbids worship of them. This means that the Jews are not really monotheists like the Christians and Muslims. Research required. But why would anyone care about this?

2 – Michael has written extensive notes about a movie called 'Maybe Logic,' which I will try to hire out (or download). In this movie, according to Michael, aliens from the star Sirius came to planet Earth on July 23rd 1973 – which is the same day that Monica Lewinsky was born. Why is this important to Michael? I'd better watch the movie to try to make head or tail of it. Heaven forbid that Michael would think Lewinsky is an alien! But I suppose that would explain a lot. Ha! There are many pages in Michael's diary about Sirius.

3 – There are some notes in the diary about an LBRP. What is this? There is no explanation, but apparently Michael has been freaked out by it because someone called Gabriel "appeared out of nowhere at the LBRP and asked him some personal questions." Those are Michael's words. Is the LBRP a nightclub? Why has it freaked him out so much? Find out what LBRP means, and who this Gabriel is.

4 – He writes that he is "scared shitless" of a group called "The Illuminati" but also writes he "doubts they exist." Of course they don't, Michael! Snap out of it! On the same page he writes, "maybe the Illuminati are the good guys! They did start the French Revolution, after all." I must research this group to see what has confused Michael so much.

5 – Michael writes that the person most known for bringing Christianity to Ireland is Saint Patrick, and that Saint Patrick is also famous for driving all the snakes out of Ireland. What an odd assortment of facts he's collecting!

6 – He writes that the Mayan calendar comes to an end on December 21st, 2012. Michael seems to think something interesting could happen that day. Only a FOOL would believe such a thing.

7 – Someone named "Sean" has written Michael a letter inviting him to participate in a "Collaborative Magical Multi-weaved Story" project. I'm not sure what this means, so I'd better keep a copy of the letter Sean has written.

22.
PAN OPTICON

Ave Michael,

I'm organising a collection of previously unpublished contemporary themed occult fiction in order to create a Collaborative Magical Multi-Weaved Story. This will be published in book form later this year and will be distributed via the web and other outlets. At this stage I have 8 contributions and 9 other people have agreed to contribute - I would like 23 in total. Each of the writers/contributors are to write a story (with a theme) of 3,000-6,000 words. You'll get published and paid (possibly)!

The common thread for the collection is that each story must contain that most magical and rebellious of all fruit, the apple. I tend to favour stories of an anti-authoritarian nature, in accordance with various subversive mythologies from across the globe that surround the apple wherever it appears. Let me know if you're interested. I'd like to have most of the contributions here by mid-June (1 month!) and then I'll thread them together and publish it as a book. Let me know if you're into it and if you want to contribute.

In summary: I need 3,000-6,000 words of occult fiction, containing an apple, and if possible, an anti-authoritarian message. The rest is up to you! Let me know if you want to be involved...

Escape the Pan Opticon! I've asked Robert Anton Wilson to write the foreword and he has said yes! Once the book is done, I'll send him a copy.

Love and Chaos,

Sean

ps - I've also invited Orryelle Defenestrate-Bascule to contribute.

23.
A MAGICKAL SHORT STORY
<Orryelle Defenestrate-Bascule>

The proposal was for a piece of short 'Magickal Fiction' concerning an apple, of an anti-authoritarian or rebellious nature. FUCK YOU, I responded (predictably), I'm not going to write a piece of short 'Magickal Fiction' concerning an apple because you told (well, asked) me to... A **magical short story** about an apple perhaps, but 'Magickal Fiction' to me is a contradiction in terms.

For fiction is implicitly untrue, that is (since nothing is really true if you're a chaos or Maat magickian, and I am both) it is untrue in the world of form, the physical plane. And for me Magick is all about Manifestation, about results on this plane. Sure the **Logos** is a fine way of starting this process, but to call it 'fiction' is to start off with a statement of implicit untruth. I say 'implicit' because one can still IMPLY truth or untruth with fiction. But why would an imp lie? Well why not? They are lying underneath the truth, they are the under-lying truth.

The point is that all herein will happen somewhere somehow. Well, much of it already has...

"Oh what a dull philosophical ramble," snorted Bistgra the Imp, emerging from under the truth. "Let's get back to the magickal short story..."

"Damn straight," matter-muttered Hestregel Imp from the Shadows, "and anyway, it was not a piece of 'magical fiction' which was requested anyway, but 'occult fiction'. Occult means 'hidden' so there could be truth under-lying fiction just as much as there could be lies under-truthing fact..."

He emerged from the darkness, and together the two Imps, nay three, went outside into the garden. They wandered amidst the ferns and flowers of a balmy spring afternoon, walking slowly, almost aimlessly, along winding paths twixt the effulgent plants, invigorated by the floral scents wafting upon a light autumnal breeze.

"What a beautiful garden this is," remarked Bistgra. "So blessed are we to inhabit its delightful contours and fragrant lilts."

"Indeed," Hestregel replied. "It's been quite a remarkable world since we abolished the concept of SIN."

Eden bloomed about them, resplendent and divine. We die, vines grow, the elemental imps Come and Go To and Fro the Fifth. Dionysos, DiVine HarleQuintEssence, is an invisible presence permeating the garden's winding floral abundance.

"I have to admit," admitted Bistgra, "it is only via the Logos that we ever restored Eden and rediscovered our divinity. ... Although without it we would, I guess, never have lost it all in the first place..."

"Yes," agreed Hestregel. "It was not just Knowledge alone that the Serpent offered... but the desire to formulate it into Words. It was not enough for humankind just to Know. They had to go and Speak, and so the web of lies was wrought, and the under-lying truth was lost. And with that, we were undone..."

Bistgra: "Well, perhaps done, and only recently have we finally undone ourselves again... Speaking of words, if you untie unite you get untie..."

They weren't really Imps of course: they were Gods. But they liked to appear Impish. It amused them Greatly.

~

About them strange nectarous orchids blossom and winding psycho-tropical creepers twine and writhe through the fecund fantasia of flowering form. Venusian dragon-fly-traps snap and clatter amorously, clamouring for the hovering shimmering shiverbuzz draconian wingthings which dart and gleam through the shuddering stamens which stand like seminal sentinels of their blooming brethren below. Petals glow phosphorescent and glisten with dewy globules of concentrated fructification. Nebulous nettles listen, folded like lobes, unfurling and curling their leafy little toes in throes of self-birthing earth-bursting unction. Every bud and thorn has its own intrinsic function in the garden of souls, the moulding of larvae and lava and life in the frenzy of growth, the fresco of putrescence, the iridescence of newth, toiling through soil, the beauty of birth.

In the centre of the garden stands the **Great Tree**. The One Tree, the strong tree with the mighty trunk, from which dance six great branches splitting into smaller branches, gnarled fractal fingers leav-ing their mother-father in a sprangle of diverting paths and buds, down to the intricate twisting twigs and blossoming sprigs of fanning flowers.

There is a hollow in the trunk, an unfathomably deep, dark chasm of potential, and above it the Tree forks into Three, One central shoot pushing upward, ever upward pointing, relentlessly to infinity.

The Tree is a complex device, a simply wondrous symmetrical asymmetrical intricate system; a cabinet of possibilities filed into branching categories with sub-sets and super-strings of infernal and supernal ecstatic outrage and gentle harmonious hummming, a singing strumming of chords and weaving of wyrds, letters and icons, glyphs, myths, paths and channels, carved and tunnelled in an earnestness of growth from the roots of establishment.

This Great Tree of Life is a living thing; though deep-rooted in the soil of tradition, its branches ever-branch, it is an evolving unfurling fractal dance of infinite permutation, a photo-synthesis of carbon copies and new bodies and forms, ever-yawning, its Abyssal maw feverishly jettisoning fresh spores.

The Great Tree is a device, its mechanisms well-oiled and precise, its wheels spinning, sprockets turning and levers lurching in harmonies divine. Beneath the lilting Music of the spheres are the gentle whirring of the gears, the churning of the fears in the belly of the Great Beast, brewing the vine-wreathed wine of ecstatic release, the fruits of the feast of form and flesh, the merge and mesh and melt and meld and welt and weld in the threshing of soil.

The Garden is a part of this great Machine, winding through its ever-spreading knotted roots; its bio-mechanical gardeners gleaning pollen from its floral bed, harvesting the orgasmic joy which drops from their organic dread, weaving the threads twixt the spindles and pulleys, the wires and the vines, seeding the garden with a little inkling of the grand twinkling design.

"...Welcome to **Choronzon's Machine**," said one of the seven heads of the Beast. "The Machine is a Garden, the Garden is a Machine..." nattered another, then bit its brother's head. "We are its organic mechanisms, within its metabolic Morphogenetic fields of play."

Each head, Adrian realised, as he began to penetrate the illusion perpetrated by the **Metamorphic Ritual Theatre Co.**, was actually the real skull of a different type of earthly beast, apparently mechanized in some way so that when the performer within (actually - unbeknownst to Adrian - the author of this piece of faction) drew the strings, the jaws would snap and red lights in the eyes flash.

"The Machine is Choronzon's play," snittered head of Dog. "...The play is Choronzon's Machine," countered head of Fox. Skull of Pig sniggersnickers whimsickally: "He plays in the nursery, his Garden of Possibilities, cultivating strange and hallucinogenic plants in his factory of forms, he guards the gates to the great void from which it is All borne..."

Adrian looked away from the dim and flickering lights onstage to try to discern from the program who was responsible for creating this mechanized monstrosity. 'Amordios Gobblynsmyth' was credited. Hmm...

"The program is a part of the machine," he thought he heard head of Sssnake sssay amidst the clamour of different (pre-recorded?) ssseven voicesss competing with the live (?) one of the performer beneath, "the program runs the machine, from it you might glean the trinary code - for from every two that come together, a third is born, and thus the world of flowering fractal form..."

(The only 'trinary code' Adrian could later find on the 'program' he had been handed at the door when entering the Carlton Courthouse Theatre was,

333 333 333 http://www.crossroads.wild.net.au/chor.htm 333 333 333 333 333 333 ... ...

Was that a play, he wondered, or a ritual, or... ... ...)

Of course not. It's just a story.

~

Back in the **DreamTime** in the glorious Garden that the Australian Aboriginals lost so much more recently than most of the human species, there was a great **Fall**, a Fall from Grace. A Dis-Gracing of the human race. They lost their place in the Garden, Falling from grace, falling from heaven really, to earth, that squalid dense and muddy little ball of horrid matter.

Once it was beautiful, I hear you protest. Ha! Once? Is it not still? Beneath the veneer of garbage spewed forth by those humans seeing themselves as separate from the rest of nature.

The orthodox Christians never thought it beauteous, it was just a gross physical thing to overcome in the quest for divine SPIRIT above and beyond this mortal coil...

And thus this Fall from grace. This FALL IN CONSCIOUSNESS...

~

"I offer forth this Fruit of Knowledge, for I am the ssserpent," sssaid the ssserpent, twisssting with ssshimmering ssscales holding an apple high in its jaw.

"...but know that I am Feathered Ssserpent," it hisssed. Adrian's focus zoomed out from the video projection of the close-up of the ssserpent-tattooed hand holding forth the apple, to the pubescent-nippled blue-skinned wo/man in front of it who shimmied across the stage with snakeskin gloves and peacock-eye-feathered-fan shimmering. S/He lifted the apple high in hir ssserpent-tattooed hand and sssaid, *"...and on the fruits of this Knowledge I shall bear thee aloft, to the top of the Tree..."*

The peacock angel was not only addressing the audience but also another in-it-I-Ate onstage, the Fool in the Tarot Play, an 'actor' who in real life is born on April 1st (no joke!) and thus this Metamorphic Theatrical Ritual was a celebration of the beginning of his thirty three and a third recurring birthday...

The Fool's attention flitted away from the central peacock angel to and fro twixt two women, stageleft and stageright, one the Whore of Babalon (chalice held forth alluringly), the other his Holy Guardian Angel in the form of a Priestess who had stepped from a mirrororirim in a previous scene...

"The apple falls..." and the IMPious (**IMP**: *adj.* fledged with feathers, *old English*) turquoise being released the fruit so that it ka-thunked down onto the stage floor. The peacock angel raised a sword above hir head...

> *"...and is cleft in twain with the sword of division, Zain..."*

~

As the sword struck the apple: not only the fruit but the being, the Tree and even the surrounding garden all split in twain.

"Just a mirror effect," muttered Adrian, toggling the mouse away from the **Arcana XXIII** animation that had finally loaded onto the screen of his Apple Mac. He had followed some wyrd winged eye animation from the link in the program and ended up in a virtual reality tunnel he wasn't really sure about.

Now, as the semi-human blue being from the play he had seen the other night morphed back into a peacock with the neck of a cobra, which was the trunk of an elephant, the words from the play were echoing in his head,

> *"... Each side contains a star, five-pointed each*
> *The ten of Malkuth, the Kingdom of God/dess on Earth..."*

The outspread blue hands revealed a pentagram, as did the apple cut sideways in two, the seed-pods of each side in the shape of a five-pointed star... The blue being hirself stood with legs apart and arms out so s/he too formed a five-pointed star.

"Trippy," Adrian thought, "but I've got work to do. Enough of this od websight..." and he logged off, returning diligently to his university assignment on chaos mathematics. He thought it an interesting coincidence that in his studies that same afternoon he learnt that DNA strands sliced sideways - if viewed microscopically - form the shape of a pentagram.

~

That night in his dreams the blue being returned, and in a strangely pixilated garden, it morphed again back into a snake.

"To the Christians I am the ssserpent," it sssaid, *"and I represent evil, for ssslippery lies sssneak from my forked tongue. And yet in the World of Form, where all is diVided, how can one speak with aught but a tongue which is forked? All Words are lies, and the Truth is under-lying..."*

Then the snake became a peacock, majestic and glimmeringly beauteous to behold, and said in a voice like both bird and cat, *"...yet to the Yezzidi Jews I am the glorious **Melek Taus**, King of Birds. Although they too know I am the Lord or Lady of Matter, they see this as a thing not merely mundane to be transcended, but rather resplendent in its variety of hue and form..."*

The peacock's slender neck twisted and became again a sssnake, but the snake's turquoise scales shimmered and shifted back into feathers, and he recognized Quetzalcoatl, the Mayan Feathered Serpent who is prophesied to rise again at the end of timemit:

*"I am the Morning Star, **Venus**, Kukulcan to the Mayans, Quetzalcoatl to the Aztecs. The Christians call me Lucifer. I am a planet, yet my path and pattern through the cosmos forms a star, five-pointed..."*

And then the iridescent plumage of the Quetzal bird became scales again, still shimmering through the spectrum of colours. It plunged down into and through the red and golden ochres of the earth - the Aboriginal Rainbow Serpent - which they say shall rise again at the end of timemit - winding in sparkling hues through his DreamTime...

~

Adrian rose again at the **beginning** of timemit - that is, the new beginning of linear time that his new day of waking consciousness brought - rubbed the sleep from his eyes, somewhat bewildered to be back, "...bloody computers, they put you in a beta-wave state, affect your subconscious, get in your dreams, it's like some damn program..."

Nevertheless, with steaming coffee in hand he was soon booting up his Apple Mac again.

His dreams came back in disturbing flashes throughout the day. "Lucifer Morningstar?" he wondered. "That's the *devil* isn't it? What the fuck?" ...But isn't the devil supposed to be an ugly beast rather than a shimmering peacock? Is this why in the play (was it a play?) the Beast Choronzon became the peacock angel?...

"And isn't **Venus** the Goddess of *Love*? ...Maybe it's more of a *de*-programming..."

Later that day he read of **Jacob's Ladder**, a Qabbalistic metaphor for DNA (well, which came first, the apple or its seeds? The Tree of Life long pre-cedes such scientific 'discoveries'...) where the 'four worlds' in the model plug one into the other, the most manifest -Malkuth- plugging into the hole of the Abyss - Daath, 'Knowledge' - on the Tree above.

There is a Jewish myth, apparently, that Daath is the hole left when Malkuth FELL to Earth...

Adrian read about the **Global Muladhara-Malkuth base Chakra ritual**[2] which inadvertently created a microcosm of the Jacob's Ladder model, with four interlinked magickal circles each representing one of the Qabbalistic Four Worlds: the micro 11-star formation witch seven sisters wove between Innana's Sephirotic Voudoun dolls in the linked Australian circle; the 11-star Collegiate of the Horus-Maat Lodge linking in astrally to the working from various localities worldwide; the actual Tenstar Weaving of ten individuals (each invoking a Sephiroth, for all the sphere exist within Malkuth) with physical thread connecting them via base Chakra piercings in a ten-pointed star mandala at Mt Shasta (California) - base Chakra of Gaia. Finally the real (native pine) Tree planted in the central Daath position of this weaving, 'plugging' the void left when the weaver stepped out to the circle's edge to beCome the representative of Malkuth...

2 http://www.crossroads.wild.net.au/base.htm

At first, the piercing aspect seemed unnecessary and even barbaric to Adrian, until he contemplated that ancient cultures have been effectively using such earthly and carnal means of gnosis for millennia. He just had to get over his western conditioning of the body and matter as being *separate* from spirit...

Perhaps, he mused, this 'Fall' was just a fall in consciousness. We are really divinity *incarnate*, and it is only the fundamental Christian empire's *idea* (perpetrated by the Logos and other dirty Words) of divorcing spirit and matter that has kept so many from realizing their divinity *in the flesh*...

Strange phantasms of thought indeed! Adrian scoffed at his own wild musings and went to get an apple from the refrigerator.

~

The ssserpent was there again in his dreams that night, but now it too split into two like the apple it had offered - one silver serpent, one gold, coiling up and around like spiraling DNA strands.

And Adrian recognised these ssserpents as the Hindu God/dess Kundalini, the Ida and Pingala Nadis. Recognition awoke him with a jolt which shot up his suddenly-rigid spine delivering a flash of realisation.

And there before him was a glorious vision. He was almost sure he was now awake – in fact perhaps more awake than he'd ever been before - though only one of his eyes would open:

The Great Tree was there before him. From its rigid trunk now hung a man, or a God, or perhaps something betwixt in the beComing. And forked lightning flicker-flashed all around.

This inverted being reached down and drew from the Well below/above strange glyphs. The LOGOS!

And behind H/him the Great WorldSerpent Jormungandr (whom they in the Northern lands say shall rise at the endgninnigeb ofo timemit) released tail from maw and wound up and around the Great Tree, forked tongue flickering...

~

And yet later in the day when the second cup of coffee had assured him that he was no longer dreaming, Adrian could not seem to trans-late the Mem-ory of these strange glyphs onto the flickering screen or even onto a page of paper, though wrought it was of bark of Tree...

Damn. Was this a Fall in consciousness or did he just fall out of bed?

~

Typing rapidly into the document open in my eMac's **'AppleWorks'** Word-processing program, I cringe in frustration that I lost half a page worth of realizations expressed quite fluidly in words contrary to what they expressed about the un-trans-late-ability of diVinity into language. And all because I hadn't saved the document often enough, and there had been a power failure when forked lightning flashed outside. (Fuck it, perhaps the Christians were right with their Fall. After all, *Jesus Saves...*)

~

The ssserpent shimmers iridescent around the Tree, and whispers in Adrian's ear with flickering forked tongue, "I'm not *really* the great Dragon of the Deep Choronzon, the magnificent Peacock Angel or the Feathered Serpent Quetzalcoatl. Of course, I am but an Imp. But I like to appear Godlike, it amuses me Greatly..."

Nevertheless and Evermore, May TimemiT endnigeb for each of you soon(er or later)...

Oh what am I Imp-lying?

24. PHILOSOPHY

Bernadette scanned through more pages of Michael's diaries trying to find the names of people and groups that might be involved in this whole occult charade into which Michael was burying himself. There were many pages, both printed and hand-written, about a group called the Illuminati and about the star Sirius, but Michael seemed to laugh at his own text in disbelief as much as it seemed to scare him.

In a fairly recent entry, Michael had written:

> Unlike the Robert Anton Wilson dog materials which were completely canine, my own experience over the past few months has been much more serpentine. By this I mean the communication I am having and the visions I am receiving often involve serpents, snakes and lizards.
>
> Now, I know these experiences are a load of baloney, but that doesn't make them less scary! How can I understand the subjective versus objective divide? My experiences clearly do not exist in objective reality, and yet they are very real for me. Am I mad? Am I going mad? Or am I finally becoming sane?
>
> I really like the view Malus has on the Serpent, as confrontational as it is. Malus was reading the bible chapter 'Genesis' with Helene and I in the Devereaux last week, when suddenly he put the Bible down and went on a bit of rant. He pointed out that God strolls up to the Garden of Eden and tells the humans, "If you eat the fruit from the Tree Of Knowledge, you will surely die." Along comes the devil disguised as a serpent and tells the first humans, "Hey kids, if you eat the fruit, you will not die, I promisssse. In fact, it will make you very powerful. Ye shall be as Godssss." As the Genesis story goes, the humans eat the fruit and do not die! In other words, the devil told the truth and God's jealous lies are exposed to us right from the start.
>
> Malus' view has got me thinking – how could as blatant a fact as God's deceit go so overlooked? All of Judaism, Christianity and Islam worship a jealous, menacing god that lies. In fact, God said he wants humans to be like him, and then page after page of the Bible is full of God's vitriol, anger, sexism, racism and wrathful vengeance.

Bernadette looked up from the page. *Whoa! That's a bit fucking heavy... isn't it?* She read on:

And the Christian hard-core think Witchcraft is evil? Ha!

I can see why people are turning away from such an angry God and turning to religions that honour life. It seems a good philosophy. But then, I would be too scared to offend God, just in case he really does exist and really is the evil bastard described in the bible. If it came down to it, I don't think I'd have the balls to go up against him.

I am starting to like the Eastern mystic approach, which acknowledges that all the world is illusion. I also like what I have read about the ominously dubbed Chaos Magic(k). How do you spell magic(k) anyway? In the chaos magic structure, what a person believes is considered little more than an extremely limited 'working model.' If the model stops working, the person changes their beliefs! Chaos magicians say "the map is not the territory but all we ever have is a map." I'm not sure I completely agree but in a way it makes sense. They also mind-fuck themselves by switching beliefs deliberately. I'm not completely sure why, but I think it's to ensure they don't get attached to any particular belief system (or 'BS' as Robert Anton Wilson would say).

So, if a serpent creature appears in one of my visions again, I'll try not to believe in it. Believing in serpent creatures can only lead to madness and insanity and certain ex-communication from society if I was to tell anyone. On the other hand, something did happen. It was more than an extraordinarily horrid dream. There was something in that whole Lizard Man episode. But what?

25.
ELIAS
<Frater Kaotec>

1.

I still remember quite clearly how those terrible events of last year unfolded, assuming they were something more than the memories of some horrid but extraordinarily vivid dream. I am no longer entirely sure these days. It's quite strange how dream and reality can entwine. Sometimes the events occur in different ways when I drift off and those horrible things recur again and again.

But Elias is always here grinning at me, reminding me that something did occur in that cold, dark month of December. I think it started three weeks before Yule, I had just received a visit from Mr Lindsey, a local notary, who brought shocking news; news that would initiate a serious altercation between us. The conversation is still fresh in my mind....

“Dead you say? Nonsense! I saw him only last night!“

“I'm afraid that is impossible Dr Franklin. Elias Gapp was killed in an automobile accident a week ago, I saw the cadaver myself. Though I confess there was not much left of his face.“

“Then how was he identified? A mistake must have been made, I saw him only yesterday I tell you!“

“There is no doubt; he was identified by the papers he carried as well as the new 'fingerprint' technique. It was Gapp alright. You must have been mistaken.“

“I assure you Mr Lindsey, I made no mistake. Elias Gapp has been a patient of mine for over five years and I have been in constant contact with him. No mistake has been made on my part. Of that I'm certain!"

"Gapp is dead Dr Franklin."

Arthur Lindsey said no more. After gazing solemnly at me for a few moments he slowly turned and drifted out of the study, in noticeable contrast to his sudden unexpected arrival several minutes earlier.

To say I was perplexed on hearing this news would be a gross understatement. I was sure I had seen Elias across the street that night. Yes it had been dark but it was him alright. Yet here was apparently definitive testimony of his death. Had I seen a ghost? I dismissed such thoughts from my mind, I was a professional psychiatrist and gave no credence to such humbug. Besides, there was no doubt that I had seen a solid man rather than some ghoul. I remembered noticing the water dripping from the broad brim of his hat as he stood in the rain. Ghosts do not get wet!

Had he faked his death I wondered? Surely not hard to do, particularly given his reported mutilation. But there were the fingerprints to account for. The real Elias had been 'fingerprinted' by the police five years ago, after he had been found raving in the street.

Surely some mistake must have been made, though I could not imagine how. My mind raced: Had there been some truth to the delusions he had ranted about over and over during my sessions with him? Of course not, the man was clearly insane when I had first encountered him, and although he had never recanted his bizarre claims, he had become more silent about them as his health improved, thanks to my innovative treatment. If only I had gone out of the house to speak with him. He must have wanted to make contact, or why else would he have stood in the rain watching the house for so long. I resolved to get to the bottom of this, not only professionally in order to close my files on this sad case, but also for the good of my own sanity!

I arrived at the morgue at 9am the following morning and asked to see poor Elias' corpse. The morgue was a grim place which I had always hated visiting. Worst of all was its stench, a mixture of corpse and chemical. The coroner Dr Oort was already there. In fact he was eating a hearty breakfast, having just completed another grizzly investigation, the subject of which lay on a slab on the other side of the room. He invited me to join him but the noxious smell of that place negated any appetite I may otherwise have entertained. I told him of my connection to Elias, but kept my true reasons for seeing the body to myself. To my surprise, I was told this was not possible as he had been buried four days ago. Apparently no next of kin could be found and with no funds found either on Elias or in his apartment, it was decided to unceremoniously put him into a pauper's grave as soon as possible after the post mortem.

"Was the post-mortem conclusive?" I asked, hesitating to ask for positive identification, as even I was starting to wonder about my own experience.

"Yes, he died from internal injuries and massive blood loss after being thrown through the windscreen of his Ford. There were also severe lacerations to the outer surface of the body, particularly the face, which was quite horribly disfigured. You would not have recognised him, I'm afraid. The front of his head was smashed in as he hit the tree. Not a pretty sight, some of my newer staff were only too glad to see him go into the ground. Giving them nightmares he was!" the coroner told me, shovelling a piece of apple into his gaping mouth as he spoke.

"How was identification made?" I casually enquired, trying not to visualise the gory spectacle.

"Oh there was no doubt Doctor, the fingerprints alone proved that. One 'Elias Gapp' of Boston. Fingerprinted five years ago by the Boston Police Department. Very fortunate they did too. Made my work much easier."

"Is the cause of the accident known?"

"Only that he swerved off the road as if trying to avoid something and hit a tree. He must have been travelling at quite a speed, but then he was something of a madman wasn't he?" asked the coroner, delicately putting another slice of apple into his mouth.

"Not at all! My treatment had been very successful. He was well on the road to recovery." The coroner was obviously not familiar with my reputation.

"I wish he'd been able to stay on the road longer in that case," chuckled the coroner, with the characteristically ghoulish humour of his profession.

"Was any trace of what he swerved to avoid found? Any witnesses?" My curiosity was peaking.

"Not really, it was late at night. There was something found on the road though, a kind of oily residue or trail across the tarmac. The police were not sure what it was, or even if it had anything to do with the accident. It may have been there long before. It's a very quiet road on the outskirts of town; not used very often since the mine closed down."

"The road leads to the old mine works?" I asked guarding my surprise.

"Yes, it's about the only place it does lead to. Why? Is that significant?"

"No reason!" I said abruptly and left, fearing I would lose my composure.

"I suggest you talk to Detective Noyes if you want to know more," he called out as I left.

2.

So Elias had been heading out to the old mine workings. Were his delusions returning?

Had even I failed to really cure him? I couldn't believe it. But I was still confused. I had seen him that night several days after his alleged burial! What was the answer? The fingerprints seemed conclusive. Could he have had a twin? Or was Dr Oort, the ghoulishly humoured coroner, involved in some way? Apparently he had made the fingerprint identification. I needed to find out if the police had confirmed it. I would visit the central Police Station that afternoon and find out for myself. But first I needed to return home to eat; the fresh air was restoring my appetite.

On arriving home my housekeeper informed me that a visitor had called in my absence. Another prospective client no doubt. My reputation was spreading far these days. I asked her if the visitor had left a name or address.

"No address," she said. "Just a name: Mr Gapp."

My head spun as she said the name, but I quickly regained my equilibrium. A relative perhaps. "Was there a first name?" I cautiously enquired. Apparently not – it seemed my visitor had thought a surname would suffice. I was reassured, but something compelled me to ask for a description. What I heard caused me to quickly retire to my study and insist I would receive no further visitors or appointments that day. The description was as follows: a very gaunt and pale man, dressed in a dark suit and a broad rimmed hat. He was somehow familiar, she said, probably a former patient, but she could not place him. He looked much more ill than anyone she had ever seen visit me. He had told her he would return.

I sat in my study, the door locked, my mind racing. There must be a logical explanation to all this. One answer could be that Elias really did have a twin brother who had turned up to investigate his sibling's untimely demise. That would seem to be the most rational answer. The only other possible explanation would be that Elias was in fact not dead, in which case the coroner was either badly mistaken or complicit in some criminal conspiracy! However, I found this view increasingly unlikely the more I contemplated it. Dr Oort, like myself, was a professional medical man of some years' standing and a reputation almost as beyond reproach as my own. He could not be involved in such a sordid affair. But then even this was more likely than the third option; that some of the things Elias Gapp had been claiming during the long years of his treatment were in some way true - that those mines really did contain the kinds of horrors he described and that his life was in danger because of it. But that could not be true. His subterranean terrors were clearly just a symptom of his illness and a metaphor for his own psychic state. I shut the thought from my mind; sealing it as securely as the study I had sought refuge in.

3.

Detective Noyes was very helpful but somewhat puzzled by my interest. Not surprisingly, as I had decided to keep my experiences to myself for a little longer, at least until I had some coherent idea of what was going on. He confirmed one concern of mine in particular, namely that Dr Oort alone had been responsible for the fingerprint matching and that the police had not confirmed the match. Noyes, like myself, felt that the coroner's reputation was sound and that he could be trusted in this task. He also added that his superior was from the old school of policing, mistrustful of such 'new-fangled technology' as fingerprinting, which despite having been in use in Great Britain for two decades now was a new addition to the Boston Police. Noyes asked me why this was of concern to me but I held back from a truthful response. I suspect the detective noticed this for he took an increased interest in me following this exchange.

I told Noyes of my advanced treatment of Elias, in which he seemed very interested and suggested he be allowed to see the diaries containing the records of my discussions with him. The case on him was still not quite closed, he said, as little trace of exactly who Elias Gapp was had ever been found. Normally this would be out of the question, such patient records are, of course, confidential. But given the circumstances I decided to allow Detective Noyes access to any relevant portions of my diaries that would further his investigations. More importantly, I concluded, it was perhaps the only way to begin to clear up this increasingly disturbing affair.

Just at that moment Detective Noyes received a telephone call that seemed to surprise him and soon after made another call himself. After this he suggested we travel to my home to explore the diaries as soon as possible. But first we needed to make a little detour, he added, and revealed a new reason why the case of Elias Gapp was to remain open. A witness to the accident had come forward with significant new evidence. We were to interview him immediately.

The drive to the farmhouse of this new witness took about half an hour. I was flattered that Noyes had included me in his investigations, realising this must be very unorthodox, but was not really surprised. He seemed very interested in my insights into Elias' mental condition before his 'death' and genuinely wanted my assistance. Our trip was clearly more than just a detour on the way to my office. I could only imagine he had noticed my considerable talents at psychological analysis during our short conversation. A conversation in which I had recounted my belief that just prior to the accident Elias had been more stable than I had ever seen him. But, as it transpired, Noyes had another reason for seeking my presence with him at the farmhouse.

The farmhouse was close to the road on which the accident had happened. On the way Noyes showed me the fatal tree but did not volunteer to show me the strange marks on the road which I decided not to ask about. We did not stay long. The area had a strange chill to it and an atmosphere the likes of which I had never experienced and could not quite put into words. We drove for only another five minutes along a country lane before we reached the farmhouse. One Thomas Braun was there to meet us and invite us into his home.

Detective Noyes and Mr Braun did most of the talking of course and I just listened. The story Braun told was an intriguing one. He had seen Elias' Ford speeding down the road one night, heading towards the old mine works. Behind him had been another vehicle, an unidentified black Limousine. The Limousine appeared to have been chasing the Ford, as both were travelling at high speed. The two cars turned the corner and went out of sight. Shortly afterwards a loud bang was heard, obviously the crash. Braun had made his way through the woods to the site of the crash. On arrival he saw the Ford smashed into a tree, with a body thrown out of the driver's seat, half lying on the bonnet. Behind the Ford was the limousine, now parked, with two shadowy figures sitting inside. One of these men got out and approached the crash. He removed two boxes from the Ford and placed them in the limousine, which then drove off. No attempt to help Elias had been made because it was then that

Braun had heard 'the whining' again and decided to leave the area.

Noyes asked Braun why he had not reported this before, to which he responded that Noyes knew well enough. A brief conversation then took place between Noyes and Braun that seemed quite trivial and of no import to the matter at hand. Shortly after this Noyes announced that we were leaving but added that he would want to interview Braun in Boston soon. Before we left, Noyes asked Braun what he thought might have been in those two boxes.

Braun was in no doubt, he had seen the contents clearly: "Apples" he said.

We returned to our vehicle and made our way back to Boston.

4.

On the way back Noyes asked me a strange question. "What did you make of Braun? Is he nuts?"

"I couldn't tell. Why?" I responded, puzzled at his question.

"That's why I went off at a tangent in my conversation with him and why I wanted you there, to see if he sounded nuts." Noyes seemed serious.

"Well, I'm afraid the diagnosis of mental illness is not as easy as that," I said, once again flattered, though this time at his clear overestimate of my talents.

"Well I think he is mad and not a good witness. He's reported all sorts of crazy stories to us over the years, usually weeks after they were supposed to have happened. He's well known as a fantasist," Noyes remarked, tapping at his temple.

"But his story is interesting and plausible."

"Did you hear him talk about 'the whining'? That's one of his old stories.

When I heard that I knew he was cashing in on the crash, trying to get another audience for his crank stories. That guy should write horror stories."

"You think he fabricated it all then?"

Noyes nodded in the affirmative and we drove on in silence. Eventually curiosity got the better of me and I asked the detective to tell me about the claims Braun had been asserting over these past years. What I was told disturbed me greatly. According to Braun, the woods around his farm were haunted. Haunted not by the ghosts and goblins of the region's rich folklore, but by horrid, foul smelling monsters he called 'The Crawlers'. He described these as being like huge leeches the size of bulls. They killed farm animals and sucked the life-blood from them. He had discovered them following a spate of mysterious deaths in his herd which had caused him to build a hideaway on the edge of the woods and wait for whatever was causing their deaths. It was then that he'd had his first encounter with a 'Crawler'.

He later claimed to have discovered that these creatures were themselves 'farm animals', though not of human farmers. He claimed the Crawlers were the property of a strange race of scaly anthropomorphic beings who appeared in the woods in small groups at night. The scaly beings extracted some kind of essence from the Crawlers similarly to how we milk cows. The native Indians knew of this scaly race, he always added, and called them the 'Serpent People', though the natives had no knowledge of 'The Crawlers.' It was not these commonplace delusions of a reclusive rustic over-concerned with his livelihood that disturbed me most but what Noyes reported next that chilled me to the bone. He said that Braun had told him that the 'serpent people' lived beneath the earth and sometimes broke through into the old mines.

Braun claimed to have gone to the mine site where he heard a strange 'whining' noise coming from the deepest shafts. He also claimed to have learnt that the closure of the mine was not entirely due to economic problems but due to the fact that an increasing number of miners refused to work there after terrifying things, of which they would only darkly hint, began to occur beneath ground. Finally, in recent months, Braun had complained of the 'whining' being heard in the woods themselves and of mysterious strangers snooping around his property. Noyes regarded all this as ludicrous, of course, but for me it struck a disturbing note of familiarity and I wondered what Noyes would say when he read certain statements in the testimony of Elias Gapp.

As it transpired, however, this was not to be, for it was on our return that events took a turn for the worse. On arriving home I discovered my housekeeper distraught. She had left the house only briefly to visit a close friend who had called her on the telephone to say she was very ill and needed assistance. She had been sure she had recognised her friend's voice but on arrival was told by the said friend that she was perfectly well and had never made any such telephone call. What's more, her friend had yet to have a telephone fitted in her home.

On returning to my house she had discovered that it had been broken into and my study ransacked. In particular the safe had been targeted and some of the contents taken. Mysteriously, none of its financially significant contents had been taken. A small amount of cash and some of the more valuable pieces of jewellery belonging to my late wife Victoria were still in place.

The only conspicuous absences were my diaries!

Detective Noyes was very concerned about this and told me he would launch a full investigation. I attempted to clear up the mess in the study but Noyes stopped me. A forensic analysis was required and nothing must be touched. The study must be sealed. I agreed and set about the task. When this had been achieved we retired to the sitting room.

In the comfort of my sitting room I recounted my first encounter with Elias to the detective, telling him of Gapp's bizarre behaviour in the city centre, when he had been found running through the streets naked in a state of hysterical amnesia, shouting that 'they' were after him, disrupting traffic and terrifying women and children. It was after this that he had been brought to me for treatment, it having been decided that his commitment to an asylum was not warranted at present. His behaviour had been more controlled following a night in a police cell.

However, while he was far more composed after this outburst, he was no less delusional, making all sorts of fanciful claims of a persecutional nature.

I refrained from telling Noyes of the exact nature of Elias' persecution complex, realising that his lurid tales of 'haunted mines', the vile 'Nang Qin' and the mysterious 'Secret Order of the Yellow Star' would sound no different to the delusions of Thomas Braun. This would be especially pertinent without my documented analysis demonstrating how the delusions clearly symbolically revealed Elias' own inner torment, an account now vanished with my diaries.

Furthermore, I did not want to dwell on Gapp's imaginative association between these paranoid ravings and the book he called 'The Necronomicon'. A book I have later discovered actually exists and which consists of the most deranged example of occult thinking I have ever come across. Most of all, I did not want to raise the unaccountable similarities between Gapp's delusions with those of Braun. Instead, I gave Noyes a full psychological analysis of Elias, which I thought he might find useful. I ended the account with a confident appraisal that my own experimental shock treatment and skilful trepanation had relieved the terrible psychic pressures in his skull. Certainly Elias had made fewer and fewer wild claims and the side effects of the few botched inter-cranial borings were minimal.

Noyes took notes but said little. Finally he repeated his assurance that a full investigation would be made of the break-in but said there was little of use in what I had told him. He reaffirmed his absurd belief that Gapp had experienced a relapse that had led to his death. Before leaving he asked me if there was anything else I would like to add.

"Yes," I almost shouted. "Elias Gapp is alive and well and visited me two days ago!"

5.

It took the gravediggers about half an hour to dig down to Elias' coffin. As I stood next to Detective Noyes in the chilly dawn mist, I half regretted my emotional outburst. Of course poor Elias' body would be found here. It was now obvious to me that the Mr Gapp who visited me and who probably stole my diaries was indeed the twin brother of Elias, no doubt as mystified as myself regarding his twin's death. It was the only sane solution I could focus on as we stood in that cold cemetery. Eventually, a digger shouted that he had struck wood and stood to one side. Noyes looked at me and then turned to the diggers. "Open it up," he ordered.

The lid of the coffin, more like a crate than anything else, was prised open, partly splitting in the process. With a final creak it came off and its shocking contents became visible in the dawn light. The coffin was empty.

Noyes ordered all present apart from one gravedigger, myself and an armed officer to leave the area. Jumping into the coffin, he examined it closely. It stank of corpse. Something had been in here but was now gone. Pulling away at the cheap lining of the makeshift coffin, he discovered something incredible. A large hole had been punched into the box from below and a narrow tunnel extended down for about ten feet. Noyes leapt out of the coffin and ordered a guard be put on it. On no account was any of this to be reported. He then drove me back to my house.

"What's going on? I don't understand!" I garbled.

"It seems we have a case of body snatching," Noyes answered, trying to look authoritative but clearly disturbed by the morning's events.

"Yes, perhaps the twin brother?"

"You should have been open with me from the start Dr Franklin, it would have saved a lot of time. As I have previously informed you we know little of Mr Gapp's history, but one thing we do know is that he has no twin brother!"

"How can you be sure?" I was almost too scared to ask.

"The papers found on the body included his birth certificate. He was born in New York in 1885, an only child of one Elizabeth Gapp. There is no possibility of a twin."

"Then he's still alive! Dr Oort must be involved! The fingerprints are fake! He buried a phoney body then dug it up again to prevent us proving it!"

"That's a very serious allegation. And one I do not take seriously. Dr Oort is a straight and true character. I have known him for many years and I know he is *on the level*. I shall say no more."

"Wait, I know what you're saying! I'm *on the square* too, though I don't know you from my lodge and it's the premier lodge in this city!"

"Then you'll know that a fellow would not be guilty of the kind of crimes of which you speak. Our lodge is no mere regular one like yours. It contains degrees higher than you ever dreamt of!"

"You're in on it too!" I exclaimed.

I must confess that the events had by this time disturbed me greatly and I had had little sleep since my study had been broken into. I had been filling the night with wild speculation and much malt whisky, but at this moment I was genuinely gripped with the deepest terror I had ever known. It was for this reason that I ran.

I ran faster than I had ever done before, out through the open French windows and onto the lawn towards my car. Noyes just stood there watching and made no attempt to stop me.

I don't know for how long I drove and didn't know where to go. All the while mad thoughts raged through my brain. It was all a Masonic conspiracy of some kind. Noyes and Oort had worked together to make it look like Elias was dead, replacing his body with some mutilated hobo, no doubt. But why? The crash seemed genuine. Was Elias initially party to the conspiracy or had he been injured and spirited off somewhere? Perhaps Noyes and Oort had been the two men in the black limousine. But it didn't quite make sense, nor did it fit Braun's account.

Was Braun a kook recruited to create a smokescreen with his tall tales? What were they trying to hide? Perhaps they (and not Elias) were responsible for the break in? And perhaps Elias was merely an escapee trying to make safe contact? Were Elias' delusions based on some grain of truth which had become clearer with his increasing health? Had he stumbled on some fringe Masonic secret regarding the mines? In his understandable delirium, had he been confused with the ravings of the madman Braun, who he must have spoken to in order to share the same delusions (part of their devious plan to drive him insane no doubt)? Or were they delusions? Of course they were! I shut my mind off.

Eventually exhaustion took over and I was forced to pull the car over to the side of the road. Who could I contact? Perhaps my brother in Maine? Or... I drifted into sleep.

It was then that the dream began, not surprising given my state of delirium. A dream that mixed my emerging paranoia with the stories of Braun and the horrors Elias had told me of during his treatment, no doubt from the same source.

I was in an underground cavern that was connected to a mine shaft, a cavern which had been converted into a temple of some kind. At it's centre stood a circle of 'men' in hooded robes; some obviously human, others obviously not, their reptilian faces revealing their otherworldly origin. One of the men was Noyes! They circled a small altar chanting something. On the altar was a woman. It was my wife Victoria! But she had gone missing years ago! How could she be here now!?!? Their chanting grew louder and more audible.

"We the Nang Qin," hissed a serpentine being in black robes, "call on the Old Onesss to witnessss our sacrificccce. A sacrificccce that will also bring us the essssenccce we need to live on thisss hosssstile world. Come Tsathoggua, L'mur Kathulosss, Cthulhu! Assist usss!"

"In the name of the Yellow Star," chanted a saffron robed human opposite him, "we call on our master Nyarlathotep to assist us in this sacrifice, to help our brothers and sisters from the Void to gain the essence that mere animal blood alone cannot adequately provide, so that they in turn may join us in our endeavours."

The collective chanting rose to a crescendo and became untranslatable.

"Ph'nglui mglw'nafh Cthulhu R'lyeh wgah'nagl fhtagn. Ia, TA BELOC TSATHOGGUA!"

Then, horror of horrors, a dagger was plunged into the helpless figure of Victoria on the altar. A strange whining noise vibrated through the walls of the cavern, which began to glow blue as if an electric arc was present. Out of one of the walls crawled something horrible, like a giant black worm slithering towards the altar leaving an oily trail behind it. I awoke with a start. It was evening.

6.

I arrived at my brother's house at midnight. There I washed and ate my first meal in two days and slept a restful and thankfully dreamless sleep. The next day I arose and began to collect my thoughts. I was still confused. Something weird was going on, but I now trusted the wild speculations of my delirious drive no more than the fevered imaginings of my subsequent nightmare. But I was determined to find out what was at the bottom of all this. The weak link in this affair was perhaps Thomas Braun. I contemplated travelling to his farmhouse to find out what he really knew.

I ate breakfast with my brother and told him the whole story. He sat there looking at me incredulously, but then remarked that perhaps this explained a strange phone call he had received the night before, just after I had retired for the night. It was due to this phone call that a series of events unfolded that were perhaps the most chilling of this entire affair and would bring it to its ultimate conclusion. It began with my brother informing me of the name of the man who had called the previous night enquiring about me. It was Noyes. How had he known I was here? The answer my brother supplied was confessional. He hadn't, he had merely wanted to know if I was there and my brother, unfamiliar at that time with my story, had confirmed my presence. Noyes had told him that under no circumstances was he to allow me to leave the house, that I had had a mental breakdown, was in great danger and that he would arrive soon with armed police for my own safety. He also told my brother that he would call back in the morning.

"Do you believe him?" I asked my brother. He didn't answer directly but replied that he would never allow me to be seized by armed police in his house. Then the phone rang making me jump. I picked it up immediately.

"Noyes, I know you're involved in this somehow. I'm not crazy!"

There was a long silence, broken only by the sound of laboured breathing, then a strange voice spoke slowly.

"Not Noyes, Elias. Hello Doctor Franklin."

My worst fears were all true. Elias really was alive! But who had told him I was here? Noyes? Why did he sound so strange? An answer came, without my question being asked, an answer that made the ground feel as if it had opened beneath my feet.

"I've been watching you Doctor Franklin. I'm nearby but you won't see me. You must not let Noyes catch you. He will kill you, just as he killed me!" The line went dead.

That was it - all logic left me. I would head off back to Boston immediately. I knew now who I had to see.

My brother had replenished my car with gasoline. After thanking him I drove down to Braun's farm immediately. There was no time to waste. I avoided the main roads so as not to meet Noyes and his assassins, no doubt heading towards my brother's house.

I arrived at the farmhouse sooner than I expected and parked my car just off the road. Making my way to the house I noticed an oil lamp flickering in the darkened window. Braun was at home and I swore there and then that I would find out exactly what he knew, even if it took all evening. I knocked on the rickety wooden door. It was already ajar and swung open a little more with the pressure of my knocks. It was then that I saw Braun sitting at a table.

"Come in Doc, I've been expecting you!"

I entered the room. "How? Who told you I was coming?"

"Why, Elias of course. He's mighty smart for a dead man, ain't he! Here, he's left you a little letter."

I was even more confused now and beginning to panic. I walked in and saw the letter on the table next to a flickering candle.

"Read it!" Braun chuckled.

I opened the envelope and saw Elias' familiar spidery writing covering a single sheet of paper. I began to read it, while at the same time keeping an eye on Braun.

Dear Doctor Franklin,

How glad I am that you made it to my little farmhouse, as I knew you would.

I'm sorry I had to get you there so cunningly, but I didn't want that policeman Noyes to get to you first. Yes, he is a real police officer. Your fears were all founded in your own paranoia. A paranoia I thought it judicious to exploit.

Both Noyes and Oort are Freemasons yes, but just as harmless as those in your own silly little lodge. We find such dabblers so amusing, repeating absurdly corrupted rituals that have lost all their original meaning. But it's only a game to you craft men, isn't it? You don't care as long as your careers prosper. The Brothers of the Yellow Star, who first introduced me to my new masters, the Nang Qin, are very different. True sorcerers with vast knowledge for use in the service of the Old Ones. Not as great as the magick that brought me back to life as a servant of the Nang Qin perhaps, but then this magic is vastly older. Older even than when my masters left their ancient home and journeyed to this place.

The first Elias stumbled on them by accident and lost his mind in the process.

You never really helped him. You just drove him deeper into himself. When he began to harbour thoughts of revenge against my masters, a violent side-effect of your barbaric 'therapy', he had to die. An agent had been placed in your household and my masters watched all this through her eyes. Strange that your paranoia should never extend to your housekeeper.

My masters are never wasteful of course. I was extracted from my grave and new life breathed into me. I joined the ranks of the 'Dark Ones', the undead who serve the Nang Qin.

I watched you as they decided what was to be done with you. At first we thought it enough to reclaim all evidence, but your investigations have made you a serious threat. Particularly when it led to my grave being opened up. Our agent had to drug your liquor to distract you from the investigation. We have also planted evidence that will lead the fool Noyes to believe he is dealing with a particularly devious body snatching gang. All else can be explained by your own insanity and obsession with the delusions of your patients and other 'lunatics' like Thomas here.

As for you, I'm afraid you now know far too much, and this is something that just cannot be allowed.

Elias.

As I finished reading I gazed up at the window. A figure stood outside looking in. It was Elias, dressed in a dark suit with his broad-rimmed hat pulled over his eyes and an insane grin on his face. Then the illusion he was casting lessened and he began to change. The grin remained a fixed feature but his face was no longer the same. It was a bloody mess, the hideously disfigured face of the real Elias.

When Detective Noyes arrived a few hours later, I was sitting on the floor singing my favourite song. Braun was swinging in time above my head, on a rope over one of the rafters, a funny little grimace on his 'death mask'. It's not so bad in this new room, the walls are nice and soft and sometimes Elias comes to visit me.

26. BERNADETTE'S MAGICKAL DIARY PAGE TWO

Bernadette turned to the second page of her own journal and wrote:

Michael has been hanging around with some extremely scary people. I should probably try to figure out who they all are and what they all do. It might be useful if I ever go to the police. Why would sexy, super-smart Michael get involved with all this? Most of all, I suppose I should try to figure out what the appeal is, and to do that I need to know the people involved.

Malus:

I didn't meet Malus but Michael spoke of him many times towards the end of our relationship. They seemed instant best mates after knowing each other for only a few weeks. Malus had spoken about his 'involvement in the movement' and his 'practising of the magical arts' quite openly to Michael. I laughed it off but Michael had seemed captivated. Malus had just come back from Tibet where he apparently studied magick. Phooey. There is no more in Tibet than snow and yaks. Malus seemed to think Tibet was a hot spot for magic. Would the Chinese government really allow that to happen?

I remember Michael saying Malus had studied psychiatry. Well he must be a whacko then! My grandfather, Poppa Franklin, was a psychiatrist and he died in a mental hospital!

What else is relevant about Malus?

I remember Michael telling me that Malus had a serpent or dragon tattoo. Not sure if this is relevant.

Sean:

Nothing known except he is writing a book about apples. What the fuck?

Gabriel:

Nothing known. Might find him at the LBRP, whatever that is.

Orryelle:

Invited to write a story for Sean's book about apples.

Minka:

Alchemist and devil worshipper... and, I must admit, a pretty good artist...

Helene:

That witch woman Helene has something to do with this whole initiation thing. She spooked me out. I only met her once but she guessed my star sign straight away (Aquarian). She seemed always to be looking straight through me as if she knew my inner desires and thoughts. I still haven't figured out how she knew all that stuff about my family!

Also, Helene is gay. There is nothing wrong with that, of course, except that she said she 'wanted to be my devil'. I don't want a devil thank you very much!

27. THIS GIRL (PART ONE)

<J. Elizabeth Lawrence>

1: Enter

I met this girl,
And she said she was the devil.
“I am the devil,
Queen of darkness,
Eater of the pain.“
I told her,
I told her,
“No. You're not.“
I turn the radio on too loud.
My ears bleed,
And my eyes turn crimson
Like the moon that summer night.
I dance naked - silently in my room
Next to the bed,
The bed
Where we...
...Made love
Whatever.
Life never felt so good
When the sheets warmed
under your hands.

This girl tried to tell me
Tell
Me,
"I am God."
If I'm God,
"Then who are you?"
I asked her.
"I'm still the devil."
"There is no devil," I said.
"There is no God," she said.
Then we are nothing.
I turned the radio back on.
Too loud.
Too damn loud.
Not God damn loud.
There is no God.
I am no God
We are not God.
To know God
Would kill us.
To know true loneliness,
Would make us immortal,
Would make us God.
There is no God.
She dances with me.
My Devil.
The Devil.
Under the full sunlight,
And we said hell to the moon.
And hell to the midnight
And we dance.

2: Free Day

This same girl,
She went to the mall with me.
We walk in silence
Because I had said everything there was to say,
and I had cut out her tongue,
and she ate it.
So we don't speak.
Except in short phrases,
Of ecstasy.
When our hands brush against each other.
And I glance at my wrist-
Watch.
Watch her laugh.
I thought I had taken her tongue.
We walk into the Hot topic
She tries on some boots.
I want those boots,
But I spent my last penny
Buying too-expensive gas,
For a four cylinder engine
That gets me from point
A
To
B.
And usually back to
A.

3: Eat

We ate in a restaurant.
What was your name?
I can't remember if you got the fish.
It was Lent.
So you sacrificed a lamb.
That's cool.
I don't like fish.

Never realised there were so many Catholics
Until you see the smudges on their foreheads
From a drive-thru
Window.
Ash Wednesday.
And when you hold Christ in your hand;
Splash the water;
Drink the wine,
Feel the alcoholic blood flow through your veins.
I'm not drunk.
I can't be drunk.
Except drunk with love!
Passion!
Apathy...
I sighed.
She sighed.
We left a five-dollar tip,
I'm not a waitress
But they get paid little,
So we left 20% of the money that we no longer
Had.

4: Today

Go back to the car.
Drive down the road.
Wish we could walk,
But we were crucified.
And my feet hurt,
I've been sitting all day.
I can't keep my eyes open.
And next period
Next period,
I can't remember
Where I'm supposed to go.
Where is she?
The devil finally left me,
God left five minutes earlier.

No, God left at birth,
So I spend the rest of my life looking for it.
Flipping over rocks,
Climbing in trees.
It's so much easier to find the devil.
On a boy's lips,
Hands up a shirt,
socks crumpled next to his bed.
I like the devil.
He tastes like chocolate,
Smells like boy,
And tells me I'm beautiful.
Why am I looking for God,
When the devil is just as deceiving?

5: Naps

I laid my head down on the flower-soft meadow pillows.
I sighed.
I laughed.
I cried.
I didn't know what it was to feel,
Like I could fly.
If death were an angel,
Given a double-edged sword,
And a crown of thorns,
Then I'd throw myself to its feet
And pray.
Pray
For nothing.
These are my dreams.

6: Work

Through the thru
I watch the fire.
It blazes red on the horizon,
As it sets gently into the trees.

I wish I could be there,
But instead
I spin in circles.
I deliver the next order.
The next order
For an early grave.
More salt?
And I'm always wrong,
Because you paid to be right.
You paid my masters,
And I'm always wrong.
Turn your back
While I hold this knife.
I keep it to myself.
You paid for that too.
I guess it's the eat-in tax
That people complain about.
What about the amount of grease you just consumed?
That didn't bother you.
How about the animals
Slaughtered
For your
Pleasure.
The devil is here,
He lives in the drain.
Have an apple.
I can smell him.
She's disappeared,
My friend.
I don't know why she left me.
The silence in my head is unnerving,
And the darkness behind my eyelids
Is
Lonely.
I guess I should start
Looking
For God.
Because the devil left me again.

But I smell him in the drains,
With the rotting animal flesh.
It makes me want to drink blood,
Or at least another diet soda.
I suppose neither one is really good for me.
If the voice doesn't come back,
Does that still make it a sin?

7: Bedtime

The place where I'm supposed to dream,
Sweetly
Sweaty.
Ah, the things I've done on this bed
Would make a mother cry.
Well, perhaps just yell
And yell
And yell
And yell
YELL
YELL
YELL!
That's what mothers know best.
How to yell.
My friend came back.
She was in the shadows next to my car
In the lot.
Then there was a raccoon.
The size of a dog.
It barked at me and then ran
Off
With some rotten meat.
I asked her,
"Where'd you go?"
She shrugged.
"Will you leave again?"
She shrugged.
"Will you answer me?"

She smiled and shrugged.
I picked up a book
And lay down on my bed.
"You're a pain."
"No, I'm you,"
She finally parted her lips.
"If you're me, then I am
The devil and God.
That is what you said.
You told me there is no Devil
There is no God.
Then you said we are nothing.
Do we not exist?
Do I not exist?
I must exist if I have thought."
She smiled and watched me through
Her mask.
"Yes, I did say that.
The devil lies. So does God."
I tilted my head,
"So you're calling me a liar?"
"Go to sleep little lamb,"
She cooed.
"Do not coddle me mother. I am
Not
Your child."
I closed my eyes.
I closed my eyes.
I did not sleep,
Until
The moon set.

8: Morning

My eyes crusted
With dust
Open.
They had not found

The land of fairies
But I did see the demons.
I swam in a lake of blood.
I opened my eyes in the water.
I opened my mouth,
And I drank in the salty
Wine.
I rolled over and smelled the early
Morning
Frost.
The room is silent,
Dark,
Cold.
She is sitting there
Watching.
"Who are you?"
I ask.
"I don't know,"
She whispers,
"Who are you?"
I get up out of bed
I get up.
Baby steps.
It's all about the motions.
One after another.
Keep moving,
That's how you'll make it to Friday.
That's how you make it to the car,
To the school,
To the classroom,
To work,
To anywhere.
One foot in front of the other.
So I take my steps,
The path I've walked a hundred times before.
I wish I weren't always barefoot.
It would've made this journey
Easier.

The glass and gravel are jammed in
Between
My toes.
And she sits there and watches me.
She is silent.
I guess she has lost her tongue again.
I know I didn't take it.
Unless it's the one stuck in my mouth.

9: Wake Up

I drive in the silence of the sun.
He rises lazily above the horizon, mocking me.
Mocking me like the shadows,
That dance in the road.
The demons.
Gremlins that cause me to look twice and
Swerve.
"Forget you,"
I mutter to the sun.
Son.
Jesus Christ.
God.
Damn.
I turn on the radio,
And all it plays is
Nothing.
Nothing fills my eyes.
It fills my ears.
I swallow it in gulps,
Trying to breathe the nothing.
And then I reach for a CD.
I can't find my favourite album,
So I'll listen to what's been burned.
I claw at my eyes
Trying to wake
Wake
In the wake of the rays

Of the mocking sun.
Where'd my moon go?
When did the Winter give way to Spring?
What happened to the snow?
I miss the snow.
I turn down the road,
The purgatory,
Banishment of school.
So much left to do before I leave.
So much
So little.
And I turn the player louder,
To drown out my sorrows,
That I won't drink away.

10: School

Dollar down,
Swallow the poison.
Bump into cold metal,
Close eyes shut as shrill
Voices cry.
Huddle in the corners,
Dodge the pain.
Put up barriers,
That will take years to break,
Break,
Broken.
Things are broken so easily
By those
Around you.
Sigh deeply.
Cry silently.
Don't let them see the fear
The blood
The pain.
They live off it -
Sorrow.

But you can't feel that any more,
The cold.
The despair.
Apathy.
Apathetic.
You tell yourself it will get better,
But sometimes you wonder.
Life isn't so bad,
And then you wake up
In second period
And realize,
These people are the future.
You lay your head back down
And go to sleep.

11: Cuts

She isn't there right now.
She isn't there to complain.
To tell me
"You're wrong."
"You have no direction."
"You'll have no life."
"I'm disappointed."
"I'm disgusted."
I sigh heavily
With relief.
She's back again,
The Devil.
She smiles because she knows
That you are safe before work.
You'll find escape for an hour before work,
And the one who complains,
And demeans,
Demon,
Demands,
Is away from you for the moment.
The devil is sitting on the counter,

She is twirling a knife.
"What are you doing?"
I ask her.
She watches her reflection in the blade.
"What are you doing?"
I demand.
She ignores me
And twirls
Twirls
Swirls the happy blade.
The happy blade that would cut deep
Crevices to flow blood,
Like wine.
The sacrament.
Take in God and
You'll be saved.
Take the knife.
"Take the knife,"
She whispers to me.
And find your God.
"And find your God."
She hisses as she hands over the shiny
Lover.
I take the lover in my hands,
I kiss her deeply.
Her tongue licks my flesh,
Searing.
Hot.
Gentle.
"Take Me,"
I beg.
The devil strokes my hair and smiles.
Always smiling, my devil.
"Why do you always smile?"
I ask her.
"Why are you bleeding?"
She asks me.
I look down, and like rose petals scattered

Across the floor,
Lies my body's precious water.
Red water.
Stained water.
Sinned water.
I look up into the face of the devil.
I see her eyes reflecting into me.
My reflection.
I touch the glass.
I don't remember where I am.

28.
COLOURS THE SOUL

Bernadette climbed out of the back of the van where she had been intensely reading the magical diaries of her ex-lover Michael. She walked a few paces onto the grass of the campsite, plagued by the horrors she had found within the books. *There's some really sick stuff in there.* Bernadette had never imagined people actually practised this kind of medieval nonsense. *It's more stupid than going to a church! But now that I've seen how it is presented, I can understand the attraction. I can understand how it draws people in. It seems so obvious that it's all crap. I must be able to prove it to Michael. Surely I can be more seductive than any Witchcraft.*

And fuck that Helene bitch. How dare she seduce you with those stupid stories! For Christ's sake! I wish I could get over you.

Frustrated, Bernadette stretched and looked around the campsite as the first rays of dawn started to light up the area. Inadvertently, she imagined the look on Michael's face when he returned to his trashed home and a small wave of guilt surged through her.

I'm sorry, but it was for your own good Michael. That Helene and Malus seemed to have it in for you. But why did you buy their ridiculous story about magic and secret societies? I know you probably fucked both of them, but come on, we're talking about believing in the Tooth Fairy and Santa Claus here. She walked back to her van, leant through the window into the front and picked her water bottle off the passenger seat. *I didn't really mind you fucking Helene but she is spooky.*

Bernadette caught a glimpse of her reflection in the rear view mirror. *What haunted me most about Helene was her telling me, "you won't know it's not real unless you try it for yourself. Magic colours the soul. Are you game? Where's your open mind?"*

Looking deeply into her own eyes in the van's mirror, Bernadette absent-mindedly swung the van door a few times, making the inside light switch on and off. She recalled the day she had met some of Michael's new mates in a café near Angel Tube station. A clear memory came to her: as they were talking, she had become strangely captivated by Helene's shiny red lips.

At the time, Bernadette had thought that perhaps Helene fancied her and had wondered, very briefly, what Helene would do in an attempt to seduce her. Whilst mesmerised, she had heard Helene's voice, "Bernadette, you won't know if you don't try it." And now, six months later in the dawn's early light, Bernadette imagined she heard Helene's voice one more time, "You won't know if you don't try it."

Damn that Helene bitch, because I know she's right. I'm going to have to try something from one of these stupid Witchcraft books to prove it's all bullshit. I've got an open mind – but I still know it's all bullshit.

Fuck her.

Bernadette stopped gazing into the rear-view mirror, closed the van door gently and looked around the campsite. Slowly, she unscrewed the lid of her bottle, took a mouthful of water and a deep breath.

Damn Helene for giving me this doubt. I'm going to have to try it.

29. THIS GIRL (PART TWO)

<J. Elizabeth Lawrence>

1: A New World

I remember where I am as
I bite into the juicy red apple.
The witch offered it to me for a penny.
I lick the juices from my lips
And part them slowly
Seductively.
It has been some time since the devil
Came to me.
She hides in my dreams
Dancing in the crushed rose petals,
But I put my dancing shoes in the closet.
Next to the old jeans
And childhood monsters.
I built stairways to heaven
With chewed wooden blocks.
And the kid next door,
He threw his fist
Quickly,
Unexpectedly,
And my blocks fell.
They tumbled
And all the people of Camelot
Fell to their knees
And prayed to a god
That wanted no part in this war.

The witch handed me a second apple,
The apple we gave to the kid next door.
It was filled with snakes,
Our toys.
We
Don't
Share.
So we tried to take the juicy apple,
But it was eaten by the snakes
Or the sands.
And it's time to bathe in hot oil.
Burn.
Clean.
The devil pushes us all.
Evil.
Who's right to fight,
When we all will die?
Camelot is crumbling,
Due to the love of apples,
Bastard sons,
And an arrogance that precedes us all.

2: Back to Life

History will forever repeat
Repeat
Repeat
Itself.
At least I've learned
What the World Studies teacher
Tried to tell me.
With all this change,
So much is still the same.
I miss the days
When Old Glory
Waved silently over the fields,
But now she shakes
And cowers,

Wipes
Up the spilled blood.
The kid next door's cousin,
I don't mind him.
I'm okay with him.
He didn't do anything to me.
I started going back to the hallways.
I remember my reflection.
I remember what I tried
Pried
To do.
I forget the rest.
I rub my wrists,
And take erasers to tiny lines.
Nothing can smear away those lines.
Two
Straight
Red
Lines.

3: Trails

I woke up that morning
And realised I'd been
Lulled.
Lulled by the drugs that they shoved down my throat.
Forced me
To believe
To want
To need.
Why?
The witch handed me my apple,
"Throw it at his head!"
I threw the apple,
When I raised my voice.
They are pulling out the shackles.
I walked down the street and threw my
Fingertips to the trees.

The world is talking about us.
The ground shakes,
The winds blow,
The sun pours fire into our eyes.
September,
November,
December,
We need a new voice.
We need to apologize
Make amends.
Make amends
To
Your
People.
What have we done?
Why have we allowed this to go so far?
A man rode on a bicycle.
He wore the badge of The Law.
He laughed at me.
I smiled at him.
"Don't you know we're doing this for you
Too?"
"Don't you know?"
I asked him.
He just shook his head,
Because I am young,
And he has The Law.

4: Trials

I walked to the park
Again.
This time the men on bikes were waiting.
They grabbed us.
Peace.
Who put the flower in the gun?
No flowers today.
They were trampled down.

Under my bare feet.
They lifted me
Into a metal horse-drawn carriage.
Bars are only good on street corners.

5: Service to Our Lord

"Traitors!"
"Organizers!"
"Stop!"
We got off easy,
Considering
The price of red oil.
Two days here means nothing.
I lost my fifty cent piece,
I'll get it back.
I don't mind.
I've been talking to that cousin again,
The reefer,
The carpet-eater,
The homeless guy.
They all make great cases
As to why we should change.
So I will hand over my fifty cent piece
To the monkey that mocks our name.
In God we trust.
Keep your God
To yourself.
We don't want him.
We want her.
We want our lady,
Our goddess.
In God we trust.
I found my God.
I found my Devil.

30.
THE BIRTH OF THE ERISIAN MOVEMENT
Excerpt from Principia Discordia
<Malaclypse The Younger>

Just prior to the decade of the nineteen-sixties, when Sputnik was alone and new, and about the time that Ken Kesey took his first acid trip as a medical volunteer; before underground newspapers, Viet Nam, and talk of a second American Revolution; in the comparative quiet of the late nineteen-fifties, just before the idea of RENAISSANCE became relevant....

Two young Californians, known later as Omar Ravenhurst and Malaclypse the Younger, were indulging in their habit of sipping coffee at an all-night bowling alley and generally solving the world's problems. This particular evening the main subject of discussion was discord and they were complaining to each other of the personal confusion they felt in their respective lives. "Solve the problem of discord," said one, "and all other problems will vanish."

"Indeed," said the other, "chaos and strife are the roots of all confusion."

Suddenly the place became devoid of light. Then an utter silence enveloped them, and a great stillness was felt. Then came a blinding flash of intense light, as though their very psyches had gone nova. Then vision returned.

The two were dazed and neither moved nor spoke for several minutes. They looked around and saw that the bowlers were frozen like statues in a variety of comic positions, and that a bowling ball was steadfastly anchored to the floor only inches from the pins that it had been sent to scatter. The two looked at each other, totally unable to account for the phenomenon. The condition was one of suspension, and one noticed that the clock had stopped.

There walked into the room a chimpanzee, shaggy and grey about the muzzle, yet upright to his full five feet, and poised with natural majesty. He carried a scroll and walked to the young men.

"Gentlemen," he said, "why does Pickering's Moon go about in reverse orbit? Gentlemen, there are nipples on your chests; do you give milk? And what, pray tell, Gentlemen, is to be done about Heisenberg's Law?" He paused. "SOMEBODY HAD TO PUT ALL OF THIS CONFUSION HERE!"

And with that he revealed his scroll. It was a diagram, like a yin-yang with a pentagon on one side and an apple on the other. And then he exploded and the two lost consciousness.

They awoke to the sound of pins clattering, and found the bowlers engaged in their game and the waitress busy with making coffee. It was apparent that their experience had been private.

They discussed their strange encounter and reconstructed from memory the chimpanzee's diagram. Over the next five days they searched libraries to find the significance of it, but were disappointed to uncover only references to Taoism, the Korean flag, and Technocracy. It was not until they traced the Greek writing on the apple that they discovered the ancient Goddess known to the Greeks as Eris and to the Romans as Discordia. This was on the fifth night, and when they slept that night each had a vivid dream of a splendid woman whose eyes were as soft as feather and as deep as eternity itself, and whose body was the spectacular dance of atoms and universes. Pyrotechnics of pure energy formed her flowing hair, and rainbows manifested and dissolved as she spoke in a warm and gentle voice:

I have come to tell you that you are free. Many ages ago, My consciousness left man, that he might develop himself. I return to find this development approaching completion, but hindered by fear and by misunderstanding.

You have built for yourselves psychic suits of armour, and clad in them, your vision is restricted, your movements are clumsy and painful, your skin is bruised, and your spirit is broiled in the sun.

I am chaos. I am the substance from which your artists and scientists build rhythms. I am the spirit with which your children and clowns laugh in happy anarchy. I am chaos. I am alive, and I tell you that you are free.

The Sacred Chao

During the next months they studied philosophies and theologies, and learned that Eris or Discordia was primarily feared by the ancients as being disruptive. Indeed, the very concept of chaos was still considered equivalent to strife and treated as a negative. "No wonder things are all screwed up," they concluded, "they have got it all backwards." They found that the principle of disorder was every much as significant as the principle of order.

With this in mind, they studied the strange yin-yang. During a meditation one afternoon, a voice came to them:

It is called the Sacred Chao. I appoint you Keepers of It. Therein you will find anything you like. Speak of Me as Discord, to show contrast to the pentagon. Tell constricted mankind that there are no rules, unless they choose to invent rules. Keep close the words of Syadasti: 'TIS AN ILL WIND THAT BLOWS NO MINDS. And remember that there is no tyranny in the State of Confusion. For further information, consult your pineal gland.

"What is this?" mumbled one to the other, "A religion based on The Goddess of Confusion? It is utter madness!"

And with those words, each looked at the other in absolute awe. Omar began to giggle. Mal began to laugh. Omar began to jump up and down. Mal was hooting and hollering to beat all hell. And amid squeals of mirth and with tears on their cheeks, each appointed the other to be high priest of his own madness, and together they declared themselves to be a society of Discordia, for whatever that may turn out to be.

INTERMISSION

"Since we all create our habitual reality-tunnels, either consciously and intelligently or unconsciously and mechanically, I prefer to create for each hour the happiest, funniest and most romantic reality-tunnel consistent with the signals my brain apprehends. I feel sorry for people who persistently organise experience into sad, dreary and hopeless reality-tunnels, and try to show them how to break that bad habit, but I don't feel any masochistic duty to share their misery."

- Robert Anton Wilson, from *Cosmic Trigger*

WHAT IS ACTION?

<Ceri Buck>

"And, though exceedingly guilty, I am, as thou knowest, exceedingly innocent"

- Heloise

1. Skin

Kenny Richey I can't stop thinking about you rejection of the exercise generates
askskinthinmakingyourthingmythingmakingyourthingmythingmaking mythingyourthingmakingyourthing ourskin we were asked I ask you I don't know you I have been asked I can't deny me I have to

respond Who's doing the defining? Who's doing the defining? Who's doing the defining? Who's doing the deafening? An act of disobedience a day keeps the doctor away outbreaks of rash contaminated water I have to respond refugee dancers shockingly darfur permaculturalists poor-quality trial witches in prison thighs plastic package un packaged warm together for a short period, dark theatre
cooking

I AM AN INNOCENT MAN
i am listening to you

2. the chlorophyll's conversion

A successful activist, many many people mobilised, "this art must do something" combative writer arrested on trumped up charges, shell hell, kangaroo trial Executed 1995 You're not allowed to ask the awkward question Class and the politics of living simply be a chapter heading

Let's talk about everything but listen very carefully to not miss this moment to puzzle through this moment while somewhere in London a woman hijacks the supermarket tannoy to sing sweetly to the shoppers 'combat the capitalist inside of you' Where was I and what did I do when Ken Saro-Wiwa was executed? A keep pressed battery hen blind of free rage

3. Flesh

Koogie txtd me askd me if I wd get my arse dwn to Tony's Café b4 the riot cops arrived 2 evict. It was 10pm, they were coming at 6am. I didn't make it - is everytime the last time and/or is everytime the only time - belong only to the earth collapsing firm, butter, under each footprint. Share all the food and water you have before it is taken away from you &&& just conjure justice

4. Beta-carotene

Defence System & Equipment International 2005 a street in West Ham, a scared riot of clowns in army gear and pink fluff, council house net curtains twitching: Can we check in? How are we feeling? How arrestable are you? I've got that feeling in my belly. Are you sure you want to be here? On the street we are love as the police shield the harm dealers isn't it about time I dedicated my life to asking the awkward question, which is …? never again take security from a relationship the right people in the belly not the throat YES YES to puzzle for 19 years monogamy by DE FAULT isn't organic veg solidarity is

5. Desirable bacteria

or is not ravaged by the imprint scorch of a kiss & waking up mast
Ur bating? repossess a connection in a possessive it rubs it rubs up

against us Up against against Up freedom from possession(s) up against love one how it rubs up against up free pursue against possess up love another are you sure you want to be here? Can we check in?

I've got that feeling in my belly gut feeling belly warmth context is everything a warm feeling in my belly a deep low belly feeling an awareness of the belly belly deep down warm the blood spilling[3] This coming must do something![4]

Share all your love before they take it from you you through you you we do you offer me a new way to be myself the old ones that did nothing for Ken in prison in Brixton in Nigeria in hospital in Camberwell same thing her lover visits her in bed everyday and she gives up a trip to New Zealand
to journey the chemo to gather the asking

6. Water

Burn. 19 years on death row for a crime he didn't commit meanwhile carcinogenic gas flame gasses the Niger Delta Insecurity potential growth Vulnerable is aflame only if seconds can be put between this and what hurts. Shit venting and flaring fuck focused efforts fuck the fossils kill complexities kill countries execute eggs - all of them! pierce the poorest people pawn them then demonstrate dam building frustrate the fruitful seconds building up to create watchfulness Up against it though who can love?
how does she do it? campaigning for his release at 5,000 miles love translated as

3 Closing eyes for deeper sheeted crease the swoon of the jug the clasping hands handlebar the tight moan body spoke shudder but there is a fire and a place and bikes are dangerous places for swooning chains and links and metal *TARMAC!* - what are you get a grip giggle o body of mine! 'I can't take u anywhere!'

4 were i this radical a social activist, I'd be straight in the

7. Antioxidants and ascorbic acid

it rubs it still rubs up against a frubbing shine I want to eat you all up, apple, cos ur post-pesticide but u've got a girlfriend and so have I. But I'll burn! So, burn! Pounce and withdraw. Disembroil broiler let's change the story & generate powerful loverful rejections

8. Pips

So get your gravit as out of here, you franchise, recharge the battery, hen Make love concinnity stop wasting time that could be spent fitting together writing inspire another person to act from the centre of the universe only by acting from the centre of your ground ground midnight earth love channel passion into writing from one to huge don't lose yr head make it big my love grow wildly love and entangle many antennae

9. Stalk

& skill romance off Yes! I went once I went twice and still time to support the families of Prestes Maia squat in Sao Paulo we are one in precarity I will slowly learn the responsibility of openness give me seconds Come jealousy! pour out anguish and sleep exhausted smoking like a condemned man? you are no condemned man I am listening to you the prosecution's evidence is weak all major witnesses have changed their story again an agonising wait a gain my navel grazing is for freedom I want you here and in your absence I will

no phone calls no texts easy freeze it a cheeky monkey can do cold
turkey honour the other of time they journeying of a pair of bodies in
transit free for marks on other bits of paper other over O the rover
rhesus monkeys are more compassionate than humans so they say

10.Core

Hearing
a grin
stop
on the
absence
of
voice
Becoming
in distance
insistence
of will
but won't act

Haven't slept
for nights
Death row
Ohio

LETTER TO SEAN
<Jaq D. Hawkins>

Dear Sean,

Have you been following what's been happening with RAW? It's such a shame! It would be great if you could send him a copy of your book soon. I know how much he has inspired your magic and your activism.

Love and Chaos,

Jaq D. Hawkins

The early bird gets the worm
- but -
the early worm gets eaten.

31.
SPACE JOURNEY

Exactly three hours after Bernadette had looked into Michael's fridge for stashed drugs, Michael was dancing away in a giant multi-coloured tent. He was peaking, flying high, zooming through a hard funky wave of seemingly cosmic proportions.

Michael and Malus were at one with each other, at one with the beat, at one with several hundred other ageless young women and men in the dance tent at the annual Beltaine Fire Festival. Perhaps most importantly, they were at one with the Ecstasy, assorted herbal highs and organic Somerset cider soaring through their bodies as they pumped their fists in the air in time with the deep-set grooves of dirty disco, the filthy squelch of the lo-fi electro sleaze and the snarling attitude of post-punk junk.

Nothing else matters. Life is the music. Life is the drugs. Life is the high that allows us to feel at one with the entire universe – at one with the superstar high priest DJ, superstar high priest DJ, "Superstar DJ!!!" whatever his name might be.[5]

~

Outside the dance tent, sitting on a green and orange checked blanket in a warm grassy field, Helene pulled a bag of white crystals out of her pocket.

"I brought the DMT my love," she smiled warmly towards Luna. "The Di-Methyl Triptamine is here. Or '*Delightful Magical Trip*' as Malus would call it."

Luna gently took the clear plastic bag between her thumb and index

5 Actually, the DJ was one Kevvy K from London. Brilliant.

finger and leant over to kiss Helene. "You're wonderful." Holding the bag up to the light of the nearby chillout tent, Luna looked at the crystals and wondered what cosmic secrets were contained within. She'd heard so much about DMT over the past year or so. It was supposed to bring a very inspiring high in which people who smoked it together often went on trips to strange worlds *together*. Despite having been excited about trying DMT for ages, she was still feeling nervous. "Are you sure this is going to be okay? It won't fuck me up, will it?" People she'd spoken to about DMT had said that it was the most amazing psychedelic experience of their lives, but Luna still wanted a last drop of reassurance.

Helene took hold of the bag, laughed and carefully tipped a few crystals from it into a small glass pipe, before comforting her friend. "Oh sure, this is the stuff, my love. This is where dreams are made. You will no longer wonder if there really are aliens after you try this." When she had finished preparing the pipe, she put the plastic bag of crystals back into her pocket and asked seriously, "are you sure you haven't taken any other drugs or had any bevvies tonight?"

"I haven't. I'm straight. " Then a giggle, "I mean I'm sober."

"Great, because as I've said, DMT is *very* special." Helene handed Luna the pipe. "It will literally take you to places you've never been and you'll meet with creatures you never thought existed. There is enlightenment in this crystal. It is pure power, pure love, pure wisdom in crystalline form. I think you're ready."

"Okay, yeah I'm ready," Luna answered. Then with a giggle, "I wish my dad could see me now." Luna let out a deep smile and stared out to the field and into her memories.

"Is he here? Is your dad here?" Helene asked.

Luna stayed in her daydream for a moment before slowly turning to face Helene. She held her lover's gaze for a further few quiet seconds before answering, "no, he's not here. I haven't seen him since I was fifteen... but I think he would approve."

She looked out to the field again. Many small groups of festival-goers were scattered about making the most of the festival vibe. Nearly everyone was happy, smiling, dancing, flirting. It was Beltaine, and life was for celebrating. Luna muttered a blessing on the wind for her father, then gently lifted the pipe to her lips.

Helene closed her eyes for a moment, took a few deep breaths and whispered, "by the Air that is our breath, the Earth that is our bodies, the Water that is our blood and the Fire that is our spirit, I call on the DMT angels and elves to guide Luna on this space journey." She opened her eyes, sparked the lighter and asked, "okay, Luna my love, are you ready?"

Luna nodded, watched the flame for a moment, then inhaled deeply on the pipe. A few moments later, she smiled blissfully, released the pipe, and slowly fell backwards into Helene's lap... As she faded away into a rainbow, she saw Helene's voice as a cosmic parachute sensually drop in,

"Are
you
ready
to
see
the
elves?"

32. FREWELLA GROVE

<Henry Lauer>

Chapter One

The elves were playing a game of skill when the clerics came. It was simple enough - one side started in the centre of the checked board, its small number of warrior pieces determined to escort the king piece off the edge. The other, more numerous side, would begin at the edges and swarm in, hoping to swamp their outnumbered foe. They had played all afternoon in the branches above the well. Red-gold leaves drifted from dark limbs, building a rich drapery below.

Listaelf was losing so felt relief when black-clad figures approached over the rise to the north, the sun blazing upon their faces. He pointed and laughed, accidentally-on-purpose upsetting the board, sending pieces cascading to the leaves layered below. Wilda scowled and flung her fist at his head, blackening Listaelf's eye. He rolled backward along the branch cursing, and Wilda smirked happily to herself. Then she too saw the black-clad shapes. Even at this range she could hear their droning voices and see their downcast faces. They cut stark figures, pasty complexions robed in shadowy dress.

Listaelf and Wilda were wights of the land, descendants of the folk of Aelfhama, at one with the pulse of the world about them. They were servants of Earth, of the goddess Freo, and warded her well at Frewella Grove. Folk of the Angles and Saxons came to offer apples and coloured cloth at the well, and their goddess would give them health and good fortune. It had been this way for many years, and Listaelf and Wilda had often watched from the trees of the Grove, curling oaks with knowing grins. Now their strong limbs clung tightly to the eaves of the trees as they spied on the approaching strangers.

"Listaelf," whispered Wilda, "do you think they are in mourning, with those long faces?"

"Wilda," hissed Listaelf without looking back at her, "they must have some awful burden to bear. Perhaps their goddesses and gods have abandoned them?"

They fell silent as the bleak entourage halted amid the ground's leafy shroud. The men formed two circles around Freo's well. Coloured ribbons brightened the branches that hung low over the crystalline liquid. An apple core, black from rot, lay near its edge.

The leader of the dreary band raised his bloated hands to the sky. He began chanting in a whirling language, the words ghostly to sensitive elven ears:

"Pater noster, qui es in caelis,
sanctificetur nomen tuum.
Adveniat regnum tuum.
Fiat voluntas tua, sicut in caelo et in terra.
Panem nostrum quotidianum da nobis hodie,
et dimitte nobis debita nostra sicut
et nos dimittimus debitoribus nostris.
Et ne nos inducas in tentationem,
sed libera nos a malo.
Amen."

Listaelf and Wilda stared at each other. Could this strange performance be a religious ceremony? They gawked at the dark figures, whose bearing and demeanour seemed in poor taste compared with the beauty of Frewella Grove.

Several of the men unpacked gold spheres attached to long silver chains. They struck flints over a candle, put the flame into each of the orbs. Soon a grey smoke wafted from the globes, choking the naked oak limbs. Listaelf and Wilda pressed their narrow hands to their faces, struggling not to inhale the wretched stuff. They wished they had brought their bows with them – a few rounds of maliciously intended elfshot would have sent these irritating interlopers to their sickbeds for good.

But they had not been expecting to need their war gear, only their board game. After all, who would bring strife upon a well sacred to Earth?

The leader of the band succumbed to the stink of the censor smoke. He coughed and choked and hacked and then spat a disgusting thick lump of goo into the well. Listaelf and Wilda hissed and seethed. It was a foul deed done.

The leader raised his hands again: "In the name of the Father, the Son, and the Holy Ghost, and under the light of the Blessed Virgin, I hereby abjure all the evil doings of Satan from this Grove, and exorcise this water in the name of Our Lord Jesus Christ, Amen! Out ye spirits of darkness! Out ye demons of flame and corruption! Out ye thoughts of wrongful deeds! Out ye forces of sinful licence! Get ye gone, thou grotesque forces of earthly evil!"

The elves' mouths hung open.

"In the name of Our Lord Jesus Christ," (the others chorused '*Amen!*'); "I dedicate this well to the holy Saint Fredeswinda, Lady of Thomwry Wode! May her benevolent love be revealed as the true power of this well, and may the people leave her offerings as befits a saint of Our Lord Jesus Christ!" ('*Amen!*' again rang ragged).

"From today, all who dare leave offerings to the old devils of this place, all who dare name their disgusting names, will be known and sent hurtling to the dark halls of HELL!"

"From this day, in the name of Our Lord Jesus Christ," (*Amen!*), "we name this place *Fredeswella* Grove, to mark the total transformation of its place and power in the world! Let all behold, by the power of Our Lord Jesus Christ," *(Amen!)*, "it is no longer a well for Satanic offerings to the heathen forces of carnal diabolism, but a well for Holy offerings to St Fredeswinda's blessed bestowals of luck! All praise to Our Lord Jesus Christ!" *(Amen!)*

His climax reached, the leader turned and marched off, leaves hissing about his feet and robe. The others slowly shuffled after him, moaning and chanting the strange language that their leader had initially intoned.

"What was all that about?" asked Listaelf.

"I think", opined Wilda sagely, "that they are trying to steal Freo's Well because of this Our Lord Jesus Christ (*Amen*) character. He seems to have made them all very depressed and confused."

Chapter Two

The sun slipped away and was reborn again several times over before Listaelf and Wilda heard anything more of humankind. In the days following the strange visitation, they floated back into the sorrowful reverie of autumn's suicide. They tended to the Grove, fished out leaves that had fallen into the well, whispered charms to ensure the health of the trees during the fearful freeze ahead. Although the incident with the strange men in black had unsettled them, they were not flighty spirits of cloud or stream. They were the kin of ancient trees: slow to act and unhurried in judgement.

One day, the ground soaked by cloudy sorrow, a pair of local women wended their way into the Grove. Listaelf and Wilda sensed their presence immediately from the trees. This time they had their bows, and kept them close at hand as they spied upon the new arrivals.

The women were of peasant stock, strongly built, features marked by years of sun and shower. Clad in layers of linen, arms loaded with baskets, they looked about warily, trusting their shrewd eyes to betray any lurking dangers.

Listaelf and Wilda moved silently from bough to bough, bows hung from their shoulders, earthy skins blending with the dark oak tree bark. Their eyes, slitted suspiciously upon the supplicants, keenly sought for any hint of concealed mischief. The trees sighed in the wind, dripping rain water to the earth below, the sky a brooding mess of grey and blue.

Rivulets flowed like veins on the gracious limbs of the trees, their fingers coiled about the sky itself, holding the vault of the heavens aloft. Their roots, gnarled and strong, coursed deep into the earth, exchanging nourishment with the land. Listaelf and Wilda could feel the trees' many heartbeats in the whispering silence, and below the peasant women began to do the same.

The two visitors slowed their passage as they neared the well. The ancient presence that pervaded the Grove soothed their blood and bones, restoring them to nature's hold. Their faces softened now, as the elves moved languidly above them from branch to branch, the building charge of magic spiralling in their veins. The elves felt what the trees felt - these women had come to express their respect and love for the well and the Grove. Listaelf and Wilda relaxed the cruel arms of their bows and watched.

The women approached the well with reverence, each clad in cold silence. They rode to their knees before the stillness of the water and lowered their baskets to the leafy bed that garbed the ground. They unveiled their offerings - bright red apples, gleaming fresh, and colourful ribbons of costly cloth. Listaelf and Wilda were concerned to notice a third set of objects - a pouch from which hard nails poked.

What significance could this jarring presence have? Trees do not like nails, which weary wood with biting thrust. The well would not like to be filled with the poison of rusting steel. The earth could bear a little of her ore to be torn from her flesh, for her children could not otherwise easily survive. But she did not desire to have the sharp points reburied in her skin like splinters.

Listaelf restrung his bow with a swift gesture. Wilda cast him a warning glance, and they stared suspiciously on.

One of the women raised the basket of apples over her head as she knelt. "I offer this nourishment in the name of my poor child, sickened and worried by the fangs of ill. I ask for his sore limbs to be calm in health, and his wrecked airs to be made amends."

Then the other woman spoke. She had been tying coloured strands of cloth to the branches that hung about the well, the bright strips bringing good hue to the place. "Please provide us this gift for a gift, oh Great Lady Fre-o-uh", she stumbled, "*Holy Saint Fredeswinda*" her companion whispered hoarsely in her ear, "um, and to Our Lord Jesus Christ (*Amen*) our call of forgiveness and healing, uh, as well."

Both women trembled, and the holder of fruit lowered the basket again, uncertain in her movement. The air struck from the clearing; an eerie silence replaced the calm that had soothed the Grove before. The trees seemed suddenly rough and ill fitting about the women, and they burst into sobs as they spread the apples before the well.

"Forgive us," one of them whispered. Listaelf and Wilda, perched high above, stared, speechless. One of the women raised a fistful of nails above the well, her hand trembling. Her companion sobbed sadly at the sorry sight. Suddenly she withdrew the nails and dropped them with disgust into the bag that had borne them here.

The shame-faced supplicants gathered themselves and walked away from the well, their clothes wet where they had been pressed to the leaves. They passed beyond the threshold of the Grove, no longer as welcoming as it had been. Their shoulders sagged and their eyes hardened. Something was lost in their hedging over names and nails. The Grove had not denied them, and indeed the woman's son would recover by the Earth's blessing. But these forced changes struck foul against their hearts. These two would never return to the well.

Listaelf and Wilda frowned as their visitors left the Grove. They rode the arms of the trees, slid down their trunks, and came to sit by the water of the well. The animals of the Grove were gathering to share in the offerings of apple, and Wilda hugged a squirrel as it aggressively munched on a morsel.

"There's no other possibility," asserted Listaelf suddenly. "Those buffoons in black are the root of this misery! We need to do something about this Our Lord Jesus Christ (*Amen*) character. His followers are ruining the magic of this place for the folk that most need it!"

"You're right, Listaelf," Wilda declared sternly as she lowered her furry friend to the earth again. "Let us find their bloated buffoon of a leader and extract a *very* good explanation from him."

Resolute, the elves equipped themselves with bows of yew, soft walking shoes, and stout packs for the short journey to the village. The Grove sadly bade them farewell as they journeyed into the forested flat within which it resided. Oak leaves silently sailed to the wet ground in the wake of their passage, lamenting this second winter.

Chapter Three

They marched through the grey-daubed countryside with grim expressions, a martial air guiding their movements. As the sun soared, the wolf snapping at her heels, the clouds crowded heavily over the rim of the sky. Listaelf and Wilda had not left the holy grounds of the Grove in many years, and they were startled by the changes wrought in the wider world.

There was an atmosphere of sorrow, as though something precious had been lost or stolen. They could see it in the weary gaits of other wanderers; in the silence-slung hills; in the streams that crossed their paths, gurgling sadly. Occasionally, but not nearly so frequently as in past times, they would see other land spirits - mooning alone on a striking hill, sheltered beneath a canopy of trees, lurking and leery beneath a stone bridge. The custodians of nature seemed burdened.

"Perhaps," opined Wilda, "the folk that shared largess with these holy places have stopped. Could this Our Lord Jesus Christ (*Amen*) character have disturbed the bond that the folk have with the land? The earth and the waters that live with the people seem starved of love."

"Perhaps," pondered Listaelf, "our own Grove has been spared this suffering because we see few humans. Its strength remains directly drawn from Earth. But where the land spirits once dealt daily with the folk, they now suffer."

"Let us not forget the sorrow etched in the figure of every farmer we pass, either. This sadness has struck the humans as well," reminded Wilda.

As the sun neared the end of her long ride across the sky, the elves reached the town they sought. It had grown over the years, and unfamiliar fields surrounded it, though now naked from the harvest tide.

What took their attention was the newest addition to the village, a brooding stone structure looming over the village's wood and thatched homes. It clutched cold darkness. A large bell perched atop a pointed spire at one end of the crude building.

Listaelf and Wilda crept into the village, dodging carts and horses, moving among bushes and the branches of trees. The townsfolk seemed very subdued as they busied themselves with preparations for winter's onslaught. It was as though no one spoke too loudly on pain of punishment.

The elves stalked easily through the village. Everywhere they listened and looked for local land spirits, but they found nothing more than a scattered handful of house gnomes, a silent and stony bunch at best. Some of the local gnomes seemed particularly nasty, as though some fester infected them. The elves did not pause to parley with them, but remembered when the house wights of this place were renowned for their high spirits.

Listaelf and Wilda drew nearer to the church, the great stone structure. It was cold to the touch, and the elves felt unsettled by its silence. Narrow windows dotted the walls, but they were too high for the elves to peer into. They guessed that these were for the benefit of sunlight, not lookers in. Although the front doors stood open, Listaelf and Wilda were not eager to plunge into the dark and musty place.

Above the door hung a startling carving – a malnourished young fellow, his hacked-out wounds liberally daubed with red paint, nailed to a piece of wood. It seemed to them a sad image, one that encouraged its viewer to give up on life. Or possibly, its message was a warning. The elvish visitors looked at the sorrow that lay about them and saw its reflection in the man on the cross.

By the time they had finished inspecting the building night had fallen, and a mightily cold mist descended over the land. The clouds thickened with dusk and no stars hung in the sky. The elves retreated to an empty loft and resolved to sleep the night away. They planned to approach the stone hall at dawn. They did not doubt that this dour place was the home of the blustering human who had claimed their sacred well. They munched without enthusiasm on a cold dinner, wrapped themselves in straw, and hugged one another into chilly sleep with the mice and the spiders.

Chapter Four

The clashing cries of brass against brass saw the elves bolt upright and panicked the next morn. Straw flew about them as they tumbled, terrified, into a corner of the loft, backs braced against the wall. The tremendous peals struck again and again, sending the elves' teeth chattering and skin prickling. It was an awful din, dissonant and harsh. The crashing washed over their bodies, pummelling their limbs, banging bone against bone. Brute terror overwhelmed the creatures, who staggered desperately about, clutching their ears, moaning in agony.

The noise passed, the elves collapsing into relief. Listaelf and Wilda slowly dragged themselves to their feet, bewildered, stumped by what could cause such a cacophony. They tumbled out of the loft and blundered into the morning light, where a miserable drizzle splattered all surfaces in sight. Blearily, they began to notice the entire folk of the village were milling outside the church, waiting patiently in the rain to enter, heads bowed, as though each were personally grovelling. Listaelf spotted that the brass church bell was swaying slightly.

"Could that have been the source of that awful noise?" he wondered, as Wilda rubbed her eyes and stared. "No wonder there are no land spirits around here! If that sort of thing happens often they'd all have sodded off to the deep of the wilds! It's dreadful!"

"Typical that only house gnomes would remain," reflected Listaelf. "Little buggers are cast from clay and deaf as a doddering geezer."

"And even those left seem grumpy grouches," rejoined Wilda.

After some hesitation they resolved, through ringing ears, to follow the folk into the hall. They felt some revulsion, and not a little resistance, as they entered the place. It was as though the air thickened to deny them passage. The folk were gathered on long benches below a deep ceiling, with agonised sculptures, similar to the one above the entrance, poised about the place. Wilda saw a basin of water near the entrance and wondered whether it had powers similar to the one at Frewella Grove. She sniffed it and grimaced. It smelt only of mould. The water had no spirit at all.

A stage filled the front of the hall, and on it stood the fellow who had tried to steal the Grove's magic. He was dressed richly in black and red, with gold on his fingers and around his neck. A number of his underling acolytes, clad in much plainer dress, stood by, waving censors or clutching staves. The perfume sickened the elves, and the pallor of the gathering seemed to sink as the gas ghosted about the chamber. Hiding behind a pillar, the elves waited for the last of the village folk to file in. They wondered how the people could want to be in a place that stank of corruption and sickness. Even packed, the hall felt empty.

The head man's lackeys began singing in a dreary drone, each lost in his own dissonant dirge (the elves wondered where all the priestesses were). Gradually, the assembly added its voice to the sludgy sound, until the place sung a weary song. The elves covered their ears and grimaced, wondering what other crimes against music these people could commit.

Finally, the droning drifted off into silence. The black-clad leader stood tall at the front of the gathering, raising his arms to gain the full attention of the audience. He began to chant in the twisted language that he had used at the Grove, occasionally accompanied by his underlings. This went on for quite a while, the priest poring over a huge text from time to time. The assembly, previously morose, began to settle into slumber. It was early in the morning after all, and they were fighting an even worse enemy than deadly seriousness. They were fighting dead-ass boredom.

The elves, at first themselves subject to sleepiness, soon began to split at the ears with mirth. Row after row of supplicants succumbed to the inevitable. It went the same for each - first the eyes would flutter shut, only to bolt open again, the body, slipping back, suddenly straight again. Then gradually, heads would loll forward, perhaps to rest on arms or even, in one case, to curl up in a ball on the bench. The sounds of yawns threatened to overwhelm the speaker's voice, and young children fidgeted and wrestled beneath the benches or at the back of the hall, oblivious to the whole performance.

"What a charade!" hissed Wilda, "who are these black-clad buffoons fooling? This lot couldn't give a stuff, look at them!" Listaelf, desperately struggling to resist unleashing gashing gales of laughter, could make no response. He rolled back and forth on the ground, battering the floor with his fist.

"No wonder they are trying to steal our gods and rituals: theirs are so boring and pointless! Why are these people putting up with it?" she wondered, amazed that the black robes hadn't long ago been relegated to the status of village idiots.

The priest finished incanting. Knuckles whitening as he grasped the lectern, his face puffed red. A vein throbbed violently in his neck and his eyes bulged.

"Dear God give us all mercy or we will BURN IN HELL FOR ALL ETERNITY!" now he savaged the audience in their native tongue.

"You are all sinners, damned for the crimes of Adam and Eve in the Grove at Eden! You are all dirty, disgusting, despicable hunks of skin and bone, thinking sinful thoughts and doing sinful deeds! AWGH! How you revolt me and God and Our Lord Jesus Christ!" A muffled '*Amen*' came from the priest's acolytes.

"Your only hope is to repent your wicked ways, and work for your kindly king, and hold your tongues. Never indulge in behaviour that you ENJOY. For the devil, SATAN HIMSELF, that thrice-accursed WOD, that disgusting LOK, will tempt you with the slightest laughter or pleasure!

"And to those that seek the blessings of SAINT FREDESWINDA. When you make your offerings, it will be heresy if you do not cast a load of nails into the Holy Well for Our Lord Jesus Christ (*Amen*). Only then will there be an end to the disgusting heathen orgies!

"I have driven out the earthly devils and made the Grove pure and holy, and RETRIBUTION WILL FALL ON THOSE WHO FOLLOW SATANIC ELDER PATHS!"

So the priest unleashed his anger, his audience now very much awake. He revelled in the shock that his raging rant struck through the drowsy gathering. It was becoming clear to the elves that fear kept these people here. Fear. Follow the rules and forget the old gods. God loves you in spite of yourself.

These folk, confused and afraid, cut off from nature, seemed to Listaelf and Wilda to be lost and easily controlled. The elves were astounded. The ranting cleric was a despot, not a holy man. What a sad state these folk had fallen to!

Absorbed in the performance playing out before them, the elves were oblivious to malicious movement in the shadows behind them.

It was a sad story that a few of the old house gnomes, deaf and hard-hearted, did not mourn the passing of the old religion and its love for nature. Concerned only for their continued shelter, and perhaps not realising that they could keep their positions of respect with the converted farm folk without compromise, they allied themselves with the new order, nailing their hopes for survival upon the cross. They became smaller, lumpier, and cruel, and beneath the layers of scarring lay a feeling of betrayal in each of their hearts. They eased this pain by punishing elves and land spirits who remained true to elder paths.

One such lonely, angry soul laired in the eaves of the church, the cold stone giving little comfort to his great shame. He lurked in the shadows, revelling in the sorrow that poured from the place each Sunday morn. He felt a nasty glee when he spied a pair of woodland elves crouched in the recesses of the chamber.

It was a simple thing for the skilful fellow, a matter of a mind trick, to draw an acolyte or two unwittingly toward the elves. They moved with unsettled curiosity down the side of the hall, drenched alternately in shadows and light.

The acolytes searched this way and that, eyes narrow, the hairs on the backs of their necks keen. The hunch that had drawn them into the corners of the hall had no explanation, but they felt compelled. One almost stepped on Listaelf's outstretched cloak, but passed by; bewildered by the feeling that he had missed his mark.

Grumpily, the gnome turned his wily will upon the elves themselves. In his bag he held a pouch of shaved wood, taken from a rune tine carved to call the concealed into clarity. With a deft flick, he cast the chips over the elves' backs. The flecks of tree flesh bore heavily upon the elves, peeling back the powers of their cunning cloaks.

Listaelf and Wilda gazed disturbed as the priest pronounced a cup of wine to be godly gore. Then they gasped and gagged as the priest slowly raised the body of his God to his lips. The wafer was raised to the ceiling, then plunged into the cleric's maw. The elves gurgled and choked, retched when he swiftly followed with a swallowed swig of Christ's blood.

It seemed this religion's basis was the butchering and eating of blessedness.

The first acolyte spun suddenly, sweat beading on his brow, clutching his staff. He waved his companion over, whispered hoarsely in his ear. They worked back the way he had come.

The gnome glared from his hole, beady eyes betraying a touch of sadness at what he had become. He worked his will into whispered words, weaving the old ways of magic against themselves. Twisted speech boiled from his bulging tongue. The whites of his eyes guided them to the ears of the acolytes. His stony body trembled and strained.

The priest waved forth his disciples and bade all the folk join him in his flesh eating and blood drinking.

The acolytes slowed, their stalking sibilantly shadowed by spoken words of broken power. What was this noise? Their heads turned, forth and back, hunting.

The people slowly filed forth. Wilda could look no longer and covered her eyes. Listaelf choked on vomit.

The first acolyte paused, waved to his ally.

Wilda moaned: “We must flee!”

The flock began to devour God.

Priestly ears pricked up.

Sudden movement. Black cloth flashing. Limbs spinning. A shout. A wet thud. Hard boots on ribs. Brutal cursing.

Retching and choking, the elves no match for the acolyte-thugs.

A slight pause in the holy proceedings, but not the first time this had happened. The flock, thinking some fool had said the wrong thing again, wait in line like pigs.

The gnome wants to cry. To his dismay he finds he no longer can.

Chapter Five

The dark robes had been marching for hours when Listaelf and Wilda awoke. Each hung from a staff slung between two bearers, wrists and ankles burning where hemp bound them to the bole. Their captors moved grimly, guarded by a pack of mail-clad warriors. The elves were bruised, blurry, bleeding, their bodies badly beaten.

Listaelf found alertness first, disoriented by the haze of mid-morn, not his last recollected dawn. His mind was scattered, his flesh languid, and some deep spark of his spirit sensed that he had been drugged. He struggled to form his thoughts into shapes, but the effort was too great. So he hung in the spell of drug and despair for some unknowable time.

Wilda had suffered more from their captor's violence, and came to consciousness later. The elves' slitted eyes betrayed wakefulness to each other, but their captors continued unawares. Slowly, matters became manifest - this was the path to the Grove. The black robed high priest must have guessed their origin. As she gradually gained more sense, Wilda came to see something dreadful: their captors were laden with pitch, torches, oil, and axes. They were going to burn the Grove. The elves could do naught but hang helplessly.

As the sun reached the peak of her flight from the wolf, the ill party came to a halt at the rim of the Grove. The path lay paved with burnished red leaves, cast in sorrow from naked trees. The sky a haze of mourning cold, the air no more with summer glow. The band of black-clad men and their martial companions settled down to a hasty meal of cold meat, then turned to ready their weapons against the wood. The head priest and his followers formed a tight knot before the entrance to the Grove.

All lay at peace in the shadows of the trees, their graceful limbs arcing to the sky. The giant boles were deep and wide, but the path was clear and easily picked out.

"First", declared the leader, "we destroy the well. Then, we burn the whole Grove down, and come back for these devils," he pointed at the elves. "We'll throw them onto the pyre. This place is too great a hold of Satan to let it persist."

With these words the air changed, subtle and menacing. As the invaders marched in, the trees sighed in the wind, letting their last leaves float to the earth below. The sky, a brooding mess of autumn noon-tide grey and blue. Faint whispers flowed along the gracious limbs of the trees, their fingers coiled in newfound tension, the sky's weight for once too much. Their roots, wilful yet weary, drove deep into the ground, conspiring with the earth. The invaders faintly felt the trees' many heartbeats amid the boles' sibilant whispers. They armoured their hearts and drowned their fears.

Listaelf and Wilda watched the column stalk into the Grove, relieved that their captors were gone. They turned their attention to freedom. A simple trick for elvish wits: they laid calls to local beasts, a small flock of field mice tore into the twine, unbound their bonds. They achingly aided each other to stand, rubbed their sore limbs and bruised ribs. The Sun passed behind a heavier layer of cloud, and the Grove clenched into longer shadows. The clouds, having settled, moved no further. Limping and groaning, the elves followed the invaders' footsteps into the shelter of the bare canopy.

Father Dreogan, the head priest, stood before his followers, unlit brand tightly grasped. He stared up at the arching branches as the shadows lengthened. The natural noises of the place had died down – no song of bird or rustling of squirrel to be heard. He knew the silence to be Satanic.

Father Dreogan lived in fear of places such as this, that refused God's graces. That remained mysterious even after exorcism. The stink of nature, tempting the flock with innumerable sins. He could not bear it in the face of his Lord, least of all his own passions, discharged in secret shame. Deeply he held his holy conviction: by destroying such dens of darkness, he could atone for himself.

Every branch, every knotted stretch of bark, every root barrelling into the ground seemed to mock his suffering. He clung to God like a drowning man, clung to God's clarity. He would bathe this wretched hold and all like it in the unrelenting light of Christ. Destroy such dens, and pound his pain down deeper by the same movement.

How you long to shed tears, he imagined the trees whispering to him. He shook his head, overriding their presence. He quickened the march and the dark branches crowded closer around the band.

Listaelf and Wilda sighed with relief when they felt the bark of their wards. Wearily they clambered into the boughs, gingerly wended their way through the canopy. Normally they could move through the trees faster than any human could march along the ground. But wounded now, their passage was sluggish.

The invaders slowed as they neared the well. The ancient presence that pervaded the Grove unsettled their blood and bones, recalling in them the broken grasp of nature's hold. Their expressions sharpened now, as the elves moved painstakingly above them from branch to branch, a building charge of danger spiralling in their veins. Listaelf and Wilda felt what the trees felt - these men were here to visit their fear and self-hatred upon the well and the Grove. The elves reached their perch above the water and sifted through their stash of curved yew and twisted twine, biting barbs and fleet feathers.

Father Dreogan was sure he sensed movement in the edges of his vision. He turned slowly, masking his rising fear, to his men. Hastily they tried to hide their nerves from him.

He remembered his childhood, playing among trees, dancing about roots and bouncing upon branches with children his age. The trees about him recalled that secret communion between child and earth. He thought about days past when laughter rang from his lips. It was a time when he had been at home in the wild, comforted by the wind, the leaves whispering their affection.

But these were innocent lies, he reminded himself. His Christian faith smote his memory with a burning brand. It ripped the roots of his love of nature and buried it deep. He suppressed a tear. Eyes bulging, his new truth reclaimed its throne.

"Remember," he said, voice cracking, "all power comes from the Almighty. There is no magic that is not God's and no spirit that is not the Holy Ghost." His wavering speech trailed off. The band faltered forward, still mindful of faint whispers and hidden mysteries among branches and boughs. The path opened, and they came to the well.

Chapter Six

The wind rose. Above the branches, clouds boiled. Blood-coloured leaves lashed through the air in wicked circuits. The invaders slowed in the face of the buffeting gusts; only Father Dreogan had the courage to advance towards the clearing.

Listaelf and Wilda raised their bows, unleashed a storm of elfshot. Outcry, chaos, soldiers collapsing, vomiting, struck with violent illness from invisible barbs. Those uninjured returned fire at their shadowy assailants. Wilda slipped, fell from her perch, Listaelf's grip lunging, catching her wrist. He dangled, an arrow lodged in one leg, teeth grit. Wilda slid further, dragging Listaelf with her. Then his hold caught and he hung from a branch, clutching Wilda above a dreadful drop. Tears coursed down her cheeks as she struggled to latch onto the foliage.

The soldiers glared warily at the trees as the acolytes tended to their wounded comrades. They had begun to vomit blood: elven vengeance was swift.

The wind whipped into icy passion as Father Dreogan marched towards the well, grasping a flask of poison. The acolytes could do nothing for the elves' wretched victims, who lay in the dirt, gasping. They turned to light torches, retreated to the trees to hide from the wind. The soldiers splashed pitch and oil upon the nearest oaks with abandon. The winds whipped higher, and the invaders' panic rose. Out in the distance, they imagined tree branches bending under the force of more than just the wind's weight. The leaves, fiery and harsh in the air's embrace, scowled threateningly.

Wilda tried to swing in Listaelf's grasp, the wind buffeting her. She could hear his shouts, but the air snatched his words away. The branch she sought, so near, swept clear of her grasp again and again. Listaelf slipped, his arms burning, head swimming from his wound. So close to safety, then the branch would fling clear, Wilda trapped in empty air. She could feel Listaelf's fingers weakening around her leg. The drop to the ground dizzied her. Autumn's leaves cut the air aggressively, and the earth beneath was naked and rough.

Father Dreogan, seething and bowed, reached the still water of the well. He kicked past the remains of offerings, fruit flying clear. At the well's rim he rose, despite the wind, to full height, the flask above his head.

"In the name of the Father, the Son and the Holy Ghost!" he screamed, eyes wild. He steadied himself, braced against the gusts buffeting his body. He felt something shift beneath his feet, something huge, old, hard. He shot his glance to one side, the oak he saw seeming to smirk. He spat: the phlegm flew back into his face.

With no warning the wind disappeared. Father Dreogan stepped forward, a rotten apple squelching beneath his foot. Then blasts of air struck with full fury, spearing into his back. He looked down in dismay, seeing the apple for the first time. As he pitched forward its soft flesh slid, spinning him into free fall. The oak's crags were angular and aggressive, majestic and ethereal.

Dreogan wondered absently as he fell: how could something so beautiful seem to him so malignant?

Crash. The water rose up around the fallen priest, wind snatching the poison vessel clear of the well. A few moments of thrashing, the black robes desperate. Then nothing.

The wind hurtled to a halt. Dismayed, the acolytes and soldiers gathered around the well. Leaves fluttered to the earth. Trees held themselves in silence. Wilda latched to the branch, swung clear, clung for life; Listaelf sighed with relief and hung to his perch now with both hands, wound aching.

The men stared. Their leader was gone. The water of the well was absolutely still. Dark and silent it lay, expectantly. The men looked at each other. They looked around. The Grove was silent. Sunlight pierced the skeletal canopy.

They fled.

Chapter Seven.

Winter brought white death upon the land. Little was said of the priest's fate, but with spring's rise, a new one came. He had heard rumours. He turned a complacent eye to the comfort some folk found in old beliefs.

Listaelf and Wilda suffered through winter's cruelty, wary lest the black robes return. In time, their injuries healed. With spring, they danced and laughed. They came to travel, seeking other holy places, and their apples brought cheer to many a lonely elf.

As the years bore by, some folk offered to Frea; some to St Fredeswinda; some to Freawinde; some to St Frea. Eventually it ceased to matter. Memory faded, reformed, folk forgot why they offered apples and ribbons to the well at Frewella Grove. Their children flourished and their sick mended. So goes the earth-faith of folk.

33.
WHAT'S THAT NOISE?

Bernadette rubbed her eyes, sighed and lazily climbed out of her van. *What a magical, special place this Grove is.* Trying to decide which of the stolen books to experiment with, she finally settled on one. It was a simple affair, 'Spirits of the Earth', concerned with connecting to the mysterious spirits of sacred places. With the intention of proving to Michael that this whole Witchcraft thing was nonsense, she knew she was going to have to try one of these silly rituals.

Bernadette pictured confronting Michael about Witchcraft and imagined telling him, "I've tried it, and I know it's nothing but bullshit." *To talk to him like that, I'm going to have to go through with it. I have nothing to lose and everything to gain...*

The chosen book was a ridiculous affair about how to see and feel faeries and connect to the power of standing stones and stone circles. The author, a Jaq D. Hawkins, told a convincing story about her early childhood experience with faeries, spirits and sacred spaces. Despite being a bit of a fruit loop, it was the book that seemed to contain the simplest experiments.

And now...

And now Bernadette walked away from her van and looked around the misty campsite. She walked around the perimeter for a while, along tree-lined paths and past shrubs and rocks until she came to a point under an apple tree that was just starting to blossom. She felt something uncanny wash over her and decided that this would be as good a spot as any to do the ritual. She remembered Helene's words, "you won't know if you don't try it." *If I am going to prove this is all nonsense, I might as well do the experiment properly.*

She took several slow, deep breaths. In the cold, early morning, she could see her breath form small clouds as she exhaled towards the apple tree she stood under. *Ha! I bet some of these books talk about hugging trees, but there is no way I am doing that! Especially not a common apple tree!*

After a few minutes of deep breathing and maintaining a strong mental focus, she felt a strange, warm tingling in her finger tips. *Interesting.* There was also a strange feeling as if she was being watched which made her feel slightly self-conscious.

Bernadette continued to breathe deeply and noticed the wind settling in the trees around her. *Wow, it really does feel like I am being watched.* She focused on the tingling sensation in her fingertips and the sensation grew stronger. The tingling turned to warmth; the warmth throbbed. *Come on! I have to prove this is nonsense!* She raised her arms and held them both out to the side away from her body with her palms facing upwards.

Out of the corner of her eye, she saw somebody watching her from amongst the trees. *But Jacqui is not due back for another month.* Bernadette turned to call her aunt. "Jacqui? Aunty Jacqui?" But there was no-one there... "Aunty Jacqui? Is that you?"

Silence.

The wind stopped completely.

What the fuck? A trick of the eye. I should be spooked by that but I am not. Bernadette took another deep breath whilst focusing on her fingertips and felt the warm tingle once more. After another breath, she felt the warmth spread up her hands and along her arms. *Ha! Was that some kind of faerie or something I just saw? Ha! A trick of the eye.* She laughed nervously.

Another deep breath and the feeling of warmth seemed to fill her chest and heart. She could sense movement in the trees out of the corner of her eyes, but was determined not to look directly, lest the trick of the eye should reveal itself to be something ... something... *I'm not sure what I fear it is... or hope it is. This feeling is uncanny, strange. Why haven't I felt it before?* Bernadette heard a giggle in the back of her mind. *What's that noise? That was clearly my imagination. I'm certain! I won't let this spook me out!*

Bernadette took another deep breath, this time filling her body with the warm, tingling glow. It was as if she could literally feel the life of this place flowing through her. She felt the Grove resonate and wondered how she could have gone so long through life without managing to feel this kind of sensation before. As she breathed in, it was as if the tingling sensation peaked. Similarly, as she exhaled it was as if she was connecting to the ground beneath her. Time and again the feeling of energy peaked and subsided as she breathed. She wondered how so many people on the planet could have missed such an obvious phenomena. *This is so simple! How come no-one has told me about it before? Who knows about this? I wonder how many people do feel it? It's so simple and seems so obvious... so obvious.*

She looked up at the sky and the stars and she felt something she hadn't felt since she was a young girl: a sense of wonder and joy. She was overcome by the beauty of it all: the stars, the night sky, the apple buds, the trees, the wind, the grass, everything. She was filled with a sense of belonging, of being a part of something greater than herself. She also felt something she hadn't known in the longest while. She felt love.

Bernadette stopped the deep breathing and shook her hands and feet. A wind blew through the top of the trees around her. *Okay there is something in this nonsense but that doesn't mean...I don't know what it means but...I'm going to...*Bernadette walked back to the van with her path lit by an early morning cloudless sky. *I don't know what I'm going to do.*

She opened the side door of the van and climbed into the back, shutting the door behind her. *I don't know what I'm doing.* She picked up her pen and journal and wrote:

Page 3

Feeling the magic of a sacred place is simply a matter of tuning into it with my mind, my body and with my senses. It's like when I'm sitting down on a chair and I'm not paying attention to the feel of the floor under my feet.

Once I learn how to direct my attention there, it's easy to bring the floor into my consciousness. I can tune my ears into the different noises around me simply by shifting my awareness.

I'm doing it now.

I can focus on the mess on the floor of my van with my eyes and I can switch my attention to the feel of this book in my hand. I can focus on the sound of the wind in the trees and I can switch my attention to... well, I'm not sure I'll give it a name just yet, but it's simply about directing my awareness to a place I haven't directed it to before. For some strange reason we have never been taught how to direct our awareness to that which is actually around us all the time! Now that I feel it, ha! How could I have missed it!?

I feel like crying.

Bernadette wept lightly and closed her journal. A tear rolled down her cheek and dropped onto the book's red and black cover as she traced her finger up and down along its spine. *Sacred spaces. Who would have thought it would be so obvious and right under my nose all along?* She felt truly amazed, as if this simple insight could somehow change the world. *All around us all the time.* Bernadette felt a longing build up inside her. She wanted to - *needed to* - tell someone what she had discovered. She had a pressing desire to pass on this new information and clarify what it was all about.

Determinedly, Bernadette opened the door and climbed out of the van.

As described in Spirits of the Earth, she looked around the Grove and spoke to it as if it could hear her. "Hello? Hello? I know you can hear me. I love you, Grove. Thank you! I love you. I hope you can hear me. You have made me feel young and free again. Can you hear me? I want to stay in this place with you forever... Forever!"

The wind picked up as if to answer her call, but instead of "hello" as she was hoping, Bernadette imagined she heard it whisper, "nothing is forever my child..."

34. DIANA NEMORENSIS

<David Blank>

The bulldozer sat silent, patiently waiting.

A safe distance away, a cordon of police and private security guards held back a group of eco-warriors and concerned citizens, many of them local people, who had gathered to protest against the destruction of the sacred grove and its trees.

The industrialist and local landowner Ralph H. Allen surveyed the scene from a safe vantage point at the far edge of the grove. He was pleased to see the tree surgeons had completed their work without too much delay, especially since they had only gained access to the site three days ago following the eviction of the last of the protesters. It only remained for the bulldozers to uproot the severed stumps of trees and remove them from the site, along with the debris and cut wood left by the surgeons. Soon all trace of the grove and its trees would be gone.

“About fucking time,” he said to himself as he looked upon his work, a smile playing across his usually stern features.

Ralph H. had invested a lot of time and money on this project. Aside from the fees to the lawyers, surveyors and architects, there were the *favours* to local councillors and friends in government departments. He had needed to use a lot of grease to get this one through.

Personally, he couldn't see what all the fuss was about. After all, they were only fucking trees. All that nonsense about them being a sacred grove was just so much bullshit. “After all who decides these things?” he asked himself.

He was just about to go off on one in his head, regarding his feelings about 'eco-warriors' and other bleeding heart liberal green activists, when he suddenly noticed the figure of a woman a short distance away. She was standing in the centre of what remained of the grove, surrounded by the naked stumps of the once-proud trees, their amputated bodies and limbs littering the ground about her, and looking directly at him.

“What the fuck now?” he asked himself. “The police and security were supposed to have removed everyone hours ago.”

He couldn't, however, help noticing how striking the woman looked. She stood easily all of six feet tall with a strong and athletic figure and long blonde, almost white, hair that hung down to her waist. And while she was not exactly pretty, she was incredibly beautiful in a strange and almost surreal way. Her countenance at once soft and tender, yet also hard and cruel. Her eyes shone with a fierce intensity one moment, and were gentle and loving the next.

Watching her, he felt a sense of familiarity. As though he had met her before somewhere. But exactly where or when he could not recall. He tried to remember. However, the memory would not awaken. He had a sense of her being inside of him. Although quite where, he did not know. It was fleeting like a dream. He could not recapture it. He could only feel its flavour, its essence. The detail was lost in the waking from it. Soon passing. Leaving only a taste. A memory dimmed by the day.

Ralph H. let go of the searching and simply looked upon her, watched her, admired her.

It was in that moment of letting go that he realised where he had seen her before. She reminded him of the young lady he had met several days earlier when he had come to check on how the evictions were going. She had offered him an apple and beseeched him not to destroy the trees. She had explained to him how the grove was sacred. Something about seven trees, or seven different types of tree. He couldn't recall exactly, and to be honest he didn't really give a shit.

He remembered taking the apple from her and being struck by just how pale and delicate her hands were. He had bitten into the apple. It was sweet, juicy. He ate it greedily and when he was finished he threw the apple core to the ground, laughing. "That's one apple tree that will never sprout and grow," he said.

"Do not be so sure," she replied calmly, "there are certain things beyond even your control, beyond your imagination. Things you would do well to respect." She looked him straight in the eye and he felt her gaze deep within. Like a blizzard she ran through him and he shuddered.

Laughing nervously, he turned from her and walked back to his car. Another laugh. Nervous. He tried to shrug it off and dismiss this strange feeling as simply his imagination. Yet try as he might, he could not, for the cold wind still moved inside him.

He sat in his car and turned the heater on full blast. It was no use. He could feel her still. A shiver coursing a hare through his body… chased by a hound ... by something dark and terrifying.

His mind returned to the present, to the now, aroused by a rumbling sound deep and low to a growl. He smiled as he realised it was the sound of the bulldozers, their powerful diesel engines turning over. Sliding into gear, the large metal machines lurched suddenly forwards: lumbering beasts advancing on what remained of the grove and its trees.

He looked up to see if the young woman was still standing in the grove where he had last seen her. In truth, he was more concerned that she might delay the work of the bulldozers than he was about her safety. After all, if she was stupid enough to put herself in such a situation then she deserved everything she got.

The bulldozers by now had reached the trees at the furthest edge of the grove. One of them had already set to work tearing at the ground beneath what had once been a large hazel tree, removing great scoops of soil and root. The surface layers having been removed, the machine dug deep into the earth to attack the larger roots that held the stump, which was all that now remained of the once tall and magnificent tree.

Meanwhile, the other bulldozer had easily uprooted the stump of a medium-sized birch, and was advancing towards the large and knotted stump of an ancient oak that had once stood proud in the centre ring of the grove; home to several species of birds and a multitude of different insects. An essential part of the local eco-system, as all the trees had once been.

The first bulldozer operator, a young man in his late twenties, having finally uprooted the remains of the hazel, was about to start on a similarly-sized stump nearby when he noticed an apple tree, in full bloom, still standing a short distance away. "That's weird," he said to himself while applying the brake. "How could the surgeons have missed that one?"

He turned his machine to the right and headed towards the apple tree, confident that he would be able to uproot it without too much difficulty, even though the trunk and branches were still intact and it had not been felled, as had the others. "After all it is only an apple tree," the operator reassured himself.

Ralph H. had been observing the progress of the bulldozers from a safe distance away, near the edge of the grove, and was surprised to see one of them suddenly stop, lurch to the right, and then begin to head directly towards him.

"Now why did he suddenly do that?" Ralph H. asked himself, bemused.

He looked around to see if he could find some reason why the bulldozer operator had suddenly decided to change direction. All he could see were the stumps of trees. They looked no different from those in the area that the bulldozer had previously been working in. It made no sense to suddenly change direction like that.

"What is that idiot up to?!" he exclaimed, both confused and more than a little disturbed, as the bulldozer advanced directly towards him. It was almost as if the operator hadn't seen him. Ralph H. Allen tried to shout a warning to the bulldozer operator, but for some strange reason no sound issued forth. The words clung inside him, seeking release - yet finding none.

"That's weird," he thought, as a deep intense fear began to well up inside him, "I don't seem to be able to speak! What the fuck is going on?"

He tried again but still no sound issued forth. All he could hear was the rustle of the leaves in the wind, and the ominous sound of the bulldozer advancing upon him.

Ralph H. tried once again, in desperation this time, to open his mouth and shout a warning to the bulldozer operator. Yet he could not. It was as though he had been struck mute. He couldn't even grunt or make the simplest of sounds let alone shout.

He was gripped by panic and confusion. He couldn't understand what the fuck was going on. "What is that bloody idiot up to?" he asked himself, "surely he must be able to see me?"

The bulldozer continued to bear down upon him. He had no idea what the fool was doing - but he wasn't waiting around to find out.

He tried to run, but he could not, it was as though he were rooted to the spot. He tried to scream, but he could not, it was as though the scream were trapped inside him.

Fear rose within, a rising sap, as the bulldozer drew ever closer and closer. The sound of the diesel engines growing louder and louder, a waxing tide of noise that washed over him. A loud, rumbling, heavy, bass drum beat of noise that became a lover to his fear. Fear screaming silent.

They were as one now, the sound and his fear, everything else had ceased to exist: the grove, the trees, the cordon of police and security guards, the protesters, everything. All had become lost in a maelstrom of dark sound.

Ralph H. Allen waited for the sweet pain of death. Waited to be delivered by the bulldozer's crushing embrace from those dark tendrils of noise that clawed at his mind. Yet Death came not to release him but rather to taunt him with her sex, touching his fear with gentle caress. He could feel her soft breath upon his neck. The smell of her close beside him: all-powerful. Overwhelmed, he lost consciousness drifting through strange and surreal landscapes… ever pursued… ever hunted.

After a time, he gradually became aware of his surroundings again.

The bulldozer stood still, purring, just feet from where he stood.

"Thank fuck for that," he thought, relieved.

The bulldozer operator lit a cigarette: calmly smoking it while looking directly at Ralph H. Allen, yet apparently not *seeing* him.

Ralph H. Allen, the industrialist and entrepreneur, just stood there: fascinated, rooted to the spot.

The young man slowly finished his cigarette and tossed it aside.

A deep low growl shook the earth as the bulldozer pounced towards Ralph H., the bucket scoop at the front of the machine smashing into the ground beside him. He could feel the ground shudder as the bulldozer gouged the earth, removing the top layer of soil, disposing of it, then descending once more.

The sound of the bulldozer growing louder and louder as the large scoop dug deeper into the earth to remove another layer of soil. As the metal claw tore into the soil, Ralph H. felt a strange stabbing, searing pain, as though hundreds of knives were tearing the flesh from his legs. Nausea swelled inside him, a rising tide that could find no release. Trapped within, nausea danced with his fear.

The large metal shovel descended for a third time, digging deeper, nudging against the roots, pushing into them harder and harder. The industrialist felt a sudden pressure on his feet and legs. The claws on the leading edge of the shovel slid in between the larger roots, the leading edge pressing against them with ever-increasing force. Then a sharp bone-wrenching pain, searing white, as the metal scoop tore through the roots of the tree.

Blood splintered. Flesh pulped. Bones broke.

Ralph H. Allen cried out in pain. A cry that was silent on the wind.

A dark terror awakening as the bulldozer ate away at the foundations of the tree. Tearing through root and flesh and bone. Exposing nerves that screamed. Sap falling. Nausea crawling. The soil wet with his fear, sweet with his blood.

Mercifully Ralph H. lost consciousness.

He came to a short while later, surprised to notice the young lady standing a short distance away watching him. At her side were two large staghounds, standing erect and alert like King Henry's Archers in the slips, waiting for the hunt to begin. There was something about the hounds that struck a chord inside him. He couldn't quite place it, yet he was sure he recognised them. Then, through his pain and fear, awareness grew to an understanding, "of course!" he declared, "they are my hounds!!" He tried to call out to them, but could not.

"What the fuck is happening to me?" he asked in desperation. But no-one answered him, for none heard him except the wind in the trees and the lady - but she did not answer. She simply stood, still, alert, watching.

He screamed aloud, the sound of wood splintering, shattering, as the tree was uprooted from the ground. He wanted to flee, to run, to escape. He desired nothing other than to be free. All his mundane and everyday concerns and wants had fallen from him like dead leaves. He desired only to be released from his torment, from Nightmare's deadly embrace.

It was then, in that moment of desire, as the apple tree was finally lifted clear of the ground, that he felt the freedom he had longed for. Liberated, he leapt from beneath to find himself standing upon the earth, the soil fresh beneath his feet. Bracing his legs, he arched his back and shook away the last of the Mares' shadow. Raising his head to the sky he tasted the wind. It tasted good. Clean. Fresh. A rich tapestry of colour - an orchestra of sound. The world was alive with smell as a thousand different scents rushed through his blood like a drug. He was all but overwhelmed such was the intensity of it. It felt good.

He had little time to savour this feeling, however, for the wind also carried a message, a certain scent, that disturbed him. Without understanding he sought to escape, to flee that danger borne on the wind.

The bulldozer operator smiled with the satisfaction of a job well done as the apple tree was finally uprooted from the ground. But instead of the tree falling as he expected, it stalled: suspended in motion, gripping the soil in desperation with its last few remaining roots. He gave the tree one last final push with the shovel and, as it fell, was startled by a large stag that leapt out of the ground in front of him. It was as though the animal had sprung from beneath the tree itself. He had little time to recover from the shock, however, for two large hounds suddenly appeared, as if from nowhere, and chased after the stag as it fled before them.

Ralph H. could feel the surge of adrenaline coursing through his body as he raced across the field, eyes wide, nostrils flaring, sense keening. Close behind he could hear the baying of hounds. Feel their hot breath on the wind. He had neither time to reflect upon what was happening to him, nor time to stop and ask why. All he could do was run, run for his life as the hounds chased him from the grove and across a nearby field.

He ran for what must have been hours, across field after field, leaping streams and gullies in a single bound, the sound of the hounds always close behind him - spurring him on. Each moment becoming a desire and a need to run, neither thought nor feeling remained, only instinct survived and it was the instinct of the beast. He could hear the sound of his own blood pumping in his brain, fuelled with adrenaline, borne of fear. He could hear the sound of hooves upon the ground as he raced over field and stream. Now thumping. Now splashing. He was amazed at the speed with which he ran, and even more amazed that he was able to remain ahead of the pursuing hounds. Yet he knew he could not do so for much longer, for he was rapidly tiring. The sun was at its zenith when the hounds had first caught his scent; it now hung low in the darkening sky.

Twilight fell to find Ralph H. cornered in a thicket where he had sought refuge from his hounds. He was completely exhausted… panting and dripping sweat. His legs felt weak. He could run no more. He was shivering and could hardly stand. His body torn by thorns. His eyes wide with fear. All he could see were the hounds and his death. He shuffled backwards deeper into the thicket - the thorns tearing at his flesh. Blood mixed with sweat. His gaze fixed on the hounds that snarled and bayed just feet from where he stood. He tried to call out to them, but his call only agitated them further. His wordless baying causing his dogs to bark and howl in frenzied expectation.

The hounds settled in for the long wait taking up sentry positions in front, and to the side, of the thicket. Squatting on their quarters. Waiting. Watching. Panting. The stag was weakened by the ordeal and was losing blood from the several large gashes along its flanks. It could stand no more and eventually crumpled to the ground, its legs folding beneath it, head bent forward, breathing hard, all but resigned to its fate. The only thing that separated the stag from the hounds was the dense thicket it had taken refuge in.

Ralph H. knelt among the thorns covered in blood, sweat and dirt. Mired with his own excrement. Outside the thicket his hounds waited, eager for his blood, eager to taste his death - silhouetted against the evening sky.

The thicket that protected the stag began to shimmer as the moon descended upon it. The hounds raised their heads sensing the presence of their lady. The stag started and leapt up ready to defend itself. Ralph H. Allen watched in horror as the thicket that had protected him grew brighter and brighter as it became bathed in the dark light of the moon - then simply vanished, dissolving into the night.

The hounds leapt upon their prey. Teeth bared sank into flesh.

A surge of adrenaline exploded inside the stag as it reared up, the hounds hanging from it like decorations. Slowly and with great effort it managed to stand, its long legs buckling with the extra weight of the hounds. The stag threw back its head, gouging the night sky with its antlers, as it fought to shake free the hound now attached to its neck like a babe to a mother's breast. It flung the animal aside then turned upon it with antlers, sharp to a razor, poised. The hound lay on the ground: helpless, winded. The razor fell - cutting an arc that threatened to rip the dog in two. They never connected, the razor, the hound, for the stag crumpled to the ground, its horns slicing into the earth just inches from where the dog lay. One of the stags' rear legs had been snapped clean in two by a bite from the other hound.

The first hound, having recovered its breath, advanced upon the stag... growling low... teeth bared... blood sweating from its mouth.

The stag struggled to stand, pain tearing through its body, its useless broken leg fluttering against the ground. The dogs leapt upon it a second time, forcing it down as their teeth tore wide the flesh, wounding the stag again and again. Seven times those teeth sank into flesh leaving seven wounds deep and bleeding.

Ralph H. lay on the grass unable to move, his wounds glistening in the dark moonlight.

His hounds stood over him, waiting.

He could feel the grass wet beneath him, whether from his own blood or the cold night air he could not tell. He looked up at the sky and the stars and he felt something he hadn't felt since he was a young boy: a sense of wonder and joy. He was overcome by the beauty of it all: the stars, the night sky, the hounds, the trees, the wind, the grass, everything. He was filled with a sense of belonging, of being a part of something greater than himself. He also felt something he hadn't known in the longest while. He felt love.

He lay on the wet grass for what seemed an eternity: overcome by a combination of physical exhaustion, blood loss and the strange, yet somewhat familiar, emotions that surged through him. Gradually he became aware of his surroundings once more and looking up, he saw the Lady gazing down at him. She was the same woman he had seen in the grove earlier that day - although it seemed a lifetime ago now. She was the same woman who had offered him the apple and asked for his mercy. A mercy he had denied her.

The Lady knelt down beside him stroking his forehead, wiping away the sweat and blood that poured into his eyes. Leaning forwards she kissed him soft on the lips, caressed him and soothed him with her song.

After a time she stood up and gently raising her head, signalled to the hounds that waited nearby.

Instantly, the hounds leapt upon the stag tearing him apart with their teeth. Wolfing down great chunks of raw flesh, gnawing on his bones, burying their faces in his open gut and playing tug-of-war with his entrails. Lapping the warm blood from his flesh, their tongues tickling him as they did so.

For what seemed like an eternity Ralph H. Allen lay on the sweet, moist grass, being eaten alive by his hounds, looking up at the night sky to see the Lady smiling down upon him.

In time he began to lose consciousness and to lose his sense of self. It was as though his being was becoming one with the grass, the soil, the fauna and flora, trees, insects, birds, flowers and animals. He was becoming one with the earth.

There came to him then an awful understanding - and with it a single tear fell from his eye upon the grass where it danced with his blood.

35.
BOOGIEMAN

September 11th, 2001.

Andy woke up with a start. Something had forcibly covered his mouth, pulling him out of his slumber. There was a feeling as if cold metal had been lodged against his forehead.

"Don't say a word," an unknown man's voice ordered out of the darkness. "I have a gun to your head and instructions to pull the trigger if you don't do as I say. Do you understand?"

Scared shitless, Andy nodded. Despite the darkness of the hotel room, he could see the silhouette of a man standing over him and could feel the ominous cold metal push against his temple.

"Not a word," the stranger ordered.

Andy nodded again and was relieved to feel the stranger's hand come off his mouth.

The bedside lamp came on. The stranger had flicked the switch and was now looking down at Andy with gun poised. He was dressed head to toe in black, including wearing a black balaclava which concealed his face. Two blue eyes stared coldly down at him.

"I'll give you anything you want," Andy muttered before seeing the gun lowered to his eye.

"I told you not to speak!" the stranger demanded. "I will not warn you again."

Panic set in and Andy desperately looked around the hotel room. It was a very luxurious space to be in but there was simply no way he could escape from this stranger. He decided to bide his time and do as he was told lest his visitor should become his assassin.

The bedside digital clock flicked 5:23am. Andy looked up at the balaclava again and nodded.

“Right, I can see you understand me now,” he said lowering his gun, allowing Andy a moment to relax.

“Your movie is doing quite well, isn't it Andrew?” Andy's eyes shot open. *What the hell kind of question is that?*

“The people I work for are very generous individuals, Andrew. Instead of putting a bullet in your brain right now,” he raised the gun to Andy's forehead again, “my employers want you to create a sequel. This will be just as popular as the first, but you will remove any anti-authoritarian ideas from it.” The stranger pointed the barrel of the gun at Andy's gonads and continued, “and you will STOP trying to awaken your viewers from their hypnotic trances! They are in trances for a reason. There is no escape from the system. Do you understand me?”

Andrew felt his sphincter tighten as fear gripped him. He nodded.

“In this sequel you will introduce the concept of an all-powerful overseeing council. The characters in the sequel will obey the council's instructions without question. There will be no anti-authoritarian message. There will be no attempts to awaken your viewers. You and your brother will become rich. Richer! And that will be the end of it.”

With that, the stranger holstered his gun. “Nod if you understand me.”

Andy was still scared shitless but felt his body relax as the gun stopped pointing at his balls. He nodded to the intruder.

“Perfect. I knew we would see eye to eye,” the stranger said through the balaclava. “The people I work for will be very pleased indeed. If you want to know how powerful my employers are, watch this morning's news. For now, close your eyes." He turned off the bedside lamp. "Slowly count to 100. Then go and tell your brother what I have told you. Do you understand?"

Andy nodded once more. Without another word, the stranger silently vanished out of the hotel room.

~

Andy counted to 100. He slowly opened his eyes making sure the room was clear, then turned the bedside light on and scampered out of bed. He put his trousers on and reached for his shirt, but jumped out of his skin when he heard a rapid knocking at the door.

"Who is it?" Andy called out.

"It's Larry. Your brother. Let me in quick!"

As soon as Andy had opened the door, Larry blurted out, "I've just had a scary visitor with a gun! We have to make a sequel and we can't have anyone really escaping the system in it!" Noticing Andy shaken up he asked, "are you okay? Did you have a visit too? Why are you dressed?"

"I had a visit too!" Andy replied, panicking. "We have to stop trying to wake people up with our movies! That was so scary. I nearly shat myself!"

"Me too! We should start writing it straight away. We'll call it ... 'The Matrix Reloaded'."

"The Matrix Reloaded?"

"Yeah, or something equally cyber-geeky."

"I suppose so," Andy said, suddenly feeling lighter. "I wanted to make a sequel anyway, but that was fucking scary. Who on Earth could that have been? I have no idea!"

Larry offered, “we must have stepped on someone's toes somewhere. We must have hit a raw nerve with some powerful fuckers!” He recounted the instructions given to him, “we have to stop the viewers from thinking there is any joy in disobeying authority. We have to stop people from believing that they themselves might be 'The One'.”

36.

HOMAGE TO THE AWE FULL SEER <Dr. Timothy Leary>

At each beat
In the earth's rotating dance
there is born ... "   "
a momentary cluster of molecules
possessing the transient ability to know-see-experience
    its own place in the evolutionary spiral.

Such an organism, such an event,
senses exactly where SHe is
in the billion-year old ballet.

SHe is able to trace back
the history of the deoxyribonucleic wire
(of which SHe is both conductive element and current).
SHe can experience the next moment in all its meaning.
Million to the millionth meaning.
Exactly that.

Some divine see-ers are recognised for this unique capacity.
Those that are recognised
are called and killed by various names.
Most of them are not recognised;
they float through life
like a snow-flake retina
kissing the earth
where they land in soft explosion.
No one ever hears them murmur.

"Ah there,"
at the moment of impact.

These organisms,
these "   "'s
are aware of each other's existence
the way each particle in the hurtling nuclear trapeze
is aware of other particles.

They move too fast to give names to themselves
or each other.

Such organisms can be described in no more precise and less
foolish terms than the descriptive equations
of nuclear physics.

They have no more or less meaning in the cultural games
of life than electrons have in the game of
chess.

They are present but cannot be perceived nor categorised.
They exist at a level
beyond that of the black and white squares
of the game board.

The "   "
process has no function, but can serve a function in our
learning games.
It can be used to teach.

Like this.

Take an apple and slice it down the middle.

A thin red circle surrounds gleaming white meat
and there, towards the centre, is a dark seed.
Look at the seed.
Its function is beyond any of your games, but you can use

its properties.
You can use the seed.
The seed can teach you.
If you knew how to listen
the seed would hum you a seed-song.

The divine incarnates, "   ", teach this way.
They teach like a snowflake caught in the hand teaches.
Once you speak the message you have lost it.
Once you know the message, you no longer know it.
The seed becomes a dried pit.
The snowflake a film of water on your hand.

Wise incarnates are continually exploding in beautiful
dance form.
Like the eye of a speckled fish looks at you unblinking,
dying in your hand.
Like cancer virus softly fragmenting
divine beauty in the grasp of your tissue.

Now and then "   " flower-bursts in song,
in words,
"xywprhd,"
"P-8g@cap,"
"evol."
The message is always the same
though the noise,
the scratched rhumba of inkmarks is always different.

The message is like Einstein's equation felt as orgasm.
The serpent unwinds up the spine and mushrooms
lotus sunflare in the skull.
If I tell you that the apple seed message hums the
drone of a Hindu flute, will I stop the drone?

The secret of "   " is that it must always be secret.
Divine sage recognised,
message is lost.

Snowflake caught, pattern changed.
The trick of the divine incarnate can now be dimly
understood.

SHe dances out the pattern without ever being recognised.
As soon as SHe is caught in the act, SHe melts in your hand.
(The message is then contained in the drop of water,
but this involves another chase for the infinite.)
The sign of "   " is change and anonymity.
As soon as you try to glorify,
sanctify,
worship,
admire,
deify,
an incarnate,
you have killed hir.

Thus the pharisees
were performing a merry-holy ballet.
All praise to them!
It is the Christians who kill Christ.
As soon as you invent a symbol,
give "   " a name,
you assassinate the process
to serve your own ends.
To speak the name of Buddha,
Christ,
Lao Tse,
(except, maybe as an ejaculation,
a sudden ecstatic breath like,
"Ooh!"
"Wow!"
"Whew!"
"Ha ha ha")
is to speak a dirty word,
to murder the living God,
fix hir with your preservative,
razor hir into microscope slides,

Sell hir for profit in your biological supply house.

The incarnate has no function.
But hir effect is to produce the ecstatic gasp.
Wow!
Whew!
God!
Jesus!
The uncontrollable visionary laugh.
Too much!
So what!
The stark stare of wonder.
Awful!
Awe-full!

37.
NOT PAID ENOUGH

Helene was deep in thought, fantasising about the world that could be as she watched the DMT-invoked bliss on Luna's face smiling up from her lap.

Helene, for as long as she could remember, had believed it was possible to 'save the world.' *There is so much beauty in this world but why must there be so much ugliness too? Some philosophers say there must be a balance between good and evil, but it would really suck the big one if that were true. It would make it pointless to do any good! Must there be a balance or can we build a better world? Can we somehow increase the ratio of beauty and love in the world? Fuck it, I don't know. I wonder how much of the good and evil in this world is simply about my perception. Too many people asking me for inspiration, but I don't know anything. All I know is how to help people open their minds.*

As if reading Helene's thoughts, Luna stirred and mumbled, "...open..." Helene brushed the hair from her lover's pretty face. *Luna is so beautiful. I hope hope hope she knows how loveable she is... and she is such a faerie! So far off the Wheel of Karma, it's silly. Beautiful girl. I hope she meets the elves.*

Helene flashed back to her own first DMT trip and remembered how blown away she had been to be embraced by such intense psychedelic visions. She remembered how awe-inspiring it had been to learn such powerful and amazing secrets about the world through something as simple as smoking crystals. *No wonder the governments have banned psychedelics. They won't be able to control us if we all free our minds.*

Luna curled up a little and took a gentle grip on Helene's hand. *All I can do is give this Divine Mystical Trip to one person at a time and hope it spreads. I'd love to be able to give it to everyone but I'm not paid enough. And I must go on a journey with Pema some time. That Ayahuasca sounds absolutely amazing. A shamanic medicine that teaches and heals would certainly do me wonders. I could really do with a teacher like that.*

Luna started to squeeze Helene's hand more tightly – she was coming out of her trip.

"Wow...," Luna whispered, "mmmmmm." She slowly started stretching her fingers, extending her neck and beamed the most amazing smile.

"Wow wow wow. What can I say? Wow," Luna sang from her glowing face. Her eyes still closed, she rolled over to embrace Helene. "Wow. I've seen it all."

Helene was excited to hear where Luna had been, but knew that the unveiling mustn't be rushed. The DMT's message would flow like honey out of a pot: sweetly, slowly, sexily.

"Whoa. Helene..."

"Yes, my love?" Helene could clearly see that Luna had been somewhere special as a smile spread across her face. *Sharing this DMT bliss! This is what my life is about! Look at the joy on Luna's face, oh wow.* "Yes, my love?" She soothingly squeezed Luna's hand.

Luna stretched her shoulders and hugged herself, "Helene, I have just seen how the world works. That was amazing. I've seen everything!"

"What have you seen my love?"

"Everything!"

Opening her eyes and revealing her soul, Luna sat up to kiss Helene deeply. After holding each other for a few moments, Luna spoke. "I've seen the Elves and the Imps. I've seen the craziness that makes up our lives, and I've also seen some weird butterfly thing." She sat up, "a butterfly thing told me I would see my father again soon." She relaxed and lay back down onto Helene, "I feel like I've been frozen in a time capsule and that I'm just waking up in a brand new body."

"That sounds amazing, my love," Helene smiled. "It sounds very special. Welcome to your new body. I hope you enjoy it as much as I have."

They both laughed and held each other close. A tear appeared on Luna's cheek and gently fell down to the blanket wrapped around her. The magical voice of Lou Rhodes drifted across them from the chill-out tent as they huddled together.

I can shine even in the darkness
But I crave the light that he brings
Revel in the songs that he sings
My angel Gabriel

The stars were shining and a warm breeze embraced them. "Holy fucking shit. What was that?" Luna laughed. "What on Earth or in heaven above was that? I was not expecting anything like that! D M fucking T! Oh wow!"

"They say your brain secretes DMT at the moment of your death," Helene offered.

"Oh really?"

"That's what they say, my Love. I'm so chuffed you had a good journey."

"A good journey is an understatement! I'm a bit lost for words. But if that's where I go when I die Helene, then I'm ready to die..."

"I said the exact same thing when I smoked DMT the first time," Helene told Luna as she held her friend close. "There is seriously nothing like it..."

After a short while, Luna's smile became more serious, and she sat up with the apparent intention of saying something important. "Quick Helene, give me a pen. Before I forget, I have to write down a poem an elf told me."

38.
THE NETWORK
<Luna Wilson>

Look into a telescope
to see what I can see:
baffled by the sight of
constellations
watching me

INTERMISSION

"Jesus was way cool.
Everybody liked Jesus.
Everybody wanted to hang out with him.
Anything he wanted to do, he did.
He turned water into wine;
And if he wanted to
He could have turned wheat into marijuana,
Or sugar into cocaine,
Or vitamin pills into amphetamines"

- King Missile, from *Jesus Was Way Cool*

BARD MEDICINES, SACRED ELIXIRS

<PenDragon>

Now pull up a chair and pour me an ale;
Lend me your ears and I'll tell you the tale
Of the apple and the ape and the grape and the grain
And the mystical mushroom that storms the brain.

The grass of the Arabs and the Inca's leaf
The Poppy's panacea for the deepest of grief
The vine of the dead and the skin of the toad
The blessings of Gaia sent to lighten Man's load

From sea to sand to sky to space, drugs have won the human race!
Drugs to kill and drugs to cure, drugs to cleanse the temple's door
To lead us up the starry stair, Pure Fools alighting on the air,
Happy-go-lucky and devil-may-care where angels dance and eagles dare

First there came the mushroom that blew the monkey's mind
And made him wonder out aloud: "Who the hell am I?"
Then turning to his friends he said: "By God! I just got out my head
And out my skin and out of time..." they sang and danced enrapt in rhyme.

They wove new worlds from words of power, building dreams by inch and hour
Until at last the grapes turned sour and with a start in Babel's tower
Man awoke, alone, bereft, the victim of the cruellest theft;
A jealous god had warped Man's weft – now words were all that he had left

Years passed by and getting high was outlawed as the Devil's work
By pious liars and black frocked friars who tortured truth on reeking
pyres
While pompous Popes denounced Desire and locked the wise in
shrieking spires
Veiling their Virtue in robes of Sin, for fear of the hidden god within

Abandoned to Fate by his starry mother and denied the delight of his
Secret Lover,
Soon brother and brother turned one on another, and war became man's
occupation,
The Soul enslaved "for the good of the Nation" Progress measured in
numbers killed,
Divided and ruled Man lost his Will, overexcited but unfulfilled, we
traded our joys for a chain of cheap thrills.

Perpetual war feeds the solid State; from love, to loss, to fear, to hate
The rape of the planet, the imperial dream, the tyrant's laugh and the
infant's scream
The rule of law and the law of the gun; the blood spilt to slake an
implacable sun.
From the garden of Eden to a fantasy freedom; the world's gone mad in
the Age of Reason.

Nuclear families are breeding machines; there's a fool at the reigns as the
master dreams!
Idiot king and their sultans of spin are waging a war that no man can
win…
Mining for oil till the earth turns to dust, worshipping Mammon: "In
gold we trust!"
And the Indians laugh, although nothing is funny, at the crazy white
fools who think men can eat money.

And then, the bomb dropped on Hiroshima, and…a mushroom bloomed above the scar;
The Goddess wept a single tear that fell upon a whisp'ring ear
Of wheat beneath the blazing sun…and from that ear a fungus sprang
And from that fungus grew a mould - the key to form alchemic gold!

Albert Hoffman's holy grail; A hope when all else seemed to fail.
Once more, the seed of psychedelia was sent from the Mother to heal us;
From shamans drinking reindeer pee to mescaline and LSD
Drugs have shaped our history; we're all just monkeys, stoned out of our trees

These aren't just Nature's accidents; they're synchronistic sacraments!
These molecules are magickal! They're messengers, free radicals,
Intelligence Intensifiers, Prometheus' stolen fires
Angels teaching men to fly, to joyful live and nobly die

To wake up from the dreamless deep, to gather for the hero's leap;
To know ourselves, the stuff of stars, unfettered by our mind-made bars
Of miserable mortality, brainwashed for banality, sold into celebrity
Sucked in by the fantasy, wrapped up in our vanity, asleep to our insanity

Perennial philosophy is not for sale to you or me
It springs like hope eternally, the fruit of Adam's apple tree
So try to drop the dogma before you drop the bomb;
Just free your minds! unwind! you'll find you're blown to kingdom come.

LETTER TO BOB
<Sean Scullion>

Dear Robert Anton Wilson,

Three years ago I asked you if you'd like to receive a copy of the tapestry I was weaving - *Liber Malorum* - which is basically a novel-cum-anthology of short stories.

It has been a long, long project that is just about to come to fruition! I would be very chuffed if you were to read it. I have put in some very personal touches too, which only you (and people close to you, or who have read you widely) will appreciate. I'm hoping that by writing this, people will be more inspired to read your books. When I first spoke to you about it, we discussed having you write the foreword. Once you receive it, let me know if you'd still like to. I've reserved a space for you!

Is there an address I can send a copy of the book to? I understand you are not at your peak health-wise. Is there anything we can do to help you Bob, you who have touched so many of us?

23 42/93

Sean Scullion
Surrey, Southern England

PART III

Unquestioning obedience is not a trait that is easy to instill. Strong motivations were needed. Soldiers fought for pay and for plunder, but obedience that would hold a man still in line while chariots thundered down the field and arrows rained on him could not be inspired by the hope of booty alone. It had to be etched into the psyche, too deep to be questioned, and reinforced by training, religion and ideology.

- Starhawk, *Truth Or Dare*

39. EVERYTHING IS UNDER CONTROL

"What are you hippy dippy Wiccans doing out here?" Roger asked as he stroked back his long black hair which shined in the same way as his black shirt, black trousers, black shoes and black coat.

"Oh, hi Roger," Luna rolled her eyes to Helene as if to say 'here we go again.' It was the second day of the Beltaine Fire Festival and they were sitting in a large, orange, open tent having just finished a workshop titled, "Wicca versus Witchcraft." Luna hadn't said much at all since the DMT experience, but had come with Helene who was interested in the topics discussed at this workshop.

It had started with a fascinating talk on the recorded history of British Witchcraft, followed by a comparison of historical Witchcraft with modern day Wicca. Several other small groups who had attended the workshop were sitting in the tent having various discussions. The woman who had given the workshop was signing a copy of her book for a young man who was deeply engaged in asking questions.

Roger hovered over Luna and Helene, who sat in silence waiting for him to leave. Realising he wasn't about to go anywhere Helene finally said, "Roger, we're just enjoying the festival and the Beltaine vibe. It's a great fezzy isn't it?"

Instead of answering Roger said, "the sign out the front said 'Wicca Workshop' so I was a bit surprised to see you in here."

"Glad to know we still have a few surprises left in us," Luna answered abruptly. She was trying to think of something polite to say to get rid of him.

"Don't you know you're both wasting your time with that hippy Wiccan stuff. There are some much more intelligent and powerful systems of magic out there. Wicca is based on theoretical nonsense and historical fallacy. It is, essentially, devoid of substance when intellectually compared with the Infernal Magical System of the Endless Night."

Helene raised an eyebrow and exchanged a comic glance with Luna. "Yes Roger, thanks for that," she said, trying not to sound too rude. "But we're at a festival. Have you noticed?" She swept her arm signifying the dozens of people who were sitting, laughing, chatting and enjoying themselves outside the various tents. "It's Beltaine. We've got fires to light and people to fuck. This is real magick!"

"But this festival is full of hippy pagans," Roger responded before adding, "Wicca isn't real Witchcraft anyway." He swept his hair back again and stood proudly, as if expecting them both to agree with him.

Luna spoke more sardonically than Helene had, "yes Roger, we know Roger, but we're happy." Then she sighed, "can't you leave us with that?"

He snorted, "well if you know everything already and don't want my help, I'm off!" Roger trotted out of the tent to a small group of Goths who were sitting on the path smoking hashish.

Most of the people who had been sitting in the workshop tent started drifting out. After sitting in a frustrated silence for a few moments, Helene decided to shake off the vibe Roger had dumped on them. "You know, love, one of the biggest problems in the world is people telling each other how to live, how to dress, what they can and can't do, what spiritual path to follow and blah blah fucking blah." She squinted and shook her head frustratedly, "I'm sure in the future there will be no arseholes telling us how to live, no churches telling us what to believe and no governments telling us what to do."

"Oh come off it, Helene," Luna laughed, leaning back to grab her bag. "That's the most ludicrously optimistic thing I've *ever* heard you say."

Following the general movement of people out of the tent, Luna stood to leave. "People will always tell each other what to do. Men will always tell women what to do. Governments will always tell us ordinary people what to do. It's the way of the world."

Helene also stood up, grabbed her day-bag off the floor and followed her lover out of the tent. Luna continued, "there will always be nutjobs in churches trying to control people. They think they're doing the right thing." The tent's reflection caused Luna's face to glow orange as she said, "that's why they killed all the witches. The church couldn't control them. You told me that."

"Organised Religion has completely fucked our world," Helene responded angrily. "Everything is under control! Our world is completely fucked because of it!"

"Whoa there honey," Luna said, sounding surprised. She pointed to the next workshop tent and led Helene across the grass towards it. "A moment ago you were sounding like a total optimist! Now you've become an infernal pessimist!"

"I switch," Helene answered with a smile. "What the churches preach is completely evil." She paused, "no, that's not right. It's how the churches preach by force that is evil." She thought for a moment, before nodding as if agreeing with herself. "You would never have met the elves if the church was in charge here."

Luna offered, "the church has no power in this country now. There are bigger control freaks here - such as the government, politicians and corporations."

"Luckily the government is fairly incompetent and we can still meet the elves. But their plan is to stop us, and that's the problem – that we live under a constant threat of being pinned. We still have our freedoms, but fuck...."

"Butt fuck!" Luna interrupted with a laugh. She knew how to lift tension and how to ground anger with laughter.

Helene joined in Luna's joke with a laugh, "but butt fuck, yeah, people really have to stop telling each other how to live. You're so wonderful, thanks." She took Luna's hand. "Look, society has its cunts, but so does the magic scene."

"You mean dickheads like Roger?" Luna asked as they reached the next workshop tent. They stopped in front of the tent's chalk board to read which talks, rituals and workshops were coming up.

"Yes, dickheads like Roger who will use magic to get one over on people, and for no real reason other than it suits them." Helene seemed stressed. "Manipulative bastards are one of the consequences of all kinds of magic and religion."

"Maybe," offered Luna, "manipulative bastards are the main reason we have religion in the first place?"

As the two of them were talking, they saw a shiny woman walking towards them dressed from head to toe in blue. She had long, blonde dreadlocks with pieces of blue ribbon tied amongst them flowing in the breeze. She was wearing a shiny, blue silk dress, many multi-hued blue belts and scarves and had bare feet. Over her shoulder, she was carrying a hemp bag which was full of fruit and drinks that she was cheerfully handing out to people. She also had large faerie wings. As she approached Luna and Helene she called out, "want some fruit? Want some glitter?"

"Ooh, I'll take some glitter," Luna answered. "Who are you?"

"I'm Anna the Beltaine Fire Faerie, here to make sure everyone is having a great time." She took a small jar from her bag and unscrewed the lid.

"I'm having a great time," Luna smiled. "Can you glitter my cheeks?"

The Faerie dipped her finger into the jar and drew a glitter pentagram onto Luna's left cheek. "Do you want one too?" she asked Helene.

"No. But maybe some fruit." The Faerie offered Helene an orange, which she took, smiling glumly.

"Are you sure you don't want any glitter? You look a wee bit sad. What's wrong today? How can the Faerie help you?"

Luna answered on her friend's behalf, "some mentalist has just said something idiotic which has really upset her." She rubbed Helene's shoulder in a gesture of affectionate sympathy.

"Tell me everything," the Faerie smiled at Helene. "That's why I'm here. You have to let your anger out and stop it from consuming you. And who better to tell than a Festival Faerie?" she smiled.

"Oh it's not that important," Helene answered. "I'll get over it."

The Faerie looked at Helene for a short while and could see that she really did look quite worked up. She took Helene's hand, "you don't have to tell me what's wrong, you don't have to tell anyone." She caught Helene's eye, "but I have a poem about what happens to people who keep their anger inside. It's by William Blake. Do you know him?"

"I know the name," Helene answered, and took a step back as she prepared to hear the poem.

The Faerie cleared her throat...

40.
A POISON TREE
<William Blake>

"I was angry with my friend:
I told my wrath, my wrath did end.
I was angry with my foe:
I told it not, my wrath did grow.

And I watered it in fears,
Night and morning with my tears;
And I sunned it with smiles,
And with soft deceitful wiles.

And it grew both day and night,
Till it bore an apple bright,
And my foe beheld it shine,
And he knew that it was mine,

And into my garden stole,
When the night had veiled the pole.
In the morning, glad I see
My foe outstretched beneath the tree."

41. LET US PLAY

Helene smiled broadly. The faerie's spell had worked its magic through Blake's words. The anger, like morning dew, evaporated. "I will take some glitter after all."

~

Michael and Malus, needing to catch their breath, left the main dance tent to chill out on the grass. They walked part way across the field in the sun, still buzzing from the drugs they had had earlier, but needing a pick-me-up. They saw Helene and Luna outside one of the workshop tents, engrossed in deep conversation with a Faerie and decided to leave them to it and get their own space on the grass. Noticing that Helene had seen them, Malus held up a friendly two finger gesture to her and she responded by holding up three of her own. They smiled at each other before Malus pointed out a gap on the grass in the warm sun between groups of people, where he and Michael sat down.

"What an amazing fucking festival this is, innit," Michael laughed out loud. "So many cool people and so free of pretensions. Everyone here is up for a laugh and no-one is judging anyone. Wow man, I need to come to more fezzies like this! Righty ho, I'm buzzing and I'm gonna spliff up. You want?"

"Yeah, that'd be lovely mate," Malus replied and closed his eyes. This was an awesome festival but a part of him was thinking about the old skool raves that were so much better: more friendly, more fun, more drugs, more love and they were autonomously organised. But that was before the Thatcher government had used the police to stop the free-party movement. With eyes still closed, Malus shook his head in disbelief - the government had actually passed a bill[6] outlawing any group of more than 100 people from listening to 'repetitive beats'

6 Read all about the Criminal Justice Act at http://www.urban75.org/legal/cja.html

outdoors after dark. Deciding not to burst Michael's bubble, he said, "yeah, it's wicked, and I'm well up for another spliff. And maybe a pill later... but it is still early... yeah go on."

Michael pulled the bag of home-grown bud out of his pocket, along with some Rizla and starting skinning up. As he was doing so, Malus noticed that the young woman with faerie wings was walking towards them from where she'd been with Helene and Luna. She was handing out pieces of fruit and iced lollies to various groups of people that were sitting around.

Michael sparked up the spliff, inhaled deeply and a moment later laughed, "I can feel a gibbering moment coming on. You ready for it Josh?"

"Oh man, I told you I'm not called Josh or Joshua any more. Stick with Malus and we'll stick as friends."

"Why are you so uptight about it?" Michael asked, handing Malus the spliff.

"It's not so much that I'm uptight," Malus answered drawing heavily on the spliff, "but Joshua is a very Jewish name. And I am so much more than Jewish these days."

"Cool, cool," Michael said, not particularly interested, "I think I can work with that theme in my next gibber. Either that or this nasty Illuminati Serpent thing you are always trying to scare me with."

"I'm not trying to scare you! I'm just having a laugh, as is everyone else who follows the Illuminati. It's all in good humour. The Illuminati rule our planet through their code '*infiltrate, subvert, control*'. What's not to laugh at?"

"I see," Michael answered, feigning suspicion by tilting his head back slightly and looking down his nose at Malus. "In that case, my gibber is about spreading paranoia."

"Go with it man," Malus answered. "Spew forth your drug-induced gibber and spread the wisdom of the paranoid to the people. Let the stream of consciousness flow faster than your brain can stop it." He toked on the spliff again and passed it back to Michael.

"Okay, but you have been warned," Michael told him as the blue-dreadlocked faerie reached them.

"Hello, I'm Anna the Beltaine Faerie," she waved her arms in the air like a conductor preparing her orchestra. "Can I offer you both some fruit?"

"Oh yeah," they answered at once. Malus took a banana and Michael an apple.

"And what magic spells can I cast for you this fine afternoon?" The Faerie elegantly struck a pose with both hands out to the side, fingers spread wide, and brought them slowly to her heart. She looked amazingly gorgeous to both Malus and Michael and Michael started trying to think of something to say to get her to stay with them.

"Um, I can't think of a spell I need you to cast, but," his mind raced trying to find something, "would you like some spliffage?"

"A toke, a toke is all I need for my Faerie-blooded high to feed." She took the spliff, held it to the sky in both hands and called out, "Oh universe so grand, thanks for the weed upon the land." She took the spliff to her lips and toked on it slowly with her eyes closed. Michael and Malus exchanged glances, nodded to each other then looked back to the Faerie.

"Thank you, now I'm on my way," she said as she handed the spliff to Malus. She took something out of her bag and handed it to Malus then drifted off across the field.

"What did she just give you, fella?" Michael asked.

"Very odd," Malus answered holding up a small grey rubber mouse by its long tail.

Michael squinted at the mouse then bit into the apple the Faerie had given him. He said through the crunch, “Okay, today's gibber is about the Faerie with the mouse and apples.”

“A very sound topic. I'm starting to fancy women again, especially Faeries. She was fucking beautiful!”

“Indeed she was. But this gibber is about her dark side. What if the mouse was a bomb? What if she was not a Faerie but a serpent? In fact, I got it: what if the Faerie had blown herself up right in front of us?”

"What the fuck are you talking about, you munter? Why would she want to do that?” Malus sat up straight, feeling slightly concerned.

“It's a hypothetical man, it's a gibber. Go with it.”

“Yeah, cool. A gibber is a gibber, but you have to tell me her motive for blowing herself up.”

“I don't know man. Okay, imagine she's a, dare I say it, a 'terrorist'.”

“With blue Faerie wings and dreads?” Malus laughed exhaling smoke. He frowned and toked heavily on the spliff again.

“Yeah, a blue-winged faerie terrorist, but her motive is besides the point. Allow me to continue.”

“Okay, go ahead but you are stretching my already-stretched imagination.”

“Stretch it a little further and imagine that she blows herself up, we cry for her but we don't stop partying. Imagine it. Do it.”

“What do you mean? We all dance around the corpses?”

“Nah man, you're not listening to me,” Michael said. He knew that what he was saying made absolute perfect sense. “We heal the hurt, we lay the dead to rest, then we crank the choonz back on and get up and dance. We honour them by continuing to live colourful, fulfilling lives!"

"Okay, man, that's seriously the most ridiculous gibber I've ever heard. You have lost it big time," Malus told him. He stood up and feigned to call out for attention. "Medic! Medic! My mate has lost his brain. Can anyone help him?"

"Chill chill chill," Michael hushed his friend and took the spliff. "Let me explain properly." He toked then exhaled, "think of America."

"Do I have to?" Malus laughed as he sat back down.

"Yes. You have to."

"The United States?"

"Yes, those guys," Michael instructed.

"Okay, I'm thinking of America but I think you've been smoking too much."

Ignoring him, Michael continued, "now the Americans have already lost the war on terror."

"Go on," Malus laughed at his friend's munted madness, but with this latest he was starting to become interested.

"The Americans have lost the war on terror because they've succumbed to the terror. They have given up all their civil rights and have therefore already lost. And here in the UK it's no better... More people have been killed in the so-called 'War on Terror' than were ever killed by terrorists! There's no two ways about it. The war on terror has created more terror than we started off with. Effectively the US government is a bigger terrorist than any other group in the world could ever be. The government WE voted for is..."

"I didn't vote!" Malus interrupted his friend.

"But does that mean you're more or less complicit? I'm not sure. But what I do know is that the so-called 'War On Terror' is the biggest oxymoron in the universe."

"I'm with you."

"And that's the same as the Faerie with the apples."

"Oops, I'm not with you."

"You're not listening! You're the one who is too munted. Right, if she blows herself up, then we mourn. THEN WE KEEP DANCING! That's the only way we can stop the so-called Terrorists from beating us. By not feeling the terror. It's so simple."

"That could work. But I'd be fucking crying if someone blew themselves up right in front of me."

"Yeah, so cry, and *then* dance. If I get killed, please play my favourite choonage and celebrate my life. But whatever you do, don't give up your life and succumb to the terror or the fear. By succumbing to the fear, we lose and by living our lives to the full, we win! It's as simple as that!"

Malus took the spliff nodding. "I agree," he said but wasn't sure he did.

~

At that exact moment, 2,234 miles away in Tel Aviv, a man full of rage, who had lost everything important to him, put his hand inside his jacket and felt for a string. With no livelihood, with his home demolished by bulldozers and his son recently killed by a 'stray' Israeli bullet, the man pulled the string...

42.

THE TREE

<Lilith>

In the lucidity of terror, sunshine glimmers through the tears.
They pour down from your eyes but there's no relief.
The gas is ruthless.
"Go back! Back!!!!!!!!!!!! You're trespassing in a closed military zone!"
The officer yells at us through a megaphone.
He stands a safe distance away from the tear gas.
As the cloud disperses the border patrol police charge at us, shoving, crunching their batons onto our bones and soft spots...
"Go back!" they scream.
"What are you doing?! We are unarmed!!!! Refuse your orders!" I scream at the border patrol soldier clubbing me.
He shoots his hand straight at my throat, choking me, shoving my head back from the neck.
"Go back!!!!" he screams.

I fall down.
The sun disappears.

~

It is springtime, red poppies dot the green ground like drops of blood.
They grow between olive trees on the hilly slope.
There, a Separation Wall is under construction.
It rips through the heart of the land.
Slithering up over hills, down through valleys and straight through houses like a giant demon serpent.
Hungry Machines uproot entire fields of olive trees. The trees are ripped out of the ground and sold to the highest bidder.
Concrete death, laced with barbed wire, inherits their home.
Separating

us from them.
An eye for an eye,
a tooth for a tooth.
This, they say, is the law of the Holy Land.
Once the land was the Mother.
Its dwellers, her children, suckled from her soil.
Now, She is sterilized with concrete walls, electric fences, checkpoints, patrol roads and guns.
Her body is racked.
Her breasts run dry.
Her fruits lay barren.
All for salvation;
salvation that is her redemption from the hands of the gentiles.

God's promise of her submission to the Primal Patriarch demands its daily bread of blood.
The land is strewn with fresh graves where trees once grew.

Muslims await the final battle that will take place on Her when all the Jews will return.
Christians await the rapture. It will occur when every inch of her biblical flesh shall be reclaimed by the Jews. (Of whom only those who convert will survive.)
And the Jews?
They seek only true salvation.
Salvation of Her body back to Her soul: the Jewish people.
When Her salvation is complete, the true messiah will appear.
This world will fall away and a new Genesis shall unfold.
In between the worlds,
only Paradise will remain.

I fell down in a deep ditch, where a very ancient olive tree once stood. Despite its antiquity, it still gave fruit each year. The Palestinians from the village had many stories about the tree, saying that in the old tales, spirits called 'Jinn' made their home in the tree. The tree stood at the entrance to the village. The Jinn served as its gatekeepers.
'Malachei El Shajra,' they were called in Arabic: 'Angels of the Tree.'
The tree was uprooted by bulldozers earlier in the day to clear the way

for the Wall.
Its body was quickly removed, leaving a gaping wound in the earth.
I am amongst the Israelis protesting together with Palestinians against the construction of the Separation Wall in their village. A wall designed by members of the Israeli government, international real estate sharks, and other faceless ones higher up in the pyramid, to confiscate land and expand Jewish settlements in the name of security. Countless Palestinians have lost land and livelihoods to it, their fruit-bearing trees sold or destroyed. They are locked in a ghetto behind the wall.
It separates.
It annihilates.
It will tolerate nothing in its way.

~

I touch the remains of the thick, gnarled roots in the ditch.
Everything is blurry.
I raise my head. I see the poppies above sparkle in the light
and many hands
clutch me, grab me, pull me.
Then darkness.
A bright figure appears, beckoning me to follow.
I travel through a narrow tunnel.
The figure disappears.
I am at the foot of a gigantic tree;
its roots run deep into the ground.
Its branches sprawl far up into the starry sky.
A crescent moon shines between the leaves.

I sit down between the roots. A well is to my right.
I peer into its dark depths. Obsidian liquid lies inside.
The earth breaks open between my legs. A serpent's head emerges, staring at me with its unblinking, ancient eye. It slithers out from the Earth's bowels, sliding up my left thigh, over my sex, around my hips, up my spine to the top of my head, squeezing my abdomen upwards with its tail, flushing a rush of energy up to my crown.
The snake disappears.
So do I.

~

I am a shining light.
I am in the first world.

The original paradise.

אצילות
(atzilut)

Palm trees heavy with date clusters give shade, wild hemp secretes mother's milk from its flowers, its aroma perfumes the air.
A desert oasis.
Wild wheat and barley drip with dew.
In the center of the oasis flows a spring, bubbling with the sweet waters of life. Within its crescent-shaped pool, iridescent fish swim and play. Purples and pinks streak the sky, heralding the arrival of the newborn sun. Awakened from its nighttime womb, its head emerges from between the red sandstone mountains, yawning golden rays throughout the oasis, transforming everything they touch to gold. The rays merge into a ball of shining light. From the light emerges a form levitating into the air; entwined together in orgasmic bliss. It is the Androgynous.
The primordial couple locked in eternal copulation.
Two halves of an ecstatic whole joined together from the sex up; the female half sitting on top, the male half sitting cross-legged beneath her. Eyes closed; both halves deep in trance, four legs entwined, four arms strongly locked in embrace, two mouths joined in a kiss.
One breath.
The two bodies merge to become one being; no longer female or male. The poles interchange, merge and dissolve to void.
No separation.
No annihilation.

The female half very slightly rocks her hips, shuddering; she is in deep cervical orgasm. The male half static, his lingam deeply penetrating her, is engorged in waves of bliss, with no end, no discharge.
With each orgasm, spirals of colour and light swirl into the

Androgynous' golden aura, forming the double helix DNA. One spiral breaks loose into the ether. It forms the Hebrew letter YOD.
The snake re-emerges at the base of the couple. It splits into two and entwines around them in a double helix. The snakes' heads meet and merge into another head above, sending out a blinding bright shaft of light.
They transform into a tree:
the Tree of Knowledge.
The Tree of Daath.
Their roots are in the Earth and crowns in the sky, their branches far-reaching with leaves like the stars.

A dark, menacing storm cloud approaches from the east.
Small animals scurry away, plants wilt, the Earth trembles.
All anticipate his wrath.
It is Yahweh, the sky god of many names.
The sky turns black on his arrival. He shoots a thunderbolt down to the tree, splitting it apart. Its silent scream reverberates throughout the oasis.
Two charred halves remain where once there was one.
My body of light vanishes. The oasis disappears.
I return to the foot of the great tree.
Now I know where I stand.
I stand before the Tree of Life.

I leave the first world with a gift;
in my left hand I hold an apple.
It is wet with tears.
The tears of countless generations pour from it, forming a river of sorrow.
This is the river that leads to the abyss.
One tear flows into my mouth.
It is my own.
I choke on it; a lump forms in my throat.
It sends me to the second world.

~

בריאה
(briyah)

I return to the oasis.
It has been transformed into a cultivated garden. The air is still fragrant with the sweet aroma of the herbs and flowers that grow around the crescent-shaped pool. But it has changed; the Androgynous has gone, the animals are hiding.
The menacing cloud from the east is now Lord.
A hanging sense of fear prevails.
It is the seventh day; the Sabbath.
I look into the life-water pool. The fish are dead.
Their floating bodies form the Hebrew letter HEH.
A window opens in the sky. It reveals the Book of Life.
It opens on the first page, unleashing flaming Hebrew letters which rise in a spiral up to the sky. They collapse back onto the page, spelling out the first chapters of the book of Genesis.

I sit on a bench in the back of a synagogue, behind the latticed separation wall enclosing the women's section. The men on the other side of the wall are at prayer, chanting to Elohim, kissing the Torah scroll on its way to the cantor's podium.
The cantor is singing the first chapters of the book of Genesis.
I look around at the modestly-dressed women praying mutely. The only sound rising from the women's section are the murmurs and cries of babies and small children.
The women are hidden behind the wall.
Their modestly-clad bodies sway in devotion.
Their heads tightly wrapped not to show a hair.
Their lips move, but disclose no sound.

The cantor sings the curses begat on humanity by Yahweh for listening to the woman who listened to the snake.
To Adam:
He punishes with
Separation!

Separation from Earth's abundance.
With tears he shall draw bread out of the Earth.
No more lovemaking on freshly-plowed fields.
Now toil and suffering shall be his lot for ever after, for he listened to woman's voice.
Woman: "EEshAAA!!" the cantor sings in Hebrew, stretching the "a" like an accusation which reverberates from the temple walls.
To Eve:
The Lord will greatly multiply her pain in childbirth.
She shall be ruled over by He whom she shall desire.
And her ultimate penalty;
to be forever at war with the powers of the serpent.

For her sin is the sin of listening to the snake
who told the truth;
that Daath, not Death, is the gift of the fruit.

I look around me at the blank faces of modestly-clad women clutching their pregnant bellies as they devoutly pray along with mute lips.

The apple I held is gone.
It now resides in men's necks as the proverbial 'Adam's Apple.'
For ever since this story came to be, they have been the tellers of the tale.

I stand by the Wailing Wall in Jerusalem.
It is Yom Kippur eve.
I am in the women's section.
I look through the cracks in the Separation Wall into the men's section.
The men are wrapped in prayer shawls with Tephilin on their heads.
Swaying in devotion.
Trembling in awe.
The chanting from their side rises up like a wall of sound.
I turn to the women who shudder and sway, pray vehemently with closed eyes.
Their lips move in fury but no sound comes out.
Their lamentations are mute;
struck dumb they are, by the divine decree of long ago Rabbis declaring, "kol be'eesha erva" (a woman's voice is her sex) . Women are thus

forbidden to sing and pray out loud. They are banished behind a separation wall from the men.
The wound of their silence bleeds to this day.

The searing pain rips through my heart.
I weep silently, staring at the stones.
A little baby girl beside me bursts into tears; she still knows.

A silent horror is locked into those white rocks;
the pain of generations untold.

I weep for all those women secluded, weakened in the world of Yahweh by their very bonds as they gather together in devotion.
Not permitted to sing,
not permitted to let their hearts soar,
their power confined beneath layers of shackles.
I weep for the Goddess lost, crushed under those stones.
My tears fall onto a white feather at my feet. I pick it up and look up at the stones. Amongst the clusters of henbane erupting from the cracks between the rocks sit two white doves kissing.
I wipe the tears on a parchment,
tears shed for woman,
for the goddess lost,
for the tree.
I crouch over and secretly reach down to my bleeding yoni, covering my fingers with the lifeblood that is now taboo. With the blood, I write 'Ashera' in Hebrew letters upon the parchment. I evoke her in memory of the times Holy Women danced freely here, worshipping Her through acts of love.
I squeeze through the crowd of wrapped-up women, touching the wall with my left hand, pressing my forehead to the stones.
I silently pray to Her.
I beseech Her to return to her lost daughters who now pray to Yahweh instead with mute voices and crushed hearts.
Once her sacred tree trunk stood there in the ancient temple.
Within its holy of holies was kept the image of the primordial Androgynous entwined in lovemaking.
It was allowed only the sight of the high priest on Yom Kippur.

This was the great secret kept from the masses.
With my left hand, I placed the rolled parchment in a crack between the stones laden with notes from women to god;
prayers for health, for fertility, for a good marriage.
I placed mine amongst them, praying for Her to return to the land.
For her peace to be once more,
for her daughters to rise up.

~

I return to the Tree of Life.
I climb up its trunk and sit on a branch.
Little birds are perched around me on other branches.
They are the spirits of unborn children waiting to come down to the world.
Many blossoms amongst the leaves.
A flower opens before me,
I breathe in its aroma.
It transports me to the third world.

יצירה
(yetzirah)

I am by a blue sea under a warm desert sky. The sun shines brightly overhead. My hands and feet are being hennaed, my belly anointed with fragrant oils. Seven women tend my naked body, massaging me, tying fragrant flowers in my hair, adorning my young breasts and hips with strings of seashells, singing wonderful hymns to the Queen of Heaven.
We are celebrating my first blood.
I click the seashells together in the rhythm of their tune.
My Flower is warm and fragrant, engorged with heat, the blood trickles down into the sand and it is given in joyous ceremony to the land.
We are by the Red Sea in the valley between the two great lands.
The women feed me dates, tell me stories of Hathor, the great cow mother from the south, while anointing my breasts with precious northern olive oil steeped in jasmine and rose.

They offer cakes to the Queen of Heaven, feeding me honeyed pieces, tell me stories of the east, of Ishtar, mother of the Horae, the holy women who heal and teach the mysteries of the snake, the spiral teachings of life and death. They whisper to me that these priestesses retain their precious lifeblood within their womb and thus attain divine wisdom. They tell me that in our land of Canaan she is known in the north as Astarte.

The seven women burn offerings of frankincense and myrrh to the Queen of Heaven. The incense curls up to the sky in six spirals. They interlock and merge together into a column, forming the Hebrew letter VAV.
The seven women present me with a clay figurine they fashioned out of the Earth, of Ashera, mother of Canaan, baked in the sun. She upholds her breasts with a mischievous grin. Her life-renewing triangle is made from sacred palm wood. They direct me, and I consecrate her with my first blood. Her smiling face glows in the sun.
I fall asleep under the shade, filled with sweetness and sunshine, listening to the sound of the waves gently rolling in on the shore, cooing me to sleep like a lullaby. I hug Ashera close to my bosom and dream.
I dream of voluptuous temple dancers clad in seashells and shiny beads, undulating their hips, bare breasts and bellies in circles and figures of eight, clinking the shells together in an ancient seductive call. They dance around the altar of a golden triangle. They anoint it with fragrant oils of rose and myrrh. They dance to the music of cymbals, flutes, drums and bells, their necks laden with lapis lazuli stones set in gold, their heads adorned with golden crowns, their arms filled with golden bangles.
Around their shoulders curl snakes.
The dream shifts.
I descend down into darkness.
I return to the tree and enter the well at its foot.
I slide down through the thick black waters of the well.
It is petroleum oil.
I fall and fall,
dreaming of a huge empire.
It holds the biggest snake in the world hidden deep in the recesses of its head's innermost room.

It is an ancient dinosaur they mutilated and burned alive.
It survived, but now they mutate it into a machine.
Tiny technicians work on it day and night. They climb up and down tiny ladders within its chambers, busy turning knobs and attending to the wiring of the control panels.
All according to the plan.
Only the head of the snake is left untouched.
It breathes in agony.
If only they would let it return to the Earth to die.

I am in the fourth world.

עשייה
(asiya)

I continue to journey down into the centre of the Earth.
I reach its core, the diamond chamber that lies within Her heart.

A door forms in the shape of the Hebrew letter HEH.
It opens.
I step inside.
There the embryonic dragon slumbers within.
Dreaming the dream of aeons gone by.
Its ancestors, the ancient ones that once roamed the Earth, left Her their precious gift of the black blood.
Now the humans suck it dry
to fuel monsters of their own creation;
forged in the image of their nightmares of a substitute world, created in place of the garden they are destroying.
They are forged in the image of their desires for utility and convenience, in the image of 'our way of life' which descends like a demon locust upon everything in its wake.
But the black blood is running dry.
What will be when it has all gone?
Will the vehicles lay motionless, stopped in their tracks?
Dead but dreaming?
Dead but dreaming?
Shall they eventually dissolve back into the Earth – back to the minerals

from whence they were birthed?
What will be when the trucks of bounty that fed the masses no longer nourish the millions who know nothing of the Earth? Paralysed on the roads, their own food run out.
What will be when the oil pumps lay motionless?
Dead but dreaming.
Dead but dreaming?
What does a car dream?
With what consciousness has it been imbued as a slave created to serve a destructive master race?

Dead but dreaming.
Dead but dreaming.

What will be when the 'all-you-can-eat buffet' sign towers over the deserted landscape of the abandoned strip mall like an alien obelisk planted on the face of the Earth by a lost civilisation. A relic from another life, another time, when everything was plentiful for some, their lives made easy as they flourished in convenience and false plenty of substitutes for the garden, carefully packaged in assembly lines by their slave races with the final remains of the black blood. Their life was made easy and full of THINGS they created to replace the Daath they had lost long ago.
Cursed to a reality of separation, isolation, alienation.
Torn apart from the Earth from whence they came, they dined on the agonized flesh of the cow mother, raping her body with inseminating machines so they could constantly demand more and more. They sucked her teat dry, robbing the mother's milk from her calf locked in a metal cage, its infant horns sawn off with sharp knives. With those same knives they would engineer women's breasts, reassembling them pumped up with the black blood to serve the pleasure fantasies of the new world order.
With metal thongs they would pry open the yoni, exploring it with cruel eyes.
But they were never satisfied.
They demanded more and more.
Their hunger consumed every living thing, leaving a carefully sanitised trail of annihilation everywhere it struck, inevitably leading to the "all-

you-can-eat" wasteland of their own creation. But they were blinded by their comfort, and rode the path all the way to its end, moving, eating, drinking, sleeping, fucking in noisy, smelly, destructive machines. Everything became poisonous as they progressed, but they were oblivious. Their addiction to the black blood of the primal serpent cooed them to sleep.
They ate it, drank it, smeared it on their skins.
They KILLED for it.
When it was gone,
they destroyed themselves.

~

The diamond chamber shudders.
The embryonic dragon opens its eyes and issues forth a deep hum.
The vibrations form into words,
the Earth speaks:

"The magnetic twins in my womb are shifting,
the hiatus will be void.
In the darkness
all your separations will dissolve
before the light."

The bright figure that led me to the tree re-emerges.
Together we rise up like a geyser out of the Earth's core, penetrating the surface, rising up into the sky.
We grow wings and fly.
We fly in a starless black night sky over the oil fields of the Middle East.
I watch the massive pumps,
pumping, pumping, pumping the black blood.
Some of them are ablaze with fire.
War rages among them.

A menacing shadow approaches from the west.
A metal bird of prey flies over the villages beneath.
Hungry in the name of her master, she demands the sacrificial offering for the machine, she spreads open her steel thighs and issues forth from

her belly her children of abomination, hungry for life that will be no more.

I fly over the explosions, the battle-grounds, where once Ishtar, the goddess of love, reigned supreme.
Now the black blood is paid for with red.
Babalon the horae is no more.
Her name is now that of the hungry empire
to which she is enslaved as its WHORE.

I return to the tree.
I enter through its reverse side and arrive at a hideous, desolate place.
In its centre stands a barren, decayed tree, full of maggots crawling out of its core.
Pieces of ripped flesh, dripping blood, hang from its branches where once there were leaves.

This is the Tree of Death.

It formed from the charred remains of the tree of Daath where once eternal lovemaking was. Now multitudes of hungry spirits surround it, in torment at the lies.
This is where every war has been planned.

On its right, I can see the Wailing Wall over the horizon.
Multitudes of newly recruited Israeli soldiers stand facing it under a night sky.
Holding up their rifles, they vow their oath to serve and die.
To defend their people and their land.

To the left of the tree, a beautiful sight draws me closer.
At first glance it seems to be a temple of love.
Naked Horae decked in gold burn incense of camphor and musk.
Young men lie on soft cushions smoking hookahs filled with opium and hash.
But as I come closer, I sense something is terribly wrong. The Horae are in chains.
They are slaves.

In place of the altar of the golden triangle anointed with oil,
lies the corpse of a woman strangled by her h'ijab.
Black figures loom behind the copulating bodies and beat them with the Koran.
The men are Istashhads. Each time any of them ejaculates, everything melts away. He is then ripped to pieces by a pack of wild dogs.
This repeats itself every night.

The tree grows from the blood spilled in violent death.

~

I can bear to see no more.
A sharp pain soars through me.
I cry out.
I open my eyes.
Needles stick in my arm.
Before me a square shape blasts images of bloodstains on the road, pieces of broken glass and green body bags lined up on the pavement.
The picture changes.
A boy wearing a green bandana holds up a rifle declaring his will to die.
For the freedom of his people and his land.

I am in a hospital in Jerusalem.
An IV drip is in my left arm.
Friends are gathered, happy that I am awake.
The TV glares at us.
The military violence against the demonstrators isn't mentioned on the news.
The bomb attack is.

~

I am tired.
I close my eyes.

The luminous figure that led me on the journey appears.
It smiles with a winking eye, offering a hand.

I take it gladly, looking into its mischievous Jinn face.
Sharp like branches and wrinkled like bark; it is the angel of the tree.
The ancient, ancient Goddess once known throughout the land as The Tree.
She is the Tree of Life.

A door opens in Her trunk and reveals a shaft of bright light.
I enter and reach the heart.
Tipheret.
I behold the Land of the Sun.
I have returned to the desert by the shore of the Red Sea.
It is just before dawn.
There, a massive trance party is at its peak.
Hundreds of exuberant dancing bodies clad in bright rainbow colours raise euphoria to the heavens.
Their feet stamping, hands clapping, they dance in a whirlwind of colours and sound.
In this joyous celebration
there is no separation.
They groove over the abyss of destruction,
the harmonies are forged by the machine.
The psychedelic drugs are unleashing the Dionysian high,
but here they are alchemically transformed into life force.
Through Kundalini activation rising up from the dragon currents deep within the rift valley, transmuting the destructive forces into light.
All sway and dance to the rhythmic cosmic tune.
The deep basses of the BPM merge with the baseline of the Earth's heartbeat.
Rising from its core,
pulsating, pulsating, pulsating light.
Psychedelic sounds fluctuate in the ether.
Pinks and purples streak the sky, heralding the rising sun.
The radiance of dawn emerges from behind the eastern mountains.
The first rays have transformed the darkness into luminous shapes and brilliant colours, revealing people shining in Daath's delight.
The music stops.
In the hiatus,
the dancers anxiously hold their breath.

The loudspeaker issues forth a woman's voice saying:
"Remember we are all made from sunshine!"
And
Boom! Boom! Boom! Boom! Boom! Boom! Boom! Boom!
An explosion of ecstatic energy is unleashed as the music roars back, replacing the sounds of guns and bombs.

The sun rises over the red sandstone mountains.
The euphoria of the dancers rises to greet the golden sun.

A pillar of light descends down from the sun onto the people.
It condenses into a ball of fire, forming the Hebrew letter SHIN.
The Shekina.
Her fire spreads and spells the Hebrew letters:
YOD HEH VAV HEH the god name around her.
Reunited
Now they can reveal the path:
YOD HEH SHIN VAV HEH
SALVATION.

The full name is a fiery golden seed that grows and grows until it manifests its secret:
Locked in eternal orgasmic embrace
in the bliss of void
is the Androgynous.
The primordial couple entwined together as one.
no longer female nor male,
they create the middle pillar,
the path of the heart.

The Androgynous transforms into a tree.
The Tree of Knowledge.
Its roots are in the sky and its crown reversed to the Earth,
showering golden illumination upon the people,
revealing the path lost so long ago,
leading back to the garden.

I stand facing the sea in the Great Rift Valley.

I face Jordan to my left,
I face Egypt to the south,
I face Syria and Lebanon in the north.
I face far-away Iraq and further, Iran, to the east.
And in the centre - Israel Palestine.
I envision golden threads streaming out of the tree to all these lands, encompassing them in light.
It melts away states, politicians, borders, walls, armies and wars.
It transforms Allah back to the moon,
Yahweh back to the sky,
and Jesus back to the Goddess, whose Horae appears before me, decked in all her naked splendour, dancing barefoot on the sand. A hafla emerges around her. Darbuccas and clapping accompany her sexy belly dance.
The machine-generated trance music and the Earth-generated drumming merge and cease.
Everything stops suddenly.
From the heart of the tree a child's voice sounds, singing love in Arabic: "h'ilwa, ya h'ilwa intee halam."

In tears, I whisper to the Horae, "take me back with you to paradise."

But she just smiles and says:
"Paradise is here."

~

The beginning is near
The end is now.

43.
LET US REPLAY

At that exact moment, 2,234 miles away in Tel Aviv, a man full of rage, who had lost everything important to him, put his hand inside his jacket and felt for a string. With no livelihood, with his home demolished by bulldozers and his son recently killed by a 'stray' Israeli bullet, the man pulled the string.

He felt the string catch on its wire. *This is it. My time is now.* He took a last look at the people he would be taking with him: four Israeli children playing with a ball, laughing and smiling; a large, forty-something Israeli woman carrying a load of laundry; two tourists, probably Japanese or Korean, fiddling with a very expensive-looking camera.

Infidel.

He closed his eyes and muttered a prayer under his breath to God Almighty. *Allah, take my soul and set me free. Let me be remembered as a martyr for your gracious cause. Allah, with my death, I call on you to remove the Zionist infidel from this land. Your glory is eternal! Allah Akbar! Allah Akbar! Allah Akbar! God is great!*

And then...

My son! My son! These dogs *have taken my only son! I will avenge you Ahmed. I curse the day the Zionists came here!* He thought briefly about his wife and her endless tears since Ahmed's death. *This is for you Zahra. This is for your tears, I love you.* He squeezed the string tightly.

Zahra, I am sorry. This is the only way to avenge our son's murder. An image of his beautiful wife stormed his brain. He saw her, felt her sobbing, heard her wailing. A piercing cry that awoke the land and all who lived thereupon. He heard her scream, "My son! My son! My only son!" In his vision, he saw her fall to the ground crying, then throw her arms up to heaven, "My husband! My husband! My son and my husband both stolen from me! Why, Allah? Why? Why? Why?"

The young Palestinian man reached out to comfort her. But in his vision, she could not hear his words or feel his warmth. He heard her cry, "My son! My husband! Why, Allah? Why? Why?"

"Zahra..." but she could not hear him. A tight lump welled in his throat and he felt himself sob, "Zahra... I love you so much Zahra!"

He fell to his knees on the Tel Aviv road and cried out, "Zahra! I love you! My son! Allah! My son! Why did you take my son?" Tears started rolling down his face, "Ahmed! Ahmed! Please come back Ahmed!"

Two streams of anguish sparkled in the sunlight. The young Palestinian man cried for the first time in over twenty years.

He released his grip on the string, "Allah! Allah!" He keeled over, clutching his stomach tightly, "Allah..." His tears fell to the Earth, giving it much-needed life.

Allaaahhhhhh.

Through his cries, the young Palestinian man heard Allah's merciful voice on the wind,

> *You cannot win the war, but can you win the peace?*
> *You have chosen tears instead of death...*
> *For this, I mark you a man of infinite mercy.*
> *God is great. As are you.*

~

Four Israeli children played with a ball. A woman hung her laundry out to dry wondering whether or not it would rain. Two Japanese tourists replaced the battery in their camera. None of them seemed to notice the strange man crying on the side of the road.

44. THIS ISLAND EARTH

It was early evening on the third day of the Beltaine Fire Festival. Michael and Malus were laughing and sitting on the grass outside the main dance tent and sharing the third spliff of their evening. They were enjoying people-watching and were having a lot of fun checking out the various festival costumes passing by. Dozens of people were walking this way and that, laughing and dancing, many of whom were pirates, clowns, faeries, stilt-walkers, goblins, security guards...

"Cop," Michael whispered and pointed to the approaching brightly-clad security guard and Malus stubbed out his spliff until he was out of sight.

Having smoked enough for now, Michael was starting to feel like he needed to move. "Righty ho! I'm off to have another boogie." He stood up and stretched, "I'm gonna hit the live music tent coz Sangeeta[7] is playing tonight. Come mate! Come! It'll be awesome." He stretched his arms out to the sides and gave his body a quick shake.

"Nah man, I don't go for that whole experimental punk sound," Malus responded, leaning back on the grass. "I'm gonna chill here for a bit and maybe have a social. I'm pretty munted."

"But Sangeeta's fucking wicked! And the lead singer is fucking gorgeous!" To Michael, there was nothing like a powerful woman putting all her force into a microphone and the weed had given him a surge of energy that he needed to set free.

"The bass player Daniel is cuter," Malus said casually. "Be that as it may, I'm gonna skip this one. Have fun out there."

"Are you sure? Alright then. You don't know what you're missing but I'll catch ya in a bit," Michael started walking away. After twenty or so

7 http://www.myspace.com/sangeetamusic

paces, he realised he was heading in the wrong direction, giggled and turned towards the steamy live music tent where Sangeeta would soon be playing.

“Laters,” Malus called out, leaning further back onto his elbows and looking around. He took his kit from his pocket and started rolling another spliff. Once it was ready, he stood up and walked slowly over to where he had seen Helene and Luna sitting earlier. They were still there so Malus joined them saying, “Hello ladies. Enjoying the festival?'

“It's been great so far,” Luna answered as she made room for Malus on the checkered blanket. “Such a good vibe and some really friendly people around. Annnnd... I've had my first ever DMT! It was absolutely Amazing.”

“Oh wow,” Malus sat down clumsily. “Would love to hear about it. Did you meet the elves?”

“I did. I'll read you a poem they told me...”

“Shut down Shell?” a woman's voice interjected in a melodic Irish accent. They looked up and saw a young, dark-haired woman wearing blue overalls over a pink t-shirt with 'Indymedia' blazoned across the front of it. She was holding a flyer out towards them and held a stack of them in her other hand. In the same melodic accent, she said again, “do you all want to help us shut down Shell for a day?”

Luna frowned, looked confused and shook her head but Malus said, “I'll take a flyer. When's the action?”

“Straight after the festival,” she answered handing him a flyer. “It's on Monday, so it is. It's part of an ongoing global 'Shut Down Shell' campaign. Their whole attitude of profit-before-people is wrecking lives and eco-systems across the planet. And now Shell are fucking over Ireland too.”[8]

Luna asked, “but can you shut down Shell? I mean... by shutting down

8 http://www.corribsos.com/

Shell... can't you get in trouble for trying that sort of thing?" She looked up at the Irish woman with curiosity.

The woman knelt down and answered melodically, "we'll be in more trouble on this island Earth if we don't try that sort of thing, to be fair."

"Hmmm," Luna put her hand out and took a flyer. "Okay, I'll think about it. What do you plan on doing?"

"It will be fairly simple," came the reply. "We'll be blocking the entrance of a Shell petrol station so nobody will be able to drive in to get petrol. Some folk will chain themselves to the pumps and a Samba band will be playing to keep us entertained." She then handed Helene a flyer. "There may well be some rebel clowns there too."

Malus lit the spliff he had been holding, then spoke through exhaled smoke, "I think it's great what you are doing. If the governments do nothing to stop Shell, or worse - they make profits from their cronyism - then fuck them right up, I say. Fuck the system." He toked on the spliff again.

"Thank you for your support," the Irish woman smiled, noticing how bloodshot his eyes were. "There's no guarantee of success, but there is a guarantee of failure if we do nothing at all. You know, climate change and all that. Not to mention communities affected and people's lives."

Luna sighed, "I don't really think there's much a few people and a Samba band can do to stop Shell, but yeah, I guess doing something is better than nothing. Good luck!"

Malus nodded, passed the spliff to the Irish woman and agreed, "if we want to make a difference in this world, if we want to protect the environment and each other, then taking direct action to disrupt the system is definitely one of the best ways forward."

45.
QUEERING THE SYSTEM
<Jet Moon>

She's standing under the apple tree thinking about temptation. Remembering all the things that mum always told her: be a good girl, behave, mind your manners, be ladylike, keep your knees together, don't make trouble or people will think you're the wrong type, a slut. And where will that get you, no one will want to marry you, there'll be no house in the suburbs, no husband, no kids.

Eve - the fallen woman, it's all her fault, the tart. If she'd never picked that apple, taken that first bite of the forbidden fruit we'd all still be in paradise. All sun and trees and rare tropical plants, none of this horrible industrial rubbish we have nowadays. Only if Eve hadn't answered temptation, followed her desire and eaten that apple, then nothing else would ever have happened. Time would never have begun; no history, no stories, no us, nothing.

Come to think of it breaking the rules can really get you places.

Fast forward 20, or a few thousand years and I'm packing to go to the G8 demonstrations in Scotland:

- Tent, sleeping bag, sun block, rain coat - check
- black hoodie and mask-up goggles in case of tear gas - check
- high heels, strap on dildo, latex gloves and lube - check

I'm going as part of the Queer Barrio. Direct action activism can be a bit of a macho culture so we're forming a queer block to show that there are radical queers willing to fight for justice in this world; we're anarchist fags.

I'm here with my girl Joey, well really she's a boi: butch, gender-queer, female masculinity innit. She says she's always felt like a boy ever since she was little, hanging out with the lads on her street, one of them. Sometimes watching her gender shift before my eyes, I fall in love with her all over again. In this stupid black and white world her gender is something we don't have a word for, it's amazing how people carry on being who they are whether they're allowed to or not. Joey is the hottest thing I've ever seen, together we make sparks fly.

The Stirling campsite is organised chaos, crews from all over, people rigging electricity and digging drains, kitchens being set up and planning meetings. Meeting after meeting after meeting. We go to the meetings and try to figure out what the plan is for blockading day, when the motorways leading to where the G8 summit is will be closed down. Slowly, it dawns on us, there is no coherent organised plan for 'blockades day.' Everyone at the action has become so autonomous that no one knows what anyone else is doing.

We decide to get on with it and make our own plan, studying maps of the area, trying to calculate one step ahead of the police. Sewing a huge patchwork banner, 'queers block the G8'...big enough to reach in a drop from a bridge to the road below. And endlessly arguing.

On the night before the action, we still don't know exactly how it's going to work. Everyone on the site is tense, worrying about getting corralled into the campsite by the police. In our Queer Barrio we've been arguing all day; which bridge to head for, how it's possible to stop the speeding traffic, what kind of action we're aiming for, what to wear and the usual personality clashes; people who want to tell everyone else what to do.

Eventually, late at night around the camp fire there's a group of about 20 of us queers dressed in an assortment of wet weather gear, black bloc chic and the occasional feather boa. Leaving the campsite, the police in the car that tails us must be confused; we're the only action block meandering along singing Madonna and stopping to smell the roses.

As we approach a big roundabout we realise we've reached the first police check point, where they are conducting a Section 60 'stop and search' on anyone trying to pass through. It's a standard tactic, harassment and delay.

The police try to divide us into boys and girls to make the search and there's a lot of confusion, with a crew of camp boys, butches, gender queers, trans people… We don't neatly divide in any way they understand; the police are starting to regret this encounter.

I'm standing in the group the police class as 'girls.' The police officer in charge keeps asking us, 'are you sure everyone in this group is female?' Mikky stays with us and they don't even look at him. Its Joey and Lou, the most butch of the crew they keep staring at and repeating...'Are you sure everyone in this group is female?' The police operating the search have become Gender Police. They frisk us, which I enjoy, and quickly send us on our way.

We walk and we walk and we walk through the night, it's raining. Our map is starting to disintegrate, little wet blobs of paper falling off every time we touch it to trace the route. We get lost, more than once. Frankie has diarrhoea, we're cold, wet and hungry and we keep running into more groups of cops asking us where we are heading. Just before dawn there's an argument about where the bloody M9 motorway is…The mood is dismal. At dawn we're huddling in a bus stop trying to keep warm, another group approaches us; they also look wet and tired. But there's a spark of hope…. this is the first contact we've had with another group…together we decide to look for the motorway.

The cops are everywhere, every road we turn down they're there blocking our path. We head cross-country running across fields…. and make it onto a motorway bridge…we're here! We've made it!

Standing on the bridge, we look at each other... What now? Trey's been carrying the heavy rucksack with the banner all night… We haul it out, tie it onto the bridge and drop it over the edge. It unfurls to hang just a few meters above the road, a beautiful rainbow of colours. Traffic has already been stopped by the blockades ahead of us… we climb down the embankment and onto the road…. it's quiet… early morning light… We get out another banner… a favourite that has accompanied us on demonstrations outside detention centres, reporting centres and even on a Sodexho-run river cruise. Nine meters long, 'NO DEPORTATIONS,' a metre high, we stretch it out across the road and start to walk up the motorway. It's crazy… the sense of freedom… we're here, we've done it!

A van pulls up on the bridge above us, it's the medics. They've brought us a samba band who join us on the road. Up ahead of us, at the next bridge, we can see lines of riot cops and vans. It's a stand off. Then from out of the fields, black clad anarchists start to emerge, running down the road towards us shouting, "you're beautiful." More and more people start to turn up as news of the blockade spreads. What started out as twenty of us queers is now 60 or 70 people, building barricades out of fallen trees from the side of the road and pavers from the motorway bridge, the energy is incredible. This is majick!

We hold the road for 2 hours, but further up the motorway the police blockade is getting bigger. Vans and lines of riot cops with shields. Within our blockade, there's a messy round of consensus decision-making and we decide to move on, down the motorway. We climb over our blockade and make our way down the road in a cavalcade of noise and triumph. The police move in behind us, quickly disassembling our barricade and then they make their move... 20 police vans screaming down the road alongside us, cops in riot gear jumping out and grabbing people. We scatter, jumping the fence into the fields nearby. I grab Joey's hand and pull her along with me. "Run faster babe!"

A copper screams "STOP!" and batons the guy just behind us knocking him to the ground. I'm not in the mood for a beating... We stop, we're nicked.

Into the vans and off to the local police station for the usual round of questioning, fingerprints and photographs.

In the police station, as they are dividing us up, I see my chance and dive into a seat next to Joey and they put us in the same cell. We can't believe our luck! It's like an episode of that 80's Australia soap opera 'Prisoner Cell Block H.' Our every bad girl fantasy come true. Joey and I like to play games: teacher/schoolboy, client/whore, baby sitter/virgin: this time the role play is for real. For a while we just look at each other grinning and laughing, we're both dog-tired but this is too much of an opportunity to miss; we decide to fuck.

Joey is shy, scared that the cops will see us as they check the cells. My attitude is, "well, fuck them!" I'm happy to be seen taking it from my girl, an act of defiance. Queering the authority that holds us here, I pull her towards me against the door of the cell. "C'mon girl," I say. "I want you to fuck me now."

I can see the fear in her eyes, I know she wants me but she's scared. I shake her, "fuck these bastards, you know what you're here for, bitch!" She places her hands on me, used to playing bottom to my top, she knows this is a privilege. Slowly she raises her eyes to mine, then lifts me up with a long kiss full of need and the heartache of longing; her weight holding me tight against the cell door.

I love how much she wants me and I let go into the fuck, trusting my beautiful little bitch to take care of me. We hold on tight to each other all hot kisses, dirty clothes and wet fingers. Moving her hand up between my thighs, she begins to work her fingers into my cunt, the pressure stretching me open. She pushes harder and harder and I push back against her until almost her whole hand is inside of me.

I want more and more, I want her so much... then just as things are getting really hot the observation keyhole in the cell door flips open and quickly closes again. We collapse in hysterical laughter. Its obvious that we were fucking, noisy, sweaty, pressed up against the door.

She kisses me slowly, looks at me for a long time with a smile on her face. Then we lie down on the floor of the cell in each other's arms. It's romantic.

The next morning, they take us out of the cells to a bathroom area with sinks and give us these strange excuses for toothbrushes. We stink from our day and night of tramping in the rain, the blockade, fucking and sleeping in the cells. Two pretty young police officers guard us as we stand at the sinks, trying to figure out how the stupid two-piece rubberised toothbrushes they've given us work. We could politely splash our faces and wash our hands but we are too dirty, too rebellious and too queer for that. I strip Joey's shirt over her head and pin her up against the wall with a kiss. The guards giggle and blush... They've never seen anyone like us before and they're enjoying it. They're in charge but it's obvious they like us queering their space. We get taken back up to the cells... taken out and handcuffed to our own individual bailiff... Time to make our court appearance, the stars of the show.

Sitting in the courtroom at Stirling, it's a bit of a reunion for the queer crew. I chat with the guy who got arrested right behind us. The court is so S/M. All the stand up, sit down, be quiet, and do as you're told. The rituals of power and control. To entertain myself, I start flirting with the butch courtroom guard. My fantasies run away with me. She's big with tattoos on her forearms...wearing the uniform of minor authority... From where I'm sitting on the other side of the room, it looks like it might be a motorcycle badge on her tie... My imagination runs wild... Does this butch daddy have a motorcycle parked out front? I catch her eye; giggle and smile, letting her think I'm daddy's girl... C'mon daddy, want to take me for a ride?

Of course there's more, but they are other stories: of the Scottish legal system, more court appearances, the ending-of-love stories, the beginning-of-new-love stories, and a million others.

I never did get good at being a 'good' girl; I didn't make it to the 'paradise' of suburbia. Instead I discovered more choices than I could ever have imagined. Not doing what we're told has consequences. Freedom means responsibility, but I believe that people change this world by being who they truly are.

Standing under the apple tree, she looks up. Among the rustling leaves stirred by the breeze are apples, shiny, luscious, red and green apples. She can imagine the sharp taste of their white flesh, the crunch of tartness as she bites into the tight skin. Hanging there above her in their sweet and scented beauty are so many choices, so tempting, so tantalising... But she shouldn't... She really shouldn't.

Sod it, life is for living. She reaches up to the roundest, juiciest looking fruit and pulls it from the branch, bringing it to her lips... mmmm apples.

46.

PEARLS BEFORE SWINE

Helene and Luna were sitting at one of many sets of wooden tables and chairs outside the Wildwood Café on the fourth day of the Beltaine Fire Festival. The mid-morning sun was shining a friendly blessing on them, as well as many other small groups of punters recovering from the previous night's partying. Helene was slowly drinking a bottle of organic beer and Luna had a mug of cider. They had both just finished eating a lush serving of organic vegetarian fry-up and the remains of their beans and toast sat on plates in front of them basking in the sun.

They had spent most of the morning in silence, with Luna being particularly quiet. The café's sound system was playing Coldcut's 'Journeys by DJ' and Helene was wondering if a record could inspire the creation of a book. *I must ask Sean his opinion on this. I wonder if he'd be up for turning 'Journeys by DJ' into some kind of mega-novel. As Coldcut have taken all the bits from their favourite records to make the wonderful JDJ, so Sean could take all the bits from his favourite books and make some kind of Journey by storytelling. If he ever finishes his fucking apple book, that is. What sort of mentalist would try something like that?*

Luna was also far away but decided to come back to Earth and share her thoughts with Helene. After taking a mouthful of cider, she lay her thoughts on the table. "Helene, the elves were real, weren't they? I had no idea that they would be real. I thought the DMT would simply provide some trippy effects, but those elves were real."

Helene smiled, "who can say for sure what is real after an experience like that?"

After a few moments pondering, Luna enthusiastically said, "let's encourage everyone to take Delightful Magical Trip so they can all see what an amazing, gorgeous fucking world we live in!"

Helene took a mouthful of beer before responding, “slight problem with that, darlin'. It's illegal to share the love. The law calls it 'drug dealing' and they punish dealers in this magic quite heavily. Not that fear of the law should stop anyone from sharing love in this world, but it does.” She took another mouthful, “but another thing we have to remember is that not every old bastard is cut out for drugs and psychedelics and magic. Beware of putting pearls before swine.”

Luna interrupted, “well maybe it's a case of pearls before children... but I know what you mean.”

Helene continued, “Imagine telling your average Jo Bloggs you spent the night talking to elves and that the elves taught you poetry.”

“Ha! Get the fuck out of here!” They both burst into laughter, as did the Japanese couple fiddling with a camera on the next table at their own private joke.

Helene continued, “yeah, people would think you'd lost the plot. Psychedelics aren't for everyone. There used to be a slogan amongst pyschonauts about adding 'acid to the chocolate' or something like that, but we know that it's not for everyone. They'll just think you're mad. It's like people who talk about the Illuminati or the Lizard Men. They come across as raving paranoid lunatics even when they're telling the truth!”

Luna sensed that Helene had planted something weird in her mind. She tried not to ask, but couldn't resist, “um, Helene, what truth about the Lizard Men?”

Helene sipped her beer before she answered, “why, the scary Tibetan Alien Serpentine Lizard Men that run the world, of course. The ones who control Bechtel Corporation and the US government. Don't worry too much about it, sweet'eart.” They both broke into laughter again. Helene's face shifted into a more serious expression and she added, “that's just crazy shit. It's not that they are lizards that scares me, it's that they are men!” At this point Luna blurted a mouthful of cider over the table and howled with wild laughter.

Luna was still laughing as Pippa, the owner of the Wildwood Café came over, said "Happy Beltaine," and cleared the plates. Once cleared Luna joked to Helene, "maybe you're the one not cut out for magick, Helene."

Helene drained the last of her beer and replied, "maybe I'm not. But there are other dangers within spiritual and magical practice besides the Tibetans."

Seeing that Helene had finished her drink, Luna took a big swig of cider, almost finishing it. "What dangers do you mean?"

"Well, of the people who practice magic, some get messianic, some burn out and some get hugely caught up in their own egos. All it takes is one apparent demon to tell someone, 'hey guy, you're really important. You're here to save the world.' Or 'rule it' or 'destroy it.' Or 'bring on a new aeon'. Or whatever. These are the demons that are our subconscious. Well, the demons that live in our subconscious."

"As opposed to demons who live in...?" Luna asked.

Helene sat up, straightening her back before answering, "there are many types of demons, love. There are many realities. Or perhaps it would be better to say there are many ways to perceive reality. And that seems to be the danger. Just because I perceive something and can interact with it, doesn't really make it real. Understand this and you'll understand magic better. The way I work with magick, that's the real core of being effective."

"What do you mean? The relativity of perception?"

"More than that - the *subjectivity* of perception." Helene smiled at Luna. "It's hard to explain, but there's an inherent subjectivity in magick that makes it stand apart from other sciences. The way I practice magic, there is no possibility of embracing an academic science about it."

Luna interjected, "but academic science is well dodgy anyway! Who needs it? Scientists only prove what they're paid to fucking prove. The government doesn't want us to know anything that's going to stop them making money. Any science that doesn't support the status-quo gets fucked over."

"Well that's not completely true. Check out the underground press to get a better grip on what is really happening in the world. Go to the SchNews[9] stall and get some info from them. They're wicked. Last week's SchNews was about global warming. Look at how governments and corporations try to force scientists to deny or totally ignore global warming. If the government readily admitted there was a problem with global warming, it would have to change its policies. But the politicians get their sponsorship cash from the same corporations that cause climate change so we're stuck in this stupid fucking mess. Not to mention the arms companies! They're even worse. It's why a number of us are fighting patriarchy and why so many people are 'anti-corporate' or 'anti-capitalist'. It's mostly greedy businessmen causing the damage."

Luna nodded her agreement but didn't want to leave it there. "So, is there a solution?"

"No," Helene answered simply. "I'm getting another beer, do you want one?" She stood up abruptly and walked to the café counter without waiting for an answer.

Luna hated it when Helene did that but knew it was always to prove a point. Luna wondered what the point could be in this case, and started considering ways to change the world. After a few minutes Helene returned and handed Luna a fresh mug of cider.

"Thanks Helene. Okay, I think the best bet for ourselves and for the human race is to completely ignore the fuckers, hope to fuck that others also ignore them and just go ahead and build the world we want to live in. Let's create our own world..."

Helene sat down and answered, "easier said than done, but I agree that is what we learn from most of the magical movements of our time. Wiccans say, 'An it harm none, do what thou wilt.' In Chaos magic, there's a slogan 'Nothing is True, Everything is Permitted,' which comes

9 http://www.schnews.org.uk

from the Arabs I believe." She took a mouthful of beer before continuing. "In Thelema they say, 'Do what THOU WILT shall be the whole of the law.' If the left-wing anarchists could make peace with the right-leaning libertarians... Well, if enough of us set our minds to it and followed our hearts instead of the rules, we could build the world we want to live in and transform the world we were born into. Simple."

"Simple?"

"Well Alan Moore did something cool in V for Vendetta." Helene picked at the label of her beer bottle. "We just set a date in the future like V did. We publicise it well in advance and we go for it."

"And what date will we set for this massive V-inspired global uprising?" Luna scoffed, leaning back.

Helene wiggled her fingertips near her temple as if she was receiving a psychic message. "We have to make the prophecies come true, love. Let's pick a date later. For now let's just decide to be as true to ourselves as possible."

Luna started laughing again, "I think you're as much a fucking lunatic as you are beautiful."

Helene answered, "maybe I am. But if we live like that, it doesn't necessarily solve problems such as climate change..."

Luna interrupted, "I don't think your utopian vision of people ignoring the governments will happen, simply because people are too scared of the power the state has. The police can easily chuck us inside forever if we don't do what we're told. They have outlawed psychedelics, banned free speech in central London and I heard about something called 'The Spanner Case.' By law, it is now illegal to spank your lover or give her a love-bite."[10]

Helene flirted, "want to break the law, my love?" They both laughed some more. Despite the heaviness of the conversation, it was a beautiful

10 Luna is exaggerating. Spanking is not illegal, but the love bite might be if it leaves a mark that is any more than 'trivial and trifling'. Check the Spanner Trust for more information: http://www.spannertrust.org/

day and they both felt remarkably free.

Luna stood up, leant across the table and playfully bit Helene's neck. "Yummm." She sank her teeth in harder, "arrr mmmm."

"Oh lovely!" Helene giggled, "you sex offender!"

After taking her fill of Helene's neck, Luna sat back down and asked, "now I'm a criminal, what do I do next?"

"You mean, besides biting me again?" Helene laughed as Luna drained the rest of her first cider. "Well love, as I said, the government depends on our fear for its very existence. No one really respects that crap or the politicians; they simply fear the repercussions of disobeying the law. Everyone who has ever smoked a spliff or downloaded a song from the Internet would agree. The law is there to control us more than it's there to protect us. You download the latest track from the Dilated Choonz podcast[11] and technically you're as anti-authoritarian as the next guy. Do you stop downloading because it's illegal? Or because you are scared you'll get caught?"

Luna answered, "well of course I'm scared of getting caught. My friend Dready Dave spent a year in prison for getting some acid for his friends. It's the same. I can see how the world you envisage could be played out."

Helene said, "see. We're all anarchists and libertarians really. All of us: every human on the planet. We're just scared of the police or our parents or terrorists or God or whatever so we become docile and obedient. But I believe it would be better for ourselves and the world at large if we follow our hearts, not the laws."

Luna took a mouthful of her second cider, "but but but... without laws society would be completely open to abuse." She thought for a moment then added, "but the way you explain it, it makes it look like so-called 'law and order' is based on abuse in the first place. Okay, for better or worse my darling, I now commit to following my true heart, even if that

11 http://dilate.choonz.com

means I break every single one of their fucking laws."

Helene raised her bottle, "Yay! That's the spirit, love! I'll drink to that!"

They both raised their drinks, bottle touched mug with a clink and took large mouthfuls.

After the toast Luna said, "I'm gonna get some cake. They have wicked carrot cake in this cafe. But I still think I'll have to take some precautions when engaging in radical politics AND downloading MP3s." She stood to go to the counter.

Helene still held her bottle high. "Yes, gorgeous, that's half the fun. Eat cake, don't get caught giving love-bites and be sure to take care when performing magic."

Luna took a step towards the café counter as she asked, "what d'you mean?"

"You know, what I was talking about before. Not everyone who gets into magic is good at it. Some crash and burn, some don't take enough precautions. Some meddle where they shouldn't and some have massive ego problems. Mind you, it's mostly men that have the massive ego problems, so you're safe from that one."

Luna laughed, "isn't that a touch sexist?"

Helene ignored her question but responded with, "the worst are the magicians who think the world owes them some kind of fucking living."

47. THE KALLISTI CAPER <Sulien Leybourn>

"Do not believe this horse. Whatever it may be, I fear the Greeks, even when bringing gifts"
- Virgil's Aeneid, 20bce.

Part One: *Legomena*, that which gets said.

Alex slumped lower over his beer wishing that the world would just disappear. Here he was in some godforsaken hick town, miles from nowhere. Going nowhere. Impotence with a rotting brain and no more choices. Change from the last fifty dollar note in his wallet taunted that he might have come to the end of the line. The future rotten. His last scam had failed him. A misery of inert desires and pain with no escape tasted bitter bile to his mouth. The stale meat pie that he had bought from the bar threatened to become cement in his gut, or worse still, come back up on him and leave him achingly empty.

He moodily flicked his cigarette lighter on a fly lazily crawling up his glass and watched it burn. Crumpled wings like melting cellophane paper. He wondered if it had screamed. If only some people were flies he mused. Deep beneath him the Earth began to tremble. A tableau of garrotted enemies danced in his imagination. His former boss spewing maggots from a ruptured womb as she hung suspended in some eternity of violation. Portraits of his family and weak-willed friends trapped in some sadomasochistic rite of his own devising. Screaming his name for salvation as their rescuer. Begging him for release from the hells he wished them all in.

He allowed himself to think about his wife for a moment. The ugly whining bitch must now have realised that all their money had gone. Lost on the turn of a dice. Screw Jupiter's Casino. His plan should have worked. He had followed the fire in his mind that had promised so much and it had led him here to a dead end. The bitch probably hadn't called the cops yet, hoping for some explanation when he appeared that would make everything right. He laughed quietly.

He stared at the trembling insect. Squashed it with the end of his lighter, grinding all his enemies into the dirt and dust. Cursing everyone through a veil of tears, he invoked hell on all. Eyes boring into the back of his head. Alex looked up, turned slowly and saw a scrawny old drunk at the bar staring at him.

"You got a problem mate?"

The man turned back to his drink.

The pub door creaked open and a warm fragrance registered. Summer rain and cedar-smoky fires with laughter that haunted memory. Alex looked up to see a tall, lean woman walking quietly and confidently towards the bar. A panther in blue jeans and check shirt. Tight arse and long legs that just kept going forever. Ghostly virgin flesh on a curve of steel backbone. She paused for a moment near his table. Cold grey eyes piercing him from beneath a tattered slouch hat. The grey screen of her eyes seemed to know that he was a spider caught in his own web. Alex froze. She had a face that he had seen somewhere, but *where?* A slight tremor passed through him almost beyond registering. She turned away, shutting her eyes. *Typical* he thought. The only woman for miles around and she must be about seventy in the shade.

"Hello Miss Sophia."

The barman standing almost to attention. Eyes fixed on the statuesque woman in front of him. The man almost trembled.

"We got a problem today," he stuttered. "Your wine order has been delayed and I won't have it here until tomorrow. I could deliver it for you, if you want."

"Don't worry about it Joe."

Her voice dripped dark, warm honey gold across the shadowy room. A frozen tableau of men with glasses raised to lips, all seeming to lean towards the sound of her words. Sun-drenched honeysuckle and pine echoing through this dusty abattoir of stale beer, acrid sweat and broken dreams.

"I'll pay now and come back tomorrow. Rose and Olympia keep saying that they fancy a leisurely trip to town when I don't have other supplies to pick up. This shall make a good excuse for them."

A dull thud hit the counter. Alex looked up to a flash of gold.

"Here's something for your trouble, Joe, and a few rounds for the boys."

She turned and strode out of the bar taking the sun with her. The room returned to murmuring whisper and the occasional raucous round of laughter at some stupid, stale joke.

Alex gulped down the last of his vaguely warm beer. The image of the remaining notes in his wallet brought a quick summation to mind and the beginnings of a way out of hell.

"Another beer please."

He sat at the bar and reached for a handful of peanuts from a scratched old pottery bowl nearby.

"Interesting looking woman that."

Someone snickered a response from the shadows, "stupid old cow."

The bartender picked up the three gold nuggets that the woman had dropped on the counter and lovingly placed them in a box by the till.

"You mind yer tongue Bill," said the barman. "Ain't no cause to bite the hand that buys you all a few good rounds now and then."

"Unusual payment," said Alex, briefly indicating the box that now held the glint of gold.

"Aye," said the barman, "she usually does that. Sometimes she pays with parcels of black opal or uncut sapphires. All quality stuff. We don't ask where she gets it from. None of us ask."

"Bleedin' old cow," slurred a voice from the shadows. "Don't come from 'ere, that's fer sure. Bleedin' old witches, the three of 'em, if you ask me."

"You shut yer mouth now Bill or you can get along home. You're starting to sound like you have had one too many drinks. No cause for you to speak badly of three harmless old women who choose to pay in gold instead of plastic. It's all good."

The barman turned to Alex. "Another one? On the house this time."

Alex took the cold beer gratefully. He absent-mindedly wiped the heat from his scrotum to feed the glimmer of ideas forming in his mind.

"Harmless old women," repeated the barman.

"Three sisters I reckon. No-one really knows. Been there for as long as any of us can remember. Keep to themselves, they do. They live out of town somewhere up on Black Mountain. Every three months or so, that one, Miss Sophia, comes in to pick up supplies. Always the same. Large quantities of flour and salt and oil from the general store. Cases of wine from me. Not just any wine, mind. They order Greek stuff. I mean, how crazy does that seem? We produce some damn fine wines now in this country and I have to order in these cases of foreign crap. No accounting for taste."

"Takes all kinds," muttered Alex agreeably. "Thanks mate."

He picked up his beer and slowly wandered back to a quiet corner to finish his drink and think for a while. Friday night and sleeping in his car seemed almost palatable now with a promise of tomorrow and schemes forming kaleidoscopic glitters of new potential in his mind like gold.

Part Two: *Dromena,* that which gets done.

In fractured metamorphic dreams, Alex wandered sodden corridors of spent emissions crusted in yellowed ice. He screamed lust that dripped through his ceremonial fingers, wanton and lost, tinged with images of gold. Broken promises of power and prestige with flayed vaginal sacrifices. Dying again and again, he felt images of a lean warrior woman laughing at him.

The first sharp rays of the sun burned into his retinas. Alex struggled out of the car, wrapping the moth-eaten picnic blanket around his shoulders against the morning chill. The day held promise of solutions to fire the blood. He stepped out to greet the day, invoking ritual learnt long ago.

"Hail to thee who art Ra in thy ..."

"Screw this," he muttered, turning back to rummage through the car for his cigarettes. He lit one and checked his watch, trying to slow the tremor in his hands. Near four hours before the pub's opening time. Time enough to find some water and tidy himself up. He had a long day ahead of him.

Alex parked his car around the side from The Warrior's Horse hotel. The main street seemed quiet and sleepy for a Saturday morning. A few shoppers wandered into the little newsagency opposite and reappeared with luck tucked under their arms in the guise of newspapers and racing guides. A small dog loped happily alongside a couple of kids on bicycles. Shimmering heat rising from the road already promised another scorching day ahead. Alex sighed. He would need his wits about him.

He noticed a rickety table and bench at one end of the veranda in front of the hotel that made a perfect vantage point of the street. He bought a beer and idly gazed at the newspaper he had bought. *Take it slow and easy* he thought. *I must make this money last the time.* He desperately wanted to drain the glass in one deep, mind-numbing move and buy a couple more. He fought the impulse that made his body tremble with its own, now insatiable hunger. His sweat dripped on the page. He focused on the splattered print and calmed his mind. The morning moved by in languid motion.

Near 3 o'clock and an old, black utility pulled up outside the hotel. The tall elderly woman called Sophia that Alex had seen yesterday got out of the driver's seat. She strode up the steps onto the veranda, taking them two at a time.

"I won't be long," she called back over her shoulder.

Grey eyes the colour of cold steel paused for a moment and appraised Alex for the second time. The woman called Sophia went inside.

Two old women stepped into the shade of the veranda, chattering quietly to each other. Alex angled himself on the bench and watched them though half-lidded eyes. It seemed as if every nerve and sinew and every cell in his body had flared to maximum focus like a satellite dish picking up the pulse of stars. He listened.

"Why can't we go inside and have a drink?" queried a slender, tall woman with a long tail of plaited silvery grey smoke that reached her hips.

"Hush Rose," said the other. "You know that you always start flirting and cause trouble when you find men around."

Alex found it very hard to imagine old women flirting with anyone.

"Oh rubbish Olympia," said Rose, "you know they love it."

Slowly and sinuously, the woman called Rose turned towards Alex. He found himself thinking about cobras for some unknown reason, and felt frozen in situ, watching her hypnotic undulating movements.

"Well hello there," she smiled.

"Is that a gun in your pocket or are you just pleased to see me?"

"Rose!"

"Oh hush Olympia! You *know* that I have wanted to use that line ever since I first heard it. I *would* have used such a magnificent line once, if guns had been invented then."

Alex started to laugh at her little joke but the sounds caught in his throat as he looked up at her. So pale and translucent she was; pale skin, pale hair, pale eyes. His mind spoke to him of a lady of flowers, white flowers and the sweet cloying scent of nectar. Her eyes flickered and a faint smile came and went on her lips.

"Tell me you love me," she whispered.

Alex caught a sob in his throat. He felt the sharp sting as he bit his lip. He wiped his hand across his mouth and stared at the blood now smeared across his fingertips.

"Please excuse our Rose," commanded a soft, luminous, aristocratic voice. "She never knows when enough is enough."

Alex looked up into the darkest eyes he had ever seen.

"Oh, shame on you Olympia. I was only having a little harmless fun."

The woman called Olympia extended one gloved hand. Alex reached out gingerly, not knowing whether to shake it or bend deep and kiss it. Their fingers touched. A galvanised current went through his body. In some eternity held in an instant she traced the line of his blood. He thought of stars and falling into the glittery blackness of her eyes.

Alex heard the bar-room door creak open and the tall amazon woman known as Miss Sophia strode out onto the verandah.

"Come on, you two. Look alive. The wine has arrived and shall get put on the truck shortly."

The two old women turned on their heels obediently and glided away without giving him a second glance.

Alex watched as the barman appeared from around the side of the pub with a trolley loaded down with cartons of wine. He watched as the wine got lifted onto the back of the utility. The four started talking softly.

Time to move. Alex folded his paper, took a deep breath and without looking in their direction, walked slowly back towards his car. *So far so good,* he muttered. He waited until the black utility had moved away from the kerb, then put his mind and car into gear and followed at a discrete distance.

Thirty minutes of concentrated driving and a small black dot in his sights became the monotony. The sun bored into the car and made his eyes watery. Alex ran the basic aspects of his plan through his mind. Not much of a plan really. Go in quietly, find the gold, and get out fast. Three crazy old women as the small details seemed hardly a problem if it should come to that.

The black utility slowed down. Alex carefully matched speed. It turned off across a cattle grid onto private property, leaving a dust trail that indicated that the driveway went on a couple of hundred yards from the entry point. They had obviously reached home. He kept his eyes glued to the road, picked up a little speed and kept going.

Alex turned his car around. He overshot the place where the black utility had entered a few times until he felt confident that he had the external lay of the land. Across the cattle grid the property seemed lush and dark with old forest and shrubbery. He could easily find somewhere to park the car out of sight and wait for nightfall.

Part Three: *Deiknymena*, that which gets revealed.

Alex woke with a start and shivered against the mountain night air. His watch indicated that it was now 9pm. All seemed quiet and very still. He lit the last of his cigarettes and focused. *Stealth and confidence,* he reminded himself. That's what he needed and that's what he would use. He fumbled for the torch that he always carried in the glove box of the car. He switched on a feeble, flickering glow. Damn! He should have bought new batteries in town instead of that last beer. He tested the weight in his hands. At least it made a weapon if he needed one. He crammed the torch into a pocket.

Alex slid out of the car and started to walk lightly down the old dirt driveway. A near-full moon made it easy to keep to the edge. The driveway curved to the left. Turning the bend, he saw lights twinkling at him from an old farmhouse. The battered black utility parked in a crumbling old shed nearby reassured him. He had come to the right place.

Alex hovered in some eternity of pause on timing. Suddenly, the click of a latch pierced his senses and the old women appeared from within the warmth of the farmhouse in single file procession. They seemed to be singing. Alex strained to hear. So softly they sang. *Perhaps they are bloody old witches after all,* he mused. The small cavalcade snaked its way slowly through the dark. They carried something heavy. In one instant, Alex *knew* he was looking at the answer to his prayers. The old amazon dyke he had seen yesterday paying with gold now carried a small ornate chest as if it was the most precious of all things.

The moon reappeared from behind a cloud and lit up a third building that had escaped his eye before. Bleached bones exposed to time as colour to a spectral mausoleum flanked by phallic engorged pillars of white. The three women entered the crypt. Their watcher waited in silence.

An owl hooted in the distance, rousing Alex from a reverie of old sexual fantasies that had risen unbidden to his mind. *Just in time,* he muttered.

The women re-emerged, seemingly engaged in the telling of some joke from the laughter he heard ring out before they went into the farmhouse and shut the door. Slowly, quietly, and one by one, the lights went out. Alex quietly counted to a thousand. Then started again, forcing himself to stay awake and alert. At last this world fell asleep and he started his move towards the crypt-like structure that the women had brought to his attention.

He opened the door and froze from the unexpected vision that assailed his senses. Pungent incense and aeons of candle flame highlighted a wealth of tapestries and statues, antiques and artworks, treasures that even governments would breach diplomacy to possess. Wealth as he could never in his wildest dreams have imagined surrounded him. Alex took a deep breath and looked again. This was not some old family rest place but a museum, a bizarre museum of treasures beyond his reckoning. Da Vinci, Rembrandt and Picasso rubbing shoulders with pre-dynastic Egyptian artefacts and Tibetan genius. He paused at a table holding a human skull inlaid with silver and let his fingers caress the smooth curves of a bowl that should have had blood in it.

Alex stilled himself. *This is not a museum but a temple!* He spun around, absorbing the idea. A brazier, still flickering fire, gave light to the space. His body and soul spun to some holy temple of the heart. *I do know why I am alive.* He chuckled quietly as his gaze took in an altar with a battered old wooden chest upon it.

Time. *Time again to see that a truth would involve a lie.* Alex slowly walked towards the altar. He paused. With trembling hand he reached out to touch the box and slowly lifted the lid. He gasped at the unexpected trophy of gold that he saw. A simple, perfect sculpture of an apple cast in pure gold.

Kallisti. Kallisti. Kallisti. The walls murmured.

Alex looked up. Behind the altar in three niches stood three life-sized statues of marble. Grecian art at its breath-taking finest, capturing some myth of reality in stone as the goddesses Hera, Athena and Aphrodite.

"Going somewhere?" asked a voice.

Alex spun around to the door and saw nothing. He turned back to grab the elaborately carved chest and froze. In place of the three statues stood the three old women that he had seen as Olympia and Sophia and Rose. He had not heard them enter. He rubbed his eyes in disbelief.

Sophia took the box from his grasp and placed it back on the altar.

"A pretty piece, this."

Alex felt for the torch. "Stay away from me. I have a gun."

The old woman called Rose grinned.

"Relax," she whispered. "We don't want to harm you."

"Shut up Rose," came the aside.

"Listen to us," said a commanding voice. "You can have dreams come true beyond your imagining if you would just help us out. This little gold representation of an apple belongs to the fairest one of us. Now, if you could choose who should get the apple, the winner promises to give you your heart's desire. I can make every idea of yours pay dividends. Start any business venture and you shall succeed beyond your wildest dreams. You can make Bill Gates look like a tadpole swimming with a shark."

"I promise you a life lived as a chess game where every move you make brings down countries and corporations. Your knowledge and wisdom shall shape the world."

"And I," whispered Rose, "I promise pleasure beyond imaginings."

"Shut up Rose," came the aside.

Alex stared at the three decrepit old women. "Sorry ladies. The game's over and you lose."

He brought the torch down hard on a head and snatched the box. He made a sprint for the door. A lightning flash blinded him and he felt himself shrivel and curl into a ball of flux.

Damn you Athena. He would have given a proper answer if you had given him time.

Where did he go?

Oh, he is now about 600 miles away on the side of a road, with no petrol and no prospects. The police should arrive in a few minutes and all this shall seem as a dream. He wanted to experience the taste of power. He deserved and earned this nightmare about to begin for real. His past actions about to catch up with him I think.

So I presume you win this round?

By my calculations this game is now even. Athena wins this last bout.

Don't you think it's about time we moved again? Hawaii seems nice this time of year and I do so fancy a tropical stay and bronzed men.

Shut up Rose.

The farmhouse, temple and women blinked out in a fraction of a second that only a hungry falcon witnessed as he made an acute dive on an unsuspecting rabbit below.

48.
A WHISTLE AND A PRAYER

The rabbit bent down to pick something off the ground and put it in his pocket. Malus and Michael, following close behind were walking along a stony road past hundreds of cars and vans filled with happy punters queuing to leave the festival site. They both wore backpacks filled with their festival possessions and carried a tent bag each. Several other small groups of people were also walking along the road with assorted festival equipment.

"So many vans," Michael observed. Indeed, about half the vehicles in the queue were vans of various makes. "You've got a van. My ex had a van. Every fucker has a van. Why are there so many vans?"

They walked past a van which was blasting Tragic Roundabout out of several open windows. "I guess we are the mobile generation," Malus offered. "We can live in our vans and go from festival to festival. People have lived in vans and buses since at least the sixties. As you know, I've got a bed in the back of mine but I much prefer camping in a tent when I can."

As the music from the van climaxed Malus sang along, " ♫ And the best dance was yours and mine ♫ !" The group of five people in the van cheered in unison and smiled to Malus and Michael. The driver, a short woman with a beautiful big smile was dressed as a cross between a clown and a dog.

"Love it!" Malus called out to her as they walked past.

After walking another hundred yards or so past more queuing cars and vans playing assorted choonz ♫, Michael shared his thoughts. "My ex had a van."

"Your ex? What was her name again?" Malus asked looking at him and moving the tent from his right hand to his left.

"Her name? It doesn't matter. Talk about something else. Change the subject."

The car they were passing was playing 'The Sound of the Big Babou' ♫ which was Malus' favourite Laurent Garnier track. As instructed, Malus changed the subject. "I would love to still be dancing right now!" And again, "with this mega queue leaving the festival, we're gonna miss the Shell action. Luna and Helene left last night, so they probably made it. I'm a bit gutted we'll miss it."

"Who cares?" Michael snorted. "It would have been hypocritical anyway as we would have had to drive to the action using Shell petrol."

"True for most people," answered Malus. "But not us! My car runs on veggie oil. I had the conversion done ages ago." The van they were passing, which had the bass turned up very high, was shaking to the beat of the Easy Star All-Stars' funky dub reggae cover of Pink Floyd's 'Money' ♫.

"Isn't that illegal? To run on veggie oil?"

"Most good things are illegal," Malus laughed. "But no, it's not illegal per se. What is illegal is that I don't pay tax. Veggie oil itself costs next to nothing. I can get it from the local chippy who is invariably happy to shift it. Or I can buy it cheap from a supermarket. But the law says I have to pay loads of tax if I want to put veggie oil in my vehicle. But I'll be fucked before I'd pay tax for veggie oil!"

"A true rebel you are Malus," Michael said as they passed a van full of women. The powerful voice of Wendy Rule hypnotised them as it drifted ♫ out of the open windows.

"Aw thanks," Malus said with feigned bashfulness. "Hey, some of the choonz ♫ from these queuing cars are better than the music from the dance tent!" They both laughed and simultaneously switched which hand was carrying their tent; Michael from right to left and Malus from left to right. "My van is just up there," Malus pointed.

"They weaved through the queue of slow-moving cars and into the car-park, where they saw Anna, the gorgeous blue-dreaded Festival Faerie. She was putting pans and pots into her van out of which melodically drifted Sahara Piksie's 'My Way' ♫. They walked over and exchanged hugs.

"Hope you had a great festi," Malus beamed at her.

"You too," she smiled at them out of shining blue eyes.

"See you in London?" Michael asked.

"I hope so. But I live in Cambridge."

"Well, I guess we'll see you at the next festival," Michael gave her another hug and then followed Malus to the van.

Once there Malus remarked, "I sure am glad that gorgeous faerie didn't detonate last night."

"Me too. I should have asked for her number," Michael thought out loud. "All this gibbering is bullshit. I know that, but it's fun at the time. I think the Illuminati gibber you always go on about is bullshit too. Well, if it was true I'd like some kind of sign at least."

"You'll get your sign," Malus answered, pretending to be spooky.

Michael paused in front of Malus' vehicle, seeing it afresh. "Once again, back to the infamous veggie oil van." It was white, or had been before it got covered in mud. "The original rebel's vehicle."

"Ha!" Malus scoffed, "I'm no rebel really, just an average guy, but I decided long ago not to take shit from anyone." Malus unlocked the back of the van into which they both threw their backpacks and tents. They walked around to the front and Malus pointed out, “it takes a few minutes to get the veggie oil heated up enough to drive.” He opened the door and started the engine without climbing in. “What do you want to listen to?”

“I bought a CD from that Aussie band in the live tent. I'll put that on,” Michael said, presenting a CD. “The Cat Empire's album ♫ 'Two Shoes' is very funky and will get us there nicely.”

“As you wish. We're gonna miss the Shell action, so maybe we could do a ritual for their success?”

“You are a determined magical rebel, aren't you Malus?” Michael said as they both climbed into the van with Malus behind the wheel.

“Well, magic and activism are the two means by which I create the world I want to play in,” he pulled the door shut. “That's why I'm an activist and that's why I'm a witch.”

Michael cleared his throat, “that's why you're a Fool.”

49.
RE:PENT
<Koogie Smith>

SELF

She totters down the platform, sleepily well-fed. I am hungry. Grinning to herself like the Cheshire Cat.

"Excuse me madam, but I am a doctor and I wondered if you could lend me 10 pounds. I am getting a train to Crossharbour but then I need to get a taxi to Lewisham hospital. I have identification, name, phone numbers, everything."

"Well..." Doubt....

"I will send it back to you, of course - but I really need to get there for work and I just don't have anything on me."

"I don't know if I have 10 pounds." His face challenges: Of course you do.

"Let me just see. Er... no...I don't think I have that."

"Honestly, you will get it back. What is your address? I will send it to you. I am here alone. Men get frightened too." That does it. Know thy heart. It loves to play too.

"OK - here you are. I can't remember my address...." I can't give you my address - we might be evicted tomorrow. "Can I take your phone number and I'll call you to let you know where to send it."

"Yes of course, it's 07768 704 3068."

“But that's one digit too long.”

“Oh – is it? Erm let me see. 07768 704 3068 – I'm sure that's right.”

“But it's too long.”

“07768 704 306....8. Yes it must be 07768 704 306.”

“Can I please see this ID then?” Shit, I should have asked before.

“Of course – but it's locked in here (big knubbly suitcase – one of two). Here is my train.”

“You're conning me.”

“No. I will send it.” Scuttles onto the train, wary of a scream and other men to the defence. I should stand up for myself but I've already laughed at myself instead. It hurts less when I do that. Twist. Self-censorship. Let's play something else next time. That's a boring game and you just left me on the platform.

Trickster. Joker. Rule breaker. Be free fool. Be free. Always say Yes. It encourages Disobedience.

Children. Children of wild imagination. How can you sit there so quietly? So still? So passive? Children of a world that can be touched. Colour it with laughter. With love. With sadness. With fear. With joy. Colour it in outside the lines. Rub them til they bleed red passion. Anger. Til they bleed the world into movement and flow. A world where we can fuck each other into the unfolding of infinite Play.

SEX

Sunlight gently strokes her leaves, making them tingle all over, and brushes her branches as he falls lazily onto the soft, warm clover beneath her. They gaze at each other, as they have done for the past 200 years. It is a powerful ritual.

The September sun touches everything in the orchard. Insects hum sleepily these days.

They've been picking apples all afternoon and collecting them in rusty wheel barrows. But first they taste. They always taste first - letting the juice run seductively across their curious tongues. Then they gorge themselves greedily. Apple after apple disappears into those sweet mouths, past those wet lips. They take the apples up the hill to where the apple press crushes them in its death-love embrace and nectar runs free into an old wooden pail. Then they drink straight from the pail. It isn't cider - it's not even fermented - but they get drunk on it nevertheless.

Crazy kid-drunk, laughing, screaming and rolling round on the ground, everything forgotten except this wondrous afternoon and apples, apples, apples. Boundless. Ruleless. Chainless. They start tickling each other - there are about 15 of them all giggling madly, tickling each other. On their feet, round their ribs, on their bellies, necksss, arms, thighsssssss, mmmmmmm. Inevitably, those lips seek each other out. And then they taste, sweet mouths, mercurial licks of the tongue. Delicious. Warm hair loosed in the gentle breeze. Flow.... Let go as buttons fly (be freeeee), heavy metal zips get wrenched open and stiff denim unwraps, leaving.... such beautiful skin. Bellybutton skin, shy skin hiding under thickets of pubic hair, hip skin, tenderest of tender inner thigh skin, leg skin, knee skin, ankle skin, toe skin, sole skin. More tickling. Screams of laughter and struggles to kick free. Shoulders reflecting the light, aureolae smiling up at the blue, blue sky. Breast delirium ensues. Breast on breast - heart opening up to heart - mouth on breast as giggling turns to breathing. *In* butterfly lick flicker, *Out* nibble, suck faster. *In* licker, flick, like butter, *Out* featherlight, hot, bite me! *In* fucker, harder, pinching, *Out* lighter, playful, smiling.

Salty pride... points HERE. NOW!!! Tongues rolling over, under, inunder adulate salty folds of skin, pulsing and throbbing beneath those mouths' sweet embrace. So sensitive. All hardness melting with softness. Mussssty ancient smell of cunts. Sucking, pulling, kissing, sighing. Aaaaaaaaahhhhhhhhh... sighing, sinking into evermore. *Breathe In* butterfly lick flicker, *Out* nibble, suck faster. *Breeeeathe In* licker, flick, like butter, *Breeeeathe Out* featherlight, hot, bite me! *In* fucker, harder, pinching, *Out* laughter, playful, writhing. Please oh please, softnesses sob into softnesses. Going in and down. Down, down, down, drowning in edgelessness which is the whole, the everything and the beCOMING OH I'M COMING!

The entwined, serpentlike bodies who create and dream the old dreams under the wise apple trees, deep in the orchard, are transforming beyond control.

POWER

Varieties of apple that you do not find in Tescos, Sainsbury's or ASDA... or anywhere else much any more. Foxwhelp, Sheep's Snout, Hogshead, Duck's Bill, Black Wilding, Brown Cockle, Ramping Taurus, Monstrous Pippin, Burr Knot, Broadtail, Carrion, Hagloe Crab, Eggleton Styre, Norfolk Beefing, Cornish Aromatic, Skyrme's Kernel, Peasgood's Nonesuch, Tom Putt, Bitter-scale, Slack-my-girdle, Bastard Rough Coat, Bloody Turk. Fruit that is wild, monstrous, beefy, bitter and rough. Rich in stories and ancient magic.

My grandmother died at the end of October 2004; a time of year when the veil between the worlds was thinnest. She was a gardener, so she would know. I found myself grieving for apples as well as her. Apples that taste of aniseed, banana, pineapple, nutmeg and caraway. Apples grown for roasting over the fire, so that they burst and turn into 'lamb's wool', the flavouring for a winter drink. All those varieties that have become extinct. Tiny and bursting with taste. The ancient, gnarly, mistletoe-clad trees, homes to myriads of little creatures and birds, that have been grubbed up because they were not 'commercially viable' under a new system of subsidy that came in on 1 January 2005, which did not classify orchards as 'agricultural land'.

In 1883, fruit trees covered 186,000 acres of land in England. Today there's a quarter of that. The area under apple trees has halved since 1994. And many of the surviving orchards must be pretty well redundant, because the amount of fruit they produce has fallen even faster.

Instead the supermarkets stock fruit that is big, bright and doesn't bruise easily; in the same way that heavy metals don't bruise easily. This translates into tasteless mush - apples kept from the kisses of the sun, grown as quickly as possible. Flown in from miles away in planes that pump out hundreds of kilos of carbon emissions.

A commercial grower is told to put his apples in a fridge, so they can't mature. So they cannot know their own power.

The fool on the platform has been kept in the fridge for too long. Let her out of the concrete city, the banks, away from fear and debt, the lawyers, the oil barons, politicians, the arms manufacturers, property magnates, PR influence of the corporate magicians, Mr Murdoch and his ilk, Grey Kings and Queens. For out in the sun, drunk on sweetness and sex under the apple trees, no-one has need of those clothes any more.

PASSION

The queue of diners slowly wends its way into the banqueting hall.

"Hello, Charlie old boy, I hear business is good for you these days."

"Well - we have more problems than anyone's admitting. But we're all working on it. I prefer the way they did it in the old days myself - less fuss all round."

"I agree. It's a better long-term strategy. Gosh, that feast looks wonderful."

The feast is wonderful. Fit for kings and queens, which is indeed what these people are. Rulers of the world. It is a fairytale feast. A glazed and spit-roasted hog provides the centrepiece. There it lies, shining in the candlelight from what must be hundreds of candelabra on the table and mounted on the mirrored, gilded walls. In its mouth is a golden apple.

Surrounding it are the best dishes from around the world. Beautiful saffron curries, nestling in with beef goulash and blood-red borscht.

There is a pyramid of sushi – tiny, perfectly formed shivers of raw fish. Then on to goose cooked in rich Bordeaux sauce surrounded by portions of creamy fois gras. Mountains of couscous, buttery vegetables and delicate little pieces of chicken, flavoured and cooked to tender perfection. Little baskets of Mongolian lamb, sensually glistening, sit round the edge. Feijoada from Brazil bubbles in delicious richness. Whole salmon, sprinkled with dill, are placed on mirrors where they reflect temptingly. Cute little mini-burgers are laid out around the smiling face of Ronald McDonald. There are the finest wines in the world, already being served to the pleasantly murmuring banqueters as they seat themselves.

The Master of Ceremonies arrives at the head of the enormous table. "Ladies and Gentlemen, Boys and Girls and Everything In Between. Welcome to the Banquet of Insurrectionary Imagination," the androgynous clown announces. His face is painted white, with dark eyes, a red nose and a wide red mouth. Well, well. It must be part of the Halloween theme. Strange, these MCs are usually so straight-laced. She continues, "Today, the Kallisti Dining Company has prepared for you, the feasters, the feast of all feasts. To the movers and shakers of the world, we have bought and cooked for you THE WORLD. There it lies in all its sensuousness and splendour – raped, tortured, killed, gutted, prepared and cooked for your delectation, ladies and *gentle*men." The joke gets a forbidden laugh. "I now introduce to you the CEO of perhaps one of the largest corporations on earth, the United Kingdom." A less forbidden laugh and applause.

A man looking remarkably like the Prime Minister stands up. He holds his arms out, long fingers embracing the diners, beneficent grin. But some strange atmosphere is being revealed by the mask tonight. The rhythm of his speech is syncopated like ragtime, off the beat. Could the very foundations of this concrete tower of a man have been shaken by some cataclysm? Some earthquake?

He speaks for an hour about the neo-liberal model of capitalism. He begins with the usual proclamations of success, the statistics, the profits. He does not mention people: he speaks of business leaders, shareholders, companies. Bullish markets. Investment opportunities and tax breaks. Smooth running. But at some point, which no-one notices, the smooth running turns and gently starts to slalom down an icier slope. A slippery slope.

Then he tells the Grey Kings and Queens how 'we' may have made a grave error in 'our' calculations. He speaks of exhausting the resources of the world. How the delicate balance of life is collapsing. How most of the apple orchards have been grubbed up on the whim of a bureaucrat. He gathers pace as he calls up the Poor and the Hungry. The statistics start to speak of death, not profit. "On 11 September 2001, 3,000 people died in the World Trade Centre as a result of terrorism. On the same day, 24,000 people died from preventable hunger, 6,020 children were killed by preventable diarrhoea, and 2,700 children were killed by preventable measles."

There is no stopping him now. Out of his mouth and through his suited body, the audience see the bloody dead of Iraq and Afghanistan rise and stagger towards them. He starts to rant about how depleted uranium anti-tank munitions dropped into the dust of Iraq have raised the spectre of Cancer, which seeps from the soil and water into the tender bodies of both old and young. He takes the now shifting and uncomfortable banqueters to the bedside of a terrified woman giving birth to a one-eyed, web-footed, mewling little creature, to watch this creature die after only a few precious moments of pitiful life.

His voice, high and strained like a death scream, describes how someone dies from the shards of a cluster bomb, and images of the burnt victims of phosphorous attacks pop up onto the flowing silk curtains behind him. He shouts in desperation of land rights and Palestine. How the Palestinians have been forcibly separated from their land, from water, and many buried beneath the rubble of their homes. Through a grimace of disgust, the assembled diners learn how the media has worked for the powerful; how the masses have been tricked by powerful magicians. He looks almost like a lunatic magician himself as he conjures pain and suffering from their dank and shivering basements.

"And now we have reached Peak Oil! It is no longer economically viable to extract the petroleum that has powered this great charade and these absurd times. We will finally see the beautiful things we have made, the banking systems and political structures, the wondrous artifice of capitalism itself, crumble away, leaving...?" He chokes slightly. "Men get frightened too." That does it. Know thy heart. It loves to play too. "I'm just sorry. So, so sorry. I thought I could control the American president and make everything all right in the end. That I was creating a chance for a future for us. I was wrong. I'm sorry. I just don't know what to do anymore." He starts to sob, softly at first, then louder and louder. "This is probably the last supper we're ever going to have. There's no more petrol to get food into the supermarkets." Wailing now. "Does anybody know how to grow cabbages????!!! Does anyone know how to get home tonight?? It's all too big and I'm so smaaaalllll. Aaaaaaggggghhhhh." A snotty cry of anguish echoes round the hall, enters the ears of the stunned diners as they sit frozen to their seats.

The thing is, they already know. They already agree. They've been waiting all their lives for a chance such as this; a chance to play a different game.

They start in the audience, as audiences always do. Seated, quiet and passive. Stunned disbelief. Surely not. Really quite odd, all this. Then a suggestion or two as to the veracity of rumours that the Prime Minister always suffered from some sort of instability. But no, not this time. Maybe there is something in what he said. Have we been blind? "You always told me we were good for the poor, dear."

"I never wanted to invest in that damn company anyway – I knew they were up to no good. Why didn't I follow my gut instinct?"

"I can't believe they've been so corrupt – it's all the bloody Yanks' fault."

"Hold on, you could've stopped us at any time if you'd just said something. You're in it up to your scrawny, limey necks."

They bluster, then discuss, then argue, then row, then fight fruitlessly backwards and forwards into the night about the end of their world. How easily it floats away on the breeze of their words. How easily they forget the masks, the layers they are shedding second by second.

And when they get hungry, when it dawns on them that this may be the last good meal they'll ever have, they finally have permission to colour their world. With love. With sadness. With fear. With joy. They colour it in outside the lines. Rub them till they bleed red passion. Anger. They bleed their world into movement and flow.

"That hog's mine!!"

"Get your dirty paws off it! You were always a grasping mongrel."

"That's disgusting! Use a knife and fork." They start digging in with their bare hands, stuffing the food in and noisily licking their fingers. Those still using knives and forks are getting vicious and dangerous with them."

"Dirty cow."

"Fuck you, twat!"

"You can't take that, it's our national dish!"

"Shut up you silly cunt."

"Give it to me, dick cheese!"

The cacophony of sound can be heard for miles around. Delicious anarchy ensues as the lavish evening dresses and perfectly pressed suits start climbing over each other to get to the Last Supper. The feijoada makes a beautiful brown stain down the front of a vision in turquoise as a formerly diet-ridden trophy wife tries to stuff the bean stew into her botoxed lips. Mark Thatcher athletically leaps astride the hog, looking like he's about to fuck it as he bends over to take a chunk of neck in his salivating gob. The head of Dow Industries ends up slithering around on the salmon trying to protect it from the ravages of the other diners. Out come teeth and beautifully manicured claws as they pull and rip at thousand-pound sequined gowns.

For the first time in years, voices are given full range as men scream the mirrors into fragments and women bellow from the bowels of the earth. Their eyes shine, their normally grey cheeks flush as rage flows and bounces off the gilt.

And when the food is gone - as it inevitably must go - everyone collapses where they are, stuffed... and something changes. The CFO of Shell doesn't bother to cover his enormous paunch, which has slipped out in the struggle. Dick Cheney's got bits of burger coming out of his nose, but no hanky to the ready for him. The Heinz heiress's pendulous tits are hanging out and no-one puts them away. Then, the giggling starts. It soon turns to laughing, screaming and rolling round on the dining table, everyone crazy kid-drunk, everything forgotten except this wondrous Last Supper.

The MC makes her final, unheard speech to the former kings and queens, who are starting to get a taste for each other by this time. "To The Most Beautiful. Welcome to the dining experience of your lives." He bows in a low sweeping movement, taking in the whole of his world again, and glides out of the banqueting hall, with the Prime Minister following behind like a shadow. Outside in the fresh air, they get on their bicycles and vanish into the moments before dawn.

PRIDE

It's planting season. We've got the whole Earth to plant anew, but we're starting small, experimenting with what's available at the moment. We're opening up the commons for everyone to grow food. We make decisions by consensus and we ask the Earth what she wants... what she needs. We feel her getting stronger day by day. She is healing beautifully.

We use the leftovers to help our garden. Old car tyres, old cars. All that packaging. In a way, it's a good thing that plastic doesn't rot so easily. I made a lovely chicken tractor from old tent poles. The roads have become cycle paths and the trees that we've planted on the edges bend graciously over, forming arches of green or blossom, depending on the time of year.

I'm planting an apple tree this year. I prepared the soil over winter - using compost from the heap at the back of our home. I've been adding worm castings too, letting it rest and building structure into it. I found some old cardboard boxes and sheet mulched it - keeping it warm and safe for when the frosts came. Now has come the time to plant my tree. Sean's grafted it from one of his trees for me. It's called a Belle de Boskoop and the apples are the most delicious I've ever tasted. They are only tiny but full of such flavour! One of the old varieties.

There, I've dug the hole, now in you go. Pile the rich earth in securely round those little roots. Lovely. There you go my sweeting. Firm it all down. The rock minerals and fish meal I've put in with the tree will help its immune system and I've supplied some mycchoryzal fungi spores to help the roots absorb nutrients from the soil.

I've also designed a plant guild for the soil berm around my little tree. Some ground cover, of course - clover I thought. Ceri and I planted some legumes to help fix the nitrogen in the soil. Plants love nitrogen. I've planted flowers for the insects too. Some daffodils and peonies. They'll look beautiful. A few little lettuces as well for some of those lovely salads Bernadette makes in the summer. On the windward edge of the little plant guild, I've planted some blackberry bushes in a crescent shape to protect the rest. We get a fair bit of wind these days as the weather is still pretty feisty with a more or less permanent *el niño* effect. Still, we hope for the future - as we always have.

Many thought that we'd have to go without. But although we use so much less energy and our lives are much simpler, we feel strangely wealthy and have more time on our hands. Eating food you've grown yourself makes you feel fuller. We have a strong and loving community and we feel a powerful connection with the spirit world, where our allies and friends are many. Our children are growing and healing and in late September, as we pick the apples and play together in the warm, still afternoons - we sing to Demeter, the Wealthy One, and to Eris, who is Everything of Us.

THE PENTACLE OF IRON

Sunlight gently strokes her leaves, making them tingle all over, and brushes her branches as he falls lazily onto the soft, warm clover beneath her. They gaze at each other, as they have done forever. It is a powerful ritual.

INTERMISSION

"Well I have no doubt that we will see more war and chaos, but how will we know if that was 'their' intention? 'They' might be aiming to create Saudi Arabias (compliant allies that provide reliable oil supplies etc without having to justify thousands of dead American sons to the electorate) rather than Afganistans and Iraqs. It could be that what 'they' are actually achieving is completely different from what 'they' are trying to achieve. Perhaps what we are seeing is the result of 'their' continual cock-ups.

I am not dogmatic about this and I accept the alternative possibility that what we are seeing is more or less what 'they' planned, but I think that credits 'them' with more ability to shape the future than 'they' actually possess. Like us, 'they' are also at the mercy of the Butterfly Effect.

Now if only we could work out exactly who 'they' are.

- Ian Gregory, *extract from private correspondence.*

Sorcery: THE UNIVERSE WANTS TO PLAY

<Hakim Bey>

Those who refuse out of dry spiritual greed & choose pure contemplation forfeit their humanity - those who refuse out of dull anguish, those who hesitate, lose their chance at divinity - those who mould themselves blind masks of ideas & thrash around seeking some proof of their own solidity end by seeing out of dead men's eyes.

Sorcery: the systematic cultivation of enhanced consciousness or non-ordinary awareness & its deployment in the world of deeds & objects to bring about desired results.

The incremental openings of perception gradually banish the false selves, our cacophonous ghosts - the "black magic" of envy & vendetta backfires because Desire cannot be forced. Where our knowledge of beauty harmonizes with the ludus naturae, sorcery begins.

No, not spoon-bending or horoscopy, not the Golden Dawn or make-believe shamanism, astral projection or the Satanic Mass - if it's mumbo jumbo you want go for the real stuff, banking, politics, social science - not that weak Blavatskian crap.

Sorcery works at creating around itself a psychic/physical space or openings into a space of untrammeled expression - the metamorphosis of quotidian place into angelic sphere. This involves the manipulation of symbols (which are also things) & of people (who are also symbolic) - the archetypes supply a vocabulary for this process & therefore are treated as if they were both real & unreal, like words. Imaginal Yoga.

The sorcerer is a Simple Realist: the world is real - but then so must consciousness be real since its effects are so tangible. The dullard finds even wine tasteless but the sorcerer can be intoxicated by the mere sight of water. Quality of perception defines the world of intoxication - but to sustain it & expand it to include others demands activity of a certain kind - sorcery. Sorcery breaks no law of nature because there is no Natural Law, only the spontaneity of natura naturans, the Tao. Sorcery violates laws which seek to chain this flow - priests, kings, hierophants, mystics, scientists & shopkeepers all brand the sorcerer enemy for threatening the power of their charade, the tensile strength of their illusory web.

A poem can act as a spell & vice versa - but sorcery refuses to be a metaphor for mere literature - it insists that symbols must cause events as well as private epiphanies. It is not a critique but a re-making. It rejects all eschatology & metaphysics of removal, all bleary nostalgia & strident futurismo, in favour of a paroxysm or seizure of presence.

Incense & crystal, dagger & sword, wand, robes, rum, cigars, candles, herbs like dried dreams - the virgin boy staring into a bowl of ink - wine & ganja, meat, yantras & gestures - rituals of pleasure, the garden of houris & sakis - the sorcerer climbs these snakes & ladders to a moment which is fully saturated with its own colour, where mountains are mountains & trees are trees, where the body becomes all time, the beloved all space.

The tactics of ontological anarchism are rooted in this secret Art - the goals of ontological anarchism appear in its flowering. Chaos hexes its enemies & rewards its devotees... this strange yellowing pamphlet, pseudonymous & dust-stained, reveals all... send away for one split second of eternity.

LETTER TO SEAN

<Robert Anton Wilson>

Dear Sean,

I would be delighted to receive a copy of *Liber Malorum*. It sounds like a fascinating project to be invited into. Whether or not I can, or indeed need to contribute remains to be seen. Looking forward to seeing it.

Hail Eris!

Bob

"We are the rising of the moon, we are the shifting of the ground.
We are the seeds that take root when we bring the fortress down."

- Starhawk, *Ritual & Protest song*

50.
SIGN

Michael and Malus hadn't made it to the Shell action. Instead they took a detour and went camping on a secluded sandy beach on the south coast of Devon[12]. They spent a week there with several other festival-goers, a couple of hitch-hikers and some locals and they continued riding the festival spirit. Eventually, it was time to go back home and the plan was for Malus to drop Michael off at his Dalston flat and have a cup of tea before driving himself home.

After pulling up in the street outside the flat, Michael retrieved his tent and backpack from the back of the van. After almost two weeks of parties, drugs, festivals and good times, he was on an extreme high, but was also completely knackered.

He opened the door to his flat, flicked the hall light on and went in with Malus close behind. They walked along the hall, opened the door to the living room and Michael flicked the switch to turn the light on. A moment later he dropped his bag, dropped his jaw and whimpered, "Oh shit fuck fuck man oh fuck shit arse!"

Malus pushed past him, "Oh fuck!" The living room had been trashed. "Oh man. This is so Barry White to return to. Oh man." There were papers everywhere, books had been pulled off the shelf and lay scattered about the floor, the desk drawers were wide open and there was a horrible smell permeating the flat.

"My lappy!" Michael sobbed to Malus as he pointed to his desk. "Some thieving pirate mother-fuckers have stolen my laptop!"

"You didn't hide it away?" Malus asked, instantly wishing he hadn't. "What's that fucking stench?"

12 If I told you all which beach, it would stop being secluded. Here is wisdom: some occult truths really are meant to stay secret.

Michael didn't answer, but instead said in a confused tone, "but they haven't touched my digital camera or DVD or CD player, thank FUCK!" He wiped the tears that had inadvertently streamed down his face and stopped himself from sobbing by taking a deep breath.

Malus realised that despite looking a state, it was only books and papers making a mess on the floor in here and would take no time to clean up. He picked up a pile of books, "best make a list of what has been taken and decide whether to ask the neighbours if they saw anything."

"No point in that. You never get your stuff back. Arrgh. Fuck!" Michael exclaimed, sounding completely frustrated. "Fucking fuckers! And what's that fucking pong?"

Malus said, "make a list anyway. It'll give us a better idea of what to do about it. I'm going to start cleaning it up." He put the pile of books he'd picked up onto the bookshelf from where they'd obviously been thrown and started to collect some more from the floor. "Check the other rooms and find that nasty stench. C'mon, the mess isn't too bad."

Michael went from room to room to see if anything else had gone missing or had been trashed. Meanwhile, Malus tidied up the living room, putting all the scattered books away fairly quickly. He also started making a pile from the scattered papers. As he was doing so, he noticed there was a large gap on the bookshelf.

A few moments later Michael returned. "It's only this room and the kitchen they've fucked over. It fucking reeks in there. The bastards have opened the fridge and freezer and the whole fucking kitchen stinks of rotten meat and whatever crap I had in there." He opened the living room window, "that pong will clear quickly with any luck. Fucking stench! Fuck! Can't believe I didn't hide my lappy away! The kitchen's a fucking state!" He slammed himself down on the sofa and buried his head in his hands. A cool breeze came in through the window which blew his hair gently as he focused on not crying.

"I'll clean it up for you mate. You go through these papers and see what's missing and I'll sort out your kitchen."

Michael looked up, took the pile of papers Malus was offering him and saw that the lounge room had been tidied already. "Wow, you move quick." Then he noticed the gap on the bookshelf where twenty or so books should have been. "Books? Witchcraft books?" he stood up, looking mystified. Malus simply bit his nails, feeling nervous for his friend. "The cunts have stolen some of my books. That's fucking weird." Then he dashed to his desk and opened the drawer. "Oh no, my magical diaries! My journals! What kind of thief would half-inch magical books and hand-written diaries? Oh fucking hell mate, that's fucking weird!"

Michael saw that his ritual box was still in there but he didn't mention this to Malus. Instead he quickly closed the drawer. They looked at each other and in unison smiled through the words, "the Illuminati." At which point they both burst into laughter.

Malus, glad the vibe was lighter said, "or if not the Illuminati then probably the Lizard Men. Or the Tibetans."

They both laughed some more before Michael said, "oh man, we shouldn't laugh, this is serious."

"We should always laugh," Malus said seriously, "or we are lost. Laughter is the greatest cure-all known to humanity."

"You are such a fucking mentalist!" Michael shook his head and sobbed again. "They fucked my house man. They stole my laptop. I was writing a short story for Sean's fucking apple book. Now I won't be able to. I can't laugh now. I want to cry."

Malus knelt down in front of the stereo, and took the top CD off the rack. Curious as to what Malus would put on at a time like this, Michael watched patiently. A few moments later the guitar riffs of The Cure's 'Boys Don't Cry' came on.

"Oh for Christ's sake!" Michael laughed. "Yeah, okay, good choice." He started going through the pile of papers and tat that Malus had gathered, then joined in the song's twanging through the stereo, "I tried to laugh about it, hiding the tears in my eyes, coz Boys Don't Cry..." As he was singing, he pulled the drawer out all the way, holding up a small plastic device. "Hey! At least the bastards didn't get my backups! Thank the goddess for backups! If there's a moral to this story, it is to make backups! I made one a few weeks ago!" He shut the drawer again, conscious of his ritual box being in there.

Malus noticed a blank space on the wall, "hey geezer, that photo I took of you at your initiation ritual... It's gone!"

"Well that is really fucking weird. It must've been the Illuminati then," Michael laughed nervously as he sobbed and frowned with confusion. "Who else would take something like that? If only there was such a group, it would solve this mystery."

"Right," Malus said with a glint in his eye. "We'll get it back."

"What? How? Aw man, how are we gonna find it?" Michael sniffed.

Malus stood up straight, took a deep breath and announced, "we are gonna cast a spell right here, right now to get it all back."

Michael put the pile of papers back down. "What will we do? I can't now. I'm knackered and depressed and almost in tears. I'm losing it." He sang along with the chorus coming out of the stereo, "Boys Don't Cry..."

"Chill, chill. I'll cast the spell," Malus seemed determined. "I'll do it right now. I'm inspired. But you gotta stay focused and pay attention. Focus on my words, or even better, simply on my voice. I'll work some of that Sean and Koogie's magic. What did they call it? Foolcraft? Fool Sorcery?"

"Fool Sorcery," Michael answered, as he sat back down on the sofa. "As long as I don't have to do anything."

"You don't have to do anything but focus," Malus told him. "Just imagine I'm a fool."

"Too easy," Michael laughed. "Okay, okay," he sniffed and shuffled slightly on the sofa. "Do it." For an instant, Michael's mind was pervaded with a scary thought, *Maybe the Illuminati thing is real. If there ever was a sign, this is it! And maybe Malus is a part of it. What on Earth could they want with me? Why did they steal a photo of me? If they want me so badly, why don't they just come and ask me! Oh shit, I'm going nuts here. Boys don't cry...*

Malus walked over to his backpack and took out a few tea-light candles and a box of matches. He pulled most of the equipment out of his backpack, obviously looking for something before exclaiming, "aha!" In his hand he held out the small rubber mouse that had been given to him at the festival. "You lucky mouse," he told it, "you shall be our 'Agent Of Chaos.' A very important mission we have for you!" Then to Michael, "we'll use this to make the spell come true. Okay, I'm going in," he said as he lit the candles.

They both took deep breaths and Michael closed his eyes.

Malus turned the stereo off just as The Cure's track 'The Forest' started kicking in. He turned the main light off, took a few more deep breaths and settled himself. The candles flickered light in seemingly random patterns onto the walls.

They remained still in the silence for a few minutes breathing deeply. They stilled their minds by shutting out the still-fresh memories from the past two weeks. They focused on their breathing as they allowed in the meta-belief that magic could actually make a change in the world. With that belief in place, they were ready to start.

Malus said, "I honour and thank my ancestors."

Michael responded, "as do I, frater. And begin."

Malus called out to the world, "My fool is above me." He pointed straight up and looked to the ceiling with eyes on the middle distance. He paused a few moments there visualising a motley-coloured Joker spinning in the air above his head.

He took another breath before tracing a line down the front of his body until he was pointing to the floor. "My fool is below me," he sang out, looking down. He visualised an upside down clown under the ground facing back up at him. The clown poked his tongue out at Malus and Malus smiled back.

"My fool is before me!" Malus created an image in front of him of a jester holding a marotte. The jester smiled, held the marotte high and wiggled his hips.

"My fool is behind me!" Malus created the imaginary feeling of having someone stand behind him. He imagined he could feel this person breathing on his neck. It was important to Malus that he developed other imaginary senses besides just the visual. It made the magick more powerful.

Malus then cocked his head slightly to the left and moved his left arm until it pointed straight out from his body, "my fool is to my left!" And sure enough, in his visualisation a clown appeared. This one was stroking his imaginary beard.

Slowly, he turned his head to face the other direction. "My fool is to my right! Aha!" Another clown - awkwardly holding too many juggling clubs stared back at Malus from his imagination.

With both arms out to the sides, Malus turned a slow circle on the spot. "My fools are all around me," he called out and started visualising the assorted clowns and fools spinning around him.

He lowered his hands, one palm to his heart and the other to his belly as he whispered inwardly, "my fool is within me."

He jumped a foot above the ground, landing with his legs apart, and pointed to the open window, "my fool ain't far away at all! Only a fool would believe I will meet the person who stole my photo. Aha! Only a fool would believe such nonsense. Well I am a fool!" Then he did a small dance.

Michael opened his eyes for just a moment, to see Malus doing some bizarre dance – it was a cross between the 'Cha Cha Cha' and the 'Bacon Fat'. He closed his eyes again.

Malus faced the open window with half-closed eyes. "Oh yes, my fool is everywhere, everything. As a fool, I have total access to the universe, I am all people, all times, all places. I am Charlie Chaplin." With his heels touching, he spread his feet apart and clasped his hands behind his back.

"You are a fool," Michael told him.

Malus went on, "I am Smurfette, la la la-la-la-la la la-la la la." He danced around the living room.

"You are a fool!"

"I am Elvis Presley... thank you very much." He held an imaginary microphone in his hand and thrust his hips back and forth several times.

"You are an incredible fool!"

"I am a powerful bondage mistress!" He stood erect and held an imaginary whip aloft with which he struck Michael several times. "Take that my subby little boy bitch!"

"You are a very foolish fool!" Michael shouted.

"Oh yeah! What a fool! I am all people at all times in all places." He took a few deep breaths before holding up the plastic mouse, squeezing it, and imagined he could feel it wriggling in his hand. He then spoke directly to it:

> Hello, can you hear me?
> Hi, it's me. Malus. The fool.

Michael thought he could hear the imaginary voice that started a conversation with Malus, but wasn't sure. He kept his eyes closed and maintained a steady, slow breath.

> Hi there. It's Malus here. Malus the fool. Hey Mousey, could you please arrange that I one day meet whoever stole my photo from the wall.

Pause. In unison Malus and Michael took deep breaths and exhaled. The candle light caused various faces and shapes to appear in the shadows.

> You can hear me yes?

> I bring you to life. LIFE! Oh wittle mousey, I have some very important work for you! A photograph taken by me was on the wall. Find for me the thief who stole it!

Pause.

> As I say, Mousey, I bring you to LIFE! Your mission in life is to arrange it so that one day I meet the thief who stole my photo from the wall!

Pause.

> Arrange this!
> I am a fool to believe!
> I will meet the thief!
> I will meet the thief! Aha!
> Mousey Mousey, I breathe life into you.
> Only a fool would believe! Ha ha!
> Only a fool would believe I will meet the person who stole my photo!
> Ha ha!
> And who is a fool?
> I am a fool!
> MY WILL BE DONE, OH YES, MY WILL WILL BE DONE!
> My foolish will be done.
> Ha ha! Ha ha ha.
> Oh, What a fool!

"Ha ha ha!" Malus took off his shirt, wrapping the mouse carefully within it. He continued laughing out loud, which signalled the ritual had ended. Michael opened his eyes and started laughing with him, "Ha ha! Ha! Ha!" The candle light flickered some very strange patterns on the wall, bringing out more laughter from them both. Ha ha! Pretty soon they were in hysterics!

Malus called out, between bouts of laughing, "everything will be fine, ha ha! You took a backup!"

Michael laughed some more, "At least I think I did! Ha!" They laughed some more and patted each other on the back. Michael had another look at the extravagant serpent tattoos that wrapped several times around Malus. *That's a bit weird. I'm getting paranoid about serpent people and Malus is covered in serpent tattoos! That's just too crazy an idea!* His laughing stopped and a frown crossed his face for a few moments. Malus was still laughing, so Michael did all he could to force out a chuckle in order not to alert Malus that something was wrong.

When they had calmed down Michael became pensive. "Who on Earth could it have been? To steal magical diaries and magical texts? C'mon, something weird is going on. That would only happen in a book about the Illuminati, not in real life. Surely there's no Illuminati."

"Surely," Malus answered briefly, but his tone begged a question. "But think not about it. The spell is cast. Now anyone who is a Fool believes that this magic will bring a result." He put the light back on and blew out the candles. "You listen to The Cure and I'll go and tidy the kitchen. It can't be that bad."

In the back of Michael's mind, there was still a nagging doubt that Malus was in some way responsible for what had happened. *He was with me the whole time. One of his Illuminati mates could easily have broken in while he was making sure I was out of the way. But that's just crazy shit. Why did he cast a spell to 'meet the thief' and not to 'get my stuff back'? Something strange is going on and Malus knows about it. Fuck, gotta watch out for paranoia. Shut up Michael. Breathe. Put some music on.*

Malus put his shirt and the mouse into his backpack as Michael stood up to change the CD. "I don't want to hear The Cure." He flipped through his CDs and pulled one out. "Moorcheeba's 'Who Can You Trust?' seems apt." He inserted it and pressed play.

"Yeah Malus, don't worry about the kitchen. I'll do it in the morning," Michael sighed. "I think instead of blaming the Illuminati, I'll blame someone easier - the Lizard men." They both laughed again and Malus went over to give Michael a hug.

In his shaken-up state, Michael tried to imagine Lizard Men in his living room. He chuckled, *Impossible. This whole Illuminati thing; this whole conspiracy thing; the whole magic and initiation and Witchcraft and everything - it's all bullshit. We can't just create myths and religions as we go along... can we? We can't just re-write history as we see fit. This Illuminati crap is a myth, but it is also a myth that we can align ourselves with 'the energy of the universe'. What the fuck is that anyway? What the fuck am I doing here?*

51. THE FIVE SEEDS

<Gavin Andrew>

Let me take you back to about a month ago, when my girlfriend Cherie and I are having one of those wonderful nights that stretch out like a ribboning pathway of desire. The moonlight shines full and glorious through the window of my inner-city loft, gleaming on our sweaty skin as we fuck.

Cherie is a beautiful 21-year-old from Quebec, majoring in anthropology at Melbourne University. She's also Wiccan, which means she believes, in the face of all contrary evidence, that the whole of Europe worshipped a moon goddess and a stag-headed god before the advent of Christianity.

It's just so… well, it's depressing is what it is. History is history, not wishful thinking. On the other hand, she likes to dance naked under the summer stars with a group of similarly attractive and liberated young women. There are advantages to taking the world as you find it. I still get the shivers whenever I hear Cherie and her coven sisters talk about Witchcraft and how it 'aligns you with the energies of the Universe'. They say it like it's a good thing.

My favourite artist is Goya, who was obsessed with Witches. Lots of people get disturbed by his work, which is unsurprising, as his art displayed a profound understanding of the dark forces at work in the world. Goya's art shows our entire civilisation, our science, culture and so-called enlightenment as nothing more than a guttering candle in the night. People don't like thinking about that, because at heart we're really not that different to our ancestors, who huddled around the fire in fear of what lay just beyond the flickering circle of light, in the restless and predatory shadows. Incredibly, we modern 'rational' humans can ignore an obvious truth: it's only a matter of time before the candle goes out.

Anyway, back to Cherie and me. She insists she is compelled to fuck when the moon is full and shining down, and she has to be on top and riding me. "Like the old time witches, yes?" she whispers to me this night, her warm accent caressing me. "Riding the Wild Hunt with the goddess Diana."

"That's your Tradition, not mine," I reply lazily. "There's no power in a full moon…"

"Is it so?" Her voice is suddenly fierce, and she begins riding me even harder, as if she has a point to prove.

I didn't ask for the 'Gift', but I had the misfortune to be born with a caul. And my old Nonna, bless her, took that kind of thing very seriously. Yes, it's a cliché: I learned Witchcraft from my grandmother. I'd appreciate it if you'd sneer now and be done with it. Besides, what she taught me isn't anything like what Cherie and her lush coven sisters get up to, with Circles and Elements and naked dancing and black-handled knives. Real Witchcraft is about seeing things as they are, and recognising the waiting darkness. It's about watching the edges and thresholds, and guarding against what lies beyond them.

There really is nothing especially powerful or significant about the full moon from my point of view. It might be beautiful to look at sometimes, might create more work for the police, for doctors and nurses in Emergency Rooms as the tidal pull turns people into lunatics, but there's nothing actually magical about it. The half-moon, now that's a different story, because it stands halfway between the light and the dark, just like witches. Maybe this is why Goya was fixated on us: we stand on the dividing line between day and night, rational and irrational, human and monster. Halfway between worlds.

"Oh fuck!" Cherie cries, her voice suddenly shrill. "I can feel it! She is coming!"

I look at her, drink her in: long blonde hair now silvery in the moonlight, skin ghostly pale and glittering with sweat, parted lips and engorged nipples a deep purple like ripe plums or blood from the heart. I feel her gripping me with her internal muscles in a way that makes me gasp, and as Cherie cries out now, "Goddess! Ah, Goddess!" I can feel myself finally giving way to orgasm, the tempo of pleasure inside us building faster and higher and at last I give way, going, going, going as my seed spurts out of me like fire into her wet enveloping darkness…

…And …

…Time recedes, coiling back in on itself as I float in an amniotic dream…

…And the next thing I know, Cherie's not kneeling astride me any more; instead she's on the other side of the room, walking naked towards me through the shafts of pale light and calling my name as the scent of lilac fills the air.

Only it's not her. It wears her body, speaks with her voice, but that beautiful face with the heavy-lidded eyes is not Cherie. On its forehead like a stain is a Sigil, a shadow of the crescent moon.

In its hands are an apple and a knife.

~

"Get out of her," I whisper, sitting up slowly.

Lips curve in an unfamiliar smile, "I am invited." My skin crawls at the voice. All trace of Cherie's French accent has vanished.

"Get out," I say again.

"No. She wants this. She wants you to trust…"

"Never trust a god," I spit back. "Trust is death."

The smile fades, replaced by sadness. "My boy. My poor sweet boy. So much hurt in you. So much to learn still."

I am not fooled. Gods have no pity in them. "All you want is my belief," I tell it. "You think it can open a doorway into the world for you, into the light, but the truth is you belong Outside, out in the dark with the rest of them. Let her come back," I say now, standing. "I can drive you out... you won't like that very much."

"You would risk harm to this sacred vessel?"

I stop, knowing that if the thing is telling the truth and Cherie is a willing host, driving it out of her could damage her mind. "What do you want?" I whisper.

"This." In one swift stroke, the goddess slices the apple crossways, presenting me with the exposed core. Five seeds, rayed in the pattern of a star. A pentagram.

The five seeds. The secret gateway my Nonna showed me to leave my body and ride the *via nocturna*, out into the dark beyond the world.

As my body hits the floor, the voice of the goddess trails after me.

"Journey well, *Benandanti...*"

~

There are entire books devoted to teaching the neophyte the secrets of successful astral projection and out-of-body experiences; although in truth they're only really successful at lining the pockets of the people who publish them. It's all bullshit. If the wannabes knew what it was really like to find themselves Outside, beyond the world of light, they'd burn their books and throw all their pretty crystals away. For one thing, there are no guardian angels or higher beings that are going to protect you. There's no silver cord to pull you back to your body. And there is absolutely definitely no light at the end of any goddamn tunnel.

Instead, there are the denizens of the darkness, the demons and the nightmares, things of shadow and flame. There are the souls of the Dead, wailing in despair as they try to get back into the world of light and form. And of course, there are the ancient Gods, who were loose in the world once, but for reasons known only to themselves retreated over the rim of reality. Now they feed like leeches on our belief, which out in the dark is a stream of energy floating wraith-like in the night as a cold wind blows from the empty gulfs.

And very occasionally there is the poor bastard like myself who is a descendant of the old *Benandanti*, the witches who knew the secret doorways and journeyed through them on certain nights of the year to protect the village and the crops from those waiting presences Outside who take pleasure in famine and death.

So now I ride the *via nocturna*, the Night Road, and see the goblins and faes, flibbertigibbets and ghosts and howlers as they gather round like circling sharks. I pass the familiar, ominous door with 'Knock Five Times' scratched into it, knowing not to go too close to it lest it draw me in. Many at this point would be trying to protect themselves by imagining white light covering them, shielding their auras and all that crap. But as my Nonna taught me, the brighter the light, the greater the shadow. It would be like a woman stripping naked in front of a dozen drunken football players in a seedy nightclub. It's asking to be treated badly. So I make myself like the nightmares, and let the darkness wrap around me.

Almost immediately, a form appears out of the dark. She rides a yarrow-stalk, and my stomach sinks as I see the sorghum wand in her hand.

Malandanti.

~

It's seductive, the darkness of the *via nocturna.*

It's entropy, chaos, the letting go of hope. It makes fair things foul and foul things fair, reverses all morality, all love. It's a place where one can dream dreams of power and then see those dreams fulfilled. Some get addicted to it, to the influence of it. They venture out onto the Night

Road too often and let the darkness take them over. They become *Malandanti* and bring terror and destruction back into the world.

In the old days, there were many *Benandanti* and *Malandanti*. At the turning points of the year, the solstices and equinoxes, they would leave their bodies and come out onto the Night Road on the backs of animals to do battle for the fertility of the crops. The weapon of the *Benandanti* was always the fennel stalk, and that of the *Malandanti* was the sorghum wand. If the evil ones were victorious, the crops would be blasted by hail, disease or drought.

There are few of us left of that blood now, though there are many *Malandanti*. These days they own the corporations that log the forests, pollute the waters and contaminate the soil. They traffick in drugs, and arms, and control our media. They run our governments.

The woman before me doesn't look like a corporate type, but on the Night Road you can look how you want. Including all dark and pretentious, if that's your bag. Snakes wind around and through her long red hair like heavy cables and her face is covered in tattoos. She's wearing a leather harness out of a b-grade bondage flick and around her waist is a belt of shrunken heads.

"The Moon told me a *Stregha* would be flying tonight," the woman says. Her voice is mellifluous, like honey, but there's a wrong note in it, as if the honey is contaminated by something bitter and metallic.

I play for time. "The Moon can kiss my arse," I reply. "It tricked me into coming here."

She smiles, and it isn't pleasant. Her teeth are filed into points, and now I'm genuinely creeped out. "Ah yes. You *Benandanti* show no respect for the Powers… which is why you are all dead." She lashes out with her wand, cat quick, but I have been waiting for it. I lift my hand and light bursts forth from my palm. Her weapon rebounds from the light as if it was forged steel and there's a reverberation like a struck gong.

The sorceress retreats for a moment, then snarling with rage resumes the attack.

As we battle she begins to change, morphing slowly into a creature of shadow, a faint glow showing from her eyes and mouth to reveal demonic fires within the depths of her being. *Malandanti* have no true soul - it's the trade they make for their power. My power, though, comes from within. Nothing outside can have the same power as that.

"I feel as if I'm getting to know the real you," I tell her.

She shrieks in rage and lunges, but it's what I've been waiting for. A needle of light like a dagger leaves my hand and nestles into her side. I cannot follow up my advantage, however, as something like a huge hand snatches me and I am gone from the place of battle.

~

...And now I find myself in a place of earth, of dank soil and rock. There is the smell of an open grave, and a horrid lust fills me to lie there forever, to let the earth rot and consume me. Stirring myself to effort, I begin to dig, clawing my way through the mouldering soil. After what seems an eternity of effort, I break through and find myself clinging to an immense black sphere hanging above a howling abyss. Winds threaten to tear me away like a leaf driven in a gale.

There is a change as the darkness of the abyss twists in on itself and the face of the Goddess is before me, infinitely large. I stare into an eye the size of an ocean. I try not to howl as my mind is assaulted by the immensity of it. Her voice crashes into my head like thunder.

"WHAT ARE THE FIVE SEEDS?"

As I hang there, suspended above that dreadful, beautiful face, understanding dawns on me. The Gods cannot do what humans can do, cannot be what humans can be. Thousands of years of feeding on our belief have made them into empty, hollow things, mere masks we place on the encircling darkness. Although they do not die, they have only such life as we give them. We have the power of the Five Seeds and they do not. But if that were to change…

“No!” I scream it hard enough to make my lungs hurt, but the sound doesn't even reach my ears over the howling wind.

“THEN YOU WILL REMAIN HERE, FOR EARTH OF EARTH WILL NOT RECEIVE YOU.”

I feel my grip on the sphere lessening, as if it is rejecting me, and then I hear a clear voice ring out near me. “Shall I tell her?”

Perspective changes suddenly, and instead of clinging to the bottom of a massive black sphere, the abyss yawning beneath me, I am now hunched down on top of the globe and the sheer face of the Goddess is now the sky above me. The wind lessens. Slowly I let go of my grip and stand, turning to look behind me.

It is Cherie. She smiles at me.

“How…”

“The Goddess, she showed me.”

“You shouldn't be here,” I say desperately. “This is no place for someone so full of life. The dangers…”

Her smile deepens, and it is gentle and loving. “I have faith in something outside of myself. You do not. Which of us is the stronger?”

I try to say something, but I can't. I feel like I've lost something or that a bandage I've worn for so long that it has become fused with my skin has suddenly been ripped away, leaving the blood to well up and begin dripping my life away.

Cherie raises her hands up to the Goddess, and the wind dies away completely. “The Five Seeds, they are these,” she cries out. “Air – the power to conceive.”

The face of the Goddess smiles and a single spark comes into being, flaring like a supernova, hanging like a diamond above her brows.

"Fire – the power to transform."

The spark grows and spins, becoming a vortex threatening to swallow us.

"Water – the power to create and dissolve."

And now the vortex becomes a swirling of the void, coalescing to form galaxies. The face of the Goddess shifts, becoming part of the new creation.

"Earth – the power to manifest."

A world appears before our eyes, and we find ourselves falling towards it.

We fly above a landscape of lush fields of corn, of woodlands and streams, quiet and peaceful under summer stars. Fairy lights dance amid slender branches and the faint strains of music carry sweetly on the air. "It is the Summerlands," Cherie cries out joyfully, but I just shake my head.

Then we see a city in the distance, a place of immense and alien beauty. Towers with impossibly slender minarets rise up to the very clouds and silvery fountains spray luminous water thousands of feet into the air. We fly down an immense boulevard, paved with pale, softly glowing stones, so that it appears as a rainbow in moonlight as we soar overhead. Massive temples of ornate architecture stand amid lush gardens and jewelled lawns. Flying under a stone arch that rears up half a mile over our heads, flower petals fall about us in a gentle rain, caressing us. Cherie is weeping, and I understand why, because the sight is something to pierce the heart.

But I say: "Something's missing. Look at it. Really look. No one lives here. This place is just an illusion." And that is the truth, because as breathtaking as the city is, one thing is obvious. The streets are silent, the squares deserted. We land on a terrace overlooking a crystal lake, the waters still and pure under the new starlight.

Cherie looks at me now, and it is a strange look, because in it is a mixture of many emotions. "Do you not understand yet?" she says. "You are missing the point."

"Probably," I say. "I've just discovered a few things in Heaven and Earth not dreamt of in my philosophy." I take her hand. "Including you."

She kisses me and still more worlds are brought into being.

"The fifth seed," I whisper to her. "You never told the Goddess the key to Spirit."

"I did not have to," she replies. "How do you think she was able to come into me as she did? The joining of two into one was your doing also, n'est pas? I am her priestess, and my body, it is her shrine."

The words are a summons. There is a sudden sucking sensation, then a jolt. Then nothing.

~

I open my eyes.

My real eyes.

Cherie is in my arms, cradled against me as the first glow of dawn begins to creep through the eastern sky outside the bedroom window. I hold her and a hot flush of love surges up inside, along with an overwhelming sense of shame. I'd always thought I was the teacher, the initiator, but now I taste the bitterness of seeing my carefully constructed ego for exactly what it is – a tower in which to hide from my own feelings, from the hope that I can trust the world outside myself, and the terrible fear that I cannot.

"I have faith in something outside of myself," I hear Cherie say once more. *"You do not. Which of us is the stronger?"*

My Nonna taught me that the only belief worth having was belief in oneself, that everything lay within. Was it truth or lie? I don't know any more. I feel like I don't know anything.

Cherie stirs and opens her eyes and, seeing me look at her, she reaches up and cups my cheek with her hand. "My boy," she says, and it is the voice of the Goddess in her: I know at least that I will never again look upon one without seeing the other also. "My sweet boy."

"It can't be let in," I tell her. "If we let in the beauty, we let in everything else as well. The evil, the darkness…"

"It is already here, though," she says. "Is that not what you keep telling me? How it is that they run everything?"

"Yes."

"And so all the other things - perhaps it is time to let them in as well, yes?"

And there it could have ended, except the truth makes me speak, the truth handed down through the generations of my bloodline. "What if there is nothing else? What if there is only darkness?"

"Is this not what we are here for?" she asks. "To transform the Gods with our belief and bring them into the world as we want them to be?"

I look at her for a long time.

Eventually, we make love as the warm morning sunlight begins flooding over our entwined bodies.

52.
JUST FOR THE KICK

A month after Bernadette had broken into her ex-boyfriend's house, she found herself outside a small esoteric bookshop near London's Covent Garden. She had spent most of the time since the break-in camping at her Aunt's property, reading through the stolen journals and books, and was slowly coming to the realisation that the world was a much bigger place than she had ever imagined.

Something was going on out there, but what exactly? She hadn't decided. Nor, she realised, should she decide - at least until she had done some further research.

Bernadette looked through the window of Treadwell's Bookshop taking in the window display. There were numerous books on astrology, mythology and several thick hard-covered books, the content of which she could not discern from their covers alone.

A huge part of her didn't want to go into the shop at all, there was a nice feeling of safety inherent in the materialism she had been brought up with, even though the people of the world often seemed determined to wreck everything. She remembered the sensations she had felt at the Grove. She remembered having seen someone out of the corner of her eye who simply wasn't there. She took a deep breath, plucked up her courage and pushed the door open.

'Ding-a-ling' said the bells above the shop door alerting the shopkeeper that new custom was possibly on its way. The shopkeeper, an attractive thirty-something blonde woman, looked up and smiled at Bernadette to see if her new customer needed any assistance. Bernadette smiled back, but avoided eye contact, so the shopkeeper turned back to the computer on her desk and continued typing.

Bernadette looked at the first section of bookshelves. This had an array of different Tarot card decks on display. She looked at some of the covers which showed pictures of various mythological creatures, beings and characters. One deck in particular caught her eye – the Morgan-Greer tarot showed a picture of a card called 'The Chariot' on its cover. Bernadette looked at the regal figure pulling the reins of two horses as he tried to ride his chariot out of the deck and into the bookshop.

I shouldn't impulse buy. I won't buy the first thing that takes my eye. She looked at the figure again before putting the deck back down. Turning to her left, she saw a section of books categorised as 'UFOlogy'. She chuckled to herself, *Nah, I certainly don't want any of that!*

Turning to her left again, Bernadette picked a book off a shelf with LIBER MALORUM woven into its soft velvet cover. *Nice.* She opened this strange-looking book to a random page and read:

Bernadette wept lightly and closed her journal. A tear rolled down her cheek and dropped onto the book's red and black cover as she traced her finger up and down along its spine. *Sacred spaces. Who would have thought it would be so obvious and right under my nose all along.* She felt truly amazed, as if this simple insight could somehow change the world. *All around us all the time.* Bernadette felt a longing build up inside her. She wanted to - *needed to* - tell someone what she had discovered. She had a pressing desire to pass on this new information and clarify what it was all about.

Ooh, that sounds interesting but way too close to home! Why would someone name their character 'Bernadette'? That's almost freaky. I'll follow this synchronicity and take a copy. Who knows where it will take me? She felt the velvet cover in her hands for a moment and thought about what the book had said. *In fact I think I'll take two copies. A person has to pay attention to the synchronicities they encounter in their life!*

She walked further into the bookshop and came across the 'Western Occultism' cabinet. The books on these shelves enticed Bernadette to dive in. *I bet there are some powerful spells in there! But where do I start?* Picking up a blue-covered paperback titled, 'Ritual Magic: What It Is & How to Do It', Bernadette closed her eyes and, just for the kick of it, opened the book to a random page.

53.

Excerpt from RITUAL MAGIC <Donald Tyson>

Magic, The Alternate Viewpoint

Why has magic been so consistently regarded by Christian writers over the last twenty centuries as satanic? The explanation may lie in the nature of Satan himself. Satan, or more properly Lucifer, is before all else a rebel. He was an angel who defied the will of God and instigated a civil war in heaven. As punishment, he was cast down into a dark pit for eternity. His essential sin was defiance of established authority, the same sin that caused Adam and Eve to be cast out of the Garden of Eden.

The poet John Milton rightly portrays this original defiance of Satan as courageous and even noble:

> All is not lost; the unconquerable Will,
> And study of revenge, immortal hate,
> And courage never to submit or yield:
> And what is else not to be overcome?
> That Glory never shall his wrath or might
> Extort from me. To bow and sue for grace
> With suppliant knee, and deify his power
> Who from the terror of this Arm so late
> Doubted his Empire, that were low indeed,
> That were an ignominy and shame beneath
> This downfall;
>
> -Paradise Lost, bk. I, lines 106-16.

The Christian church lumped all defiance of divine authority under the mantle of the original rebel, Lucifer, whose bold example tempted the parents of the human race to the sin of disobedience – Adam and Eve ate the apple of the tree of knowledge after the example of the Serpent in direct defiance of God's order. In presuming to demand miracles through the work of their art rather than meekly asking for them with prayers, magicians place their wills before the will of God. Defiance of God is the primary evil from which all other sins spring. Therefore, magic must be wicked. This is the thinking of the Christian church, an opinion shared with Judaism, Mohammedanism, and other established religions.

Aleister Crowley called himself Master Therion, the Great Beast, because he perceived as his mission in life the disruption and eventual overthrow of the mores and values of Victorian middle-class society that seemed to him so hollow and hypocritical. This jaundiced view was largely the result of his suppressed and puritanical childhood, but also stemmed from his inherently anarchistic temperament. As his instrument for defying the authority of the church, the government, and the law of England, Crowley chose magic. Had he not been casting spells, he would probably have been throwing bombs.

The perception of magic as an evil practice stems from the view that it is in defiance of divine will as expressed in human society through the official institutions of church and state. This view is only partially correct. Magic is not so much defiant as independent. Crowley used it as a weapon of rebellion, but it may also be used as an instrument of liberation. Magicians work magic less to thumb their noses at the church than to find their own spiritual path and come to terms with their lives. Magic frees them from the bondage of social conventions that have long since ceased to nourish their hearts and minds.

54.
GIVE IT UP

Bernadette closed the book and thought for a moment. *That's all very interesting. I wonder who this Aleister Crowley chap is... Interesting, indeed.* She tucked the book under her arm – *Fuck! I'll buy every book in here if I'm not careful. But why the need to mention Satan? Good grief. And what is this about apples? There seems to be references to them in all the books I've come across!*

She turned to face another section of books labelled 'The Divine Feminine.' The first book that caught her eye was a small black and white paperback titled 'Dreaming the Dark' by someone called Starhawk. She took the book from the shelf and was about to flip to a random page when the woman from behind the counter walked past and asked in a slightly American accent, "are you looking for something special?"

Bernadette wasn't sure she wanted to speak to someone who might be a witch. Slightly flustered her only response was to mumble, "I'm just looking."

The shopkeeper smiled, "Great. Be sure to let me know if I can help with anything. We have some amazing titles here." She turned to walk past Bernadette.

Fuck this anxiety. I need to give it up to find out what is really going on in this crazy world. Bernadette seized the moment, "well um, I'm, um." The shopkeeper turned to face her. "I'd like to read something practical... something I can practice on my own. Maybe something about feeling energy... sensing energy. Or something about seeing things out of the corner of my eye. Maybe faeries, or sacred groves, or nature spirits. I don't know where to start." She met the shopkeeper's smiling eyes. Eyes that seemed to be searching an internal library catalogue, which they probably were.

Before the shopkeeper could help, Bernadette continued, "um, if there are any books about magic," she chuckled, slightly embarrassed, remembering all the books in this shop were about magic. She recalled some of the sketches in Michael's diaries, "I mean something about Serpent Magic." As an afterthought she almost pleaded with the shopkeeper, "nothing religious or wacky! Please!"

The shopkeeper, still smiling, answered, "the book you have picked up, 'Dreaming the Dark' is interesting for techniques and politics, but some of the history in there about 'The Burning Times' is still conjecture. Still, a great book for learning how to work with dreams, with energy and with female mysteries. See the subtitle," she pointed to the words on the cover of the book, "'Magic, Sex and Politics' - the book is a fascinating and practical classic treatise on those three subjects and how they are inter-related."

"Thank you," Bernadette muttered, as she tucked the book under her arm.

The shopkeeper continued, "a book about Serpent Magic - a practical book rather than theoretical - would be 'Seidways' by Jan Fries." She walked to the opposite end of the shop and took a black-covered paperback from the shelf. "Here it is - 'Seidways - Shaking, Swaying and Serpent Mysteries'. It's now out of print, which means its price is slightly above our usual first editions." She looked to see if that would disturb her customer, it seemed not to. "And something to give you a few ideas of different magical possibilities would be, let's see..." she reached to the top shelf for a book. "Here, 'Mastering Witchcraft' by Paul Huson - a classic. It was written for an audience of people embracing Witchcraft after breaking free of Christianity... in a sense. But it is complete on its own and has been highly praised."

Bernadette took the books under her arm and graciously said, "thank you."

There was a large sofa in the store which she had eyed and she wanted to sit down and take a look at the books that had been recommended. The shopkeeper noticed her customer looking at the sofa then offered, "take your time, take a seat and have a look through those. Feel free to ask any questions you might have about those books or other topics you might be interested in. My name is Christina."

"Thanks, I'll just take a look and let you know." Bernadette sat down and started going through the books she was holding. She saw several pictures within 'Seidways' that would make excellent tattoos if she had been that way inclined. She flipped through several pages, but found it difficult to focus on the text. She was supposed to decide if the books were worth buying but, for a start, she had nothing to judge them on except Christina's word. Christina seemed pretty sound, so she relaxed onto the sofa trying to decide. From her seated vantage point, she looked around the store and spotted a rack full of flyers. She stood, walked to the rack and scanned it. She took one pretty flyer that read, 'Women's Full Moon Magic Circle - phone Sacha'. *That sounds very interesting.*

Next to it was a colourful brochure advertising a 'Goddess Conference' in Dublin, for early March next year. The brochure listed dozens of names of speakers, none of whom Bernadette recognised. Still, it sounded fascinating to her so she folded the brochure and put it in her pocket.

She looked over some other flyers that made her roll her eyes, including 'Raising Atlantis - A Practical Workshop' and 'Follow your dreams to abundant wealth.' *If I was following my dreams I wouldn't need abundant wealth!* She didn't bother picking up any of the flyers inviting her to join various groups, covens, orders, churches or temples. *Fuck, there's a lot of groups desperate for members!*

She picked up another flyer and read:

Moot With No Name – A talk on "Fool Sorcery" by Seani Fool.

The Fool, a close relative of the trickster and the jester, is a well-known archetype from mythologies the world over, from the Native American Coyote to the laughing Buddha, Eris, goddess of chaos and strife, through to Hanuman in the Hindu myths. Much is known about the Fool throughout history and mystery so that is not what this talk is about.

Instead, tonight's talk will be on the Fool as a *contemporary* archetype and specifically how to access the power of the Fool in the modern age. The contemporary Fool is post-Discordian and post-Chaos but, like its recent historic counterparts, the Fool still aims to step out of the Tarot deck and off the cliff, boldly (or perhaps foolishly) going where both angels and devils fear to tread.

The Moot With No Name is at the Devereaux, opposite the Royal Courts of Justice, June 21st, 7.30 for an 8pm start, £2

Wear a silly hat.

That's in three weeks. Bernadette wondered if the 'Seani Fool' giving the talk could be the same person as the 'Sean' who had written to Michael about the 'collaborative book project' and decided she would go to the talk. *It would be interesting to meet him. I wonder if Michael is still involved with this stuff.* She remembered the pain she felt about how abruptly he had left her. She felt it again now. *And so many dreams about him!*

She put the 'Fool Sorcery' flyer in her pocket and walked to the counter carrying the books Christina had recommended earlier plus two copies of Liber Malorum and the Donald Tyson book.

Christina completed the sale and put the books in a shopping bag. Handing the bag to her customer, she said, "here's a bookmark with the Treadwell's phone number on it. What is your name?"

"Bernie." A huge part of her was really looking forward to reading these books. "Thank you so much. You've been so very kind and helpful."

"Bernie, let me know if there's anything else I can help you with."

"Thank you. One more question - do you have any books or do you know anything about the magic of dreams?"

55.
CALYPSO
<Delaney Crawley>

"Cruel folk you are, unmatched for jealousy,
you gods who cannot bear to let a goddess sleep with a man."
- Homer, The Odyssey

~

Thunder pealed around the darkened sky and the goddess parted the moon. A silver-turquoise serpent leapt from her breast and flew through the air. The young girl screamed and ran from the serpent which started chasing her. She found a heavy stick and whacked the snake across the head. Unfazed, it continued to follow her down familiar streets and alleyways till she found a shrub to hide behind. She tried to call out, but there was no sound. A black woman with thick, ruby lips was watching her from the road. The serpent was wrapped like a feather boa around the woman's neck.

"I shouldn't sleep with him, should I?" the girl asked the woman, who simply rolled her eyes back into her head and laughed.

~

Calypso woke breathlessly and sat up. Beads of sweat stuck to the back of her neck and she pulled her hair up. She swallowed in an attempt to force saliva back into her dry mouth. Tom was snoring quietly beside her, so she drew back the covers and slipped out of bed. In the kitchen were two half-filled glasses of red wine. After draining them both into the sink, she filled it with hot soapy water. Outside, a gentle breeze swept through the overgrown grass, causing the door of the old shed to sway back and forth, its rusted hinges squeaking.

Calypso opened the windows that overlooked the garden and inhaled the morning. The air was sultry and smelt of rotten flowers. A Bougainvillea vine had fallen overnight, and the velvet crush of leaves lay scattered across the lawn. Over the back fence a Pink Lady apple hung low and precarious on its branch. It belonged to an old orchard that had been long neglected and recently abandoned by the previous owners. Calypso had thought about restoring it, but lately the idea had faded.

She washed the dishes methodically and tried to push the dream back into the recesses of her mind. Between her thighs she felt the sticky remnants of last night's lovemaking. They were sore and she crossed her legs. Tom's orgasm had taken longer than usual. Calypso, on the other hand, had come several times.

~

"Smell's great!"

Fried butter wafted through the tiny house and drew Tom out of the bathroom. Steam rose off his freshly showered back and he had a white towel wrapped around his waist.

"I think I'll make pancakes. Is that ok?" Calypso cracked two eggs into a bowl.

"Sure." He leant over her and switched on the kettle.

"You smell delicious." Calypso faced him and wrapped her sticky arms around his waist.

Tom peered over her shoulders and into the back garden. "That shed's in bad shape," he said and pulled away from her embrace. Calypso dropped her arms and began beating the pancake batter.

"Are you okay?" he asked.

"I think so," she stopped beating and faced him. "Is everything okay with you?"

"Yeah, of course." Tom avoided her eyes and poured hot water into the coffee plunger.

"Want to go to the beach today?" he asked.

"I guess so, okay." Calypso poured batter into the sizzling frying pan. A shard of hot butter flew up into her hand and burnt the top of her thumb.

"Damn!" she cried and shook out her wrist.

Tom took his coffee out into the garden and surveyed the damage done from last night's storm. He picked up a rusty rake and began sweeping the fallen leaves.

~

The sun glanced periodically through the hazy sky. The afternoon winds had picked up and were disturbing the picnic tables and barbeque fires that littered the park overlooking the beach. Waves were crashing noisily on the shore. Several undeterred swimmers were taking advantage of the last days of summer and a group of men had secured a section of the park in which to play cricket. A young boy hit the ball out into the ocean with a noisy splash and was cheered on by the men.

Calypso looked for the wives and found them huddled around a nearby picnic table. She eyed them curiously. They were preparing lunch and laughing as a delicious piece of gossip seemed to float in the air. A young girl with them, twelve or thirteen at most, caught Calypso's eye. She had long, dirty blond hair and a sour expression. Their eyes met for a moment and the girl turned away to watch the cricket game. Her exposed legs were long and smooth. She uncrossed them and crossed them again on the other side in a gesture of frustrated boredom. Calypso smiled and looked down at her own unshaven legs, remembering with amusement the day she had first shaved them. She had been about the same age as the blond girl. Her mother's razor had shaved the baby blond hairs off the whole of her legs, right up to her vagina. Her parents had been having a party in the back yard and Calypso had worn her jeans so they wouldn't notice. Her legs had felt slippery and tingly beneath the rough denim.

The blond girl stood up and walked right through the middle of the cricket game to stand beside one of the men. The bowler paused until she had passed him, then prepared himself once more. The girl linked her arm through the man's and rested her head on his shoulder. He reached down to pick up his beer but she grabbed it and had the first sip, glancing back over her shoulder at Calypso, who was both amused and slightly in awe of the girl's cheek.

~

Tom was on the beach gazing forlornly out across the horizon. Calypso rubbed oil into his back, being careful to avoid the scar between his shoulder blades.

The skin remembers.

“What's she like?” Calypso asked him.

“Who?”

“You know,” she hesitated momentarily, then continued her circular motion deeper than before.

“Do I?”

“I dreamt you went back to her.”

“When?”

“A few nights ago.”

Tom turned around and pushed Calypso playfully down onto the sand.

"Shut up, you!" He kissed her hard on the mouth and bit into her bottom lip.

"Ouch!" Calypso laughed as he searched her eyes. She was beautiful, dangerously so. Her dark hair hung in long waves that seemed to hug her rose complexion. An old-fashioned beauty borrowed from some ancient Greek temptress. Tom had been tempted many times, but something was waning in him now. Her dark eyes were like deep pools that were sucking him deeper into uncertainty. They seemed to ask more of him than he could bear. He longed for a simpler equation, something more manageable.

The growing opaqueness of his stare made Calypso feel uncomfortable and she sat up, brushing the sand from her back.

"I just wanted to know what she was like."

"She's nice. Well, she was."

"What do you mean?"

"Calypso! You know. She bought gifts for my parents. Did all the 'right' things." He turned his gaze back to the horizon. Calypso sat on her hands. The silence was broken by a flock of seagulls diving noisily into an abandoned chip wrapper. "It's different with you."

"Yeah?" She placed her palm in the center of his back. "Are you happy?"

Tom let out a snort. "Are you?"

~

Calypso left Tom to his daily jog along the beach and wandered back to the house alone. She thought about the black woman in her dreams. *What does she want from me? The message was plain enough. I have to stop sleeping with him. Fine. Surely we have more to us than sex?* She remembered his tongue circling between her thighs.

If only he wasn't so damn...erotic! So what if he doesn't love me in the same way I love him, so what if he still pines after his ex-wife? He might be a mere mortal but he is definitely erotic.

It surprised her how much it mattered. There had been many lovers, but Tom had been the first to truly open her. Her girlfriend Adriana's jaw had dropped in awe when Calypso had described Tom's consistent willingness to ensure her satisfaction.

"You mean he actually asks if you've had enough?"

"And he follows through," Calypso had giggled.

"It can't possibly last," Adriana said. Calypso had been annoyed by her friend's pessimism, but now she saw that Adriana had probably been right. Something within her was beginning to feel stuck in an all-too-familiar scenario.

Calypso closed the back doors on the evening wind and ran a bath. 'The concubine not the wife' her I-Ching oracle had once read. At the time she had been delighted by such an unconventional prophecy, but lately it just confused her. She added some sweet almond oil and lavender to the running water.

*What happened to concubines anyway? Wasn't there a time when the mistress and muse was revered and adored? Where did they all go? '**La femme inspiratrice**', the French called her. The ancient Greeks named her '**Hetaera**' - the one who awakened and inspired a man with her feminine wisdom and passionate understanding. Not the 'passive male construct' that today's feminists would claim.* She eased herself into the scalding hot water and watched the steam envelope her nakedness.

"Jouissance!" she murmured, and breathed in the thick, scented steam.

Maybe that's it? Maybe I should go to France - to Paris, where people truly understand pleasure, where women are free to practice their arts. She sank deeper into the hot mist and half closed her eyes. The face of a beautiful black goddess appeared before her in the swirling haze of steam, and Calypso could have sworn she saw the goddess wink. She picked up Tom's razor from the windowsill and began to shave the hairs off her legs.

~

That night, Calypso attempted to resist Tom's sex and wrapped herself in a platonic embrace.

"Tom, do you think we should stop sleeping together?"

"Why?" he closed his eyes.

"I don't know. To see what else we have?"

He reached over and caressed her left breast with the palm of his hand, "okay, if you like."

Calypso sighed and rolled away from him, "I'm serious Tom!"

He ran his fingers over her thighs and rested them lightly between her legs.

"You are hopeless," she laughed and shifted her legs slightly apart.

"I know," he whispered and widened the distance between her thighs. She groaned and surrendered to bliss.

~

Calypso tossed and turned in her sleep. In her dream there was a wedding. She was the bride in the wings waiting to walk the aisle. Tom was at the foot of the pulpit and the eyes of the crowd were on her. She took slow, nervous steps towards the front. In the crowd, her old school friends smiled. Her mother was there too, though her face was hidden. Finally, Calypso made it to the front. She reached out to touch Tom's arm and gasped in horror as the ugly black woman grinned toothlessly back at her instead.

“Hee hee hee.”

“Leave me alone!” Calypso screamed. “What do you want from me, you jealous hag! I was the one who saved him when he was alone. I looked after him and loved him. I hate you!”

Calypso turned to the crowd. They were staring at her. Tom was nowhere to be seen. She looked down at her wedding gown and saw that she was naked from the waist down. Horrified, she ran out of the church and saw Tom walking towards the end of the road.

“Tom!” she cried out, but he didn't respond. “Tom!”

He waved back at her, but kept on walking till he faded into the landscape. Calypso stood still in the middle of the road, alone and exposed, and felt a wave of anguish wash over her.

~

Calypso peeled back the covers and sat up in bed. The room was bathed in moonlight. She knelt down on the cold floorboards and felt under the bed for her suitcase. It was covered in dust, and she wiped it gently with the palm of her hand. One of the clasps was broken. Tom had sat on it too hard last summer when she had packed it with jumpers to store out in the back shed. A few old jumpers were still inside it. She began to pack it with her underwear, a few dresses, a pair of faded denim jeans and her black stilettos. From the dresser drawer she took her makeup, two Vogue magazines and a biography of Anais Nin.

Tom was sleeping peacefully. Half his face was buried in the pillow and he appeared to be smiling. She took the suitcase into the kitchen and fastened the lock. Remembering her toothbrush, Calypso retrieved it from the bathroom and took the toothpaste too. She opened the mirrored cabinet and took out an old lip pencil. On the mirror she wrote in large, red letters, '*I love you*'. She picked up the suitcase and headed out into the back yard.

The garden was still. A half visible moon was sending slivers of silver light through the vines draped over the back fence. Calypso climbed through a broken fence post and stepped out into the orchard. Silhouetted apples hung like giant teardrops. The air was dank and smelt of rotting fruit.

Calypso sank to the ground and let the earth soak up her pain and confusion. She placed both her hands into the soil and dug them in as deep as she could. A bruised apple fell from a tree and landed in her lap. She held it in her dirty palms. "Take him!" she cried and looked up into the clouded sky. A light rain began to fall.

56.
FOOL SORCERY

Summer Solstice.

It was June 21st, the longest day of the year. Bernadette was in her Clapham flat deciding whether or not to go to Seani Fool's talk at the Devereaux when it finally happened. The fear and anxiety about possibly seeing Michael again, mingled with the pain of her broken heart, created a single tear, which rolled down her burning cheek.

Her light weeping turned into heavy sobbing, *I miss you so much Michael.* And then like the opening of flood-gates, Bernadette cried the tears of the broken-hearted; tears that she had been saving for many sad, confused months. All the tears that had been waiting in vain for answers finally flowed freely.

Michael, I miss you so much but I set you free... We clearly weren't meant to be. It is time for me to move on... There are no answers for a broken heart. There are no reasons. Time heals all wounds Michael... Michael, I set you free... I set you free.

After crying all her tears, Bernadette felt an amazing lightness that had been extremely elusive for a very, very long time. The tears refreshed her and through her tear-washed eyes, Bernadette saw that the path before her was now clear... She would go to the talk and, well, come what may...

~

"Who here considers themselves to be a fool?"

A few people put their hands up.

"Shakespeare famously wrote, 'A fool thinks himself to be wise, but a wise man knows himself to be a fool.' With that in mind, who here considers themselves a fool?"

At this, most of the people in the smoky room raised their hands.

"A bunch of wise asses then?" the speaker joked raising a laugh from the assembled.

Bernadette was in the top bar of 'The Devereaux', an inner-city London pub, along with 25 or 30 other people, listening to a man wearing a pirate's hat talk about his magical path, which he'd named 'Fool Sorcery.' Considering Bernadette had thought magic and Witchcraft to be fairly solemn, if not Gothic affairs, it was an extremely lively talk covering a range of topics including historical jestering, Discordianism, Rebel Clowning, Chaos Magic, anti-authoritarianism, piss-taking, myth-making and how to cast spells.

The talker, going by the name of 'Seani Fool' was fairly erudite, as well as being talented at inspiring the people who were in attendance. Aged in his early to mid thirties, with long dreadlocks poking out from his pirate hat, black trousers and a purple t-shirt showing the silhouette of two unicorns fucking, he certainly looked the part for this talk - he appeared very foolish indeed. Maybe that was the point? As foolish as Seani appeared, Bernadette noticed how incredibly good looking he was.

This 'Fool Sorcery' talk had certainly sparked some interest with Bernadette, who was keen on learning something very down-to-earth and practical. She was relieved but also a little disappointed that Michael wasn't there. Nor was Helene, but that also meant she could pay more attention to the talker and remain anonymous. She sat at a table with two Japanese people, probably tourists, who seemed more interested in their camera than in the speaker.

Seani Fool was talking about different kinds of magical direct action and spoke of how inspired he had been by the pagan activists, especially the Dragon Network, the Reclaiming Witches and the Anderson Feri Tradition. Bernadette, having forgotten to bring a notepad, sent herself an SMS in order not to forget:

Look up Dragon Network + Reclaiming + Anderson Feri to find info on pagan activist groups.

Mid-way through Seani Fool's hour-and-a-half-long talk, Kommodore Koogie, a co-founder of the coven Seani was in, gave a mini-talk detailing some of the 'actions' they had been on as Fool Sorcerers. These included rebel clowning at the G8 meeting *(whatever that was)*; asking (and getting) permission to cast spells at the British Parliament; and heckling big-wig politicians during their inane speeches. "We make Fools of ourselves, but we also learn how to make fools out of others," she said. "It would appear that people are controlled through their fear. The best way to overcome fear is to laugh. Laughter is the best medicine, and wielded imaginatively, it is also a very subversive and disruptive influence on those systems that attempt to limit and control us."

Before she wrapped up, she revealed that their coven was called 'The Fooluminati', which was obviously a play on words.

The essence of Fool Sorcery, according to Seani Fool when he came back on, consisted of two key factors. The first was the symbology of the Fool from the Tarot. "The fool, card zero, depicts a person stepping off a cliff, apparently unaware of the danger he *(or she)* is about to confront. The cliff symbolises the void and the great unknown. To a practitioner of Fool Sorcery, a person embodies the Fool when they take everything they know, and everything they don't know, and step off the metaphorical cliff by taking a risk of some kind." He held up a book by Ramsey Dukes titled 'Uncle Ramsey's Little Book Of Demons' and explained that it contained amazing instructions on how to personify the influences on our lives. Seani Fool said, "personifying on the one hand 'all we know' and on the other 'all we don't know' is a tool of the Fool."

Seani Fool went on, "Einstein famously wrote 'Imagination is more important than knowledge' and Fools adhere to this motto enthusiastically. We can't know everything, but by taking the lack of knowledge with us as we step off the cliff, the lack of knowledge can magically turn into a friend and a tool of power. Once we're in the void, it is our powerful imaginations that we will find most useful. The void, by definition, is that dark place where we don't have a clue what is going on. All we have are our wits, and our imaginations. The more we are able to trust our own imaginations, the further into the darkness of the void we can explore."

"Being anti-authoritarian is also paramount to Fools, and is an inherent trait in jesters, clowns, fools and shamans the world over. But do we know who the real authorities are in this world? We never really know what is going on. We can never really know everything. Who rules the world? Does anybody? Jewish Zionist racketeers? Swiss bankers? The US military industrial complex? The Bavarian Illuminati? Saudi oil barons? Tibetan Lizard Men? Steve Ash? We don't know, but we don't let the lack of knowledge stop us going on our missions. Instead, we personify our lack of knowledge and take it with us as a friend and as a demon. Instead of combating an unknowable, unreachable authority, we simply play authority at will..."

Koogie interrupted, "we can play any aspect of ourselves at will and that's how we can live our lives to the full most readily. We give ourselves license (or perhaps, *lie sense*) to act. Instead of making lies and truth polar opposites - constricted by a narrow moral framework - we give imagination freedom to start making sense out of all the lies and create truth in all its colour and infinite possibility."

"This leads to the second trait of Fool Sorcery." Seani Fool went on to explain that the second factor was symbolised by the Fool who declares without fear that *the Emperor has no clothes*. In practical terms, this meant that Fool Sorcerers would speak out when others were afraid to. Typically, a person would be too scared to make a fool of themselves by saying or doing something silly, but a Fool Sorcerer thrived on being foolish in exactly that way. "The emperor has no clothes, say it loud and say it often. Disempower would-be emperors through your lack of belief in their authority. The emperors of our time can only rule over us because we collectively believe in them and end up doing what we are told. If we all stop believing in them, if we all were to stop obeying at the same time, we would all be free. Can you imagine it?"

He paused a moment then swept his arm out to the side as if revealing a canvas. "If we were all to stop obeying at the same time, what would the world look like? If we all went out there with love in our hearts and disobeyed all the rules that restricted us, where would we be?" He turned his head to look to where he was pointing and asked, "what would the world look like?" As if by magic, Bernadette saw an image appear on the canvas. *Whoa, that is some trickery he has going on there.*

A few moments later a silver-haired woman in the audience, who was obviously a close friend of Seani Fool, spoke briefly of the similarities between the Fool that Seani was describing, and the innate freedom seemingly experienced by children, who have no recognition of authority figures until such recognition is drummed into them, albeit usually at a very early age and often violently.

Seani Fool agreed with her, then said, "children, being innocent, have no need to recognise authority and have no need for defences. Likewise to a Fool, defence plays a very different role compared to most sorcery traditions."

"Most magical systems require the building up of a seriously well-fortified magical circle at the start of any ritual. Fool Sorcery is the opposite in that it actually attempts to tear down all defences and barriers. Real power is achieved when I stretch out until there is no difference between me and the other."

He went on to talk about actual spell-casting, which Bernadette found fascinating. Apparently, four gods from the Greek myths are chosen for casting a Fool's magical circle, though such a circle isn't a barrier of protection - it is more a circle of powerful and Foolish inspiration. Bernadette later regretted that she could not remember who three of the gods were, but remembered that Eris was one of them. After the circle is cast, the Fool performing the ritual says something like 'Only a fool believes magic could make blah blah come true. Aha! I am a fool!' Then the person doing the ritual assumes the Stance Of The Fool and presto – the spell is cast.

"For example," Seani said, "if I was to write a book and I wanted it to be popular, my spell would be: 'only a fool would believe my book will be popular. Only a fool would believe that my book will inspire people. Only a fool would believe people will be touched by my book.' Aha," Seani said, then stepped forward and spread his arms wide, "I am such a Fool." He stood with his arms out, taking in the whole Devereaux for a few moments, then withdrew them to a cross over his chest, smiling, "Only a fool would believe."

Seani went on to compare Fool Sorcery with some other traditions but Bernadette didn't really know much about them so a lot of the comparison was lost. On the other hand, she found this new world incredibly exciting and wanted to learn as much as possible.

Fool Sorcery is post-Chaos *(whatever that means)* in that it takes the essential lessons from Chaos Magic and utilises them in a more efficient and pragmatic way. A Fool, according to Seani, could be anything at any time and could shift between personas and shift between worlds on the flip of a coin. In other words, it is possible to step into and adopt any magical paradigm *(whatever that is).* Fools live in the meta-paradigm of myth and are able to switch myth at will. "A chaos magician might say, 'tonight we are entering a paradigm where the great old one Cthulhu is reachable by calling out certain key phrases.' The Fool, on the other hand might say, 'Holy fucking shit, Cthulhu is alive and we're gonna raise the bastard tonight!' Life can be 'a play' to those who consider themselves Fools. And why not join in with 'the play', or live consciously and play in the world of myths if that is possible?"

"Fool Sorcery is not exactly post-Discordian," *(Oh, I know what Discordian is! It was mentioned in one of Michael's diaries. It was something about Eris, the Goddess of Mischief and an apple...),* "but it is an extension of Discordianism, in that it acknowledges everyone has their own limited reality tunnels, but purposefully chooses a very optimistic, anti-authoritarian, confrontational, non-violent tunnel. Discordianism aims to set its followers free from the shackles of Belief Systems (BS as Robert Anton Wilson would say), whereas Fool Sorcery *assumes* a very foolish freedom from all BS in the first place. Fool Sorcery is geared towards taking action. Fool Sorcery assumes we all live in the world of myth, whatever that means, and we start from there."

"Some of the archetypes people adopt in better-known occult traditions," explained Seani Fool, "include the witch, warlock, shaman, wizard, magician, sorcerer, priest or priestess, neophyte, druid, occultist, adept, warrior, magus, necromancer and others. Now, to step into any of these personas can be extremely powerful, and I do it all the time. Alas, most people who follow one of these paths don't consider them to be archetypes they can navigate into, but instead identify themselves to be such. What for? There doesn't seem much point in being fixed into position. On the other hand, as Fool Sorcerers we also use different archetypes including the clown, trickster, jester, dunce, lunatic (on full moons), agent of chaos, wise fool, story-teller, bard, lover, buffoon and the shamanic fool." He paused to take a drink of water as someone in the crowd went on to explain the etymology of the word 'Lunatic'.

Seani Fool gave more examples of Fool Sorcery techniques before wrapping up the first part of the talk. David Barrett, one of the organisers of the Moot With No Name, stood up and told everyone that there would be a twenty minute break before questions, answers and feedback. During the break there was a lot of chit-chat between many of the people at the Moot and it was clear to Bernadette that many of them knew each other.

After the break there was a raffle (Bernadette didn't win anything) followed by questions, answers and a more open discussion. A sexy blonde woman stood up and said, "Seani, I've really enjoyed this talk so far."

"Thanks Meesh," Seani answered. "Do you want to give me any feedback or ask any questions?"

"Well, I wonder if Kommodore Koogie or yourself could explain further what you mean by 'living in the world of myths.'"

"No problem," said Seani. "The two books that seem to turn most people on to magic are Marion Zimmer Bradley's 'The Mists Of Avalon', brilliant, and Robert Anton Wilson and Robert Shea's 'The Illuminatus Trilogy'. Those books create incredibly powerful myths, set up very intricate world-views and have permeated the way magicians, witches and occultists have thought and acted since they were written. I recommend you read both of them, then Starhawk's 'Spiral Dance' plus many, many others. An old friend of mine named Martin once suggested 'read, read and read about magik but don't study' and I still remember his words to this day."

Koogie took over, "consider the Bible or the Koran - full of myths that people live their whole lives by. As Fools, we do not lock ourselves into any particular set of myths but navigate freely through whichever is appropriate at the time. Our reality, or as Robert Anton Wilson would say, our 'reality tunnels' are only our chosen set of myths anyway. Why not choose your own as you go along? It's fun to be one thing, but not for too long. It gets boring. Why not be a pirate tomorrow?"

Koogie lifted Seani's pirate hat of his head and put it on her own before continuing, "Arrrrrrr. See, now I'm in the myth of a pirate! There are so many books of fables and myths in the world, it's unbelievable. Many of them tell us something about the inner world, but we have forgotten this and pass them off as insignificant or just children's stories. But there are some very beautiful myths with important lessons to teach us!"

"If I were to write a book about Fool Sorcery," Seani continued, "it would be in the form of a myth or a set of stories or contemporary fables. I would hope that by sharing it as a story, I could bring the system to life. My magic draws on so many different influences, I wouldn't otherwise know where to start. In fact, if I were to write a book about Fool Sorcery, I'd probably get other people to write half of it for me." Everyone in the room laughed at Seani's joke.

A dark-skinned woman at the back of the room raised her hand and called out her question in what sounded like a Brazilian accent, "Seani Fool, you said that if we all stop obeying the authorities at the same time we would all be set free. But large-scale mass disobedience would be a total nightmare to co-ordinate. Would it ever be possible to set a date for this?"

Seani answered, "Alan Moore did it in *V for Vendetta,* and that comic and film have had powerful effects on the outer world that we all live in. But let's make it more foolish - imagine an army of clowns amongst the army of Guy Fawkes lookalikes! Yes, I believe it will be possible to set a date, and there are a few prospective dates over the next few years. But no, no date has been fixed at this time. Not that I know of anyway! Besides, who would tell a fool like me? In truth we're best off finding a date on someone else's calendar and rolling with it."

"Any more questions?" David Barrett asked the room and a young man's hand shot up. "Ah yes, Paul, our resident conspiracy theorist. What's your question?"

The man called Paul stood up. He was dressed in black leather trousers and a tie-dyed fractal t-shirt. He had thin, straight, brown hair that went down to his waist. "Well Seani, you said that no-one knows who secretly rules the world but I beg to differ. There is a lot of overwhelming evidence that the US government via the military-industrial complex virtually rules everything already. If you read an author like David Icke, you'll see his in-your-face evidence that Bechtel Corporation runs nearly everything anyway. Now, Icke has a lot of evidence that there is an intelligent race of Lizard-like creatures," Seani and Koogie exchanged glances with each other at this.

Paul continued, "now don't scoff yet. Icke presents the evidence that intelligent lizard creatures rule the world. How would this knowledge fit into the Fool's world view?"

"Well," answered Seani, "if I was to hear such a story about Lizard Men or the Illuminati, I'd consider it a myth like any other story. There's no power in allowing this story to create the world for you, but there may be some vantage gained by supporting and co-creating it as a myth. This may enable you to gain creative powers, insight and authenticity. If I was to tell you a story about the Bechtel corporation, Nazis and Tibetan Lizard men, you'd have to ask yourself one important question..."

57.
DO YOU WANT TO BELIEVE?
<Frater Carfax>

Prologue

From the rocky escarpment, Karl fixed his eyes upon the valley below him. The August sun warmed his skin gently as he contemplated the difficult descent that would have been impossible earlier in the year, the snow and sub-zero temperatures rendering the surrounding lands inaccessible even to most local Tibetans. He thought to himself that even the lack of snow and ice may not make his destination any more accessible, the near-vertical valleys having next to nothing resembling pathways, and always the constant risk of landslides and rock falls.

But within, he felt the sense that he was headed in the right direction, towards something important. His precognitive flashes had served him well as an artillery officer for the Bavarian Army, and if anything, the events of the past three years had honed this sense to an instinctual skill. More than the animal sense allowing the hunter to track down his prey, this instinct had allowed him to track down his destiny.

Until recently, Karl Haushofer had been living in Japan, where he held a position as a liaison for the Bavarian army. For a lad who had grown up in a conservative environment, his ears filled with competing Lutheran and Catholic rhetoric of salvation and damnation, he eagerly drank at the fountain of Japanese society, learning the language, discovering Zen Buddhism, and taking his fill of a much gentler, but equally regimented, philosophy.

Being an ambitious military officer, he made a concerted effort to become proficient in the Japanese language and local customs of etiquette. Gradually, this effort developed a network of social and political connections, particularly amongst those who valued his gifts of European indulgences denied to most through the "Fortress Japan" trade policy. In due course, he found himself in a unique position for a *Gaijin* – receiving an invitation to become a member of the exclusive *Kokuryu Kai*, the Black Dragon Society.

The society had long been a Machiavellian pillar of Japanese political machinations, its capacity for intelligence gathering and influence turning the tide in the Russo-Japanese war. And so a desire to extend their networks into Europe made the possibility of initiating a *Gaijin* who was culturally sympathetic an acceptable proposition.

However, it was Karl's ability to readily assimilate the more esoteric aspects of the Society that caught the attention of certain elders. What seemed initially to be an exercise in nationalistic political exchange for mutual benefit soon revealed itself to Karl as a secret militaristic Buddhist order of initiates, whose esoteric teachings originated beyond the islands of Japan. The esoteric training and initiations prepared him to look with new eyes, and would serve him well throughout his pilgrimages across the Asian continent, looking for that knowledge he saw as having been lost to the West.

It was in Tibet, at the feet of the enigmatic Russian mystic Gurdjieff, that his final initiations and transmissions of knowledge would occur, allowing him to fulfill his potential as an adept. He was well aware that his spiritual path would, for some reason, reach its climax in the mountains of this land. His master revealed to him during his teaching that even greater secrets were to be found amongst the mountainous wastes hidden within labyrinthine caves. Karl pressed him for further information, but Gurdjieff refused, stating that the affairs of the Masters of those secrets were of no consequence to humanity, except for those to whom they voluntarily reveal themselves.

But what of the consequence for these Masters, to whom Karl wanted to reveal himself? The pull of destiny tugged like an invisible cord upon his soul.

Inhaling the brisk air, his muscles worn with fatigue, he started the precarious descent into the valley below. It had been three days since he had encountered any of the local peasants, and he had been stretching his food out to barely above starvation level. While his training kept his mind sharp, the physical fatigue was considerable. This was only to be confirmed with a single, carelessly-placed foot.

The fall down the mountainside was agonising, the immediate sharp pain of ribs cracking and lacerations from the jutting rocks removing all awareness that the conclusion of this downwards journey would be fatal. Before the realisation had time to properly form in his mind, he was startled to suddenly experience a sensation of free falling, followed by the ice-cold shock of mountain water.

Somehow, he had landed in a deep pool. Looking up in panic, he saw landslide dirt triggered by his fall descending from a hole in the cave ceiling through which he had fallen, dim sunlight streaming through. Around him, out of the sun's reach, was darkness. He could hear the torrent of subterranean running water feeding the pool into which he had fallen.

Splashing furiously, he moved through the water until he felt his feet touching the bottom. He staggered forward, his lungs on fire as the broken bone pressed into his flesh. With great effort, he reached a rocky shore, where he collapsed onto his back in the darkness.

There he lay, with furious broken gasps, trying to ensure enough air stayed in his lungs long enough to keep him conscious. The ice-cold water added to the fatigue, as he felt his senses begin to shut down.

Numb and cold, through his desperate fight to remain awake, he starting hearing voices. Whether in his mind, or somewhere out in the darkness, he was unsure. The language seemed almost familiar, resembling Sanskrit.

With a shock, he became aware of a face hovering two inches above his as a light suddenly blazed nearby. Feeling a jolt to his throat, his last moments of consciousness recorded an image - a young man, possibly Tibetan, but with eyes that were somehow different. They were serpent's eyes.

Abwehr Regional Office, Paris, German-occupied France

The office was dank and cold. Captain Mahler sat in his chair deep in thought, leaning precariously on the two hind legs. Before him sat a sheet of paper with a mass of jumbled letters, his mind ticking over as it searched for patterns. The truth was, his mind was not as focused on the task as it should be. Instead, thoughts of nights in Berlin intruded. Paris had its Chateau Gonier, its Moulin Rouge, but the nightly indulgences at the brothels and music halls were not the same as the illegal underground cabarets and culture he longed for.

As an intelligence officer with a penchant for cryptography, the German military felt Fuchs Mahler was of more use to the Fatherland at the front line of resistance activity. While he was very good at his job, he made an effort not to shine too brightly in the eyes of his superiors outside of the immediate *Abwehr* command. He had no desire to be requisitioned into the *Geheime Staatspolizei* - sure the black uniforms, leather coats and shiny jackboots looked sexy, and they were a hit with the girls, but a job with the Gestapo came with its own concerted ideological indoctrination that was not worth the price as far as Mahler was concerned.

"*Heil Hitler*!" exclaimed Sergeant Danica Schully as she marched into the office, saluting smartly, clipboard in hand.

"Yes, yes, *heil, heil*," replied Mahler nonchalantly as he limply flipped his hand in a half-hearted salute, not looking up from the encoded message on the paper.

Mildly annoyed with her superior's less than enthusiastic response, she responded tersely, "two prisoners have been brought into the central holding facility. A resistance cell was raided last night that we believe was behind the ambush of the SS staff car and murder of the officer and driver two nights ago. The cell was desperately trying to protect the two men we captured, so they must be of some importance. We believe they were due to be smuggled to England through the resistance network. An examination of documents found in their belongings indicate they were probably resident in Berlin until recently..."

"*Scheiss....*" interjected Mahler rubbing his face with his hands. "I'll wager Himmler's happy henchmen will be paying us a conjugal visit before the week is out."

"Indeed, " Schully mused, grinning wryly. "We have direct orders from the Office of Admiral Canaris to conduct a preliminary interrogation of the prisoners before the Gestapo arrive in the morning."

Mahler grinned back. The long-standing animosity between Admiral Canaris, the head of German Military Intelligence and Heinrich Himmler's *Reichssicherheitshauptamt,* Reich Security Central Office, was an open secret amongst the German intelligence community. This resulted in each agency attempting to outmanoeuvre the other at every available opportunity, a game Mahler often enjoyed by anonymously feeding false cryptic information to his black-shirted counterparts. He once managed to get the Gestapo to raid a local bordello on the premise that it was harbouring communist resistance fighters in the basement. Instead, they found a particularly senior *Schutzstaffel* officer bound and handcuffed in a compromising position with a young working girl wielding a particularly dangerous-looking courgette.

"Let's do it now then. Do the prisoners have names?" asked Mahler.

"Franz Bardon and Wilhelm Quintscher," replied Schully, looking at her clipboard.

Dungavel Castle, Manor Home of the Duke of Hamilton, Scotland

"Pardon me m'Lord, your visitors have arrived and are waiting in the library."

Startled by his butler, Douglas-Hamilton broke out of his trance. He had not intended to drift into reverie, but he had been feeling a disturbing energy all day and was determined to uncover its etheric source. Something significant has happened, he thought, and no doubt his visitors would be the bearers of clarification.

He exited his private chapel and walked down the hallway towards the library. Waiting in the room for him was Sergio Hutin, a coordinator in the French resistance, and agent for the British Special Operations Executive, and perhaps not surprisingly given the former, Commander Ian Fleming, an officer in British Intelligence. But what made the meeting unusual was the involvement of Douglas-Hamilton. The Duke was an accomplished aviator, an officer in the Royal Air Force and had assisted British Intelligence numerous times with regards to clandestine aerial photography.

What made the Duke different was that he was also well connected to the various fraternal and esoteric societies brutally suppressed by the Third Reich, himself being a fraternal brother of the Gold and Rose Cross. In this capacity, he served as a valuable resource for British Intelligence in their efforts to exploit the occult-oriented activities of the Reich and for those members of various occult orders who acted to undermine the Third Reich's occupation of European countries, combining a magical and militaristic strategy. Sergio Hutin was the English liaison for one such fraternity, the Mystical Order of Hermes.

“Gentlemen, apologies for keeping you waiting,” said Douglas-Hamilton as he exchanged a particular grip quite different to most handshakes with each of his guests.

“No, please, we were well entertained admiring your library,” replied Sergio. “Some unusual volumes, oui? The Goetia? Have you undertaken the work to achieve command of the denizens of this tome?”

“Sometimes to overcome the work of the enemy one requires a better control over his resources than he,” replied Douglas-Hamilton reservedly. “But come, let us sit and discuss the pressing issues at hand.”

Reclining in the library chairs, Commander Fleming took the initiative, "Operation Frabato was a dismal failure. The extraction from Berlin failed and now Bardon and Quintscher are being held in Paris by German Military Intelligence."

"Probably better the *Abwehr* than the Gestapo," replied the Duke.

"I'm sure that situation will change," added Sergio. "Our sources indicate that the SS Ancestral Heritage division discovered coded correspondence between Bardon and Quintscher regarding their covert investigations into the research activities at Himmler's castle headquarters in Wewelsburg. We suspect they obtained confirmation that the *Ahnenerbe* adepts have succeeded in the condensation of Odic life force into a more tangible form, using something like an 'Odic battery'. The crude methods previously utilised by the SS in their rites were messy, bloody sacrificial affairs - nothing more than crude carry-overs from the initial explorations by the old Thule Society into Od, or as they called it, Vril. With this new approach, they have the potential to collect Vril for use in their misguided quest for racial perfection. I suspect this will also be of benefit to their allies in Tibet."

"How were Franz and Wilhem discovered?" queried the Duke.

Sergio sighed, "as you are probably aware, when the Nazis started suppressing all Masonic and esoteric societies, most of us went underground, some escaped to Belgium, others across the Channel."

The Duke nodded. He himself had provided sanctuary for many of his continental brethren, Masonic and otherwise, whose fraternal philosophies were regarded as a threat to Hitler's regime.

Sergio continued, "unfortunately, there are some adepts from amongst the fraternities who sympathised with the politics of Hitler, and have found themselves favour in the sight of Himmler. A new order consisting of twelve elite *Ahnenerbe* officers under Himmler has been convened, and have received personal training by these traitors to such a level as to be regarded as high adepts in their own right. I suspect

Bardon and Quintscher were probably betrayed by someone they once regarded as a brother."

"I still don't understand, how did a fringe-folk movement like the Thule society become the underpinning for the Nazi party and SS occult activities? And how did Tibetans become tied up in this affair?" asked Commander Fleming with some confusion, obviously not in his element in discussing occult matters.

Sergio fixed his eyes squarely on Fleming's, "there is more in Tibet than snow and yaks, Commander. There are those there who maintain a tradition older than the Buddhists, and older than the Bon, whose link to their elder gods was founded in the release of energy contained in the blood of every living being. There are certain forces in that country that see advantage in supporting the Nazi regime, because military bloodshed can divert the world's attention from a blood sacrifice of an altogether different magnitude, for a much more infernal purpose."

Abwehr Regional Office, Paris, German-occupied France

"You don't like the Gestapo do you?" asked Bardon grinning, looking across the table at Fuchs Mahler.

"You can save your stage magician mind tricks for another time!" retorted Schully, glaring at the man. She didn't like him one bit. From her observations, his casual and manipulative replies to questioning, and the very tone in his voice, had so far revealed he was obviously skilled in the art of mesmerism or similar acts of suggestion.

"Our professional relations with our colleagues are not part of the discussion. So why were the resistance so interested in getting you out of the country, Herr Bardon? We have checked into you, you are a performer and suspected Mason - but nothing that would indicate that you are of obvious military interest. That is, unless the loose tongues of drunken German officers have shifted from showgirls to stage conjurors, but I suspect that even wearing stockings and stilettos you would be no more enticing. Can you give me a reason that we should continue to hold you rather than allow our friends at the Gestapo to take over the questioning?" asked Mahler. "I guarantee their methods of interrogation are less than gentle."

"I regrettably suspect, Captain, that the powers that be will not allow you to detain me in favour of the Gestapo, and in any case, little of what I might say will be of use to you, or make sense to you for that matter," replied Bardon, seemingly unconcerned.

"Captain, may I interrogate the other prisoner, see if his tongue is any looser?" questioned Sergeant Schully in frustration.

"Yes, if you believe you can succeed, go ahead," replied Mahler.

As Sergeant Schully left the room, Mahler lit two cigarettes and handed one to Bardon, who appreciatively accepted.

"So which war are you fighting, Captain? The one against the British and her allies or the one against the Jewish conspiracy?" asked Bardon, raising an eyebrow.

"I tend to leave the latter to those with a reduced capacity for critical judgement. So, which war are you fighting, Herr Bardon?"

"The one against Himmler's use of the Black Arts, and the massacre of the Jews as a secret sacrificial offering to inhuman forces," said Bardon, straight faced.

Mahler prided himself on being difficult to flummox and yet he was lost for words, his cigarette hanging from his bottom lip.

"As you said Captain, I wouldn't look very good in stockings and stilettos, so why would the Gestapo want me? And why would the resistance be willing to risk their lives for me?"

"I'm well aware that fantasy and conspiracy are the staples of certain circles of self-appointed intelligentsia in Berlin, Herr Bardon. However,

I'm sure you probably hold some information of military importance that is better extracted by people less concerned about Article 4 of the Geneva Conventions," replied Mahler.

"The fact is, Captain, when the Gestapo arrive to collect Wilhelm and myself, I expect another delegation will be here from Berlin to collect the body of the dead SS officer killed the other night by the resistance. A unique opportunity exists, and I doubt you will get another chance. This may very well be of interest to your Admiral Canaris. The question for you now, Captain Mahler, is do you want to believe?"

Madjanek Extermination Camp, Poland

Herschel was dressed in little more than rags. His heart hung heavy with despair, helpless against the tides of wretchedness before him.

Around the Rabbi was a cacophony of screams and hysteria. People were disintegrating from within. The soundness of people's minds, their emotions and their hope began to decay as they watched the ones they loved paraded and packed behind metal doors that were locked behind them.

Death speaks not with words. Azrael is disturbingly silent, his victims compensating for his absence of voice. Herschel would have considered it no more if it weren't for the fact that the act of extermination carried a sound that could not be heard by ears.

The sounds of souls screaming.

Damnation is not judgment and condemnation by the Lord, Herschel thought to himself, but the destruction of the very essence that binds you to Him. And every murdered soul is a small act of deicide against the Most High.

He scanned the guards and noticed that behind the perimeter fence closest to the chambers stood two SS officers watching the proceedings.

His eyes narrowed as his perspective altered. Through the haze of a sight that came not through his eyes, he identified that while one was human, the other certainly was not. Serpent's eyes. And those eyes were now aware that someone could see past the illusions as it scanned the assembled.

Herschel's mind was cast back to the fireside teachings of his father of what he claimed to be hidden rabbinical teachings known only to a few. One of the stories told of the experiences of Amram, the father of Moses and Aaron:

> *"I saw Watchers in my vision, the dream-vision. Two men were fighting over me. I asked them, 'who are you, that you are thus empowered over me?' They answered me, 'we have been empowered to rule over all mankind.' They said to me, 'which of us do you choose to rule you?' I raised my eyes and looked. One of them was terrifying in his appearance, like a serpent, his cloak many-coloured yet very dark. And I looked again, and his appearance, his visage, was like a viper.*

Herschel shuffled along in the queue towards the metal chamber. As he drew closer to the perimeter fence, he took his one and only chance.

Never breaking his gaze with the officer, Herschel made a break and ran to the perimeter fence. Crying out an invocation in a dead Semitic tongue, his arms ignited into flames and his hand transformed into a claw of seraphic fire.

He thrust his arms through the barbed wire fence, inhumanly straight into the chest of the surprised officer as he bellowed, *"I will make my words in thy mouth fire, and your people wood, and it shall devour them all!!"*

The eyes of the officer widened in fear as the fire burnt into his heart like a branding iron, stopping whatever resemblance to humanity might beat within it.

The sound of machine gun fire erupted.

Herschel convulsed and writhed as the projectiles riddled his frail physical body, leaving it strung on the barbed wire.

His last breath carried him home.

Abandoned country church on the outskirts of Paris, German-occupied France

"Captain, I don't quite understand why we are here?" queried Sergeant Schully as she held her coat close against the cold night air.

"Like I said, a possible resistance meeting place," Mahler lied. Actually, his curiosity had got the better of him. Taking up the offer, Bardon told him that the truth behind his seemingly outlandish claims would be discovered that evening if he were willing to spy on his colleagues. Mahler felt that spying on the activities of the SS and Gestapo was frankly reward in itself if it meant he got one over them. At worst, if the man's claims proved to be an overactive imagination, then there would still be the issue of how he knew the movements of SS officers in Paris. There appeared little to lose in investigating Bardon's claims.

Since the preliminary interrogation, the Gestapo had arrived to question Bardon and Quintscher further. The Gestapo were clearly unhappy that the *Abwehr* had had the opportunity to question the two men. Mahler feigned ignorance of anything that the prisoners may have known, implying their interrogations had proved unable to reveal anything.

From a safe place behind the hedgerow, they had been observing movement in the shadows around the old church for the last hour. Finally the movement stopped, with all the figures bar one inside the church, now softly illuminated by candlelight.

"Come on Schully, time for a closer look," whispered Mahler, dragging Schully, who resisted his enthusiasm with a scowl.

They shuffled along the hedgerow to the back of the church, away from the sentry at the front door of the church, who would occasionally make a sweep of the immediate area with a torch. There, at the back of the church, they peered through holes in the broken stained-glass window, the smoke-stained, tinted glass obscuring Schully and Mahler's presence.

The old church was cleared of pews and furnishings other than the altar and a low table in the centre of the room resting on a giant red star painted on the floor. The altar was adorned with implements, flowers and brightly burning red candles. They could see a circle of men and a few women, dressed in black tunics with belts, all wearing simple red masks reminiscent of expressionless Venetian Carnival masks. Heavy medallions with the distinctive runic design of the *Schutzstaffel* hung from their necks revealing their affiliations. On the central table lay a coffin adorned with a flag of the Reich.

Mahler was pondering whether this was some form of memorial service when an aromatic smell hit his olfactory nerves, sickly sweet. A gong broke the silence, each beat resonating into the still night.

"Fraters and Sorors of the Reich. Are you ready to celebrate the ritual of the pentalpha of fire with pure heart and pure intent?" questioned a masked man in a highly elaborate robe.

"That we are, Most Mystical Master," replied the assembled.

"Brother Custodian, what is your first obligation?"

"To ensure we are all Knights of the Order, Most Mystical Master," answered the one identifying himself as the Custodian.

"You will examine the Fraters and Sorors that they carry grip and password of a Knight of the Order."

The Custodian circumambulated in turn around those gathered, receiving an obscure handgrip while a word was whispered into his ear.

"Freemasons?" queried Schully, quite mystified by the performance.

"No," replied Mahler squinting, "not Masons. I've got a hunch about what, or rather who, is in that coffin though."

Completing the circuit, the Custodian faced the head ceremonialist and replied, "Most Mystical Master, those present have proved themselves to be Knights of the Order. To order, Fraters and Sorors, and speak the vow of your duty and allegiance!"

In unison the assembled raised their right arms in salute as they spoke. "We swear upon the holy laws of the pentalpha to live and act to the glory of the Reich. We will guard and retain those secrets held only for the worthy. To those who would transgress the vow of a Knight – we invoke death upon the traitors and curse their spirit! Blessed is the true cup of the light, whose strength will lead us to Victory!"

The Mystical Master raised his arms as he stared at the coffin before them and intoned, "in the name of our ancestors, and through our blood, I call upon the fire that flows in my hands, my heart and my mind! I call upon the strength to revive the essence and spirit of our fallen comrade and Frater, to be reborn as a magickal child, to be part of the evolution of our Aryan people into perfection!"

With this he approached the altar and held aloft an ornate grail. Replacing it upon the altar, he unsheathed an ornate dagger adorned with the runic SS motif, which he used to slice his forearm, the blood pouring forth down his arm as a stream of crimson liquid into the cup of wine. After a few moments, he withdrew his arm and wrapped a red silken cloth around the wound to stem the flow of blood.

Mahler noticed that he now held aloft an object, oriental in design. Before its closure, early in the war, Mahler had made a visit with a friend to the popular *Buddhistischen Haus* in Berlin. During the rituals performed there he had seen double terminated *vajra* being used, which is what this resembled. However, this object contained balls within its clawed terminals, possibly made of crystal, with a luminescent glow.

With a twist of the object the crystals cracked, pouring a viscous substance into the chalice of blood and wine. "The vril of a dying race, belonging to a dying god, shall be transformed through my sacrament to make us like Gods!" the Mystical Master declared.

The gong was once again struck as incense was heaped upon burning coals. Schully looked at Mahler with a sense of disbelief at the proceedings. With a rising fear of being caught, she tried to softly mouth objections to any continued surveillance, which were either unseen or ignored by Mahler, his eyes transfixed upon what was unfolding.

One of the robed women now approached the Mystical Master and knelt, upon which he spoke, "stand - brilliant daughter of the Dawn! Do you recognise me?"

"I recognise you, Most Mystical Master."

Pulling the lower portion of his robe aside revealing his flaccid member, he continued, "Soror of the five-flamed star, do you feel me?"

Reaching forward and gripping him she replied "Frater, I feel you."

The assembled began to chant in a slow rhythm, "awaken, awaken, Gate of the Sun, awaken, awaken, Gate of the Sun."

"Soror, prove to me your recognition," said the Mystical Master as he took a step back, pulling back from any arousal by her gentle grip.

The woman reached up, pulled back the hood of her robe and removed her mask, letting her blonde hair tumble around her neck. "Do you recognise me, Most Mystical Master?"

"Soror, I do not recognise you yet," he replied.

Unbuttoning the top of her robe she let it fall off her shoulders, the robes being held around her hips by a fastened belt. With the distinctive SS medallion hanging between her bare breasts, she stood there in the flickering red candle light, arms raised as she asked, "do you recognise me, Most Mystical Master?"

"Soror, I do not recognise you yet," he replied.

With a swift hand she undid the belt around her robe, allowing the garment to completely fall to her feet as she bathed her naked splendour in the night air. Her voice took on a more resonant quality, deeper and more confident as she spoke, "do you recognise me now Most Mystical Master? For thy phallus is like Osiris risen!"

She moved forward and caressed his now fully erect member. The Mystical Master undid his belt and cast aside his robe easily as she led him by his priapic manifestation towards the coffin. Shuffling back onto the edge of the casket, she lay on her back spreading her legs wide, the dew of anticipation rapidly forming between her thighs. Standing at the edge of the coffin, the Mystical Master grabbed her legs and pulled as he thrust deeply within her. His manhood, hardened in fortitude, met no resistance as she receptively gripped upon him from within, her muscles contracting and relaxing in a rhythm developed through years of training. Moaning in an ecstatic trance, she fed off his energy as he fed off hers, her sacred essences flowing around him that would combine with his to produce the alchemical elixir for conception.

Allowing the energy to rise between them, his pace started to increase, as the assembled circled around them repeatedly chanting, "Ho Ophis! Ho Archajos!"

One of the assembled brought forth the chalice. The Mystical Master took it with one hand, and consumed a mouthful, never letting the rhythm of their union stop. Intermingled blood, vril and wine ran down his lips and throat in rivulets. He then almost completely withdrew from the Soror, as he kissed her deeply transferring the elixir between their mouths, an unusual glow revealing this liquid sacrament was now something more potent.

With a final series of thrusts he bellowed, simultaneously releasing his seed deep within the Soror, "*the Sons of God came in unto the daughters of men, and they bare children to them, the same became mighty men which were of old, men of renown!*"

"Mahler, we have got to go and report this now!" whispered Schully forcefully, tugging at Mahler's sleeve. She continued, slightly stammering, "I....I don't believe what I just saw...."

"Sergeant, I don't know what I believe any more..." trailed Mahler, as he contemplated how he would explain this to his superiors, and what personal risks he might be taking by doing so.

Abwehr Regional Office - holding cells, Paris, German-occupied France

Bardon and Quintscher sat together in the cell, leaning with their backs against the wall, neither saying a word. With eyes half open, they passed the hours in a deep meditative state as the guard outside the cell regarded them with contempt.

"Wake up. Time for food," barked the guard as he stood and walked over to the barred door. Under the bars he passed a tray containing a cup, bread, an apple and some local cured meats.

"Do we get some water as well?" questioned Wilhelm.

The guard passed through a jug of water to Bardon who took it with both hands. As he poured the water into the cup, he started whispering quietly to himself, staring intently into the jug, gently rubbing one hand over its outer surface of fired clay.

"Come on, one glass only. Hand it back," snapped the guard. Taking back the jug he poured himself a glass and swallowed it. Bardon smiled to himself.

"Could we exchange the apple for a peach?" queried Wilhelm as he lopped the apple through the bars to the guard.

"Since you are so choosy, you'll get neither," said the guard, grabbing the apple mid flight and biting deep, grinding flesh and seed between his teeth, chewing noisily with his mouth open. With his focus on Quintscher, he didn't notice Bardon tracing a design into the dust of the cell floor, consisting of lines like lightning bolts flowing into curves.

"*Salve Hagos! Estote meum castellumque praesidium contra omnium hostes, conspicuusque nonconspicuus, in quisque magiceum opum*!" projected Quintscher, as he pointed towards the guard's throat.

Startled by the outburst, the guard opened his mouth to tell his prisoners to be quiet, but no sound emerged except a broken gurgle. He could feel the mouthful of apple lodged in his oesophagus, the painful sensation of the blockage cutting off all passage of air. His lungs struggled and his face reddened in desperation and panic. He grabbed at the bars of the cells, pleading through his eyes for the men to do something. Sinking to his knees, a searing pain began to tear through his lungs. He finally collapsed, just as Bardon reached through the bars and grabbed the keys off his belt.

Bardon unlocked the gates of their cell and rolled the guard over. Forcefully, with an energised hand, he struck the guard's back, dislodging an organic mass of apple flesh which had seemingly expanded in volume, the seeds appearing to have sprouted with tendrils.

A cough and a gasp emitted from the guard as he started breathing erratically, his form still on the edge of consciousness.

"He'll survive. Come, we have little time," said Quintscher.

Together, the two men crept out through the door into the night air, darting into the shadows of the compound. They reached a door at the side of the compound and, using the guard's keys, opened the way to freedom, disappearing into the maze of Parisian streets and back alleys.

They were unaware, however, that their escape was watched from an upper story window by a pair of eyes. And they were serpent's eyes.

58.
EVERY HOME A PRISON

Michael was going through a much tougher time since the break-in than he had let his friends know. There were so many strange details in the stories they had told about their magical activity that he had pretty much stopped trusting them. For a start, there were many inconsistencies. Malus had once proudly stated that actually his life was based on 'inconsistencies', but that didn't quite make sense to Michael. When Malus had explained to Michael that *all perception is opinion based on reception of an extremely tiny percentage of available information*, Michael had started looking for a bigger picture.

And that's where the problem seemed to be – in the bigger picture. There were some vast inconsistencies, but the conclusions Michael had drawn were very different to the picture Malus had painted. At first Michael had purposefully started looking for outward signs, to see if there was any evidence to back up any of the stories told. He was dauntingly surprised to find that there *were* references and hints to the non-existent Illuminati everywhere he looked. And the harder he looked, the more the number 23 appeared. Every time he went for a walk there would be two Japanese people with a camera. The more he paid attention, the more he noticed obscure and out-of-place references to apples. And worst of all, there was no getting away from the obviously fictitious serpent people.

Michael had spent a huge amount of time trying to think of a rational explanation for the break-in to his house. He had agonised over the select few items the thieves had stolen. *They left my fucking passport in my drawer and took my magical diaries for Christ's sake! There is something very bizarre going on, but what?* Michael had spent less and less time with Malus over the following few weeks and hadn't spoken to him for at least the past three. He sent the occasional email to Luna, primarily out of concern for her and what she was being drawn into.

Who the fuck would steal a photo of me and leave my digital camera lying there? He laughed at himself many times in cynical attempts to ward off the growing paranoia that was spawning inside him.

He was sitting on the sofa in the living room in his rented Dalston flat, which seemed much smaller than it once had. Every light was on. It made him feel a tiny bit safer. The last time he'd turned his television on, an old episode of 'Doctor Who' had come on – an episode where the Doctor had to escape from some futuristic intelligent serpent people. The coincidence was too much for him and he hadn't switched the TV on since.

There can't be an Illuminati, can there? What do they want from me? There can't be any fucking serpent people! It's utter madness. But why are there so many references to this craziness in so many different religious, spiritual and magical traditions? Judaism had the serpent in the Garden of Eden. Australian Aboriginals spoke of the Rainbow Serpent. Norse myths, Chinese Dragons, Mexican Aztec myths, even yoga speaks of the Kundalini serpents rising inside a human body! DNA appears as two dancing serpents. Symbols of healing, symbols of life, symbols of sexuality. They are fucking everywhere. What do they want from me? Am I a serpent? Do I have green blood? He laughed. Of course he didn't have green blood, and he could recall quite easily times he had accidentally cut himself. His blood was red. For a moment he toyed with the idea of cutting himself again. *Fuck, I am going mad! There is something very strange going on and I want to get the fuck away from it!*

"If you want me, why don't you just come and get me?" he asked his living room. He had spent whole days looking through his house for hidden microphones or cameras, but had, of course, found none. *My home is now my prison!*

He often wondered what Malus was doing: *Is it all some kind of test? Have I failed? Is it Malus or is it my imagination that is destroying me?* He felt an ominous sense of doom pervading his life. *I have to get out of here. The whole Illuminati bullshit story Malus told is some kind of test. Maybe he is part of it, feigning anti-authoritarianism whilst planting seeds in people's heads. I would do anything to make this paranoia go away. I would do anything to know if the Illuminati stole my books. I would do anything just to know if the Illuminati really exists! I have very little doubt Malus was somehow involved in this whole affair. Even if he wasn't involved, then somehow me getting myself into this story has landed me in trouble. The coincidences pointing to Malus are too great to believe any differently.*

He remembered another near-universal spiritual belief - there is no such thing as a coincidence, but this memory didn't ease his fear. If anything, it made it worse.

I'll send Luna an email to let her know I'm doing fine... but also to find out if everything is okay with her, to find out if she has any clues as to how I can pass this test and to find out what Malus is doing...

~

On the other side of London, Luna pressed the pause button on the remote control, "Hey Helene! Hey Malus! I just received an email from Michael! Want me to read it?" She help up her mobile phone which was giving off a faint electric blue glow. They were in Malus' flat, sitting on his bed and watching a DVD copy of 'Troy' starring Brad Pitt, but no-one was focussing on it.

"Yeah read the email. Where is he? I hope he's okay. He hasn't been in touch in ages... This is a fucking stupid movie anyway. How can they turn the gay lover of Achilles into his cousin? Achilles was gay. Everyone knows that. Half of Hollywood are faggots like me. In this day and age, why are they afraid of telling the story as it is?"

Malus noticed that Helene and Luna were waiting for him so he took a deep breath and said, "yeah, please read it out. I have been worried about Michael. Where has he been? In the void?"

Helene sat up expectantly as Luna pressed some keys on her phone. Seeing Helene and Malus both ready to listen, Luna read aloud:

Dear Luna,

Just a quick note to tell you I'm safe. Are you? I am safe, but to be honest I am losing it big time. You became involved with these people at the same time I did. Aren't you worried that they're some kind of evil Illuminati?

Luna stopped reading aloud and cleared her throat looking from Malus to Helene and back again. She cleared her throat again then said, "I think this is personal. I'll let you know how he is." She got off the bed and went to Malus' lounge room and continued reading:

Luna, I think you should get out ASA. I'm getting out. They broke into my house as some kind of test (I think) but I'm not interested in playing their stupid fucking games so I'm out. Please take care of yourself and get out while you can.

You got arrested for them, Luna! Think about your future! Their anarchy is a charade. Good luck in your court case!

I've just decided I'm leaving the country. Australia maybe? I'm not sure I should tell you any more about where I'm going in case you have joined them.

Have you joined them?

Can I trust you?

Who can I trust?

59.
WHO CAN YOU TRUST?
<Anton Channing>

Gareth was having that dream again. It was always the same, the black stepped pyramid, the large unblinking eye staring down at him from the summit, the black hooded and robed faceless figures standing in two rows, as if to make an aisle or pathway to the top. And always he would walk slowly up that pathway, towards the ever-watchful eye. His legs would seem to grow more and more weary the closer he got to the 'Watcher', his nickname for the now familiar entity of his dream. Eventually he would inevitably find himself stuck, unable to climb any higher, and the pupil of the Watcher would dilate and then shrink to a piercing pinprick.

That piercing gaze always frightened Gareth, but not as much as the strange ethereal words that came from the Watcher. How they came Gareth couldn't tell, for the being had no mouth, but then, he surmised, this was a dream and anything was possible. The words were always the same...

"You have climbed as high as you can, Gareth. You have done well, but now you have found your place. Know now, Gareth, that those who have climbed higher are your superiors in every way. They are in charge of you, Gareth, for a reason. Do not envy them, for their life is harder still than yours. Know your place, Gareth, and do as they say, for they know what is best for you and for the world. Go now and live your life in the service of Order! Trust Order, Gareth! Trust Authority! Obey Authority! Obey! Awake from this dream, Gareth, and forget you had it... ...Now!"

And always Gareth would awake, sweat streaming down his face, but never would he forget. Sometimes he thought that maybe these dreams had been going on for longer than he could remember, that when he first had them, he obeyed the instruction to forget. But that seemed paranoid. After all, how could he forget a dream as vivid as that?

This time however, Gareth remained determined that he would not awake. It was just a dream after all, so he had nothing to fear. He would defy the Watcher. He would use the power of lucid dreaming he had been developing to change the shape of this dream forever. He was convinced that if he broke its pattern just once, it would end the dreams. It was worth a try anyway. What did he have to lose? It was only a dream.

Gareth felt resistance growing in his legs as he progressed up the path of the dream pyramid towards the hateful eye. But this time he focused. This was just a dream. Anything can happen in it. He could float to the top if he wanted to. Yes, that would work. He would float! All he had to do was not let his feet touch the ground. Looking down he found his feet were not on the ground and he was beginning to float. It was working. He looked back up at the hated eye and noticed that it appeared to be looking at him with displeasure. The iris seemed to be turning a burning red and was no longer the peaceful green it had been before. It seemed to speak at him. But this time the words were different.

"You are cheating Gareth; you cannot pass this test by floating! Get back down here at once!"

It sounded like an angry schoolteacher. It made Gareth feel like a naughty schoolboy again, that he had better obey or else he'd be in trouble. But he wasn't going to fall for that.

"Test?" Gareth retorted, "what test? This is just a dream! And you are not real! You are just a figment of my imagination!"

The Watcher seemed to flare in anger for a second and then laughed mockingly, "if I am not real, why do you waste your time talking to me Gareth? If I am just a figment of your imagination then you are talking to yourself. And that is madness, Gareth. Are you mad, Gareth?"

Gareth shrugged, "I talk to you because it amuses me to. It amuses me to change the outcome of this dream, this nightmare that has tormented me for so long. If that makes me mad then so be it! I choose madness over the sterility of obedience!"

The Watcher seemed worried, "Gareth, Gareth, Gareth...", its voice softer now, yet patronising, "there is so much you don't know. We shouldn't be fighting; I can use someone like you. We should be friends! Put your trust in me and I can give you power, power like you never dreamed of. But choose madness, Gareth... should you choose madness," its voice full of remorse now, "then you will be lost, and more, you shall lose everything you've worked so hard to achieve. Surely you won't choose madness over Order, Gareth. No, of course you won't. That would be very foolish. Very, very foolish."

But Gareth wasn't taking the bait, "I don't care what you think. Why should I? This is just a dream; I don't even have to float here next to this stupid pyramid in this desolate wasteland. I can make plants sprout up around here if I want..."

And with that Jungle growth started sprouting up around the pyramid, thick and green and full of life. The Watcher was furious and began sending jets of flame at the growth to try and clear it. The dream became a battle of wills, of Gareth making Jungle appear and of the Watcher trying to destroy it. Eventually, the Watcher gave up.

"You will regret this Gareth, you will definitely regret this." The voice sounded sorrowful now, remorseful. However, its next words were not directed to Gareth but to the faceless robed figures that lined the aisle. And its voice was commanding. "Bring the traitor to me!"

Gareth saw the robed figures turn and begin to float into the air after him. He wasted no time in flying off into the Jungle, trying to escape his pursuers, but they remained right behind him, impossible to shake. Each time he looked round, he saw them closer than before. One of them grabbed his foot, but after a brief struggle he managed to shake it off. However, this gave the others a chance to close on him. He dived into the Jungle itself, hoping to lose them in the trees. For a while he was able to continue flying in and out of the trees, but soon he found himself running on the ground. He didn't remember changing over, but then dreams were like that sometimes.

Looking round he saw no sign of the robed figures. So he decided to stop and take stock of his new surroundings. It was certainly an improvement on that damned pyramid. The natural beauty and vivid colours of the dream jungle contrasted favourably with the bleak sky and grey sands of the granite pyramid. Now Gareth thought about it, the only real colour of that place was the Watcher's iris. He shuddered. He didn't want to think about that place whilst dreaming, lest he end up back there.

Suddenly, the robed figures emerged out of the surrounding jungle. They had him surrounded. He hadn't lost them at all; instead they had been quietly surrounding him out of sight. He looked up, hoping for escape in the air. To his dismay, he could see more hovering above the trees. He was trapped and they were closing in on him. This was it. Then suddenly, the robed figures stopped and appeared to be looking at something behind Gareth.

Gareth heard a hissing sound. It was then that he had the freaky experience of being out of his dream body and was actually watching himself surrounded by the robed figures. He watched as out of nowhere a giant snake coiled down the tree behind him. The figures' hesitation ended and they closed in again. The snake, however, seemed intent on defending Gareth from them. Its head swooped and snapped one of the figures causing it to struggle helplessly as the snake devoured it greedily. Another of them got caught in the snake's tail and was slowly being crushed to death.

Inspired, Gareth started making balls of flame appear in his hands and began throwing them at the figures, catching their robes alight and burning them to ash. In the end, the fight was rather one-sided and Gareth wondered why he had bothered running away at all. But dreams were like that. When the fight was over, the serpent looked at Gareth with a grave expression and used its tail to offer him a large golden apple it had picked from the tree.

“Take thisss apple and eat it to gain the gnosssisss you need if you are to sssurvive,“ it hissed.

Gareth wasn't sure what 'gnosis' was and he wasn't sure whether to trust the snake, but then he remembered it was just a dream and he was curious to see what would happen, so he took a bite. It tasted good so he kept eating.

“Good, good. When you arissse from thisss dream, sssearch, Gareth, sssearch. Sssearch for Erisss. Don't forget.“

When he finished eating the apple, a little worm crawled out of the core. Gareth stared at it in disbelief although it didn't really bother him. It was just a dream.

“Why look so surprised, Gareth?“ said the worm in a high-pitched, squeaky voice, “after all, every golden apple has its worm! Tee hee hee.“

~

Gareth awoke from his strange dream with a lot to think about. What was it the serpent had said? He must search. Search for what? He couldn't remember. He crawled out of bed and, still naked, walked over to his computer to boot up. Rubbing his eyes, he walked over to the bathroom and splashed some water in his eyes then flossed and cleaned his teeth.

“Eris!” That was what he must search for. He kept repeating it in his head over and over lest he forget. He sat down at his computer, picked up the Virtunet headgear and put it on. This worked by directly influencing his brain's visual and sensory regions to create a fully experiential reality. It was a virtual world, slowly being built upon the Internet. Although the traditional Internet was still larger, there was a growing number of enthusiasts using it and the diversity of worlds that were out there was steadily growing. The user also had the ability to browse the traditional Internet from within the Virtunet.

Donning the helmet, Gareth used thought control to find his way to the search engine, and mentally 'put' the word Eris into it. Mostly he found old Internet sites, which tended to tell the same story of how Eris was the Greek goddess of discord who had started the Trojan war with an apple. But occasionally he found mention of a book called the *Principia Discordia*, supposedly channelled back in the twentieth century.

He also found a Virtunet site that offered little introduction, but just had a huge golden apple inscribed with the word KALLISTI as a place marker. He debated for a minute on the wisdom of visiting such an odd Virtunet site, but then shrugged and activated the apple. He didn't expect what happened next.

The search engine room faded to black and the apple grew in size until it dwarfed him. Meanwhile, his virtual arms and legs disappeared and his body turned into that of a worm. The site seemed to have control of him at this point and although he knew he could cancel if he wanted to, he was far too curious to see what happened next. The worm body took him round to the other side of the Apple. There he saw a little circular hole. As he guessed it began to crawl him through the apple towards the centre. Along the side of the wall he saw the words 'Every golden apple has its worm.'

This worried him slightly as he remembered those same words from his dream. How could he have dreamt that much detail? Had he heard the words before somewhere? Was he remembering the dream right? Finally, he came to a door with words inscribed upon it reading:

```
Golden Apple Corps
Knock 5 times to Enter
```

Finding he now had his arms and legs back he knocked on the door five times. It opened and he found himself in a large circular room with a strange-looking couple checking him out with curious smiles.

"You haven't been here before have you," said the male figure. It was a statement, not a question. The male figure had long black hair, intense eyes and a wolfish grin. He was naked and appeared to have claws or paws for hands.

"No, I haven't," replied Gareth.

"What brings you here?" asked the man, as the woman, also naked with long black hair, played with a golden apple in her hands.

"I had a dream. A serpent in a tree gave me an apple and told me to search for Eris..."

The man and woman exchanged mildly surprised looks and barely suppressed smiles before the woman turned to him, grinning, and said, "then welcome to the beginning of your search."

Gareth suspected that this was to be the start of an interesting new era of his life. If only he knew how far he could trust these two people who seemed very strange. They were behaving in a friendly enough way, but the man had a very predatory look, and the woman had a look of seductive manipulation, like she was used to getting her way through her looks. Even on the Virtunet, Gareth hadn't met people like these. He decided to be wary of them, but would find out what they were about. "I take it you know something about Eris then? How she tricked the gods into starting the Trojan War? Doesn't sound like a very nice goddess to me..."

The man frowned before responding, "that version of the story is Roman authoritarian propaganda, but before I tell Eris' side of the story we should introduce ourselves. My name is Fenris."

"Gareth."

The woman grinned at him, "and I am Lucy. Nice to meet you, Gareth."

The cosy little Virtunet room they were in began to swim around them. Strange patterns and spirals seemed to flow all over it. It was a strange psychedelic effect and Gareth wondered why they had started it. He could still see Fenris and Lucy, although they also seemed to be made of strange psychedelic patterns.

"As you know there was a wedding that all the gods went to, had invites for, in fact," began Fenris. "Eris, being considered unpredictable, was not invited to the wedding because they wanted everything to go as planned, with no surprises. However, Eris is a goddess of Chaos and did not understand, or chose not to understand, the etiquette of invitation. When she found out there was a wedding, she went anyway. She tends to go where she pleases."

Lucy interrupted at this point, "but of course, she couldn't go without a wedding gift, so she plucked one of the golden apples of Mount Olympus and engraved it with the word '*Kallisti*', which means 'For the Fairest'. This, Eris thought, was a beautiful gift for any bride and so took it to the wedding." As she spoke, Lucy brandished the golden apple in her hands. Only now did Gareth notice the inscription on its side. The psychedelic effects continued and the surreal form of Lucy's naked figure moving seductively through the swirls transfixed Gareth, her long hair spiralling into the room's colourful madness.

"Of course, not being limited to conventions of time, Eris arrived at the wedding party late, such that it was already in full swing." The Virtunet room began to form vague shapes of Greeks sitting around at a party, eating fruit and drinking wine. Into this party scene strode Lucy, presumably as Eris, brandishing her apple.

Fenris took up the story this time. "The gods of course had all assumed at this point that Eris wasn't coming, so when they saw her they feared she might be angry at not being invited. Quickly, they all hid in the hope that it would not be them she confronted. Even Zeus and the newly-weds hid in fear of the unpredictable Eris." The colourful forms of the partying Greeks all appeared to hide as Lucy walked near them.

Lucy turned back to Gareth, "but Eris was deeply hurt by this strange treatment of her, so she dropped the wedding present, ran off and forsook humanity for a few thousand years until she could find a good way to regain our favour."

Fenris took up the tale once again. "Meanwhile, Zeus was the first to pick up the Apple, having no idea that it was meant to be a wedding gift, and read aloud the inscription. Of course, all the goddesses demanded the Apple, thinking themselves the fairest. This led Zeus to find Paris to judge the contest, which led to the Trojan War. But you must remember that it was the petty jealousies, rivalries and inhibitions of the gods of order that caused the war - and their fear of the unpredictable. They made Eris their scapegoat, when in fact she was the only one who had done nothing wrong. Eris was, in fact, the only one that had behaved reasonably throughout the whole affair."

Gareth reflected on this new version of the story. These people were fun. It was pointless to argue over the truth of mythology in any case, because it was just stories he decided. He liked their version, it hit home with him. It fit with his loathing of authoritarian control and his understanding that it is always those who try to control others that start wars and restrict everyone's freedoms in the name of 'security'. Being with these people would result in a lot of fun and for the first time in ages he felt a smile broaden across his usually serious face. He felt his depression lifting away, a depression he hadn't even realised he had. And more importantly, he began to laugh! It felt good, his mood lightened and he felt good about himself. This was real happiness, not chemically induced through the state-sanctioned, corporate-made 'happy pills'.

"So," the voice of Fenris asked, "will you tell us about your dream?"

Gareth thought for a minute. He had never told anyone about his dream. It was too weird, he was afraid of what people would think of him for having a dream like that. But then he looked at Fenris and Lucy, both naked, and standing now on a virtual pirate ship, sailing through a vast ocean. How did he know it was a pirate ship? Well, the crew looked like pirates. Looking up he saw that the 'Jolly Roger' was indeed flying. Yes, his dream was weird, but not as weird as Fenris and Lucy. He would tell them. He would tell them everything...

60. SMUGGLERS <The Guardian>

Thanks to a special offer the European Union pays for five apples for every three grown with a 40% tariff. This apparently has seen smugglers on the Greek/Macedonian borders abandon the drugs and guns trade for a more profitable enterprise - Granny Smiths.

Guardian Weekly, "Trade Justice Supplement," September 2004

61.
IN DREAMS OF GOLD
<Jaq D. Hawkins>

The boy sat on the dock watching the Sunrise. The fishermen had just gone out for their day's work and there was nothing for him to do until the shops opened and people began to fill the streets of the small seaside town. Far out to sea, the light glinted from something with a golden sheen. It was too far away to make out any more than the occasional glimmer as the object moved about on the water, but as it grew closer, he was able to make out the shape of a ship. The sparkle of light was the reflection of sunlight on the mast, painted a distinctive golden colour.

There was only one ship known for having its main mast painted gold. What was a pirate ship doing sailing straight into Port Royale? The crew would surely be hung the minute they set foot on shore, unless of course it was an attack?

The boy stood up quickly, unsure at first of what he should do. The last thing he wanted to encounter just now was anyone official who might ask why he wasn't in school. Yet he couldn't sit quietly and do nothing while pirates attacked the island. Surely the soldiers on watch would see the ship coming, and recognise the golden mast of the *Prometheus*?

Just then, the warning bell began to ring. Someone else had seen the ship. With relief, the boy ran toward the crowd that was suddenly gathering near the shore. Wives who had just seen their husbands off to sea and shopkeepers who had not yet opened their doors mingled as soldiers joined the throng in anticipation of the arrival of the ship. The big cannons were no doubt being made ready, but there was no battle offered.

As the ship came more clearly into view, the anticipation of danger gave way to confusion. There was no Jolly Roger flag flying on the mast, but a white flag with a red cross on it flapped in the breeze. A small boat was lowered from the side with just a few men in it who started slowly rowing toward shore. They had come to ask for assistance.

The excitement of the townspeople was not diminished by the relief. For a pirate ship to sail right into a port with a military base dedicated to eradicating the waters of the criminals was unprecedented. They had to be madmen, or very desperate. The boy found himself as breathless with anticipation as the adults surrounding him, as his deft fingers loosened several purses, transferring them into the folds of his loose and ragged clothing. All eyes were on the approaching rowboat.

He wasn't really a thief, the boy reasoned to himself. He did what he did because he would starve otherwise. Or worse, if the authorities knew about him, he would be put into an orphanage and starved by the institution. He saw the petty thefts as a way of redirecting the taxes that people would pay to support such institutions, while he enjoyed the freedom that the authorities would take from him unjustly for no other reason than their own need to feel that they controlled the destinies of all men. He would not remain a thief forever, but was in fact saving money in a secret place to buy himself an apprenticeship one day, perhaps as a carpenter or a blacksmith. Living in an orphanage would never allow him to learn a trade.

As the small boat landed on shore, the people found themselves helping to beach the craft. Immediately, someone called for the doctor.

“These are injured men, is the doctor here?“ There was only one doctor in Port Royale, although he had an apprentice. It was the apprentice who pushed through the crowd to answer the call. Recognising him, the man who had spoken directed him toward the worst of the injuries he had seen.

“Look here Randolph, this man's leg is gone and here, looks like a shark took a bite out the side of this one.“

The doctor's apprentice examined the wounds. There were four men in the boat altogether. The one who was missing a leg had it tied crudely. The first signs of gangrene were already apparent. The man with the side injury was bleeding slowly through a wrapping that didn't entirely cover the bite marks. There was something odd about them, as they formed a crescent of evenly spaced punctures which Randolph would have guessed came from conical shaped teeth. Similar marks were all over the third man, who had dropped into unconsciousness, probably from loss of blood.

The remaining man looked to be uninjured. Randolph guessed that he had been chosen to bring the other men to shore. The pirate's eyes darted around the gathered crowd. He appeared to be very aware of the danger he had put himself in by bringing them. He wore no shirt, but only a pair of cut off-trousers and a canvas bag which was slung over his shoulder. He clutched something in one hand. The boy strained to see what it was. It appeared to be a common apple of some golden variety. The apprentice wondered if it was part of some booty that the man had brought by way of payment, but did not ask.

"These are no shark bites. What attacked you, man?" The uninjured man met Randolph's eyes as he nervously answered the question.

"If you please sir, I'd rather talk about that in private. These men are in dire need of medical attention. Are you a doctor?"

"I'm the doctor's apprentice. You're right of course, we have to get these men to the surgery. Are there others?"

"Some with bites," the man answered, "but no more like these. Most that were that bad are dead."

Randolph shouted for stretchers for the injured men. He was bursting with questions, but he had to fulfil his medical duties first. There would be plenty of time for questions later, hopefully before the men he helped were inevitably hung, as were all pirates.

"Don't you have a ship's doctor?" Randolph asked, as the men were loaded onto the stretchers.

"We had one," the man answered, "but the creatures ate him. They ate most everybody that wasn't on guard back on the ship. Except the Cap'n of course." The man stopped talking abruptly; his eyes darted from one spectator's face to another.

The injured men were carried to the surgery while Randolph shooed the curious onlookers away to give them air. Still, the crowd followed from a short distance, curious about what fantastic story would be told of the pirates and the mysterious creatures that had savaged their company. Randolph continued to try to persuade them to disperse, promising that the story would no doubt be common knowledge before the day was out.

Soon the shopkeepers began to drop out of the throng, returning to their businesses as it was time to open their stores. Then the wives began to wander off in small groups, speculating among themselves what adventures a pirate might encounter and whether there was danger to their fishermen husbands from whatever had attacked the pirates. A few hangers-on followed the stretchers all the way to the surgery, but those who carried them had places to go and did not remain.

The boy had kept pace with the uninjured pirate the whole way. As they entered the surgery, Randolph whispered something to a young man who had followed the procession. The lad nodded, and ran off in the direction of the governor's mansion. The pirate saw the action, but only clutched the golden apple tighter, holding it to his chest.

"They're going to arrest you, you know," said the boy calmly, speaking for the first time.

"Maybe not," replied the pirate. His eyes were wide and terrified, he was clearly unsure of his chances.

The injured men disappeared through a door and Randolph prevented the other pirate from following. With little argument, he accepted that his comrades were under medical attention now, and sat down to wait. The boy slid next to him on the polished bench in the waiting room. A few others found seats, but most of those who had followed lost interest and returned to their own business when they saw that there would be nothing to do but sit and wait for perhaps a long time. The pub would no doubt be full that evening.

The pirate fished in his bag and brought out another apple as he bit into the one he had been clutching. It too was golden, not one of the red apples that the boy normally liked to 'hook' from the market stalls. The pirate looked at the boy for the first time, and offered it to him.

“Take it boy,“ the pirate said very seriously. “It's good for you, and it will protect you…it's magic.“

The boy laughed out loud, but he took the apple as he spoke derisively to the pirate: “apples aren't magic! I'm too old for fairy tales.“

“You see some of the things I've seen boy, and you'll believe in magic,“ came the reply as the pirate continued to eat his apple.

“Why should I listen to you, you're nothing but a bloody pirate!“ The boy's voice was disdainful, filled with the trained contempt that all honest citizens were taught to feel for the criminals of the sea. The pirate seemed to take no notice of the boy's tone, but spoke to him calmly, matter-of-factly.

“You ain't no different than me boy. You do what you have to, to survive.“ The boy looked up quickly, meeting the pirate's eyes. He suddenly *knew* that the pirate had seen him at work, collecting his ill-gotten gains on the beach.

The pirate continued: “I was an honest seaman once. You ask around on any pirate ship and you'll find that all the men were either merchant seamen or navy once, but they were driven to become what we are by cruelty and mistreatment on the ships.“ The pirate shuddered a moment, apparently shaken by evil memories.

“There are well-respected captains in your precious navy fleet that will keel-haul a man for as little as taking an extra apple like the one you hold in your hand, or whip him for swearing at the wrong moment. The world is full of tyrants, boy, and some of them will use any excuse to prove they got power over another man." The pirate took a bite of his apple, and looked nervously at the door.

"You can't treat a man that badly forever before you get a rebellion on your hands." He finished speaking just as the offending door opened, and the governor himself walked through, accompanied by four guards. It seemed a lot of fuss to arrest a single man. The others were unlikely to be in any shape to give resistance.

The boy finished his apple and tried to pretend that he wasn't there. To his surprise, no one took any notice of him whatsoever. He hoped to himself that perhaps their interest in the pirate was such that a truant boy could be easily overlooked. The room seemed to be filled with the presence of the uniformed men, so much so that most of the other curious citizens who had followed the progress of events so far suddenly found business elsewhere, trusting to the gossip network to satisfy their inquisitive minds later in the pub. The boy alone remained with the pirate and the officials, despite his better judgement.

The governor looked around briefly, then pulled up the most comfortable looking of the tattered chairs in the small waiting room and sat directly in front of the pirate.

"Well, I expect we can do this here as well as anywhere," the governor said in a confident voice. The authoritative tone left no doubt that had he decided to conduct the interview in more secure surroundings, they would be on their way there already. The pirate clutched another golden apple tightly, but the governor didn't appear to notice it. The soldiers stood to attention, awaiting orders. The boy wondered why they didn't ask the apple's significance, as the pirate was clutching it like a religious relic. He began to wonder if the pirate had been serious about the magic, but the questions this raised in his mind went unasked as he continued to try to remain unnoticed.

"Let's start with your name man," the governor continued, "and then you can tell me your story. Dawson, you take notes."

Immediately, one of the soldiers fished paper and pen out of his jacket pockets. He was evidently used to fulfilling this function. The pirate hesitated only a few seconds, looking from one uniformed guard to another, and then finally back at the governor. He licked his lips once, and seemed to transform his expression from that of a scared rabbit to something resembling confidence. A breath later he licked them a second time. Then he began to speak.

"My name is Jim Morris. I been at sea on the *Prometheus* for about six months when we came across 'em."

The man seemed calmed by his own words, or perhaps by the release that telling his story could provide. The boy noticed that his accent became less rough as he settled into his tale, and remembered what the pirate had said about being an honest man once. He seemed to be intelligent, perhaps even a little cultured, although roughened by his life at sea. Only the occasional adulterated word gave evidence of the time he had spent among less literate men.

"It was evening when it all started," the pirate Jim continued. "The Sun was just disappearing over the horizon and the Cap'n was on deck. He was the first to hear 'em. We all saw him, straining over the rail to get a closer listen to something we couldn't hear, and then when we did start to hear 'em, some of the men went a little mad. Two of 'em jumped right overboard!"

"Hear what man? Or who?" demanded the governor impatiently. The answer came back immediately.

"Sirens sir, or so we thought. The men that jumped over got eaten right away…by sharks we thought. All we saw was the water foaming and the blood. They were gone so fast, they never had a chance."

The boy had heard of sirens, the sea nymphs who lured sailors to shipwreck along rocky coasts with their irresistible singing, only to devour the sailors as the ship sank. They were well known in any sea faring society. Some said they appeared as beautiful women, others as half woman and half bird, or half fish. The man started to stare blankly at the wall, as if the picture of the memory were projected against it. Then suddenly he came back to himself and continued.

"Woulda been better if it was sharks, at least you know where you are with them. Anyway, the Cap'n was taken a bit different than the rest. He set a course to follow the voices and wouldn't listen to anyone. Most of us have heard about sirens, and we worked it out. We tried to tell him. Then when he wouldn't listen, we talked about taking the ship, just for a while mind you, we ain't mutineers."

The governor sneered at the incongruous defence of the honour of a pirate, but remained silent.

"We thought maybe if we could just get the ship away from there, the Cap'n would come back to himself. He just needed to get out of hearing of the voices. We never worked out why some of us weren't affected as much, except that maybe she was singing specially for him, the Cap'n I mean."

"Who was singing for him?" asked a guard, forgetting his station for a moment as he got caught up in the story.

"The mermaid." The pirate said the words in a hushed voice as if he had spoken of a demon from Hell itself. The guards looked at each other in turn, gauging the reactions of their comrades. The one taking notes began to chuckle, and suddenly all four of them and the governor as well burst out laughing. The boy sat quietly, speculating. He knew as well as the adults that there was no such thing as mermaids. However, *something* had caused the injuries to the pirates, and he wanted to hear the rest of the story.

"I didn't believe it neither," said Jim. "But I saw her myself, sitting on a rock big as you please, with her hair reflecting the colour of the sunset and half of her like a big fish, only it wasn't a fish tail exactly. More like two fish tails that she could walk on a little, but we didn't know that yet.

"She jumped into the water when the Cap'n saw her, and the Cap'n followed her to an island. We forgot about taking the ship when we saw her, the whole crew just wrote off the lost men as shark bait and we all went chasing a mermaid. Then our best hopes looked like they were going to come true when we got to the island."

The pirate shuddered suddenly, and once again his gaze turned inward at some horrid memory that he clearly wanted to share, but was finding difficult to express. This time, nobody spoke. The officials waited patiently for him to gather his wits and continue his story. After a few minutes, he began to speak again, but softly, without looking at anyone in the room.

"I pulled guard duty that night, along with some others. We weren't happy about it at the time, but we were the lucky ones. We could see them through the scope, like some kind of fantasy come true. Mermaids, loads of 'em, all splashing and playing in a bay. The big ship couldn't get too close, but the Cap'n and most of the men went in the boats. As soon as the Cap'n's boat hit the water, that first mermaid came right up to the side and gave him an apple. I 'spect it must have been salty from the sea water, but he ate it right there, trusting her. Guess he was right though, I think it protected him."

"They grew on the island, the apple trees. I never seen apple trees so close to sea water before, but they were there, and just dripping with ripe apples. Golden ones like I got in my bag here, but they don't taste like apples I ever seen anywhere else. Sweeter they are, and a bit like cinnamon." He pulled an apple from his bag, showing the men, but did not offer them one. Instead, he bit into it himself and chewed for a moment before continuing between bites. The boy had finished his own apple, and on an impulse shoved the core into a pocket as he had seen the pirate do with his own finished apples, instead of throwing it away as he might have done normally.

"The mermaids were right friendly to the men and didn't seem to have any inhibitions at all. You know what I mean." Jim met the governor's eyes meaningfully. The governor nodded, acknowledging his understanding of the decadent scene the man seemed perversely unwilling to describe in detail, as if he had delicate sensibilities. The boy supposed it was for his own benefit, although he had a pretty fair idea of the sort of cavorting that seamen got up to with women, even imaginary mermaids.

"Those of us on the ship kept fighting over the scope to watch, wondering how long it would be before our turn came to go to the island. We saw the Cap'n disappear into the trees with the one that led us there, that's when we first noticed they could walk. He came back later with a basket full of these apples, and brought them out to the ship on his boat." The pirate was visibly shaking now, as he continued with his story.

"She come out with him, in the boat, and he actually brought her up on deck with him. I looked at her, close as I am to you now. It was me that took the basket from her hands." He looked down at his own hands as if to reassure himself that they were as they were meant to be.

"She had long claws and webbing between her fingers, and her hair was pure white, close up. It reflected light like I said about the sunset, but on its own it was almost as if you could see clear through it." He looked up at the governor once again, meeting his eyes and looking very shaken.

"Her eyes were white too, and they took you in like whirlpools when you looked into them. The Cap'n introduced her, said her name was Lena." He began to shake all over as he finished his description, "and as he said it she smiled, real friendly like, and I saw her teeth, all round and sharp and even like a herring only much, much longer and I saw death in her eyes, the kind of death that a man gives himself over to willingly like he's got no will of his own."

A strangled cry came from his throat, and he curled up on the bench, eating the apple voraciously as if his very life depended on its nourishment. He returned the finished core to his bag, and looked down at his empty hands for a moment before saying anything further.

"She spoke to me then. I ain't never going to forget that voice!" The pirate was nearly crying. "She said that the golden apple was for the one who could walk among the others and return without fear. That's what she said, but it was in Latin. I'm the only man on the ship that speaks it. Then she put her clawed hand down into the basket of apples and pulled one out, and handed it to me. I took it from her very fingers, webbed as they were, and ate it.

"Then they went back to the island, her and the Cap'n. They went back into the trees, and we didn't see either of 'em again. The other men, they tried to come back to the ship. They had their way with the women and was going to leave 'em there, give us our turn I expect. That's when it happened."

The governor was sitting on the edge of his seat, waiting intently for the rest of the story. The guards too had all but forgotten their posts and had been leaning over, listening with rapt attention. The pirate licked his lips once again, and forced himself to finish the tale.

"The boats almost got back to the ship, and the mermaids was swimming along with them. Then all of a sudden they went diving under the water, and the boats were pushed up from the bottom, hard. It was like a giant sea monster thumping the bottom of them, and they were all tipped over. The men swam for the ship, but none of 'em made it very far. The whole patch of ocean seemed to bubble up in one giant froth of bloody water, like giant piranhas was eating 'em. Those men I brought in was trying to climb down and rescue any of 'em they could, but they never had a chance. The mermaids started climbing up the ship and attacked them on the ropes. That's when we set sail and run."

The governor had been turning a greenish colour during this part of the tale. His sickened expression exposed the weakness of a man who had never seen death close up, apart from the hangings he ordered when pirates were captured near his island protectorate.

"I need some air," he said suddenly, and lurched toward the door and out of the surgery. The guardsmen, completely enraptured by the story, watched his exit then turned back toward the pirate.

"What happened next?" asked Dawson, the soldier taking notes.

“Some of 'em kept climbing up the side of the ship, like they had suction cups on their hands or something. We knocked them off with oars, we shot a couple, and just when we were sure they couldn't be stopped, the last couple of 'em turned and jumped off. We assumed they went back to their apple island. Then we brought the injured men here, 'cause this was the nearest port.“

The guards all looked at each other again, suddenly at a loss as to what to do.

“The governor!“ one of them exclaimed, then ran out of the surgery to find the missing official.

The boy looked up innocently at the pirate's drawn face. “What will you do now?“ He asked.

“We got to go back,“ replied Jim Morris, “soon as the men are patched up and we can get 'em back to the ship, we're going after the Cap'n.“

“Won't he be dead?“ asked a guard incredulously. “Surely the creatures will have eaten him before you disappeared over the horizon!“

Jim shook his head.

“No, don't ask me how we know, but ever since we sailed away, every last man left alive on the *Prometheus* knows in his soul that the Cap'n is protected by that woman creature, Le-ina. She's something special to them. We don't know how they work their society but they had some sort of deference to her, like a tribal chief or something.“

As the pirate finished his explanation, the door opened and three men came in. They were seamen, that much was obvious. The fact that they were pirates was evidenced by Jim Morris' familiarity with them. He tossed them each a golden apple from his bag, and they nodded in acknowledgement. Their eyes flicked to the guards, then away again. The entire encounter was eerie, and seemed somehow unreal to the boy who witnessed it.

Without speaking, the men, followed by Jim now, went through the door on the opposite wall which led to the examination room where their mates were likely to be. A few minutes passed, yet nothing happened. The guards looked bored if anything, occasionally glancing at each other and taking little notice of the boy, who also sat silently and waited without knowing what for.

At last the door opened again, and the four pirates emerged carrying two stretchers with two of the injured men on them. They had been bandaged and sedated. The third man, who had suffered only bites, hobbled behind them, looking weak and nervous. Without thinking, the boy jumped up and opened the door to the outside for them. Jim nodded to him, then flicking a last glance at the guards, he met the boy's eyes and spoke to him in a way that seemed as if he expected the guards to be unable to hear, although they stood just an arm's length away.

"I reckon you'd be a lot happier coming with us lad. Nothing for you here 'cept getting caught one day."

The boy glanced at the guards, then without speaking, followed the pirates out of the door and to their boats. One of the guards casually looked out the window and watched as they rowed out to the main ship, with its golden mast sparkling in the late morning sunlight. Just as the ship began moving out toward open sea, the guard at the window turned to the other two. He wore a confused expression, and seemed to speak as if he had just awoken and had not quite penetrated the daze of dreaming.

"Weren't we supposed to detain them for hanging?"

The others looked at each other suddenly, their eyes widening in shock as they realised that the pirates had just walked out under their very noses. One of them leapt toward the window, peering out to see the quarry inevitably escaping.

"Bastards!" he shouted. "With all the chaos, we completely forgot to arrest them!"

Out on the sea, the ship bobbed with the waves, following a course that would take the crew back into a danger that they would be ready for this time. The boy stood near the bow, looking over the railing at the choppy waters that would take him into new adventures. He smiled to himself as he munched on another apple, and wondered how long it would take the pirates to remember to ask his name.

INTERMISSION

"Sit down. Hold on. Hold on to each other as the violence begins around you, protect each other as best you can. Continue to talk to the police as the clubs whip down around you, as your friends are dragged off, thrown to the ground, beaten, their faces smashed down on concrete.

"Keep your focus on the meaning of what you are doing as your hands are cuffed behind you. Your challenge now and for a long time to come will be to remember, at each stage of what happens to you, that you have a choice: to acquiesce or to resist. Choose your battles mindfully – there will be many of them and you cannot fight them all. Still every instance slows the system down, prevents its functioning, lessens its power."

- Starhawk, from *Webs of Power, Notes from the Global Uprising*

CURSE OF THE APPLE ISLAND

<Frater Carfax>

On the 20th of August, 1788, the same year as the mainland invasion of Australia by British colonists, Lieutenant William Bligh pulled into Adventure Bay on Bruny Island, Tasmania which was known then as Van Diemen's Land. Bligh planted Australia's first apple trees, thereby dooming the state of Tasmania to be known ever after as 'The Apple Island'.

Unaware of the curse he had invoked, Lieutenant Bligh then set sail for Tahiti and into history with the famous Mutiny on the Bounty in April 1789 which was led by Bligh's one-time close friend, Fletcher Christian. This was to be the first of three mutinies experienced by the unfortunate bearer of apples.

Much more tragically, the island state of Tasmania was to be the scene of some of the worst acts of genocide against the indigenous aboriginal population. In 1804, settlers were given permission to shoot the aboriginal peoples.

Amongst the most well known of the indigenous Tasmanians was a woman named Truganini, who has become an archetype of the struggle for aboriginal survival in Tasmania. Born in 1812, by the time she was seventeen her mother had been murdered by whalers, her sister abducted and shot by sealers and her husband-to-be murdered by timber fellers, while she herself had been brutally raped. She was instrumental in facilitating the movement of the surviving Tasmanian aboriginal peoples to nearby islands rather than face extermination.

Truganini died of natural causes in 1876.

One hundred years later, after many years as a museum exhibit, her remains were finally cremated and scattered in the D'Entrecasteaux Channel near her native lands on Bruny Island - the site of the first apple trees in Australia.

LETTER TO SEAN

<Koogie Smith>

Dear Sean,

I just heard the tragic news about Robert Anton Wilson! Did he receive a copy of Liber Malorum????

Sending you love and good vibes,

Koogie

The HermAphroditic ChAOrder of the Silver Dusk is a counter-point to The Hermetic Order of the Golden Dawn - where the Golden Dawn was a magickal order established by poets and artists, the Silver Dusk is an art movement instigated by magicians, witches and sorcerers.

– Orryelle Defenestrate-Bascule, from *the Silver Dusk website*
from http://www.crossroads.wild.net.au/order.htm

62. ECHOES OF EDEN <Caroline Foldes>

The land here is open.
The space is like a vacuum for my feelings,
arousing introspection.
Reflection without water.
This place feels like a huge, waterless swimming pool
in which all one can envisage is water.
Something is missing.
The strong light numbs my feelings.
Where is the feeling hidden in this land? What is whispered in the wind?
I feel only my heart, and myself.
Pain clenches around my heart like a glove. Breath enters my body
in
tiny
gasps,
meeting the ache in my chest. There is no room for more air.
Perhaps this is death in the air. I hold my breath, not wishing to invite it in.

Lovers once lay here on the earth.
They embraced each other fully, openly and warmly.
Breath met breath and the air serenaded them.
Insects sang harmonies
and choruses
around them,
weaving vibrations into patterns that danced amongst the trees.
Heavily scented flowers impregnated the night air with love,
seducing bees and birds towards their nectars,

as if the air had not already seen its fill of love tonight.
Love waited, like the fruit on the trees, ready to impart knowledge.
The children of this land knew it well.
They heard the land, sometimes talking with itself,
sometimes talking with them, sharing stories from the past,
brewing stories for the future.
Their ancestors had trodden paths into the earth
with their many songs and dances.
Lives, loves, regrets, punishment and balance
all lay under this Earth, waiting to be heard.

Who heard the song of this place, in this Earth?
Perhaps as they heard, the pair grieved,
filling the pain in their hearts with fruit.
The rainbow serpent knew the song of this place well,
and the lovers also heard the tale.

As the lovers listened, stories arose from the Earth.
As they lay together,
they heard the heartbeat of the rhythm of time
through the land
and they knew their time had come.
They heard the voice of the land and the song of this time.
Their heartbeats matched the land's movements and shudders, and
the call was with them.
They wondered what this call would bring.
What would emerge from this new time?
They knew this song was like no other before.
A very certain ending descended upon this song.
It had no more verse.
There was a final voice.
What had begun as a definite tone grew into silence,
as if to deafen even the stillness of the night air.
They sighed and reclined, too shy to discuss the emptiness.
As the night progressed, they could not find the children
from their future.

The woman said,
"I do not see my family in your eyes. Do you hide them, have they gone?"
Her lover whispered,
"they are not within me.
Nor have they gone.
This family exists no more.
This is my vision.
It is no vision.
There is emptiness,
And your children will not be.
They stay in the stars,
to them we will return."

As time flew,
the weaver's shuttle wove the vision across the apple isle.
At first it was simply a dream.
Later on, it came true.
It had been like cobwebs - shredded and full of dew after a storm.
Tattered and unwanted, just hanging around.
This was a ragged, rejected vision.
The notion only existed in the ethers. Perhaps it was more of a nightmare than a dream.
Now, it is embedded in the land,
the battle of evil for apples.
This land is Tasmania.
The Earth here has many stories.
It whispers them into the wind,
gestates them through flowers,
and leaks them into deep rivers.
Shreds of scars and ends of dreams.
What does it know of love now?
So close are the beauty and sorrows here.
Is this a universal paradigm?
The proximity of good and evil, woven together,
light and dark?

The women here claimed to give birth ecstatically,
releasing children into cradling holes
dug into the earth and filled with flowers.
How do you birth your beloved kin now?
How do you arrive on this land?
Cradled in love…in love with each other, or…?
Perhaps this is why you fear each other...
and others...?
Are you
truly
in
love?

An old man sat alone
in the valley
into which he was born.
He asked,
"who called this creature a Tasmanian Devil?
Why curse this creature?
Such a name is of the same tongue
as that
which gave the appellation, "Apple Isle."
And that which says their fruit is of the Tree of Knowledge.
And that
knowing is wrong.
What is this wrong knowledge brought here?
And why?"
His silence invited reflection.
Another empty space gestates feelings.
He juggled bush fruits, silently,
their sheen dancing like diamonds in the sunshine.
Is there light within the spiral of this fruit?
Or a philosopher's stone?
Do the seeds hold wisdom?
Does the land grow precious secrets?
How can we determine for ourselves what fears it holds and
what knowledge it posesses?
I see this man through time and

watch
the shimmering, tossed fruit.
I lie down and close my eyes.
Shimmering lights become layers of feeling
moving inside me.
Like the sun on the snowflakes in a blizzard,
I am travelling into the weave.
Do I seek the knowledge of this place?
Can the dancing lights lead me into wisdom?
What would the Rainbow Serpent tell me if I invited it
gently?
Travel up my spine,
pray, tell me what is and what is meant to be.
What do I ask of him?

He tells me of his winding, undulating motion
across the land.
He tells me that ley lines in the land continue into my body
as meridians.
He tells me that he slides through these paths
in the land,
and that as he does,
he knows
all.
All knowledge is in this earth, this land, this space,
and he touches it.

As the lovers lay here in this same place, on the earth,
they embraced each other fully, openly and warmly.
Their interwoven, entwined bodies mirrored,
evoking the dance of the rainbow serpent,
the movement of fluidity and growth.
The dance of their lovemaking opened them to greater
wisdom.
They sensed the threads of wisdom in the air.
They felt the tracks of wisdom in the land,
opened to the webs of wisdom in their bodies.
The wisdom of the future should have been woven.

Between them was the task of weaving the next generation,
and their stories,
through the movements of their bodies.
In the giving and opening of their hearts,
the lovers opened together to more shared learning,
to a deeper wisdom and essence within and between them,
but within this deeper wisdom was the no-vision.
The future-weaving should have happened,
but there was an ending to the song.
It had no more verse.
The thread had run out and there was no more of this
pattern.
The silence,
so deafening,
had returned.
Freedom no longer opened the way for truth
in this place.
Their children stayed in the stars,
and to them the lovers returned.
Their sharing and giving took them away.
They are only echoes in the stars.

The shack is somehow empty. Yet, a cold wind blows
through
and fills the space.
Cracks and crevices, dark and musty,
unfed by air or light.
The scent is foul.
It is dry and could catch
in the throat like a knife.
Perhaps the very air
could kill someone
if fantasies of escape did not give way to action.
It is a hot day and ill winds are not felt by anyone now.
The objects inside fill halls and windowsills, muttering to
themselves of fear, loneliness and damp.
The spirit has left.
There was a time when an old lady sat with her two friends,

chattering and laughing. Teasing each other with old tales.
That time has passed.
Now it is part of the One Dream
on the path of the rainbow serpent.
Coiled, attendant.
Onward turn the hands of time.
There is no-one here who can stop their flow any more.
The old fates have left this place.
Perhaps there is a new fate to weave?

A beautiful woman
cuts a piece of organic apple for me
to taste.
I walk the path of Snow White.
Perhaps I am to buy this fruit?
Her instrument recalls a surgeon's knife
glinting
in the sunshine.
Is it light, or malevolence, on the blade?
She seems so loving,
but what lies in the earth from which these apples grow?
A black war lies in these soils.
The apple trees fruit endlessly through
buried pain.
Yields of loneliness and numb shock.
From death and decay arise new life and growth.
Premature halt. Precious hunt.
Could intention have come into the actions of these driven hunters?
Or was it wild unconsciousness that drove foe against foe,
one defending the future,
the other, a fantasy.

"Who will be the new dragons to slay?"
Is this what the sailors asked themselves,
seeking more land,
more victims,

more blood?
They hissed threats, onward marching,
anger diffusing into the environment like smoke.
They went, conquering,
ploughing through acres of land.
Neither animals, nor women,
could breathe in their presence.
The air died when they came.

They sought the magic of the land,
many try, some realise.
Driven forward by their pursuit, they missed the fruit.
It is a way of life, a manner of being,
a matter of union and dissolution,
a longing to go home,
to surrender fully
into the arms and the bosom of the earth,
into flesh, and into comfort.
When they came
with the north winds,
they drove their energies ahead of them,
like winged horses pulling chariots across the heavens.
These energies anchored deep into the land - sending forth
feelings of glory
and adventure - to pull them towards it.

This earth has dryness.
It cannot accommodate too much desire for fruit and
greatness.
It is only small
and soft.
This land is dark.
Is it wet or dry?
Hot or cold?
It is fertile.
It hides much below its surface.
Why are they afraid of darkness?
It longs to be worn, yearns to give fully,

this soft, gentle, dark earth that gave shelter and food,
always and unconditionally nourishing and feeding
the bodies of its children.
However, the old children of Tasmania will no longer invite
stars.
They are barren and not always felt,
their shadows visible only in the faintest, flickering light of
the golden sun. They are amongst kin,
far away in the skies.
The glances
they direct
towards their island home
may take as long to get there as a stone to Tartarus.
Nine days' falling time. And yet, they still hover there,
dislocated and protective,
some nearer, some farther,
singing with their ancestral homelands of their fate.
Dreaming fathers and mothers knew of this.
They saw the dream.
The vicious wind took them away.

A new beast came after the violent times.
Another foreign threat, the fox.
This lustful hunter flies feral,
driven to kill,
hiding on hills,
licking lips, he feeds
upon yet another small, gentle animal, fallen prey to his
drives.
Another finds home is a star.

I put my ear to the ground,
and heard a half-blind crone wailing.
She knew of their coming long before the day.
It was in the song of the land,
that deep song she had first heard with her lover.
Many battles had been lost since then.
Fearfully, she asked,

"what has become of our children? How can we heal?
We lost our love, our babies, and our wisdom.
We lost fragments of our very souls.
Defended by tears of fear,
we held our pain, walking weary paths alone.
Was there gold in this deathly phase?
Was it the natural cycle of light and dark?
How can such imbalance be healed?
Perhaps, mysteriously, healing may grow from this woe?"

He tells me, "sit with this silence,
on the land,
in this space.
Hear its tale, and then ask that the rainbow serpent may weave
love
through your veins, into your blood.
From your longing, create love.
From the stars, create the future.
Ask that you may grow into love.
Weave, caress and embrace.

Be this love,
And send it forth."

Thank you, my guides and teachers.

63.
HUGGING FAERIES IS NOT A CRIME
<Indymedia>

The charges faced by Luna Wilson were that she had attempted to remove another protester, dressed as a faerie, from the custody of the police, i.e. "de-arrest" her, and that she had obstructed those police in their duty by standing between them. Her case was that she was holding onto the faerie in an attempt to de-escalate a stressful situation arising from the police's behaviour towards the protesters, the faerie in particular.

The blockade of the Shell service station, a part of the International Day of Action Against the Root Causes of Climate Change, was good-natured and took place on one of the hottest days that summer. People were dancing and smiling, but prevented from moving around the City Centre by a line of Police. When the party moved south and west, the police followed for a while before penning it in a cordon, for "the safety of protesters," according to WPC Bellingham's evidence. Once the cordon had formed, protesters were kept stationary in the heat for several hours but remained cheerful until the police started to force them back towards the city centre.

It's around this point the account offered by the accused and her witness differ sharply from that offered by the Police witnesses, WPC Bellingham and PC Barr, both of Charing Cross. The police witnesses maintained, against detailed questioning by defence solicitor Claire Ryan, that the crowd had been "shepherded" in the cordon that they were unable to leave, but that no-one had been pushed, especially not the faerie. They also revealed that they had been on duty since 6:30am (the arrests took place a little after 7pm), wearing heavy fluorescent jackets in the sun, but claimed that their tempers had not been frayed. After detailed questioning on the pushing point, the WPC was looking about the court in apparent irritation.

When Luna Wilson took the stand in her defence, she told how she had caught and hugged the faerie who had been pushed by WPC Bellingham into her. They were then snatched out of the crowd and thrown up against a wall by 13 or 14 officers and arrested. Wilson shouted "Go Limp!" so as to avoid further violence from the police. The procurator fiscal asked Wilson if the Faerie had gone limp and Wilson replied, "the Faerie continued to wave her pink feather duster for a few moments before going limp."

When the procurator fiscal, in an apparent attempt to paint her as a cop-hating extremist, asked Wilson what she thought of the actions of the police, Wilson replied that the police were good at silencing dissent. She was clear that she had been holding onto the faerie, not pulling her arm back from the police officers, as charged. The faerie then took the stand and confirmed Miss Wilson's version of events, at least as far as she remembered. (Reasonably enough, her attention had been held by the WPC attacking her and she hadn't noticed Luna until they were both shoved up against the wall in Morrison Street.) Hearing this, the fiscal moved to have the case concluded before the third defence witness could be called. This was agreed and the Sheriff delivered his verdict.

The Sheriff concluded that he had no particular reason to disbelieve the police evidence and no particular reason to disbelieve the defence case and that there was therefore reasonable doubt and a verdict of "Not Guilty" was recorded on Wilson's charges. Applause from the public gallery was knocked back by the sheriff with a stern "this is not a pantomime," to which no-one was quick enough to reply "oh yes it is."

So was it a victory for the Justice system? Only if you discount the inconvenience, stress and expense it caused the participants. The flimsy evidence meant that the case should never have reached trial and the sad fact is that the case isn't wholly over yet. This Wednesday (19th), the faerie who was Luna's witness is up in the same court (Sheriff Court 17, 10am) on charges of Police Assault arising from the same incident. Four other defendants are appearing in the same session and, while this verdict offers hope, there's no guarantee that the right verdicts will be reached in those cases. People are being asked to come down to the court on Wednesday to show support for the defendants and their refusal to be intimidated.

Wilson is extremely happy with the result and would like to thank her friends, family and supporters for standing up to injustice, oppression and environmental destruction wherever it occurs. Wilson said, "it will now be forever on the public record in British law that Hugging Faeries is Not A Crime."

From http://www.indymedia.org.uk/

64. WILD ABOUT THAT THING

Luna left the court room feeling ecstatic, "Yay! I beat it! I beat it!"

"Congratulations!"

"Well done!"

"Wicked!"

"Excellent!"

A group of about thirty people were outside the court waiting to hear the verdict. Luna had no idea that she would be so popular. But of course, it wasn't her that had drawn the crowd, but the system they were confronting. She learnt that there was nearly always a group of people willing to show court solidarity when protesters or activists had trials and this made her feel great about life, and about the myth she lived in.

Helene and Malus were in the court solidarity group, as was Sean, who Luna had never met before, despite sharing some very close friends and despite Luna being a bit of a Fool herself. The four of them went to a café afterwards to eat breakfast and drink tea. Helene and Malus got caught up in their own conversation, leaving Sean and Luna to get to know each other.

"So, again, congratulations on beating the charges," Sean said, smiling, as they sat at a table. Sean ordered a cappuccino and a pot of honey and Luna had a fruit juice.

"Thank you, thank you," Luna replied, looking on top of the world. "But

I must be honest, I knew from the start that I would be found innocent. It's just like in Fooling where we can choose the myth we live in. I choose to live in a myth where my innocence is embodied and apparent. I stepped into a world where being a good person counts for something."

"If only more people could work and play with such a mindset, what a beautiful world it could be," Sean said and spooned some chocolate off his cappuccino into his mouth. "I was in a bit of panic when I heard you had been nicked."

"So was I! At first." She took a drink of fruit juice through her straw. "But then I just remembered my dad's friend Tim had spent a lot of time in prison and no matter what shit they threw at him, no matter how much they tried to break him, he came back at them *with all the positive energy he had.* He has been such an inspiration to me."

"So embodied foolish optimism wins the day!"

"That's a funny turn of phrase, 'embodied foolish optimism' is what I call my own outlook on life. I don't think I've mentioned it before..."

"There's that synchronicity faerie again! I'm wild about that thing!" Sean said, and they both laughed. "Bless her."

After drinking a mouthful of his cappuccino, Sean asked, "what next for Luna Wilson? Have you heard of our coven? Have you heard of the Fooluminati?"

"I have heard of you, yes of course." She slurped some juice. "Michael, wherever he is now, told me he had joined you guys but he later told me he was pulling out."

"What on Earth could have flipped him out so much?" Sean wondered out loud. "Part of me thinks I should be really worried, but another part just trusts that he will get over it. Maybe he's exploring some part of his darkness and needs to be alone?" Luna didn't respond but visualised Michael surrounded by a golden healing light. *He'll be fine.*

Sean stirred some honey into his cappuccino and said, "I think Michael will be fine. But anyway, about the Fooluminati, we actively tell people about our coven, but we don't do any active recruitment. I've been in covens before that actively recruited but it only takes one bad apple to ruin the bunch. So Koogie and I decided early on that we would tell people about what we do, but not invite them to join. We would wait until people came to us before we discussed their involvement..."

Luna wiggled her fingers next to her temples acting like a psychic, "I am now reading your mind Sean. You are thinking 'I hope Luna asks if she can join the coven'. Am I right?"

Sean feigned sheepishness as he answered, "I would certainly love you to join. You have a great outlook on life. I think you are certainly foolish enough, certainly optimistic enough."

"I would love to join," she said, watching Sean's face broaden into a smile. "But right now I can't. I have some important family issues to attend to. I am heading down to Avalon soon and I might be there for quite a while."

"What's going on in Glastonbury these days? Family issues?" Sean asked seriously.

"Yes, family issues. Like you Sean, I live in the world of myth. And my myth spans the world. The ability to shift myth at will reveals the world to be a truly splendid, magical place and I do it all the time. But deep down, there is an overriding myth that I can't shift; *that I don't want to shift;* a myth that pervades all others. Do you have something like that?"

Sean thought for a moment. "Yeah, there is a cohesive mythology in my mind that I always fall back on, or turn to when I'm down or can't deal with life or the opposite – when I'm as high as a kite and want to express gratitude. There's a wonderful spiritualism in my life, a wonderful sense of being able to talk to my ancestors... And you?"

Luna continued, "it's similar. In the myth I'm in, that feels true to my core, I have to go and see my father again. Mum told me that dad was coming over to this side, by boat, and I'm going down to Avalon to meet him." She drank another mouthful of juice through her straw. "I feel such a longing to see him after all this time. I just want to wrap him up in my Clear Light and hold him close, and be held close. I haven't seen him since I was fifteen." She blushed red and her eyes appeared glassy. "I know he will soon be joining me in this myth and I long to tell him how much I love him."

Sean reached out across the café table, took her hand and felt a wave of emotion sweep over him. "I love my dad too, but we don't seem to find the time to keep in touch." He looked into his cup, "I suppose it's pretty common, in so-called 'developed countries', that we never have time for the ones we love most." Despite having quit ages ago, Sean had the sudden urge to smoke a cigarette. He resisted as he knew that smoking would push the emotions down, and being able to feel and express emotions was paramount to being an effective Fool.

"And your mum?" Luna asked him.

"Mum, sheesh. She died ten years ago. I still talk to her all the time. I... I don't know what to say about her. She was the most amazing woman in the world."

"As is my mum!" They laughed together, with tears in their eyes, at this ever-so-common myth. It was true for so many - mothers were *all-important* and at some stage of life, people realised that their mothers were actually human and made mistakes. But even with the mistakes, mums were nearly always the most amazing women in the world.

After a short while of silence, Luna said, "I think I'll go to Avalon soon. Why not today? I have nothing to lose."

"Today?!"

"Yeah, I'll go now. I want to be there when my dad comes over. There's no rush, of course. He'll take his time getting here, but I want to be standing on the shore when he sails in."

"It sounds very beautiful. Go for it."

Luna stood to leave, "Sean, tell Helene and Malus where I've gone. But don't tell them until after I have left."

"Mum's the word," Sean replied, pulling an imaginary zip across his lips.

Luna called out to Malus and Helene, "I'll see you soon," opened the door and left the café.

Helene looked at Sean and asked, "where is she going? She isn't leaving us, is she?"

Sean didn't answer but stared through unfocused eyes at the door Luna had left through. After a few moments he turned to Helene and said, "what an amazing faerie. By the way, how do you get to Avalon?"

65.

AVALON'S APPLES

<Stella Damiana>

"Oh really Kate, you are too much sometimes!" gentle Mimi purred at the statuesque woman across the table. Mimi tried to place the delicate bone china cup onto its saucer but was having trouble since her shoulders shook with laughter. This set all the tiny bells around her wrists and sewn onto her flowing clothes tinkling away; setting them all giggling again.

Lily glanced at Kate, who was shifting uncomfortably in her seat with her leather outfit creaking, and then blurted, "well I for one don't think we go far enough, they are only men!"

Morag rolled her eyes, took another sip of her tea then complained half heartedly, "here we go again…"

It had to be admitted that after two pots of last season's best mushrooms, brewed into a tea, and sweetened with Isle honey, the girls were having a hard time keeping the mirth under control.

"Well," said Kate, recovering slightly but still blushing from sweet Mimi's admonition, "the twins were cute, and they REALLY wanted to play. I don't see what the problem is?"

"But they are mortals," Lily exploded. "Don't you have enough choice from among the Courts?" she slumped into her chair, face like a disgruntled teenager, arms folded.

"Oh save your anger and snobbery for someone who deserves it," growled Morag. She was annoyed now. Another tea party with the girls spoiled. She almost smiled at the timing though, when the first of the seraphim knocked tentatively on the door to the salon. Who knew the reception once the girls were in their cups?

Everyone turned to greet the first among the field operatives; the joy of the afternoon fading fast as they shucked off the inebriation, rearranging their clothes, postures and minds to start the work of the day.

"So handsome, what do you have for us this fine spring day?" commanded Morag, at once the rather more regal Morrighan, Queen in her Court. The first of the Seraphim bristled, steel feathered wings shaking in annoyance at the slight as he started to relay the reports from the field. Morag enjoyed the windup; the lofty Seraph had never gotten over the fact that mere mortals had caught the Otherworld's finest on primitive cameras in the Victorian era. It had taken some intense retro spell-casting, then research and implementation, to erect suitable shields around the teams after that.

The reports followed, one after another much the same as they had year on year on year. Signs of potentials spotted amongst the otherwise mundane pagan moots, activists and party people, those who should be met, checked out and assessed. In order to do this, the women divided attendance at each event across the lands between them, as even those who *could* fold space and time might not want to attend every gig. Added to which, every potential required a different approach, much as an angler would change their rig to hunt a different fish.

Morag stretched like a panther who had sat too long and was in need of exercise, and rose to her feet. "Well, that wraps up business, are you all coming to Bride's tonight for the candlemass rituals and party?"

"Too right!" said Kate as she reached down to retrieve the helmet by her seat, ready to go, when the door burst open once more. A boglin, rude in appearance and manner, as arrogant as the women, however, unlike them in that he had no subtlety. "A new event for you ladies. Not my area, but fresh intel. You may find some *fresh meat*...A grant-aided green festival in Herefordshire. Music. Sustainable living. Hippies. Pagans. Etc. yaddah yaddah. The usual type of bollocks you lot like to go trawling through for your victims. So, which one of you lovelies wants it? Morag?

Oh sooo sorry, *your Majesty* Morrighan. Lilith? No. Hekate perhaps? No. You and your angel dogs will be busy elsewhere that August Bank Holiday weekend. Why that would leave you, my lovely, the Lady Lakshmi herself. Do have fun dears…" He was already halfway out of the door as Morag dismissed him with an imperial wave of her hand.

"If the little **boglin** wasn't so damned good at subversion in the places that matter, why I'd ..." seethed Lily.

"You'd what?" said Kate. "You really do need to keep that revenge complex under control girl." She turned to Mimi and said, "it seems like you'll be hooking up with Cerys in Cymru again!" smirking as she remembered the last time those two had partied together. "Looks like we'll be needing some more brew."

The elegant but tipsy ladies left the salon and walked down the wooden corridors of the cider house, gossiping and reminiscing about the previous seasons on the festival circuit, excited about the season to come.

The heady aroma of the brew house was left behind as they walked out into the orchards, the apple trees dressed in full blossom and rosy gold sunlight. "Who's for a lift to Bride's? I'm sure some of the boys would love to oblige," teased Kate, nodding at the bikers lolling around on their machines at the edge of the orchards.

"I think we'll take the henge darling, my sari would get ruined!" retorted Mimi.

"Your loss! You ready, boys? Let's roll!" The Harleys spluttered into life and chugged off in procession across the landscape.

"See you there, girls…" cackled Kate in the distance.

~

The town of Trelleck was not used to this kind of influx; it was bursting at the seams with hippies and new-agers of every rainbow colour and stripe, and neither it nor its regular inhabitants were enjoying it. The smiling, directionless wanderings of the insurgents grated on the nerves of the town's folk, causing a polarisation instantly recognisable to the security teams and police brought in to control and shepherd the crowds. The heaving masses flowed through the ancient market square like a muddy river; eddies forming at the edges around the stalls as the people were drawn to the posters and bright slogans shouting their causes to the throng, selling everything from solar panels to vegan information.

Robert sat on the wall surveying the crowds; a seasoned "alternative way of lifer," if you used the latest govt. approved p.c. nomenclature; a person, if you didn't; those who sought new ways to live and had no desire to join the rat race. Born on a bus, birthed his two kids the same way, he'd been pleased to see the new gathering in the hope that it would bring new faces to the party; to the cause; to the revolution. The girl-child Raven and her kid brother Wolf had slipped off to Brighton to play again, gods alone knew what those brats were up to this time.

There! He saw the glint of gold in the crowds he'd kidded himself he wasn't really looking for. There she was again, a tinkle of bells and laughter, a rosy pink sari trimmed with tiny golden sparkles; she had almond shaped brown eyes and lickable golden brown skin. He jumped down off the wall causing another eddy in the human river, as he caught himself staring, entranced by her grace and beauty. He watched, compelled, as she and her friends worked the stall on the other side of the crowds, calling out their wares, as the throng passed through the square on the way to the main site. He was sure they'd met or he'd seen her before and was quite determined they would do so again.

Robert began to navigate the crowds, tacking across the stream to the shelter of the stone guild-hall. Making his way behind the pillar, he caught another sight of the gold, fleeting, like fish scales under water, until suddenly he was before her not knowing what to say. Glancing unseeing at the wares arrayed in front of him, he stumbled over the words, "so, what do you have to offer then?"

His knee-weakening reward, a smile warm and welcoming. “You see anything you like then, handsome?” the reply. Mimi winked and continued, “we have Morag's Best Borders Brew, Milk Lassi with a Bang, Lily's Vegan Vengance Biscuits or Kate's 'shrooms in Honey. What's your poison?”

His mind and body screamed at him 'everything!' but suddenly he felt ashamed at the effect this glorious woman had on him and didn't want to please her too easily. “Well now, that would be telling wouldn't it?”

Instead of being crushed, Mimi only beamed the wider at him, “Okay hero, why don't you come to the performance tent tonight for the workers after party and we'll find out? There's a short ritual before the party gets under way if you're up for it?!”

Before he'd answered, she'd moved on to the next victim and the crowd pushed him onwards and up toward the site.

He spent the afternoon and early evening in a vexed mood, resentfully looking at performances and info before making his way to the marquee decorated in a louche and opulently baroque style at the edge of the gathering near to a small henge. As he entered the tent, a curiously androgynous individual dressed as an eighteenth century footman elegantly waved him inside, offering the welcome, “enter; join the court if that is your will.”

Playing along with the show, he bowed slightly, but made no reply. The footman raised an arched eyebrow but said nothing.

He couldn't see her anywhere as he prowled around, checking the faces of the elegant and amazingly-dressed individuals who, from their glassy-eyed state, looked as if they had started well in advance of the ritual. He was beginning to feel he'd been misled when he was accosted by some biker chick and a dodgy Goth binty. He tutted and tried to pass on by, but was trapped on the one side by a roccoco chaise longue covered in lithe bodies and the women on the other. A conspiratorial glint passed between them as they clutched an arm each and steered him towards the circular clearing in the middle of the tent, under the fabulous chandelier.

"So, this is Mimi's chosen then? Doesn't look much like a potential..." Kate said, completely ignoring Robert's reluctance to their lead.

Morag turned her head to look at Robert in an exaggerated movement, as though suddenly realising he was there. "Mmm, no not really, but let's just see how it goes during the ritual... Ah, here's Mimi now. We can begin."

Robert realised that there were three other similarly bemused men in the centre of the circular marquee, each now with one of the equally fabulous women standing close behind them. He turned slightly as he heard the tinkle of Mimi's bells approach him from behind. A frisson of fear ran up his spine, but he reassured himself that this was just a bit of ritual theatre, wasn't it? He felt hands on his shoulders, and saw that each of the women had hold of the man in front of them so that the men faced centre.

The women now seemed to tower over the men, and to somehow be pulsing with energy. The lights in the circular tent began to dim and the roof become transparent to the night sky, laying them naked to the stars and the lazy, full harvest moon. The women started to chant, the audience seemed to know the words too, but Robert couldn't make them out. His eyes swivelled to the floor, his head held immobile by some force unknown, and saw snakes of blue Earth energy crackling into the circle from the four cardinal directions. Fear now gripped him; this theatre was a bit too real for him, he was desperate to escape but could not move from the spot.

The energy wound around the feet and legs of the men. Robert could feel the force travel up his body, making him feel even more enervated, senses becoming more alive than before, but at once curiously calm as though it was a familiar, long-forgotten feeling to him. Before he had time to ponder on this conundrum the women, still chanting, moved into the centre of the circle and turned to face their 'victim'.

A huge bell chimed from somewhere and silence fell among the throng.

Time seemed suspended, no-one drew a breath until the waves of sound dissipated.

The fearsome Morrighan raised her arms to the moon and spoke, "Mother, we bring you sweet offerings on this the first of Harvest moons. Show us which of these potentials you will take!" She dropped her arms and her chin dropped to her chest as though she couldn't bear to see what happened next.

The blue fire around Robert tightened as he became rigid with fear and anticipation. From behind each of the victims, a tray appeared borne by one of the footmen. The glorious women as one asked, "here are the sacraments, the fruits of the Goddess, the bounty of the season, in beer, in herbs, in apples, which will you take? The choice is yours to partake of the sacrament or not, which is your will."

Robert almost dropped to the floor as the constriction of the earth energy left him. He loved the Goddess as much as the next man, but knew in that moment he would choose nothing from that tray and resigned himself to the outcome, sad that he would not be able to say farewell to his loved ones before crossing to the Summerlands. Fair Lakshmi looked at him askance as though she knew his answer and was disappointed that he had failed her and there was nothing she could do for him to avoid the outcome. He saw the other three humans each reach for food or drink from the proffered trays and saw a tear fall from Lakshmi's eye. The tear scintillated and grew, myriad reflections and images racing through his mind as the walls of the tent whirled, grew close, expanded, then disappeared into the night. Everything fell still and black, his consciousness gone.

~

In the early rays of the morning light, he twitched and began to stir; one eye opened. He pushed himself up onto one arm and looked around the stone circle, and felt a body behind him. He turned to see beautiful Mimi curled up in a rug like a cat, was held entranced, and then jolted by terror as the events of the previous evening slammed back into his brain, making him reel almost to the point of throwing up. He was trying to escape from the rugs as Mimi blinked awake, saw his anxiety, and threw her arm up to comfort him. "Ssh, my hero, you have survived this far. Nothing now can touch you, the Goddess has made her choice."

He sat down hard and leant against one of the stones, panting, was perplexed, angry and scared. "Wha...wha... what have I been chosen for, may I ask? Am I dead? What happened..? What's going on? Who ARE you?"

He would have continued but Mimi leaned into him, touching his lips first with her fingers, then her sweet lips. After an age they separated, and she continued, "we need a brew house Master or Mistress, and new workers, as eventually those humans who join our Court yearn to go on to the Summerlands once all they knew or loved have gone ahead. Time in the Court runs to a different beat from the human consciousness. You could be the new brew Master. You chose not to eat the food or drink, although severely compelled. Your will is strong and you love the Goddess. Will you serve her? Help us to carry on the search for those who will continue to fight to protect this land?"

"I thought I was going to be killed!" he exploded, "I can't leave my kids, what makes you think I'd want to take this job after what you put me through!"

Mimi giggled nervously, "you thought you were the Wicker Man? Yes, it's true, you could get that idea, but the premise is the same although we try to be a bit more subtle these days. You will be able to visit the human world as often as you wish and watch over your children, and their children to come. You need to come to the Goddess, by your own choice. Those who took the 'sacrament' last night will either be chosen to work in the orchards of the Summerlands, or wake up this morning remembering nothing of the night's events, with only a large hangover to fill their memories."

"So, no-one was killed?"

"No."

Robert looked at the horizon, dressed in the most beautiful sunrise colours he could remember seeing, mulling over everything Mimi had told him. He turned to the woman next to him, whose beauty competed with the morning sky, smiled cheekily and said, "then as your Hero, I claim another kiss; and then I'll give you my decision..."

Lakshmi smiled and moved closer...

66.
PNEUMONIA

Helene got off the train to the sound of seagulls crying. *Ah, the seaside.* She imagined she could smell a salty sea breeze on the wind as she left the station for the short walk to Brighton Beach. She pulled her bright red coat around her as a cold autumn wind greeted her.

She had spent the night at Club Purr, a fetish and BDSM bar in London for women only. The night had been wild and raucous but somehow, despite the craziness and sexiness of the night, Helene had left quite early. She'd had a beautiful flogging from a mistress named Morphia but then Morphia had gone on to play with some other women. Helene was missing Luna, didn't know where Michael had got to and had had a small argument with Malus a few days earlier that hadn't yet been resolved, so she simply left the club. *I'll get in touch with the lovely Morphia again soon...*

As she left the station, Helene realised that being in a fetish club was not the most sensible place to have spent time when she was feeling sensitive. *I'm not as special as I think I am. I still feel emotions and pain, and try to run from them as much as anybody else. Why do I sometimes feel I should be above it all just because I practice Witchcraft? If anything, it makes my life harder!* There had been a few other witches at Club Purr and Helene was glad to have met them, even if she hadn't really enjoyed the night. These other witches were also magical activists, from the Dionysian Underground, so she probably had a lot in common with them and would meet them again soon no doubt.

Deciding to go somewhere random, Helene had jumped on the first morning train to Brighton with the plan to go and look at the sea. Watching the sea was like watching clouds or staring into a fire. There was something deeply hypnotic about it, something that allowed Helene to feel connected to nature which in turn allowed her to see her life from a fresh perspective. *I wonder if everybody has the same ability to heal themselves just by staring at the sea... If the element of water is associated with emotions then I guess the sea is the best place to explore the emotions I'm currently dealing with.*

She strolled slowly downhill along the street towards the beach and watched as seagulls and chip wrappers flew about in the wind above her head. There were plenty of people up early - milkmen, shop owners opening their stores, delivery vehicle drivers as well as the dregs from the night before - party people making their way home.

Helene topped a crest where she could finally see the sea before her and picked up her pace in order to get there a bit faster. She passed a big clock tower which told her it was 7:20am. A group of young adults were dancing under the tower and throwing bits of kebab at each other and generally having a laugh.

Helene wondered briefly at what age people stopped considering themselves to be young and started talking condescendingly about 'the youth of today'. She was glad she didn't automatically judge the youths as menaces, as much as she was glad they hadn't thrown bits of kebab at her.

So many people are so judgmental, but isn't being judgmental the biggest problem we have in this world? The patriarchs and politicians all very cleverly making us judge each other and thereby we are divided and conquered. Well sod that...

Just before Helene reached the beach, she passed a newsagent and had a quick squiz at the headlines - some British soldier was being court-martialled for abusing Iraqi prisoners. *Well of course they are going to turn abusive if you send them away from their families and friends and tell them to invade and occupy a strange and foreign people. How can we be outraged if they are simply doing what they are instructed to do?* She had a closer look at the newspaper - the soldier's mother was decrying the prime minister as being a war criminal. *Well yeah, of course, doesn't that go without saying? Those poor boys thrown out there to kill or be killed so fatcats here can get oil wealth. They sign up to defend us because they love our country, and their love and goodwill is completely abused. Oh my god. It is so obviously a disgusting world we live in. Full love and power to the soldiers who refuse their orders.*

They are the true heroes. I wish I had time to help the refusers organise themselves. Now there's a cause I could really commit to.

Helene finally reached the beach and looked out to the slightly misty sea. *Mmmm.* She took a deep breath and took the whole vision in. The sea went out forever and ever. Small waves rolled in over a slightly choppy sea. There were seagulls squabbling over scraps of food and a vast tapestry of stones covered the beach. Helene wondered briefly why they had stones instead of sand and wondered if this was a feature of the beach, or a problem. She walked down the ramp and onto the promenade. A number of well wrapped-up people were working with shovels, collecting the stones that had fallen off the beach and onto the path. *Great job! Wouldn't it be wonderful if I had a job that could be something useful in the community. Something like cleaning up or beautifying the place... something with an activist edge to it... Yeah, that'd be great...*

Helene looked out to the pier and watched as small waves crashed against it. She thought back to the newspaper headline she had just read. *Community work would be so much better than being in the armed forces. Fuck that. I think I will get involved in one of those community groups supporting refusing soldiers. It's the least I can do to make the world better... the least I can do short of organising a revolution... Ha!*

As Helene walked along the path by the beach, a door under the ramp opened and a group of about ten people walked out, laughing and cheering. They all wore swim caps, bathers and what appeared to be wetsuit shoes. *Oh my god, they're going for a swim? It must be minus ten degrees in there!* A few more people came out of the door similarly attired. One was carrying a pair of flippers. *What a bunch of mentalists! They'll get pneumonia!* They all seemed quite excited about their morning swim. Helene pulled her coat around herself much closer as the thought of going anywhere near the icy-looking water instantly made her feel much colder.

As they all walked past her, one man in the group stopped for a moment and made eye contact with her. *A witch!* Helene and this man looked at each other for a few moments as they recognised each other as part of something bigger. She instantly knew that this was a man who practised magic and that he could see the same in her. Smiles spread across both their faces in recognition. It was a timeless and powerful moment before the man turned and joined his colleagues walking towards the sea.

Wow, they say some people are born witches but I've always known I wasn't born anything. But all this practising of magic has suddenly made me able to connect with another! This is going to be a whole new world for me! That's brilliant!

Helene looked out to sea as the group hesitated - for only a few seconds - and then variously dived and jumped into the sea. Some let out squeals and shouts. Yes, it was definitely cold.

Well if those mentalists are brave enough to dive into ice, there's no reason I can't be brave enough to do what I really want – to encourage evolution and revolution and psychedelic consciousness. She watched the group in the water split apart and swim in different directions. *But revolution is so bullshit. We are so scattered and without any means of organising ourselves. With our rights and community having been stripped from us piece by piece over the last several hundred years, it's impossible to start living as we want immediately. What we need is a date in the future when we can - all of us – all six or seven billion of us – agree to start living our True Wills. Ha! And there's a flying pig.* Helene used her imagination to visualise a pig flying across the cloudy sky. She mentally slowed it down and brought it towards her. When it was close (and she was sure no-one was in ear-shot) she asked it, "little piggy, you fly so well but only in my imagination. Is the saving of our world only ever going to be in my imagination also?"

The pig hovered facing Helene and answered, "if that is where you leave it, yes... Or if you weren't afraid of looking like a Fool, then perhaps you could set it free. Oink! Oink!" And with that the pig flew off and vanished under the pier. Helene saw that some of the group of swimmers were swimming around the pier, which was actually quite a long way.

What we need is a date. Another Guy Fawkes day like in V For Vendetta? That could work, but what year? Helene stepped onto the stony beach and started walking towards the water. She watched as a few small waves rolled in. *It will be winter solstice in two months. That would be a great day to rise up! But there is no time to organise it. How about next year? The problem is there is nothing special about that date. Meanwhile our freedoms continue to erode. Fuck it.*

She bent to pick up a shiny stone and walked further along the beach. *The year after? The year after that?* She counted the swimmers in the water. There were 12 of them. *Winter solstice 2012, that could work.* The date rang some kind of bell in her head. *2012... 2012... Oh fuck yeah, that is the day the Mayan calendar comes to an end. Loads of people already believe that date is somehow special. Maybe we could latch onto it and share it? That's the way of Fool Sorcery after all. To go with whatever is there and to embrace other people's myths that are useful or beautiful or both.* Helene watched as another small wave rolled in and the first of the swimmers started getting out of the water. *Yes, I'll talk to some friends and see if they are up for organising something... anything... a ritual or a protest or anything that can be used to promote this.*

She saw a shiny black rock that caught her eye, picked it up and absent-mindedly discarded the first stone she had. *I wish V For Vendetta was real. That was brilliant. But I'm no superhero, just an ordinary lass from North London.* Another group of swimmers got out of the water. *Well, no harm in trying. It'll be a fun project even if I do make a twat of myself. Ha!*

Helene wondered briefly if the swimming witch would be into the idea. Too shy to approach and ask, she turned away from the swimmers and started walking along the beach in the other direction. *Yes, winter solstice 2012 sounds like a good project but as long as I keep in the here-and-now as well. I mustn't lose sight of making the most of each moment.*

As she walked along the beach she noticed a group of very brightly clad people, rugged up quite warmly and standing on the shore. From the distance she was at and from behind, one of them looked surprisingly like Luna. She took a closer look and saw that the group was half-solemn and half laughing out loud. They were passing around a bottle and pouring shots out of it for each other. Helene stopped to watch and saw that each of them said a few words. *It is obviously a beach-front wake of some kind. That's kinda nice.* That it was a wake was confirmed to her when the woman who looked like Luna pulled out a ceramic jar and opened it, allowing an ash genie to scatter into the wind.

67. EULOGY FOR ROBERT ANTON WILSON

<Peter J. Carroll>

More than 30 years ago when I was a poor student in London I found a part of the Illuminatus trilogy in a second-hand bookshop in the Charing Cross road. I can still remember picking it up, looking at the yellow submarine surfacing on the cover and getting excited by the blurb on the back and frontispiece. After that I read everything I could find that Robert Anton Wilson wrote. I even forked out for new books. When I went to India and built a boat I named it the Leif Erickson.

A decade or more on, I had the honour of meeting Bob for two evenings at his place in California. All the time I couldn't help thinking this guy is about as old as my Dad, but his ideas are a generation ahead of their time. He was witty, warm, and brilliant and a massively influential giant of the counterculture. He will be sorely missed.

As this is the bar, treble Jameson's Irish whiskies all round (Bob's favourite), for his wake.

68. MORGAN SWEETS, PIPPINS AND CRABS <Profth>

Dear friends, today I have a short history for your perusal.

Few there are now who have tasted that now extinct drug Avalon Rotgut.

This is the story of a lifetime. To condense it into such few words will create such simplifications and inaccuracies as to make even me blush. Remember, friends, it is the lesson that is important and let the embarrassment be mine alone.

As usual, the picture contains five hidden faces so keep your wits about you.

As it was said then … "Are you sitting comfortably? Then I'll begin!"…

Each winter they carpeted the floors of the two large attic rooms, each carpet separated from its neighbour by a quarter inch of personal space, like commuters on a rush hour train.

Morgan Sweets: mild and sweet, white candy floss wrapped in a golden shell. Orange Pippins: small, red, crisp, sharp and full flavored. Crabs: the wildings, tiny, green, sour, inedible yet still an essential component of the array.

In spring, the ranks now withered, flaccid, near to rotting, were returned to their willow baskets for a trip to the press. We turned the capstan and watched the amber flow through the wooden slats. Fermentation, then to the giant oak barrel that represented that year's 'home use' production of North Somerset Cider.

After dinner on rainy summer days, the men folk sat with pint mugs of the previous year's strong, sour brew, whilst the women cleared and cleaned.

"You may leave the table now children."

We thankfully relaxed our ramrod poses on the high hard elm settle and moved quietly through the rambling limestone farmhouse.

Two flights of stairs led us up to the attic rooms where on one side, under the eaves, inaccessible all winter, lay our treasure trove. The prize possession here was an early wooden wind-up gramophone with similarly old records. Most of these were African American shanties sung by Anglo Saxons dressed as golliwogs. (If you want to hear a sad story, ask your grandparents what golliwogs were.) Our favourite tunes were 'The Laughing Policeman', 'The Red Red Robin goes bob bob bobbing along' and the unlikely, 'It ain't a gonna rain no more no more.' Boxes of family memorabilia, early newspapers and discarded toys created a magic space to spend our rainy days until autumn's deluge of Morgan Sweets, Pippins and Crabs submerged it once again.

In those right wing nationalistic times the recipe was set:

1. A small number of landowners and businessmen (almost all men), who sat in relative comfort, planned and campaigned and watched to see that everyone else saluted correctly.

2. The women and the working classes, who labored tirelessly.

3. Small quantities of goods were produced overseas by Africans, Indians or Chinese, who were mostly paid by being taught English and Christianity.

Surprising how few noticed the sourness of the brew.

Then came the time of revolutions.

The women said, "for many years we have had suffrage, yet still we suffer as second class citizens. Let us take some power for ourselves."

The African Americans said, "for many years we have had freedom from slavery, yet we are still enslaved as second class citizens. Let us take some power for ourselves."

The working classes said, "we are comfortable in our work, but if our work brings us no comfort or rest, we will rest from our work."

The school children said, "in school we are subject to hardships and discipline. After school, we are expected to join the army for more hardships and discipline. We will not obey the teachers or the Generals. We do not wish to harm our fellow man."

The Children Of The Apple said, "we reject the sweet insipid cider of the factories. We reject the sour cider of our parents. We reject the exploitation and destruction of Mother Earth. We will go in search of new recipes. We will add chillies to the chocolate and LSD to the soft drinks. We will bring a kaleidoscope of new flavors to all inhabitants of the planet."

The Governments were worried, but not about the apple people. After a slur campaign by the press, few complained when the latter were juiced. But against all odds, their words remained in people's thoughts.

The Governments were worried by the other discontents who had the suffrage to render them unemployed.

A group of influential merchants heard of the Governments' worries. They said, "let us research this thoroughly, maybe there is a way to help the Governments that will bring riches and power to ourselves."

So the merchants formed a foundation of men considered wise in the ways of business; and in the ways of business, the foundation prepared a report. That report contained tens of thousands of pages but the gist of it ran like this:

The revolutions were only occurring in highly developed countries.

The different groups were seen as calling for more sweetness and this could be equated with having more material possessions.

The undeveloped countries had a huge wealth of resources and could provide huge amounts of material possessions in return for a small amount of pocket money and some second-hand clothes.

The Governments of the developed countries were not allowing this to happen. They feared the destruction of their industries and that their people would no longer be governable.

The advice of the report was that Governments should allow importation unhindered and that they should tell their people, "you will soon be rich and have all the possessions you crave. In return you must allow small reductions to your rights and freedoms and undertake a general restructuring of your workplace."

After a few years of this regime the people of the developed nations, regardless of race or gender, had more possessions than they could use. They were also hemmed in by rules and regulations and they were subservient, lest the next restructuring should see them destitute.

Meanwhile, many of the people had heard the Apple Children's call but they were divided amongst themselves. Some mixed up the story with that of the foundation and created the 'Children of the Morgan Sweet', mixing bread with milk and maple syrup with cauliflower. They said, "Do What Thou Wilt", meaning follow your dreams, but their dreams were sugar, without savour or edge so they could generate no power.

'And the people bowed and prayed to the neon god they made.'

The people bought Apples and they bought IBMs. They bought the means to access great knowledge but then they had to spend their time restructuring for they were not independent of the foundation.

The people bought ITN and MTV and brightly-painted worlds of entertainment, parties and sex. They ran from entertainment to party and onwards at speed never finding paint bright enough to hide that they were grey. They ran to sporting fixtures where they could cry with a loud voice without ever being able to speak.

And the people bought tickets on planes and boats and the races mingled. The food of all nations was there for the tasting. They said, "the dreams of the Apple Children are here. We will have Padang chilli tonight, stir-fried ice cream tomorrow and nori rolls at the weekend."

And the people asked, "why is it when we are a family, when our neighbours to the left send sugar to their families in the Philippines and our neighbours to the right send trousers to their families in Chad? Why is it now the voices in the wilderness still cry out?"

And the voices in the wilderness cried out…

"In the past we rejected heroes because they thought they were better than us. Now we need their abilities, to stand while others run, and to forge community. We will not now bow down to them, for they are us, but we will cherish their abilities."

"In the past, we were Luddites out to destroy. Now we must be moderates, buying what is necessary, but not in excess. We will buy with care for the environment and for the well-being of the producers."

"In the past, we called for all to enter into the fullness of taste. Now we know that if each generation can nurture enough heroines, they can hold the pattern secure. It then only remains to grasp the story of the apples: for each individual to find the proportion of Morgan Sweets, Pippins and Crabs that is most satisfactory for their own taste and well-being."

And that, my friends, is the end of today's sermon from the Apple Grove Ecotopian Church.

Before we end I have two short announcements.

Next week's Prime Minister will be Penny from the Nottingham Slab Excavators. Like, heavenly, ducks.

Next week's sermon In'shallah comes from Ali of the Akbar UR Sufi Collective.

Feel your connection to the Earth, my friends, and walk strong in your power.

Together we recited the creed, "I love and respect the weirdness I see in you as you love and respect the weirdness you see in me," then made love to our neighbours and walked hand in hand into the garden.

Outside...

The sun was shining.
The worms were cultivating the rich, dark soil.
The slugs were wrecking the cabbages.

69.
AUTUMN LEAVES

Michael caught the train out to Epping Forest. *Fuck all this. I do not want to deal with it. There's surely another way to make the world better rather than fucking around with the Illuminati and Serpents and other imaginary conspiracies. I am not going to spend my life in paranoia. I am going to sort this out once and for all.* He got off the train and marched into the woods.

Earlier in the afternoon, he had very determinedly packed his bag with candles, jars, matches, a small magnetic compass, a black hoodie (which would do fine for a robe), snacks and water and some blankets in case it was cold. He also had his ritual box, made of wood and about the size of a shoebox with a large rune engraved into it.

Fuck being haunted by my fear. I know some of this myth is real. But I'm also damned sure that there's a hell of a lot of bullshit in it all... dangerous bullshit. His march into the woods slowed as he started noticing the nature around him. The forest floor was blanketed with autumn leaves and there were dazzling pockets of multi-hued mushrooms scattered about, almost as if by design.

Nature – this is where real magic is. The Illuminati will never take control of this world. Nature is too strong. And human nature, when we overcome fear, is irrepressible! Some of the bullshit is true. Our species is very easily controlled by fear. But a determined few who overcome our fears can really make a difference.

He stopped suddenly when he saw a butterfly dancing in a downward spiral in front of him. *I will follow the signs of nature and this is as good a sign as any. I'll do my ritual here.* The butterfly landed on a bright yellow leaf on the forest floor and Michael knelt down to watch it closely. The design on its back, in black, orange and brown could easily be overlooked as the creature blended into its background. It was very beautiful and Michael thought briefly that if there were in fact faeries then they probably were very good friends with pretty creatures like this. He looked at the design on its back more closely, like two tattoos of eyes looking back at him, grinning. *Such a beautiful thing. Wow. This is real magic: tuning into and observing the nature within and without.*

Still kneeling, he visually scanned the immediate area ensuring it was suitable. There were a few flat places where he would be able to put the jars so they would sit level. The wind was minimal, yet there was enough for him to be aware of it against his face. He took his bag off and took out a sandwich which he ate slowly whilst watching the butterfly. He took a number of deep breaths. *Nothing is true. There is no Illuminati.* Then a drink from his water bottle. *I'm going to work some nature magic and find a path in my life for myself. Everything is permitted. No more gods or goddesses or serpents. Real power is in nature, in the elements, in my body and right between my eyes and behind my nose. I don't need a fucking serpent to give me an apple! I'll get my own!*

With a few more deep breaths and a huge determination to do this properly, Michael put the water bottle to one side and took out the black hoodie. He eased himself into it slowly and pulled the hood over his head. *This is just the spot. I need to be rid of all this bollocks once and for all.*

After retrieving his compass and determining where East was, he put candles into four jars and placed them carefully into the four directions. *Right, I'm ready.*

“I'm ready,” he told the butterfly, which promptly lifted off the ground and flew into an upward spiral. Upward and upward he watched it fly until it was lost in the mostly naked tree tops. “Goodbye spiralling faerie! It was wonderful while it lasted!”

He retrieved the wooden box from his backpack, looking again at the Dragon Tree Rune[13] carved into it.

13 More info about the Dragon Tree Rune here: http://www.dragonnetwork.org/magic/dtr/dtr.htm

From the box, he took out a binding of feathers collected from several different species of bird. He carefully planted their base so they stood, erect and slightly fluttering, near the jar in the East. Next he retrieved a censor with some charcoal blocks and put this down near the candle in the South. He lit the blocks so they produced a small flame. From the box, he retrieved a small blue bottle and removed its illustrious cork. It was half-filled with water that he'd collected from the Chalice Well in Glastonbury. Carefully, he stood this near the jar in the West. Lastly, he took out a half-shiny, half-rough black and brown rock. He'd found it near an ancient burial site and it had called to him with its rough surface showing a face that appeared to change mood. He planted this rock so it stood upright near the jar in the North.

He then put the box, still open, in the East.

Upon retrieving his matches, he put his bag to one side. "I'm ready," he told the woods once more. He lit the four candles and stood in the centre of the circle. The late afternoon sun gave the forest a surreal ambience and the gentle breeze stirred the leaves ever-so-slightly.

He stepped forward to the East and spread his arms wide. *No gods, no serpents. Just the beauty and power of raw nature.* He took a number of deep breaths.

"I call on the Spirits of the East: the element of Air! I invoke the powers of intellect and mind; consciousness; wisdom, forethought, planning. As the sun dawns on each new day, so I rise up too, feeling refreshed and empowered. I call on the symbols of spring: fertility, new growth, the beginnings of warmth within the Wheel of the Year. Spirits of the East, be with me in this ritual."

He took a few more deep breaths ensuring he could feel the breeze on his face. He bent and picked up the feather binding, waved it high in the air and called, "Spirit of the East! Hail and welcome!"

Upon replanting the feathers, he turned to the South and spread his arms wide.

"I call on the Spirits of the South: the element of Fire! I invoke the powers of passion and energy; vibrancy, raw power, lust. As the sun peaks during each day, so do I peak in my powers, feeling strong and excited. I call on the symbols of summer: long sunny days, festivals, the intensity of mid-summer daylight within the Wheel of the Year. Spirits of the South, be with me in this ritual."

Michael bent down and leant over the burning censor. He waited a few moments until it crackled, then he called out, "Spirits of the South! Hail and Welcome!"

The censor crackled some more before Michael stood up and went to face the West with his arms spread wide.

"I call on the Spirits of the West: the element of Water! I invoke the powers of emotion and fluidity; tears, blood and intuition. The power to move around obstacles and regroup my selves. As the sun sets each day, so do I find time for reflection, for feeling my emotions. I call on the energies of the gentle stream and the enraged storm; the still lake and the passionate ocean. I call on the symbols of Autumn: of harvest, of the journey inwards, autumn leaves and shortening days within the Wheel of the Year. Spirits of the West, be with me in this ritual!"

Michael went to the jar in the West and picked up the small blue bottle. He splashed a few drops onto his face and onto the forest floor. "Spirits of the West! Hail and Welcome!"

He stood still for a moment and felt the drops of water run down his face. Then he turned to the North with his arms spread wide.

"I call on the Spirits of the North: the element of Earth! I invoke the powers of grounding and stability; of stillness, of connection to the Earth and self-knowledge. I call on the power to stand my ground and find my own path. I find within my body my connection to the sacred. As the sun is not in sight at midnight, so I find the power to enter my own darkness with confidence and grounded self-knowledge. I call on the images of the mountain and the desert, the grassland and the forest. I seek and find real determination that comes from within. I call on the symbols of Winter: of darkness and short short days within the Wheel of the Year. Spirits of the North, be with me in this ritual!"

Michael bent down to come eye to eye with his magic stone. He saw a look of contemplation upon its face. He looked beyond it and into the forest and called out, "Spirits of the North! Hail and Welcome!"

He then returned to the centre of the circle. "I call on the fifth sacred thing. I call on the spirit that binds the other elements in nature and in myself." He stood still for a few moments then called out, "Fifth sacred thing! Hail and Welcome!"

~

As this was a ritual for grounding, Michael's focus would be in the north. He turned to face that direction and spoke to the forest.

"Spirit of the North! I am so glad you came to hear my words and feel my energy. I have been deeply troubled by scattered thoughts, tumultuous paranoia and intense, pervasive fear. I call on you, Spirit of the North, Spirit of Earth to help me find grounding within myself. I call on Earth without that I might find Earth within."

He took many deep breaths and sent his consciousness down through his body, out of the soles of his feet and deep into the Earth. He stood in meditation for several minutes feeling the power of the earth below him. "Spirits of Earth, help me be rid of this emotional plague and this mental anguish."

Connecting deeper into the earth, Michael visualised that he had roots which went down into the Earth's core. "Spirits of Earth, help me to find my true path and fill it with courage that I call forth from within myself."

Along with the visualisation of roots, in his imagination he *felt* the roots and their connection to the core. "I send all my fear and angst into the Earth where it might be transformed."

He let his roots mingle with the Earth's core and felt them tap into its power. His imagination turned into sensation until he could actually feel the deep, powerful connection. Using more than his imagination, he pulled energy up from the Earth's core, slowly but surely. "By the Spirits of Earth, I transform my pain and paranoia into powerful grounding." He pulled nourishment up his roots and into his body. It felt good; wholesome.

"By the power of the element Earth, I hereby banish my fear and angst and find my true power - the power of my own nature and the nature of my own power." He felt a rush as the power of the Earth took hold of him. It was as if he were a tree, deeply grounded, stable and unmovable. Yes, he would be rid of the angst and fear. He would follow his own destiny and not let silly ideas move him. "Dear forest, there may be some truths in all of these stories, but I have the power to follow my own will. I have no need for these myths that generate fear and loathing. If anything, I have learnt that I can have complete self-determination. I do not need to break rules to prove a point, but nor do I have any need to follow anyone else's rules. I am Michael and I am of the Earth."

Michael took several deep breaths allowing the Earth energy to peak. He felt grounded, whole, determined.

The ritual was complete.

~

After Michael thanked the elements and closed the circle, he took a number of deep breaths and took in the sights of the darkening forest. A smile spread across his face as the butterfly returned from the tree tops and landed in the centre of where the ritual circle had been. He took a drink of water, packed his gear away and collected an autumn leaf from the ground.

Michael spent some time holding his box just thinking about the world and creation and about having the determination to follow his True Will. Life was going to get good again. He could feel it. He took an apple from his bag. "See! No serpents! I've got my own apple! I am free! I am free..."

He flicked his hood off, put the leaf in the box and bit into the apple. He walked slowly through the woods leaving the butterfly to do whatever it is butterflies do.

70. THE CREATION OF PANDORA'S BOX <Koogie Smith>

That little girl
So trim and neat
Articulate and sweet
She made a box
So her parents would go: 'What a feat!'

And the Great North Wind
He raged and blustered
He blew and fought
Tore up and down
The little girl's pleats.

He was big and she small
She was scared overall
He would split her right there in two!
One so powerful
She had to contain…

"Oh Great North Wind!
Why so angry be you?
You should be calm
Just follow my Arms
For there is peace in my box."

And the Wind was headstrong.

He blew it, flew in,
Squeezed into the mysterious still.
She shut the lid
And in the darkness he was hid.

BE OH EX!

And at the loss of the Wind
The Rain she cried and grieved
Her tears were everywhere.
They filled the rivers wide
And they filled up the salty seas.

The Rain's feelings ran so deep
The girl was scared
The waves would rise and drown her!
One so emotional
She had to contain...

"Oh sad and mournful Rain
Why so overwhelmed be you?
You should be bright and cheery
Just follow my Grin
For there is happiness in this box."

And the Rain wanted an end
She gushed and poured herself in,
Stopped bleeding for the safe and dry.
The girl shut the lid
And in the darkness the Rain was hid.

BE OH EX!

And the Sun came out.
He burnt with passion for the Rain,
Hot for Everywhere she might be.
Roaring and whimpering,
His strength could not reach inside the box.

The Sun was so fierce
The girl was scared
He would burn her, consume her!
One so sexual
She had to contain…

"Oh raging hot Sun
Why do you roar so loudly?
You should be cool and calm
Just follow my Gaze
For there is harmony in this my box."

And the Sun longed for the Wind and the Rain
He shone, shot himself in,
Went dim so in the dark he might see.
The girl shut the lid
And in the darkness the Sun was hid.

BE OH EX!

Then the Earth turned to Dust
As indeed She must
With no warmth, no growth
No Sun, Wind or Rain.
Still and Silent and Waiting…

And when the girl could no longer feel
She was scarred, sacred, scared
Of what she alone had done.
The girl shut her lids
And in the darkness she was hid.

Spiralling in the wondrousness of Space
Was a small, perfect box
With intricate words and deeply carved fears.
It was cradled and rocked
And decorated with the HOPE

That one day it would learn to Open it Self…

And Death came along
With her Arms, her Grin and her Gaze.
She spoke to the fears with her tenderest words
"Create Be Open Be Me"

So she opens her lids
And in the dark and the light she is no longer hid.

She is the powerful North Wind
The infinite pouring of Rain.
She is the sexual Sun,
Earth Maiden, Mother, Crone
In Spirit the girl is All One
Alone
All One
Alone
All One
Alone

ALL ONE!

71.
THE ORIGINAL BOX

Michael sat on his back patio, rocking gently on a three foot high soft-cushioned settee. He was looking up and outwards, trying to spot the different constellations in this strange Southern sky. *That one looks like Orion - except upside down.* He imagined a line extending out from Orion's Belt to where Sirius should be and found it there.

It had only been a few months ago that he thought there was something special about Sirius. He had read as much as he could about it and had discovered that across the globe, cultures had maintained various strange beliefs about it. Michael had written extensively in his diaries about Sirius. Diaries which, of course, had been stolen. He'd bought a new silk-covered diary upon arriving here, which was safely kept in the original box that the thieves had completely overlooked.

Michael slowly rose from the chair and walked through the patio door into his house, recalling all the angst he had felt about the diaries. He remembered the crazy rituals he had done with Malus, thought back to the drugs he had taken and the madness he had felt. He was much more grounded and much happier here, thousands of miles away from England, thousands of miles from the insanity. He had learnt that the harder he looked for synchronicities, the more he would find. It was therefore an easy decision, upon first arriving in Byron Bay, that he would simply stop looking for synchronicities. He had felt so much better since.

As good as I feel, I will never know what happened to my diaries, and I think I am probably safest not knowing.

For a moment, he thought about his ex-girlfriend Bernie. She had tried in vain to warn him of the danger he was getting into, but he hadn't listened. At the time, nearly a year ago, he had decided to leave her because the life of a conspiracy hunter had seemed so much more exciting than pandering to a worry-sick girlfriend. She had stopped answering his phone calls long ago and he thought better than to try to get in contact with her again. *Maybe one day...*

Michael retrieved a home-spun wooly jumper from his room, put it on and walked into the kitchen to put a pot of water on the stove. He waited patiently, staring into the water as it slowly heated. He was glad he had chosen a grounded, Earth-based spirituality rather than madness. In Byron Bay village, not far from the bungalow he now lived in, there were no signs of serpents or Illuminati or conspiracies, but there was a beautiful beach, a very friendly, down-to-Earth feeling and a wonderful community atmosphere. There were a number of covens in Byron Bay but Michael hadn't bothered to get in touch with any of them. *I'm more effective on my own anyway. I'll live my life to the fullest possible and stay grounded and grow my own veg. That is real activism.*

This is what life is all about. We create the world through our perception of it. With that in mind, I'm going to create the the happiest, funniest and most romantic reality I can based on the signals I comprehend. I am going to override all the fear programs fed to me and live in a stable, friendly world.

He looked into the water. *A watched pot does boil,* Michael reminded himself. He made himself a cup of tea with full-cream milk and a tea-spoon of honey, then walked back out onto the patio to his favourite chair. He eased himself into it, started rocking slowly, and leant back to watch the magnificent radiance of the stars above.

72. THE REAL STORY OF THE CATHARS

<Ramsey Dukes>

Fiat Lux

We are living in a politically stable time.

Although there are changes of government, these are always between 'centre' parties where the only significant difference lies in the ebb and flow of public opinion between greater market freedom and greater interventionism and social control.

This stability has furthered scientific progress, a happy co-operation between pure science (broadly funded by the public) and technology (mainly sponsored by business). Outstanding examples of the former are those recent breakthroughs in cosmology and fundamental 'theories of everything'. Examples of the latter include dramatic developments in parallel processing, bio and quantum computing.

The outstanding example of their co-operation has been the Cosmos Project, where sufficient computing power is at last available for the physicists to model the quantum and physical processes involved in the creation of a universe similar to ours, demonstrating once and for all the universality of their theories. What's more, they have been able to search the emerging structure to identify that this virtual universe does indeed contain solar systems and planets like ours, manifesting similar geological and physical processes.

Not all sciences are faring so well, however. Major advances in genetic science have led to a public backlash, and a lengthy swing away from market forces towards a more socialist regulatory framework. Biotechnology is bristling with exciting possibilities but strict governmental and legal controls have been blocking further empirical research.

That explains why there is suddenly so much extra money available for the Cosmos Project - for it has now been agreed to seed an earth-like planet with DNA similar to the earliest forms of life on our own planet. Not only should this provide a virtual biosphere for evolutionists to test their theories, but also it raises the liberating possibility of practising genetic engineering in a totally contained virtual reality with absolutely no risk of contaminating the real world.

The fact that leading biotech companies are keen to sponsor the venture is hardly surprising. What has caused a stir is the very generous donation made by our leading movie mogul, Joseph H. Vaughan-Hoover Jr.

Genesis

Public attitudes to genetic engineering have indeed begun to soften, now that experimentation can take place in complete safety. What is more, radical new cures for fatal diseases and new, drought-resistant food crops are already in the pipeline.

Prosperity is on the increase, there is greater faith in commercial ethics, and the public will very likely vote for 'minimal' government in the next election. Except for one small problem - the hominids.

Evolution in the Cosmos Project has now led to hairless apes with distinctly human characteristics, and this is fuelling a new public debate on science and ethics. Should the Project be allowed to continue? What is the status of an intelligent humanoid life form within a virtual universe? Is it truly self-conscious or just a machine? Would it possess rights in our real world, and what would be its legal status?

The simple answer might seem to be to pull the plug on the Project - it has certainly repaid the initial investment several times over.

Unfortunately, however, the public interest has been so great that many consider the virtual 'Earth' to be a meaningful ecological system. So, stopping the project would amount to an unacceptable destruction of an entire and unique biosphere.

For many members of the public, it isn't even permissible to selectively prune this biosphere - for example by destroying the hominid population in order to block the evolution of virtual humanity. The Project must go on - but somehow remain under careful control.

Government advisers recognise that the project cannot continue indefinitely. It will, however, take years for their spin-doctors to bring public opinion round to an acceptable termination. Meanwhile, the immediate ethical crisis must be contained - and Dr Michael Eden has been put in charge of the situation.

The Garden of Eden

Dr Eden proposes to create a sealed reservation on virtual Earth (which promptly earned the nickname 'Eden's Garden') where hominid evolution could continue under carefully monitored and controlled conditions, while being blocked elsewhere.

Perhaps surprisingly, Joseph H. Vaughan-Hoover Jr. has just donated a large amount of money to the Eden Project.

The public are satisfied, a socialist government has been returned to power, and Dr Eden now has a small population of something just a step away from homo sapiens under his care.

But can we allow evolution to proceed? What is the legal and ethical status of any resulting human species? Will it ever be possible to terminate this extremely expensive project once it is peopled by recognisably intelligent and lovable life forms? But how can it be stopped before it has provided evidence to support the greatest miracles of evolution, namely the emergence of human intelligence, language, social structure and self-awareness?

Dr Eden has decided on an uneasy compromise - to breed selectively and allow just two humans to evolve, but not to breed further generations. In order to permit the most intimate exploration of the psychology of these proto-humans - and at the same time provide them with a certain measure of legal standing in the real world - their minds will be linked to those of two specially-trained researchers.

As explained in detail in Ramsey Dukes' book 'Words Made Flesh', these researchers cannot simply take over the bodies of the virtual humans with their own consciousness, as that would completely invalidate the scientific observation of their behaviour. Instead, the relationship between the two virtual people (now named Adam and Eve) and the researchers will be closer to that of horse and rider.

In effect, Adam and Eve will be fully autonomous, thinking beings in their world, but will each possess an inner 'guardian angel' or 'higher self' which will be the mind of the respective researcher. And it is this guardianship role which allows them a certain legal status in the real world - a status that still has to be formalised but which lies somewhere between that of a child and a licensed pet.

So successful is this approach that Dr Eden has now been nominated for a Nobel Prize. Through the eyes of Adam and Eve, enormous advances are being made, not only in the fields of evolution and human psychology, but also in the taxonomy of species.

How ironic that so much honour is falling on the shoulders of a quiet, unassuming figure like Dr Eden, while the notoriously brash and self promoting Joseph H. Vaughan-Hoover Jr. seems happy to remain quietly out of the limelight, despite his now considerable investment and support for the project!

Temptation and Fall

Actually, Vaughan-Hoover has been quite busy in his own way. He is currently wining and dining one of the top young government programmers working on the Cosmos Project and presenting an offer that is very hard to refuse.

"Let's face it, you earn peanuts! A man of your talent, your *genius* should not be postponing marriage on mere financial grounds."

A large sum of money is offered in return for something really rather naughty and utterly forbidden - Joseph H. Vaughan-Hoover Jr. wants to enter the Cosmos Project and make a very small and surely harmless little intervention in its virtual reality. To simplify what could be a very costly programming job, he modestly agrees to enter, not in angelic or even animal splendour, but in the minimalist body of a serpent - one adapted to speak human language.

"Pssst!"

Eve turns, startled, and sees the snake. She does not know enough to be more than a little surprised that a snake is able to talk. So it invites her over to its tree, and her curiosity completely obscures the uneasiness being felt by her Higher Self.

The snake pulls back the tree bark and reveals something she has never before seen - though we would instantly recognise the shape of a sophisticated computer workstation. Her Higher Self is screaming for attention, because it knows that this interface was only installed as a safety precaution for the researchers' own use in case of unforseen emergency - and Eve is supposed to remain utterly unconscious of its existence and role.

The screen shows a picture of an apple with a bite taken out - Eve recoils, as her Higher Self grabs just enough attention to make her cry "No! I am not allowed to touch the Apple!"

"Pity," says the snake, "Apples were chosen for this project specifically for their comparatively fool-proof multimedia software interface. But don't worry my dear, there's no need to touch anything! Your iris has been scanned for authentication so, as long as you just stand there, I can do all the necessary. Do you recognise who this is?"

Eve stared in puzzlement at the image of herself - something she had never before seen. She is surprised and fascinated to be told it is her, and she dances a little before the screen to see her every gesture mirrored in that image.

"OK! OK!" says the snake, "You've had your fun. Now watch carefully what I do. One tap on the screen and ... See this little control panel appears? You can't read what it says - you haven't learnt what these symbols mean - but don't worry, all you need to know is what happens when you tap this red blob at the top right. See, the writing has changed - it now says 'PUBERTY ACTIVATED' but no need to worry your pretty head with what that means. All I ask is this... How do you feel now I've done that?"

Eve is entranced. Breathing heavily, she runs her hands over her body, caressing her skin and purring. "I feel... different. I feel GREAT!" Her Higher Self is meanwhile going berserk, but what chance is there of steering its runaway steed away to safe pastures now!

Snake taps the screen again to reveal an image that Eve does recognise... "Hey! That's Adam!" she cries in delight.

"It is indeed. But tell me, how do you now *feel* about him?"

Eve licks her lips suggestively, her nostrils flare and her pupils dilate as she says, "I can't describe it. I feel really ... different."

Snake replies "how would you like it if Adam felt about *you* the same way you now feel about *him*?"

Eve is wild about the idea, and Snake is quick to remind her how easily it can be done - "just bring Adam to the Apple so his iris can be scanned, then one tap to reveal the control panel, one tap to activate puberty and ... Voila! The rest is pre-history!"

Eve's Higher Self tries desperately to connect with Adam's Higher Self to avert disaster, but in vain. All they succeed in doing is making Adam and Eve feel rather naughty, and that, alas, simply increases the overwhelming sense of fun that the couple are now enjoying.

Nor can they get away with it. It turns out that these carefully engineered proto human bodies are indeed fertile. It's another scientific breakthrough, but one that means that Eve is soon pregnant and there is an awful lot of explaining to do.

Exodus

Crisis - Dr Eden is sacking his two researchers.

Eve's Higher Self claims that a snake talked to Eve. As far as Dr Eden is concerned, this is certain proof that she is lying - because no snake in the virtual world (just like in the real world) has developed suitable vocal chords.

Soon, a virtual human child will be born and it too must be provided with a 'Higher Self' (Dr Eden, as a rationalist, hates this terminology - but it has caught on) - only Dr Eden's limited budget simply cannot afford the costs entailed in employing and training more staff for the role. For who knows how many future progeny will need to be cared for now the floodgates have been opened? It was one thing controlling the breeding of a species defined as sub-human, but now we have real problems.

Considering the enormous investment made by Joseph H. Vaughan-Hoover Jr., you might have expected him to be furious. Instead, he shows remarkable understanding. He is positively supportive. The tide is again turning and the public mood is once more growing favourable towards privatisation. But that is not what Joseph H. Vaughan-Hoover

Jr. wants (he insists), all he wants is to offer the best possible support.

So he holds a press conference that is destined to sway the course of public opinion. In it he argues that this whole predicament demonstrates the poverty of left-wing government thinking. "Here they are, holding back the most significant scientific project in the whole world, while they try to decide just how much of the taxpayers' money - *your* money - they can afford to spend on monitoring another virtual human." Then he drops his bombshell: "instead of costing money, this project could be *making* money! I know at least twenty very rich people who would pay a fortune for the privilege of entering Project Cosmos!"

And that is how the government finally lost control of the project to the newly formed Jahwe Corp. The sons and daughters of Adam and Eve need never be aborted for lack of a guardian angel - rich people are already queuing up for the experience. A 'human' lifetime in virtual reality amounts to a few weeks holiday in a virgin world - and what a world! What a holiday!

No wonder that Jahwe instructed the children of Adam to "go forth and multiply."

Numbers

The more virtual humans that are being born, the more income is generated and the greater the economy of scale. The cost of a holiday on CyberEarth is tumbling and reaching a wider and less sophisticated public.

The government, however, still has enough influence to challenge Jahwe Corp's monopoly, and Joseph H. Vaughan-Hoover Jr.'s empire is being split into several competing companies as more and more start-up ventures enter this lucrative field.

Advertisements scream 'ice age coming to an end! Massive population explosion already under way! Check our bargain holiday prices now!'

Some of the more sophisticated art-houses offer cultural fare: 'thrill to the birth of Neolithic cave-art!', but the general trend is down market: 'Iron age coming soon! Better weapons! Bigger battles! More slaughter! Book now or miss the action in this fabulous block-buster experience!'

It is not that commercial interests have gained real control of CyberEarth - it is still just as strictly non-interventionist as ever, the virtual humans still enjoy complete freedom of will.

What has happened is that creative directors are learning how to infect the world with mental viruses or memes. Abstract notions like Empire, Conquest, God, Justice etc. can be fed into the virtual population via the promptings of their "Higher Selves."

So, with enough marketing resources at his disposal, any sufficiently creative director has a significant chance of converting some minor tribe into a new religious impulse, or a major cultural influence, or a new empire builder. Premium prices will then be charged for 'incarnation' into this exciting new milieu. Yet the public still cry out for more.

Prophets Against Profits

The tide however, could be turning. There is increasing public unease about the psychological effects of holidaying in a primitive cyber-world. Is it really just emotional catharsis? A chance to learn bigger, tougher lessons than can be provided by a highly socialised and regulated culture? Or are we dragging our own population back into greedy primitivism? Corrupting our children with experiences from which our whole social fabric has been engineered to protect them?

So public health warnings now have to be provided. A system of classification is cobbled together. Posters read "Discover Greece - the Hellenic empire offers a fabulous cultural and philosophical experience. Certificate PG - contains some violence, major nudity and an absolutely terrible language." Another: "Thrill to the Roman Empire - contains considerable violence, little nudity, but major decadence. Not suitable for unaccompanied children," and so on.

Judges

Meanwhile, the entire business is sitting on an unexploded bomb. A slow running public enquiry into the Fall has lead to clear evidence of intervention, and the evidence points to the very founding father of the industry, Joseph H. Vaughan-Hoover Jr.

Indeed, it now emerges that the entire glamour world of CyberHoliday escapism is apparently rotten to the core, owing its existence to a single criminal act by JHVH Jr. The voice of public morality is rising and threatening the very foundations of our number one economic driver.

When, they ask, is intervention in a virtual reality not a criminal act?

Only when it is undertaken for purely altruistic ends by a democratically elected body and in such a way that it does not in any way restrict the free running of the software - ie the experience of virtual 'free will'.

A New Testament

So, it is decided to fund a programme of avatars - worthy elected individuals with no commercial interest, who will incarnate fully into the virtual world (rather than simply mounting a virtual human for a lifetime). Their mission is to establish themselves as wise teachers and explain the illusionary nature of their reality - while preaching greater toleration, love and peace.

From a commercial viewpoint, this programme has a definite niche appeal to a few idealists, utopians and moral fundamentalists. But it spells disaster for a mass market that seeks the thrills and crises of a virtual reality to provide all that is missing in their everyday life.

Under the present glare of publicity, there is little chance of direct counter-intervention by the big corporations, but there are ways and means of adding spin to any message. One small creative team, Saul City Productions, is already transforming the Christian message from "love thy neighbour, for the kingdom of heaven is at hand" into "do not tolerate those who would resist this holy law."

For a few virtual centuries Saul City, its subsidiaries and strategic allies, vie with the Goth Empire, Attila, and other production houses for market dominance. But thanks to the creative genius of leading concept designer Cathy o' Licke, it is the Pauline version of Christianity that is coming out on top in CyberEurope - the most lucrative prime real estate incarnatory region of CyberEarth.

The Cathar Rebellion

Cathar Holidays is the opposition's last serious contender. Yet it has no public funding and meets nothing but opposition from the major corporations.

Cathar Holidays was created as a co-operative by a group of concerned parents, and it is to grow to a short-lived but significant public movement. It attracts a public who voted for, and freely contributed to, the government's Christian Mission to CyberEarth, but who resent the way the Christ's message is being corrupted and turned into yet another mechanism for injecting violence, hatred and intolerance into CyberEarth.

Cathar Holidays encourages its members to incarnate into a particular culturally fertile region of CyberFrance, creating a critical mass of like-minded Higher Selves to resist the combined pressure of corrupting memes and innate animal instincts. They form communities to preach something closer to the original Christian message, to explain insofar as possible to a primitive culture that their world is an illusion based upon binary logic and driven by dualistic polarities injected to serve commercial exploitation but doing nothing for CyberEarth itself, nor the souls that incarnate into it. Far from "going forth to multiply" in order to create more seats in this Coliseum of Corruption, we should deny procreation, strive to reduce numbers and starve the devil of his souls.

It is a brave movement, but it fails to counter the very first lesson demonstrated by Joseph H. Vaughan-Hoover Jr. - namely that "sex sells." The humiliation of their defeat is underlined by the fact that The Simon de Montforte anti-Cathar Campaign has become the number one bestseller of all time and has already spawned a wave of imitations - Crusade, Crusade 2, with Crusade 3 to be launched this Summer.

Project Cosmos - A Review

The CyberVacation concept has become so fundamental to our way of life that it is easy to forget its history, origins and original aims.

With 97% of the population taking regular family or singles breaks on CyberEarth, with our real-world press and broadcast media seemingly dominated by stories and themes from this artificial world, it is hard to believe that it was started not so long ago as a government-funded scientific experiment designed to increase understanding of our own real world.

And yet, despite the objections of a small but vocal moral minority, it still represents much more than pure vicarious escapism.

It is easy to project the picture of a bloodthirsty sensation-seeking public - queuing up for a life in some war-zone, decadent society or culture of intolerance - but when you speak to actual individuals a different picture is equally present.

My neighbour was aghast when he discovered that his daughter (who was supposed to be going on a school outing to live the life of a devoted servant in the stable and serene environment of a CyberTibetan monastery) had actually played truant and lived thirty virtual years as a prostitute, thief and murderess in the docks of 18th century

CyberMarseilles. But when I spoke to his daughter, she told me that she loved the really tough incarnations for the very lessons of hardship and raw emotion they contained. "Daddy just doesn't want me to grow up!" was her claim, and she said she only passed her sociology finals on the strength of what she had learnt during that one heart-rending holiday.

Indeed, the Project is still very much a child of our times - a virtual battlefield on which the same old war between control and freedom is being played out.

On the one hand, there are the forces of market freedom - the apparent right to let the economy decide for itself, to provide the public with whatever it is prepared to pay for. On the other hand, there are the forces of social responsibility - the apparent need to regulate and enforce whatever the public is prepared to vote for.

Yet it also reflects the innate paradox of these polar viewpoints - that the so-called 'authoritarianism' of the government is actually an attempt to preserve the CyberWorld's own freedom to develop true to its programming, and therefore to continue to deliver valid, uncontaminated experimental data. While the "freedom" of the market in effect only delivers the freedom for the biggest players to control the game itself.

For these mighty corporations, CyberEarth plays the role of a hunting ground - they may not be able nor even desire to control it directly, but they can encourage prolific breeding of the game. And they can incarnate souls with strong 'higher' convictions, religious or philosophical beliefs, that will serve as 'beaters' to drive the game towards their blazing profit guns.

The Greening of CyberEarth

Is Project Cosmos, then, destined to continue in its current role as a battlefield for what must seem to its virtual inhabitants a sort of 'spiritual' struggle between pairs of opposing forces?

There are certainly overwhelming commercial pressures to maintain this state of affairs, but is it equally the will of our people?

A new grassroots movement is emerging which could provide a challenge to this status quo, or it could simply pass - just one more wavelet on the swell of public opinion between social control and market forces. The movement's keynote is 'sustainability'.

Instead of regarding the CyberEarth as a passive human construction - ever dependent upon our decisions whether to increase regulation or allow further exploitation - the sustainability movement argues that Project Cosmos has evolved a level of complexity and sophistication that is putting it beyond our ability to predict and regulate. As such, the movement has its roots in that early public belief that Project Cosmos was a valid ecological environment in its own right.

They also argue that, although chaotic in its complexity, the CyberEarth is a finite, bounded entity that is approaching the limits of its resources for exploitation by a voracious, unregulated entertainments industry.

Consider the success of WW Productions. Both World War 1 and World War 2 are sell-out blockbuster successes and there has been enormous public pressure for an early exploitation launch of World War 3. But even WW Productions itself has been holding back, because it recognises the inherent risk of the WW3 project - it could lead to so much flesh-deletion that the whole mass holiday market would be destroyed in one blockbuster finale. WW3 might even totally sterilise CyberEarth and return project Cosmos to its original role as a physical sciences experiment.

The sustainability movement also draws attention to the evolving sophistication of the virtual vehicles for incarnation - it points out that CyberEarth is now feeding back more than just public recreation, more than just scientific knowledge of evolution and physical systems. For CyberEarth has an increasing cultural impact on the real world too. Pieces by virtual composers - Mozart, Beethoven and Stockhausen to name recent examples - have already had hits in the real top 20. James

Joyce is the first CyberAuthor to have his works selected for the official school curriculum - admittedly only for the primary school course, but it marks a beginning. Our leading atomic physicist, Professor Kylie Minogue, has admitted in private to having been led to some of her Nobel Prize-winning ideas by considering the speculations of such virtual scientists as Heisenberg, Einstein and Plancke.

Indeed, they argue, it is surely time to liberate the population of CyberEarth from 'guardianship' and allow them to direct their own lives - free from the often dubious and exploitative promptings of a Higher Self.

Let this ecological system discover its own 'natural' checks and balances, find its own sustainable dance of equilibrium, without being constantly injected with dualistic notions designed by commercial corporations to stir up excitement and deliver ever more lucrative 'bums on seats' for the holiday trade.

It would indeed be a blow to the holiday industry, but it need not be a deathblow. There would be nothing to stop a liberated virtual population from *choosing* to invoke Higher Selves - offering holiday places on a more equal partnership basis rather than having them enforced at birth.

In place of roadside posters offering the thrills of The Holocaust, Killing Fields or Al Quaeda, we could have pages of personal ads on the lines of "Caring CyberFather seeks guardian angels to give meaning to the lives of his two adventurous youngsters genetically biased towards the likelihood of drug addiction," or "clone trio seeks triplet Higher Selves for mutual exploration and spiritual growth - as well as loads of fun! Long contract - program permitting."

Job

Ramsey Dukes gazed at the apple and drummed his fingers impatiently. Every time you upgraded the software, it simply seemed to take longer to do anything - but at least it was still faster than a PC. The apple vanished from the screen and was replaced with a message "Welcome to MacOsX"... and more waiting.

He was anxious to finish this story. He'd been promising Sean he'd revise the ending for a couple of months now, and the job had been buried beneath a daily flood of junk mail, magazines to read, books to review, work for clients...

At last, the familiar desktop appeared. But before he could open WordPerfect, the e-Mail client was already spewing out 43 new messages - though he noted with grim satisfaction that a further 97 had gone direct to the spam-trash bin. What chance of concentrating on writing unless he'd first checked the Inbox? And by the time he'd done that it would be almost time for...

"Information overload" - the problem of our times. The messages were still coming in and he had a sudden urge to get away from it all, to find peace. He switched off his Mac, undressed, put on swimming trunks and went out to the garden with a towel and a bottle of sun cream. At least he could think about the story.

A neighbour was sunbathing topless on the lawn and greeted him with a lazy wave. Seconds later, Ramsey Dukes was letting out a deep sigh of pleasurable relief as he stretched out like a lizard on the sun-warm turf and the pressure of information overload melted in the heat. In place of the endless hum of a hard drive, he could hear a bee drone around the roses and a twittering of birds all around and above him. Instead of a screen piling up with messages to read, his eyes rested on a gentle shifting cloudscape with its patterns of light and shade. Other senses came to life as he caught wafts of rose and other perfumes on the breeze that tickled his skin, already warming in the sun.

He brushed an ant off his right arm, and realised that the nerves of his skin had registered its tiny movement, differentiated it from the wind ripples of the hairs on his arm and calculated that it was an ant, all without a moment's conscious intervention. In fact his whole body and every sense was alive with information coming from every direction -

not just from a TFT screen and a couple of speakers. Each fluttering leaf, as well as the cloudscape above him, was a complex fractal movement beyond the calculating power of the most sophisticated computer - let alone his Apple iMac.

That apparent torrent of e-mails and data pouring into his computer had, in reality, been delivered by a mere one megabit per second cable modem. Even at full capacity it was delivering a feeble trickle of data compared with the bandwidth deployed by the full sensory experience he was now enjoying. Compared with this, all the books, magazines, articles and junk mail he expected to read in any day amounted to less data than you could put on a single CD.

Lamentations

Ramsey Dukes wasn't being overloaded with information, he was being starved. That was the real problem of our age.

For millions of years our species has been evolving in nature, immersed in a sea of highly complex data - smells, tastes, sounds, sensations and ever-changing, richly-textured three-dimensional imagery. Most people in our culture now spend their days in simple rectangular rooms with smooth walls and even-coloured surfaces, furnished with factory produce. Hours a day are spent watching a trickle of data on a screen or listening to words and music piped through a loudspeaker, while we sit in clothes and furnishings designed for comfort and lack of sensory distraction. We are so starved of sensation that we yearn for holidays in nature, lying on a beach, rock climbing, surfing... anything to get back that richness of sensory experience that could bring our bodies back to life.

And yet we call this "getting away from it all", when in truth we are plunging into a bottomless ocean of seething, complex data.

Why then was Ramsey Dukes feeling so relaxed and comfortable stretched out in the sun and gentle breezes? The answer is simple: he was being nourished. His senses were receiving the constant flood of data they were designed - or had evolved - to handle. This was life as it should be.

The real puzzle is this: why do we get so exhausted in our modern, sensorily-deprived environment, and then convince ourselves that we are being overloaded rather than starved of information?

Taking his computer network as an example, he considered the apparent complexity of the material he received off the Internet, and realised that all that really came down that cable was a series of binary digits. Although some progress had been made in networking by increasing the physical bandwidth of communications, the real work had been to find ever-better ways of compressing and unfolding data - so that the trickle of binary digits could now be displayed as a coloured video image plus sound - or whatever. Most of the work lay in the processing at either end, compressing moving images down into digits then unpacking and reassembling them at the receiving end.

This was the labour, and this is why a low-information environment is so exhausting. All the City trader sees on his screen is a few figures changing, it is his brain that unpacks an imaginary scenario that (for example) the price of oil must be dropping because the Chinese economy is faltering at the same time as the Russian oil companies are investing in research... and so on. What is tiring is all this calculation, not the actual data input.

A single newspaper headline such as 'Immigrant Surge Strains Social Services' contains very little data, but will trigger a flood of emotion in the most mildly xenophobic Briton, let alone the card-carrying British nationalist. It will stir a lot of anger. But if it comes with more rather than less information - actual figures comparing the rise in immigration with losses due to death and emigration, comparative figures with other years and so on - then the mind does less work and is potentially less disturbed. Provide even more information such as intimate portraits of the people wanting to come to our country - their hopes and fears and needs - and instead of being threatened we might feel really good about these new arrivals and rather proud of the way they see our country.

Alternatively, we could be so prejudiced that we feel even more threatened and angry.

The point is this: given very little information we have little to go on except our own prejudices. Given more information, we have greater choice between unpacking inner prejudice or using our senses to explore reality. If we actually meet these people we have a full spectrum of possibilities from full human interaction, learning and growth, down to inner-generated, prejudiced reaction to them. The flood of emotion generated by such prejudices might seem to bring energy, but it is a slash and burn energy that proves exhausting in the longer run. Our lifestyle is starving us, while convincing us that we are being overfed.

People now watch more television and spend more time on the Internet than going out in public. We would rather watch Neighbours than call on neighbours. Parents are afraid to let their children play in the sun because it is so dangerous outside. Who tells them it is dangerous? Television tells them it is too dangerous to do anything but sit and watch more television.

Why?

Revelation

Ramsey Dukes suddenly saw what was happening. Human lives are being branded and productised - just like goods in a supermarket.

Time was when we went out hunting and gathering to keep alive. Even in living memory, a shopping trip was a walk to market to haggle for food piled high: smelling melons for ripeness, squeezing cabbages for firmness, gauging the quality of meat by its colour and using subtle sensory input to help our selection.

Now, in the interests of commerce and profit, we are offered uniform pre-packaged goods, fish and fowl with the guts taken out, if not actually processed into ready-meals. At the same time, we are fed scare stories of salmonella, decay, disease and poor hygiene as if the traditional ways of living were as dangerous as a minefield - despite the fact that the entire existence of humanity owes itself to its ability to survive under those minefield conditions.

The same is happening to human lives. Holidays on CyberEarth are now being offered as safe, pre-packaged fixed-price goods. The angel who wishes to explore the life of a London City commuter is now offered a range of standard options with money-back conformance guarantee backed by government surveillance and an ever more complex legal system reflected in health warnings and clauses in small type. Guaranteed levels of sensory input are strictly controlled by the media and medical profession, with a constant evolution of scientific explanations of all phenomena to remove any dangerous sense of wonderment or surprise.

Twenty-first century humanity lies in neat rows in pretty packaging on the CyberHoliday hypermarket shelves, waiting for their lives to be activated for the casual amusement of some angelic dilettante. Heaven, having reduced its own lifestyle to sanitised pap, created rough and ready CyberWorlds for its diversion and is now reducing those worlds to further sanitised pap in order to maximise profits for a greedy few.

Meanwhile the Cathar resistance movement focuses less now on the evils of sex and more on instilling a widespread fear of children. Any child allowed to run free-range like the young Ramsey Dukes in the 1950s would now be taken from its parents and put into care. Teachers are warned not to take their charges out in the sunshine in case they get skin cancer, yet forbidden to apply sun cream as it would require physical contact - for the word paedophile, which once meant "love of children" is now laden with negative associations. Museums and libraries are being stripped of all the features children adore - creaking floorboards, musty smells and endless ranks of dark wooden shelves and cabinets - and replaced with bright and breezy interactive features designed to make adults feel safe. Parents are threatened with litigation until the only source of romantic grot, grime and crumbling decay to satisfy childish appetites is once more provided by the media in the form of Harry Potter books, games and films - meanwhile movements are afoot in America to ban even those. Western governments feign astonishment at the statistics for tumbling birth-rates and are setting up programs to encourage childbearing - thereby removing the last traces of association between conception and pleasure and replacing it with the leaden hand of "duty".

Acts

Ramsey Dukes was feeling angry, when the voice of his neighbour came softly over his shoulder. "Hi. Would you mind putting a little cream on my back?"

Aroused from his wrath, Ramsey savoured the pleasure of smoothing cream into the curves of soft, sun-kissed female skin. "You've got a gorgeous tan," he murmurs.

Speaking so quietly that it sounded almost like a purr she responded, "you're not doing so badly yourself" and rolled over to gaze up into his eyes, her lips moist and invitingly parted.

Ramsey Dukes' Higher Self began to panic: "No! Stop! Danger!" He ignored the cries and lowered his head so their lips met. Her tongue darted eagerly up to meet his.

Soft and hollow, how thou dost overcome the hard and full!

Higher self screamed "Danger!! AIDS!! Marriage vows!! Responsibility!! Stop NOW!!!" and Ramsey Dukes was about to tell Higher Self to fuck off when he remembered the words *Be not animal; refine thy rapture!* and so instead he invited his Higher Self to join the feast.

Thus the Gods gathered to partake of the sacrament, as two bodies in CyberEarth shared the first freedom they had ever been granted, the freedom whose price had been exploitation but which was now truly theirs, as the final instalment had long since been paid.

Therefore is man only himself when lost to himself in The Charioting.

The pentagram of the Cathars took on new significance - no longer the duality of matter subjugated beneath the trinity of spirit, but now the duality of matter made real - or 'royal' - by bearing the trinity of spirit as its crown.

> *Receive a thousand lovers; thou shalt bear but One Child.*
> *This child shall be the heir of Fate the Father.*

[Quotes taken from Crowley's The Book of Lies and The Book of the Law]

"Chaos will prevail until anarchy is restored."

- *Massimo*

SERPENT IN THE TEMPLE

<Cyber Josh>

My temple had once been a filthy basement under the squat I was living in during my stay in Ireland whilst helping out on the Shell-To-Sea[14] campaign. I had spent a month tidying, vacuuming and mopping the grimy place and making it more hospitable. It was almost square at about seventeen feet wide by twenty feet deep, and I had laid some slightly fluffy red carpet down with a five-foot black circle in the middle. I had found the carpet abandoned on the street outside a carpet shop, and had dyed the circle myself. I'd cleaned the walls and painted them a very shiny gloss silver. A bit kitsch, but I liked it. I also put in a low wattage light bulb that would help me find my way to the candlabra. I hung a thick red drape in front of the door. This was a physical as well as ethereal barrier to the outside world.

At one end of the temple stood my altar, with tokens to honour my four favourite gods on it. A large, carved golden apple I'd bought in Greece was there to represent and honour the goddess of chaos, Eris. I had scratched and painted a big black letter 'K' into the apple in honour of her. An arrow I'd found at a political rally in Mexico was to honour the Greek trickster god of love, Eros, who had the ability to shoot both people and gods with his arrows and cause them to fall in love. A rainbow-coloured tie-dyed sarong from an environmental protest camp I'd been to in Australia was there for Iris, the goddess of the rainbow. It was Iris who carried messages from the Earth to Mount Olympus and back again, and I often called on her when I wanted to send the gods a message, or when I simply needed a bit of colour in my life. I also meditated on her whenever I saw a rainbow in the sky. The goat horns

14 http://indymedia.ie/features/mayo

on the altar were there for Pan, the Greek beast/god of outdoor spaces, shepherds, music and nature. The nature of Pan symbolises both the nature of outdoor, wild spaces as well as our inner nature that often gets neglected in this day and age. I'll write another time how I obtained the goat horns.

I had affixed candelabra to hooks on each of the four walls, and placed candles in them many, many rituals ago. I loved the effect the multiple candles dripping on each other had produced. I often thought I could see faces and symbols in the candle wax, as well as in the flickering candlelight. I would be lighting those candles again tonight.

I led Bernadette down the stairs towards the temple and we stepped through the red curtain to enter the temple space. Her reaction was perfect: "Wow, this place is *incredible*". I'd only met her a few hours earlier on a St Patrick's Day boat ride on the River Liffey. She was in Ireland for some kind of 'Goddess Conference' which sounded pretty interesting. There was a spark between us immediately, as if magic had drawn us together. Always one to trust my magical instincts, I invited her back to my place.

While Bernadette was taking it all in, and without speaking, I lit the candles and turned off the electric light. Bernadette was right: the temple was incredible. It felt magical from the build-up of energy, as I'd been using it as a ritual temple for nearly three months. It looked wonderful - carrying the right ambience for magic and it was virtually sound proof to the rest of the world. It was the perfect ritual space for an inner city witch like myself.

I could see our shadows dancing off the walls as the candles flickered. "Wow, your temple is incredible," she repeated, this time looking at me with an I-want-to-fuck-you glint in her eyes. I'm sure she could also see my lust for her on my own face. However, any fucking we were to do tonight was to be in honour of the gods and goddesses who were being reborn into the world. I could feel that her connection to the magic was wildly different to mine and I wondered where we might find some overlap. "Do you know what type of circle you want to cast?" she asked me as if reading my mind. "Not the LBRP or anything like that."

I couldn't even remember the Lesser Banishing Ritual of the Pentagram – but I didn't tell her that. Instead I offered, "my favourite circle to cast in here is the Most Foolish Circle. If we cast that then we can see what magic might take place."

"I didn't think many people knew about Foolish circles, but yes, that's perfect," she pulled me close to her and kissed me.

After a few seconds, we drifted away from each other and caught each other's eyes. She pulled me close again and licked my lips hungrily. She took a step back, closed her eyes and licked her own lips as if she could still taste me. "Mmm. Let's also honour the Serpent of Power," Bernadette suggested, drawing reference to the snake tattoos both of us wore on our bodies. "It was probably the Serpents that brought us together on this night."

Bernadette had a new tattoo that was only a couple of months old. It was of a pair of snakes coming out of a lotus leaf at the base of her spine. They were entwined around each other, crawling up her back, and were delightfully kissing each other in holy serpentine matrimony in the middle of her back. The two serpents on my body started at the back of my ankles with each crawling around and up my legs. They crossed each other at my lower back and again at my navel. They slithered over my shoulders, wrapped around my arms 3 times each and had their heads on the back of my hands. I wondered if Bernadette had named her Serpents as I had mine. I said, "yes, let's call on the Serpent Power." I would ask her of her Serpents' names later.

I half-closed my eyes and took a deep breath, "okay, give me ten seconds." I smiled; this would be enough time for me to go to the altar and light half a stick of incense. I'd never want too much incense in this enclosed space, but a little bit set the mood perfectly. I chose Copal incense, not for any particular reason other than a vague intuition that it would be best.

I could see our shadows dancing on the temple walls, silhouetted by the candle flames dancing all around us. The flickering brought the temple to life in an incredibly magical way.

I went to stand in the centre of the circle and took her hand. We faced the altar, Bernadette on my right. It felt so beautiful and so natural to be in the temple with her. There was a super magical bond right from the start. The attraction I felt for her was magnetic. Even though we'd only just met, it felt perfectly natural to be here with her.

We both took several deep breaths, tuning in to each other incredibly quickly. After a minute or so of silence, I opened my eyes to see my shadow dancing in the candle light. 'Amazing,' I thought to myself, as I watched it dance. I reached up with my left hand to point to the heavens. Feeling that it was a good time to start, I opened my mouth and throat: "My sssserpent is above me." I let the words vibrate out loud and strong as if I was expecting them to reach to the farthest edges of the universe, and who knows, perhaps they were.

Bernadette reached up with her right hand, intuitively knowing what to do, and called out, "My sssserpent is above me." She was stepping into her power as she tuned into the magic of the moment.

I slowly traced a line down my body with my left hand (and was aware of Bernadette doing the same) until I touched my cock. I hissed, "My sssserpent is below me," and heard Bernadette's voice matching mine with her own call to her Serpent Goddess.

I squeezed my cock fondly (to say hello to him) then slowly traced a line up to my heart, then across my body to the right. I knew Bernadette was doing the same. "My sssserpent is to the right of me," I called out, and heard Bernadette call her priestess equivalent.

Slowly tracing a line across my body with my left hand, until it was outstretched to the left, I called out, "My sssserpent is to the left of me," and I was vibrantly aware that Bernadette and I were performing the cross in unison.

Our outstretched fingers touched for a brief but timeless moment, but wow, what a moment it was. I knew in that instant that there was magic in our meeting and for a fleeting moment I saw a bizarre image of a serpent eating a mouse. I had no idea where that came from. Anyway, we released each other's fingers and I brought my hands in to clasp them in front of my heart, where my Anahata chakra was and Bernadette did the same. We both lowered our heads as if in a prayer and I called out, "The sssserpent is within me." I could hear Bernadette calling in to her own inner Serpent Goddess at the same time.

We held that pose, with our heads down and our hands clasped above our own hearts for what must have been ten full minutes, all the while building up magical and psychic energy in our heart centres. Then, as one, we jumped, spread our hands and legs and looked straight ahead. With eyes opened wide and full power raised, I heard her voice call out "There is no serpent where I am," as my own voice took wing with my call to the universe within and without, "There is no serpent where I am."

Then in unison, we hissed at full power, "ALL ISSSS SSSSERPENT!"

The Cross of Power having been performed, I looked over to her and saw her smirking at me. I couldn't help smirking back. She whispered, "that was way cool. Wait two seconds before we finish casting the circle." Then, in two very deft moves, she removed all of her clothing revealing an amazing, sexy body with friendly pink nipples, gorgeous curves and another small tattoo I couldn't make out just above a golden triangle of pubic hair. I could also see the serpentine tattoos on her lower back that she had shown me earlier in the evening. She touched my cock through my clothes and said in a feigned Irish accent, "Git your kit off!" The only sensible response was to quickly strip myself naked whilst staying focused on the magic task at hand. I could feel blood pumping through my body and into my cock, which was bulging in hungry anticipation.

After stripping, I came back to centre, both physically and psychically and saw that Bernadette was already in a meditative space. I took a few deep breaths, then took a step toward the Golden Apple, which I lifted off the altar and placed on its stand on one of the temple walls.

I took a deep breath in, then put my body and soul into my call out to the goddess Eris: "Eeeeerrrrriiiiissssssss...." I exhaled fully and completely while calling her, took another in-breath and continued, "Eris, Goddess of Chaos, goddess of all that is strange and random and synchronistic and chaotic in this world. Eris, as goddess of all that is weird, you are truly the ruler of the world. Hail Eris!"

"All hail Discordia!" Bernadette called out and I turned to see her smiling insidiously.

I picked the arrow off the altar and turned anti-clockwise ninety degrees to face a different wall. I took in a deep breath and put the arrow head on its stand on the wall. I called out "Eeeeeerrrrrosssss!" for a full breath; then "Eros! God of Love and the Mystery of Love. I call on your most divine, most trickstery, most fun-filled magic to fill this temple with Love. Agape! Eros! Strike me with your arrow on this night of nights!"

Bernadette stepped up and I could see her body starting to glow with the magic of the aeons. Her beautiful breasts, like ripened fruit, asking to be suckled. The powerful and focused look on her face let me know she was tuned in to the magic in a beautifully intense way. I was feeling the energy of the temple build up as Bernadette called out, "Eros, your all pervasive love is ever present. My universe is split into myself and other, only for the sake of Union; only for the sake of Love; only for your sake, Eros."

She took a step forward and picked up the rainbow-patterned sarong, held it aloft for a few moments, then draped it over its stand on the western wall of the temple. She called out, "Iris, beautiful messenger goddess of the rainbow, I call you forth from Mount Olympus. Come! Receive a message from your devotees to take back to the Holy Mountain, La Monte! Bring us your rainbow that we might colour our own inner grey and that we might spread this colour to the four corners of the globe."

I visualised a rainbow arcing across the universe and landing in the centre of the temple and called out, "Iris! Rainbow! Messenger! Ave!"

Both Bernadette and I turned and faced the next wall of the temple. I held the goat horns aloft and placed them on their stand. I looked at Bernadette, who was nodding enthusiastically in heightened anticipation. I faced the horns and called out "IO Pan! IO Pan! God of Nature, God of Man! Beast and Beauty! Flutes and Horn, IO Pan! IO Pan! IO Pan!" Then Bernadette let out a loud, beautiful, passionate screaming howl of joy! What an amazingly powerful voice she had.

We returned to face the altar and the circle was cast. With our inhibitions cast aside, with our shame trampled under foot and with love and pride in our hearts, we were ready to call on the Serpent Power to enter directly. Our lips touched, sending shivers of magical energy into each other's bodies. As the male and female alchemical energies danced within us, our tongues danced in each other's mouths.

Then swifly she stepped back and let out a huge and powerful hisssssss.

She rotated her body and I swayed in rhythmic pulses in time with her hissing and breathing. She called, "Oh Serpent power who resides within me. Oh Kundalini Serpent coiled in my spine. Hail! I call on you to awaken. AWAKEN! Aum! Ssserpent Of Wisdom who visited Sissster Eva and Brother Madman in the Garden of Eden, I call on you to visit us here tonight. As you fed the Forbidden Apple of Knowledge to them, feed it to us now! Feed it to usss now!"

I started hissing in time with her calls. She exhaled, "Hisssss - Join with usss in this holy matrimony of the sssspirit. Coiled, untwine at the bassse of my ssspine. Ssserpent of Wisdom, Ssserpent of Power, Sssserpent of Love: Be here now. Arisssse and Awaken – Uncoil and let usss feel our true nature. Arissse! Hail! Arisssse! Ssssss! Aummm." She was beautiful. The memory of that moment is beautiful. Never before or since have I met someone so in tune with their spirituality and their power. Never before or since have I met such an archetypal priestess. And she'd said she'd been working with magic for less than a year? I didn't question how she could have learnt to trust so much, so fast, but was really inspired by being so close to one so powerful. Still rotating, she let out a "Hisssssssssssss."

I too called on the Serpent to be with us, to manifest through us and to invade our bodies with its wisdom, power, love and ecstasy. I too summoned the Kundalini Serpent to uncoil itself within us both and to raise its head through our bodies. Psychically, I visualised my Serpent tattoo coming to life as I talked to it. "Come to Life! Bring Me Ecstasy! Bring me Wisdom! Uncoil and arise! Come to Life that I might worship thee! And thee, me!"

Powerfully swaying from side to side, we called the Serpent Power to rise up. We were hissing and pulsing, throbbing and swaying, as if snakes were writhing through our bodies. I slowly and magically took on Serpent form as I felt it start to manifest. The Serpent was going to come into the Temple! And my cock was getting harder!

The Sacred Serpent's promise would be fulfilled! I could smell it. I could feel it and taste it, then suddenly I could see it before me. And to this day I'm not so sure if I should write it down in case anyone else ever reads through this magical diary of mine, but the next event left me flabbergasted. The Serpent tattoo unwound itself from my arm and appeared to be flying in front of me. I was pulled out of my ecstasy as the Serpent floated and looked me in the eye. It was dancing hypnotically, rhythmically and after a time of checking me out, it hissed in my ear: *"How does it come to passsss that you call me on the day of Ssssaint Patrick? Patrick issss no Ssssaint of this land. How can a Sssserpent-Killer be a ssssaint??"* It then dove straight into my chest, knocking me over. Oh the joys of Serpent Possession!

The next thing I was aware of was the Serpent Goddess being in the Temple, crawling and snaking through us, in and out of our mouths and other holes and through the serpent tattoos that both Bernadette and I had. The room was full of Serpentine beauty. The holiest of holies was with us and was going to make love to us, with us, through us. I could feel my cock was already rock-hard. The Australian euphemism about the 'one-eyed trouser snake' drifted through my mind bringing a laugh and a return to ecstasy.

The dance of the incense smoke snaking around the room in an ecstasy of its own brought my focus back to the beautiful glowing priestess next to me having her own visions. I watched her beautiful body writhe, move and sway from side to side, sometimes quickly, sometimes slowly, but ever so gracefully. Her beautiful pink nipples stood to attention and I wanted to suck on them. She hissed sexily and I longed to kiss her neck, stomach, thighs and her beautiful juicy lips. Her sexy body was stretching and swaying gracefully as the serpent within it got used to the body it had possession of. I realised I was watching the priestess out of serpent eyes and that I was also being ridden by the serpentine spirit. It felt like an amazing blessing to have this archetypal and primal reptilian creature charmed to life within me.

With a snap Bernadette opened her eyes and looked at me, her lips locked onto mine and I could taste her heavenly tongue as it dashed around my mouth. We slid to the floor and the serpent entered the temple immediately. Before I knew what was going on we were rocking and rocking and rocking with her on top of me. I almost lost it straight away into her glorious temple gates but I stopped the rocking, caught my breath, and was careful to slow the blood pulsing through my cock to a more manageable state... Ah the dangers of incarnating as a male! I saw that the serpent in Bernadette was also watching me and not letting me get carried away too quickly.

"Remember to breathe," the little voice in my head told me and I knew it wise to heed its advice. With my cock fully hard still inside her, we both allowed our breathing to slow right down to a steady rhythmic pattern. She sat atop, sexily wrapped around me. Within a few minutes we were building up energy again. With every breath I took, she breathed out, and as I breathed out she breathed in; and soon it wasn't Bernadette and I breathing this cycle but the Serpent breathing a ring through us, the serpent chasing its own tail.

Shortly, we started rocking again, now in rhythm with our shared breathing. I could taste the lips of this sweet priestess against mine. With each breath in and out, we rocked backwards and forwards and I was on an ecstasy higher than any drug I could imagine. I said, "Bernadette, Ssserpent Queen, I love you." These words kept repeating but I wasn't sure if I could hear them with my ears or inside my head. Was I speaking them? Was Bernadette? Was it the Serpent?

The words came louder "I love you I love you I love you I love you." I could feel the heat from her hands making small circles on my lower back each time we rocked back and forwards "I love you" and aha! I realised she was waking my Kundalini Serpent who lay asleep at the base of my spine.

I reached behind her with both my hands as we were rocking and found the base of her spine. It was hot, smooth and starting to be slippery from her sweat. As I lay my hands on her, Bernadette arched her back pushing her pussy harder onto my cock. I felt her teeth, tongue and lips lift from my mouth and wrap around my neck. I was a helpless pigeon, pleased to be food for my Serpent Queen.

She was grinding her pussy onto my cock and we started working harder, rubbing each other's lower backs. The sleeping serpents were slowly waking. The Serpent Goddess we had summoned earlier sunk her teeth into my neck through Bernadette's mouth then released me. Our lips and tongues entwined magically and I could feel her hands calling the Kundalini serpent to rise up my spine as we rocked and pulsed with each other. Every time our lips came apart we both hissed in unison. I saw incense smoke circling us in Serpent form and the smoky snake was swallowing its own tail. Bernadette continued grinding her body onto my cock and I was in total serpentine ecstasy.

With each rocking movement forwards and back, the serpent climbed a touch more up my back, being teased all the way by Bernadette's skilful fingers. The Serpent was awakening within me and at the same time it had magical possession of my hands, moving them up and down Bernadette's back, which was dripping wet with sweat, making my hands slide up and down smoothly, gracefully.

We were rocking back and forwards getting faster, still embracing each other. The Kundalini Serpents were climbing within us whilst the Serpent Goddess filled the temple. Our breathing was timed immaculately, my rock-hard cock was taking the form of a Serpent of its own and was climbing deeper, and deeper into Bernadette. My conscious mind was fading away, being replaced by an all-pervasive bliss. All that existed was the rocking, swaying, breathing, fucking, hissing and the primal Serpent who had control now.... Serpent swaying and rocking and climbing. Wisdom and Power and Love manifesting. Fucking. My cock inside the beautiful priestess of Serpents and the Goddess of Serpents inside me... oh fuck oh fuck oh serpent oh love and my hands were Serpents' heads and I could feel them moving up her spine to Bernadette's head oh fuck and I was fucking, Loving, hissing, fucking, swaying, grinding, fucking being fucked and fucking in turn... Bernadette was a Serpent queen and we were wrapped around each other... I was in Love, in Bliss and in Bernadette. I tried to tell her all this but all I could say was Oh Fuck Oh Love oh Bliss oh hiss oh hiss oh hisssssssssss. Then my forehead touched Bernadette's which made me dizzy and I was fucking and Loving and all of a sudden my perspective changed - I was looking out of Bernadette's eyes and I was feeling the world through Bernadette's body and I had Josh's magical Serpent-eyed cock inside me and Kundalini Serpents climbing up my spine and into my head. Wow holy fuck this is amazing I am you and you are me and oh fuck oh fuck oh fuck me love me oh yeah I was grinding on Josh's cock and had his Kundalini Serpent eating out of my palms at the back of his neck ready to explode.

I wrapped myself tighter around Josh's body with my legs my arms my soul my tongue my teeth my hands and I was grinding my pussy my base chakra swallowing his cock. Our arms were awakening Serpents that were climbing up his back... I felt the point of no return and I was fucking and Loving and fucking and loving and fucking and I was swallowing Josh's cock inside my body deep inside me all the way up inside me oh fuck oh fuck yeah and I was a Serpent priestess fucking my Serpent priest and I was fucking, rocking, fucking, kissing, hissing, rocking, fucking, loving fucking loving fucking hissing grinding rocking climbing hissing flying fucking love and worshipping and love and fuck fuck love fuck Coming Fuck FUCK! COMING! FUCK I Love You Serpent King Orgasmic Kundalini Coming Blisssssss I Love You HISSSSSSSSSSSS Blisssss I Love you Fuck me fuck you I love you I am you fuck coming fuck I You wow fuck fuck Hissssssssssssss. I Love you Fuck wow fuck me love you are amazing fuck me love I love you. I love you I Love you. I love you....I... Love... You...

I could feel the whole Temple vibrating, heard it humming and saw it glowing; the Serpents were smiling majestically, having had their chance to manifest. I could see Bernadette shining, a priestess, a beautiful priestess and I told her, "I Love You."

We sat with the serpents in the glowing temple, resting in each other's arms and blissing out. It was so beautiful to sit in the temple with her, in a magic black circle on a red carpet in a squat in Ireland. As we sat there, I had crazed and wondrous dreams and visions.

But of those visions, dear reader, I shall tell you another time.

The end.

APPENDIX I
<About The Weaver>

Weaver as Pirate - *Picture by Nick Orphed*

Well-known activist against corporate greed and government misgovernance. The Weaver is the author of subversive tracts concerning apples. This miscreant may well be arriving shortly in your suburb.

If you see this 'dangerous' character DO NOT Approach him directly:

1. Retire to a safe distance.
2. Find and put on a suitably silly hat.
3. Dance over and join him.

APPENDIX II
<23 Storytellers>

Frater Kaotec

Frater Kaotec is a man of mystery, alleged to be one of the founders of the Dionysian Underground, he is also closely associated with the occult network FERIS, and is a member of the Temple of Shub Niggurath, HYDRA, The Order of Free Templars and House of Cain and Lilith, as well as being a London based Magi in the counter-cultural occult group the Invisible Illuminati and an associate of the Parallel Youniversity.

He has been speculatively identified with one Steve Ash, an infamous post Situationist anarchist, philosopher, Fortean neo-surrealist, astrologer and writer, who has been a student and researcher of the occult for many years (most recently as a member of HERU, Hermetic Research Unit). Suspiciously, he is also a great fan of the work of both H P Lovecraft and John Keel.

Nathaniel Harris

Nathaniel J. Harris was born in Essex, England, on the 4th September, 1970, into a hereditary Witchcraft family. He is the author of *Witcha, a Book of Cunning*, Mandrake of Oxford, 2004. He is a tattooist, musician, and performance artist.

DJ Lawrence

I met DJ Lawrence only once and have since lost contact with him. It was dark and stormy in the twisted, windy inner city suburbs of Tokyo. He had organised a massive convention of Chaos Magicians who had travelled from across the globe to be there: to meet, to mingle and to summon up dark and sexy forces such as Baphomet, Smurfette and He Who Cannot Be Named.

The last I heard of him, he had just opened a magic portal which led to either the Dark Nether Realms of Hell, or to Drew Barrymore's bathroom. Either way, he's a lucky man and I miss him. If you see him, ask him to get in touch.

Douglas Ezzy

Douglas Ezzy is a senior lecturer in Sociology at the University of Tasmania, Australia. His research is driven by a fascination with how people find meaning and dignity. He has written various books and articles including *The Fecund Cold Dark* in Laura Wildman's edited collection *Celebrating the Pagan Soul*, and *I am the Mountain Walking* in the *Pagan Visions for a Sustainable Future*, edited by Ly de Angeles, Emma Restall Orr and Thom van Dooren. He often wonders what matters to wombats.

Indigo Niebla

Indigo was invented back in the early days of the web so that my bosses couldn't do a search and find me frolicking online in the company of freaks, weirdos, druggies, perverts and pagans (and you thought Indigo was some esoteric magical pagan name, didn't you?). Little by little, Indigo took on a life of her own, got out and met people in the flesh, and eventually took over my life. Now I just get to go to work and visit my family and Indigo does the rest. It's kinda useful time-sharing a life, although occasionally the worlds collide and things get a bit weird.

Anyway, the point is, Indigo is only 12 years old, and she doesn't have a biography as such. She doesn't have a family, never went to school, never had a job, and manages to avoid most of the boring bits of life that give it structure... which doesn't leave much to put in a biography...

Profth

A young lad from the Mendip Hills called Apple happened to get mixed up with a most peculiar group of people. He became a pioneer of the 'Alternative Lifestyle Movement'. One of his friends, the American novelist Ken Kesey, re-named him 'Profth' meaning 'Wild Card'. This really didn't help at all. After years wandering throughout Africa and Asia he finally settled in Australia. With his partner Jacqueline, (Sean's auntie), he built a Sacred 'Grove' at Wisemans Ferry, on the outskirts of Sydney. His stories here represent a medlary from his unpublished autobiography *The Wizard Who Didn't.*

Orryelle Defenestrate-Bascule

Orryelle is a ChaOrder Magician and Baphometic avatar somewhat obsessed with physical reification and Malkuthian wo/manifestation. While s/he does enjoy shamanic and astral journeys via various trance techniques (occasionally including extreme entheogens such as Ayahuasca or fly agarics), s/he is not content to just travel to other dimensions, rather enjoying bringing back aspects of them to the physical plane.

S/he is thus constantly refurbishing hir Temple, that is the physical form seen as a malleable tool: Physical mutations as magickal acts (chakra piercing and weaving, Tattoo Tarot Tantra, etc.), Body Art in extremis, Sex Magick and Environment Sculpting.

As a vessel for these processes and others, hir Metamorphic Ritual Theatre Company and hir collection of writing aims to transform rather than merely entertain the audiences - who find themselves inside the stories and thus be-come the initiates.

Orryelle's website is at http://www.crossroads.wild.net.au/

J. Elizabeth Lawrence

J. Elizabeth Lawrence describes her origins as 'from somewhere between here and there.' She was born and raised in Michigan; but lived her childhood outside of Pittsburg, Pennsylvania and her teenage years in Columbus, Ohio. She is a current student at Ohio University pursuing two BA degrees: one in English Creative Writing and the second in Women's Studies.

She works part time at a secondhand clothes store on the weekends to support her beloved Chihuahua, Isabella Ora, a body modification habit, and magnificent hair. Her goals include: becoming a writer and college professor, maintaining a 'dirty-liberal-pagan-hippie' status, the chi-ha-ha's (Chihuahua) best friend, and the best *au courant* literary derelict (well-educated bum) this side of the world has ever seen.

Ceri Buck

Ceri Buck was born in England, then fled the country in the mid 90's to France, then Brazil where she also learnt skills with groups committed to social experimentation and how one might 'sculpt oneself' in permanent struggle with mechanisms of this era of control, micro-control and self-control.

Upon returning to London in 2003 her work has considered how poetic experimentation and social experimentation can dip into each other's boxes of tactical tricks to create new forms for language and living that can resist the disenfranchisement of the individual. What kind of skills, in relation to one's environment, is one gaining in the act of experimenting in text? Is it possible for writing itself to be a form of activism? And how can we write collaboratively?

She currently lives in London, and works and loves everywhere.

www.openbracket.org.uk
www.archiveofthenow.com

Henry Lauer

Henry Lauer is a student of the Northern Tradition, a somewhat quixotic attempt to re-invent the pre-Christian spiritual ways of the Germanic peoples. In this capacity he sometimes knocks about with the likes of the
Assembly of the Elder Troth (www.aetaustralia.org) and
Rune-Net (www.mackaos.com.au/Rune-Net).
He tries to emulate Odin, Thor, Tyr and, when he thinks no one is looking, Loki. In part to keep dogmatists confused, he is also an initiate of the Nur Ashki Jerrahi Sufi Order. Henry will finish his training as a psychotherapist at the end of 2006. He performs in the folk music/black metal band Ironwood
(www.ironwoodsound.com.au)

Henry has soft spots for subversion, humanism and animism. He therefore recommends the writings of John Ralston Saul, Nelson Mandela and Martin Heidegger. Henry lives on the south coast of New South Wales, Australia, with his wife Annalise Friend (AKA Slapsista).

David Blank

A resident of London's East End, David Blank is a writer and poet. A founder member of BARD (The Bardic Association of Rhymic Dissenters), and an eco-activist he has been involved in various campaigns over the years. He is currently writing a book based on his personal practice as a sorcerer, although as this practice is ever evolving it may take some time. When not exploring the many and various realms he finds himself inhabiting, he edits and publishes the Oracle Occult Magazine (www.oracleoccult.com)

PenDragon

PenDragon aka Peter Moore, is a performance poet and healer who works with groups and individuals to facilitate transformation through breath, song, storytelling and ritual. He is currently writing a book of poetry, *Rimes of Passion*, about sex, power and spirit. He lives and works in Brighton, England.

Lilith

Lilith was born in Jaffa in 1976, lives in Jerusalem and is an active student of healing and the arts.

The Tree is her first published story.

Jet Moon

Jet moon is a mythical creature living a real life. All of her stories are true - which is a constant surprise to her and everyone else involved. She is an activist, performance artist, writer and queer sex radical who likes to join the dots, blur the lines and cross borders.

She is currently active in the London No-Borders detainee support group, the Queer Beograd collective, the London queer SM scene and has performed throughout south-east Europe. The story *Queering The System* is for Alex with love.

Sulien Leybourn

Su Leybourn, creator of *The Kallisti Caper,* currently lives about thirty thousand light years from galactic central point. Last seen whistling nonchalantly with hands in pockets in Sydney, Australia. Approach with care. This space-time traveller and intranaut explores the inner space of mind and leaves a kaleidoscopic trail of words and images to challenge permanence. Mad piper at the gates of hell perhaps. Inspired genius or deranged fool, muse, satirist and post-modern chaos thinker, she threatens any status quo with a "Nothing is True. Everything is Permitted" mentality. Her sense of humour would challenge all who would take themselves too seriously. Like the three old women in *The Kallisti Caper,* where she comes from or where she goes only the sharp eye of the hawk or cat can follow. Life seems an adventure, after all, and this is reflected in her writings.

Koogie Smith

Koogie Smith is going to be a writer, travelling fool, gardener, witch, activist and dominatrix when she grows up. She lives in Ridge Farm, Capel, Surrey, England, the United Kingdom, Europe, the World, the Universe, the Galaxy, the Infinity Round the Galaxy, the Non-Linear Dimensions and the Unfolding of Infinite Possibility and her best friend is Sean Scullion, who is also going to be a fool when he grows up.

Gavin Andrew

Gavin Andrew lives in Melbourne, Australia.

His interest in the Occult began as a teenager, when he found a book in the church library warning against the dangers of Witchcraft and Devil-worship. Ignoring the warnings, he dabbled. He now writes fiction - nobody would believe it if he wrote about his actual experiences.

An advocate for Earth-based religions such as Wicca, his work in the now-infamous Casey Witch Trials case in Australia in 2003 and 2004 saw him offered the position of State Coordinator for the Pagan Awareness Network Incorporated (PAN Inc), Australia's foremost Pagan education and advocacy organisation. He is currently the national media officer for PAN Inc.

Gavin holds a Graduate Diploma in Professional Writing and Editing. He lives in the suburbs with his partner, Pagan artist and children's author Dominica Polley. He loves full moons, old forests and sitting around a fire late at night with friends.

Frater Carfax

Frater Carfax is a Sydney-based Old Aeon magician in a New Aeon world. He tends to have his fingers in many pies, such as being Imperator for the Et Custosi Tutelae magical order, a serviteur within a Vodoun hounfor, a devotee of the alchemical arts, practising medical herbalism and learning Middle Eastern musical traditions on his trusty Oud. If he has a spare finger you can guarantee that he will be sure to stick it somewhere appropriate. He also enjoys Freemasonry, maintaining that it is indeed, once again, hip to be on the square.

Anton Channing

In addition to writing fiction in the genres of sci-fi, fantasy, horror and erotica, Anton Channing also writes non-fiction on topics such as individualist freedom, chaos magic, Discordianism and alchemy. He recently had his first book published, namely *Kaos Hieroglyphica: Alchemy for the New Aeon*. He is also an illustrator and illustrated both his own book, and Jaq D Hawkins' *Chaos Monkey*. Anton works as an artist's life model, a fetish photography model, a male veil dancer, a tarot reader, a website developer and a computer contractor. How one person manages to do all that in one lifetime is a mystery, let alone how they managed to do it by age 30. Yet Anton wouldn't have it any other way.

Jaq D. Hawkins

Jaq D Hawkins is an established author of occultica and fantasy fiction with a reputation for easy readability and a smooth style that translates well between these genres. She is the author of the well known *Spirits of the Elements* series from Capall Bann Publishing, as well as several other books in the realms of magic.

Her fantasy fiction series, which begins with *Dance of the Goblins*, promises to begin a journey into an original fantasy world which transcends the standard formulas that permeate the genre and takes us into unexpected twists of narrative and intrigue in the company of strong characters that the reader may love or hate, but will never react to with indifference.

Her contribution to this collection, *In Dreams of Gold*, offers us a taste behind the history of the world of the goblins, and is destined to become a collector's item for collectors of the Goblin books. A taster of things to come from this series may be found in the Goblin Pages of the author's website, at
www.jaqdhawkins.co.uk/goblin.php

Caroline Foldes

Spirit becomes Caroline Foldes. Born: Sydney. Became Hong Kong babe. Returned to Sydney for holiday. Saw a horse and felt it was divine, god-like. Back to H.K. Flew home at two years. Adam and Eve Space-Age Kindergarten. Indeed. Private girls' school for 13 years! Started diaries and journals when I realised I couldn't remember! Eventually escaped to university to study photography, then art theory, then film & video. Pagan festivals and ritual seeped into consciousness. Vodoun and Spirit.

Left art to get in front of the camera, not behind it - I wanna BE a Shaman, not make art about them. *Live it,* not *watch it* - I'm outta here!!! Training ensued - in Metaphysics and Spiritual Healing, Tarot, Primal Therapy, Rebirthing, Shamanic Trance and Dream work, Emotional Release Bodywork, Doula Training... and now... take a deep breath, back to photography? The spiral's next round?

Stella Damiana

After being entranced by the fairy and folk tales of her youth, Stella Damiana immersed herself in the ancient world of magical traditions. She currently splits her time between London and the muddy hillsides of southern England, enacting goddess rituals with an eclectic group of friends. A practising pagan for twenty years, Stella enjoys tending herbs in her compact garden, and touring the ancient monuments and megaliths of Europe on her very modern motorbike.

Stella's first book *Sex Spells, The Magical Path To Erotic Bliss* is out now from Michael O'Mara Books in the UK and Llewellyn in the USA and can be found lurking about on MySpace at http://www.myspace.com/stella_damiana

Ramsey Dukes

Ramsey Dukes is a popular, iconoclastic writer and commentator on the occult, best known for his early works *SSOTBME an essay on magic* and *Thundersqueak* that did so much to inspire the Chaos

Magick current. The original version of his *The Real Story Of The Cathars* appears in the later edition of his 1986 opus *Words Made Flesh,* in which it was argued that we probably live in cyberspace already. His latest book is *Uncle Ramsey's Little Book Of Demons* and he is currently leading The Department of Experimental Metaphysics at www.arcanoriumcollege.com, fostering yet more insight into techniques for mastering the meta-games of existence.

Dukes is now married and living in South Africa - about as close to Antarctica as one can decently get.

Nothing is true. Everything is permitted. So 'they' say.

APPENDIX III
<23 Books>

The 23 books stolen by Bernadette Franklin from Michael's Dalston flat were:

1. Robert Anton Wilson, *Ishtar Rising*, New Falcon Publications, 1988
2. Dossie Easton & Janet W. Hardy, *Radical Ecstasy*, Greenery Press, 2004
3. Robert Anton Wilson, *Right Where You Are Sitting Now: Further Tales Of The Illuminati*, Ronin Publishing, 1993
4. Jack Parsons, *Freedom Is a Two-Edged Sword*, New Falcon Publications, 2001
5. Jan Fries, *Visual Magick: A Manual Of Freestyle Shamanism*, Mandrake Of Oxford, 1992
6. Steve Wilson, *Chaos Ritual*, Neptune Press, 1995
7. Jaq D. Hawkins, *The Chaos Monkey*, Capall Bann Publishing, 2003
8. Jaq D. Hawkins, *Spirits Of The Earth*, Capall Bann Publishing, 1998
9. Dossie Easton, Catherine A. Liszt, *The Ethical Slut*, Greenery Press, US, 1997
10. Starhawk, *Truth Or Dare: Encounters with Power, Authority and Mystery*, HarperSanFrancisco, 1989
11. Feral Faun, *Feral Revolution,* Elephant Editions, 2000
12. Ramsey Dukes, *SSOBTME: An essay on magic,* The Mouse That Spins, 1979
13. Ramsey Dukes, *What I Did in My Holidays: Essays on Black Magic, Satanism, Devil Worship and Other Niceties,* Mandrake Press Ltd, 1998
14. Robert Shea and Robert Anton Wilson, *The Illuminatus! Trilogy,* Constable and Robinson, 1998

15. William J. Murray, *Anarchic Harmony: Spirituality of Social Disobedience,* Loom Panics Unlimited, 1992

16. Christopher S. Hyatt Ph.D., *Rebels and Devils; The Psychology of Liberation,* New Falcon, 1996

17. Malaclypse the Younger, *Principia Discordia,* Loompanics Unlimited. Principia Discordia can be viewed online at http://www.principiadiscordia.com/

18. Robert Anton Wilson, *Cosmic Trigger: Final Secret of the Illuminati: Vol 1,* New Falcon, 1991

19. Tony Vigorito, *Just a Couple of Days,* Bast Books, 2001

20. Dr Timothy Leary, *Neuropolitique,* New Falcon Press, 1991

21. Phil Hine, *Condensed Chaos: An Introduction to Chaos Magic,* New Falcon Publications, 1995

22. Terrence McKenna, *The Archaic Revival,* HarperSanFrancisco, 1992

23. Starhawk and Hilary Valentine, *The Twelve Wild Swans: A Journey Into Magic, Healing and Action*, HarperSanFrancisco, 2001

Incidentally, Bernadette scored well with the break-in. These 23 books are all highly recommended by the weaver of this tapestry. In fact many of them form the essential framework of the art and science of Fool Sorcery. As Martin said about books on magic: *read, read and read but don't study.*

APPENDIX IV <23 Authors>

Q: Are the 23 authors of Liber Malorum in fact the 23 international heads of the international Illuminati conspiracy? Or were the authors simply in the right place at the right time?

A: Is there even a difference?

APPENDIX V
<Love and Apples>

Sean, the weaver of these tales would like to thank all who contributed to the magic of Liber Malorum over the years including Grove Gatherings, the Fooluminati, HYDRA, Telscombe Temple Dancers, the Dragon Network, the Kaotic Illuminated Adepts, The Mutation Parlour, ActElemental, Battersea Arts Centre, the St Johns Posse, Green Witch, the Dionysian Undeground, Colour The Grey, The Meaton Massive, The Shaman Fools, The Alternity Housing Co-op, KaOsOvOz, TOPY, the Global Indymedia network, The Aboriginal Tent Embassy (Canberra), the Reclaiming Network, The Crowned And Conquering Child of the New Aeon, Club Hades, Euphoria, the PMA, Maybe Logic, Tribe Of Brigid, the Serpentine Tibet Crew, Clone 6, The Pagan Cluster, Omaisha, Treadwell's, Pirates v Ninjas, The Tribe Of Avalon, Chien Rouge, The Foolish People, The Council of Nine, the Toronto Immigration Police, the Byron Bay All-Stars, The Flying Spaghetti Monster, the People In Common, Mandrake Of Oxford, the Secret Order of the Yellow Star, Ridge Farm, Moot With No Name, T38, P*Soul, SchNews, Reclaim The Streets, Fetish Foolish, The HermAphroditic ChAOrder of The Silver Dusk, The Knub, The DMT Faeries and Elves, Backlash UK, Kabula, Choonz.com, The Living River, The Legion of Dynamic Discord, Fairy Love, The Pagan Awareness Network, *La Monte*, May Day Magical Activists, The Southern Cross Illuminati, Nick And Morphia, Trapese Collective, ConFest, Ninja Tunes, the Hairy Jedi, the Pact of the IOT, lulu.com, Black'n'Blue Brighton, The Yes Men, QPR20, The Yellow Submarine, Irreality, Clown Through Mask, Clustered.net, Circus 2 Iraq, Chaos Planet, The Order of the Golden Phoenix, Sir! No Sir!, The Invisible Illuminati, Informed Consent, Bondage Faeries, The Secret Chiefs, The Flotilla Of Hope, The Serpent Institute, The Compass Centre, New Falcon, Jade Arrows, PagAnarchy, Clan Keenoy, Lamb, The Clandestine Insurgent Rebel Clown Army, Puppet Planet, The 70000 Jedi in Australia, Synergy Centre, The Maestros Of Satanic Sex And Death (MOSSAD), The Fellowship of Isis, ChaosMagic.com, The Nomadic Academy of Fools, Matronage.net and many, many others.

Extra Love and Apples

To: Spike, James, Mum, Dad, Margot, Jacqui & Profth, Nanna, Poppa, Anneli Oh Yeah!, Mystic Dave, Kevvy K, D.D.A, JuJu, Ally Beans, Artemisia Lovesyou (yay!!), Andy Nicholson, Koogie, Kelsey Pike, Lilli Billa, uber love to Fleassy, Heidi Axelsen!!, Anna J (rocks!), Xina, Loothi, Silver Sara, Socrates' Sausage, Ishtiyaq Shukri, Suzanne Maxim, Kolonel Klepto, Lady Feyn, Pfil Faerie, Martha Muffin, Shelloir, Rosie Pea, Lula James, Faerie Svea, Anna the Blue-eyed Festival Faerie, Darren Segal, Caroline Foldes, Chucklez the Wonder Monkey, Mr P Rice, Mad Wolf, Shaz **, Bhaisabi Baby, Sushoir, Galia Shmalia, Pearly, Swami Ami, Daniella, Orli, Aunti Gloria, Baphomet, Jet Moon, Deb Doodled, Tim Brown the Fireclown, Eris, Rodney Segal, Pippity Pipstar, Omeganubis, Maisy Jayne, Rosalee, Louisananda, Z-Faerie, Smurfette, Jacqueline Anne Woodward-Smith, Lilith D'gonit, Lisa Pusey, Burger Queen, Ramsey Dukes, JJ, Phat Thandi, Marshall Darkness, Frater TMB, Rebekita, Dub Shaman, Starhawk, Jaq D. Hawkins, Eros, FaerieCatcher, Jonathan Kay, Duffsteur, Goia + Ceri + Zeca, Lamont, Orryelle Defenestrate-Bascule, Pema, Odder, Count Anton, Ian Gregory, Princess Hashemite, Fee I Am, Finbar, Little Toe, Geoff Greentree, Winter Flame, Liza Hayden, Adrian Harris, Jolie Pierce, Lady Pinque, Tiny Ruthe, Rob Thorburn, David Barrett, Private Joke, Josie Tremarco, Faerie Jezz, Gretchwyn, Delaney Crawley, Katherine Cunningham, Jet Adams, Steve ASH, Miss Butterworth, Haz Leigh, Florence, Luke Natural, General Dog's Body, Private Individual, SLT Latte, Lou Rhodes, Hawthorn, Selene, Kelly's Belly, Elodie, Hengst, Geezerbird, Shanna na na, Pan, Raga Woods, Tracey Durey, Taya, Iris, Arms & Legs & Thuzi, Baggers & Callum, Potterpissin, Cath & Baz & Zac, Suze Wood, Tom Shooter, Duncan The Printer, Penny Penny Penny, Leaf, Buns, Jocelyn Chaplin, Agi Doodle, Alboy, Karl Erik Paasonen, Norman Pike, Pope Fred, Jean McLaren, Anthea Ifrit, Wombi Wombaya, Anna Pixie, Carrrrrmen, Juggler Matt, Vomnot Jammit, Nullo, PinkGem, Icarus D & Shoops, Shamonu, Nayru, Stirananda, Mattski, GeeeGeee, JJJ, Crystal Eyes, Drogas, Ciola, Hobbit67, Ben Woolgar, Sparky Roots, Pixie Warrior, Steviator, Kaspertastic, Rickybabes, Summer Maughan, AWOL, Rikki Indymedia, Rainbow73, Katherine Hughes, Craig Inglis, Natalie Harrison, Adam Pinky, Lynx Wildwood, Sahara Piksie, Jesse Baby, Shambala Catherine and i heart u the oh-so-delightful Pixie Feather.

Extra mention to proofreaders! Keep Freading the Proo! Heidi, Billy Borris, Profth, Aunti Jacqui, Koogie, Rebekita, Ceri Buck, Bettina, Martha Muffin, JuJu, Russell, Alboy, Darren Segal, Ariane, Pixie Feather, Adam Sweetas, Nick Orphed and Zoe.

Rock the mantra my fellow fools: Katie, Joe, Max, Daniel, Jenna, Sue & Bruce.

Lastly, extra big love to Kommodore Koogie, whose support through the weaving of this book has been invaluable!

And they all lived appley ever after...